'... as a sophisticated and brilliantly expressed vision of ... and one can see, smell and taste the America of which he ...tes' *Times Literary Supplement*

'It is difficult to think of new superlatives to describe *Purple Cane Road* . . . [it] is written in a language which, at once sharp yet poetic, can handle with nonchalant skill anything from extreme violence to languorous ease. But this must be the best of the series . . . the final pages have an emotional impact which lifts the novel far above its genre' T. J. Binyon, *Evening Standard*

'At times Burke's writing and atmosphere remind one of William Faulkner; at other moments Raymond Carver. I cannot think of much higher praise that can be accorded a novel'
Marcel Berlins, *The Times* Metro

'Burke tells a story in a style all his own: language that's alive, electric; he's a master at setting mood, laying in atmosphere, all with quirky, raunchy dialogue that's a delight' Elmore Leonard

'That James Lee Burke has been consigned to the literary ghetto marked "crime fiction" is itself an offence. Burke is a fine writer, his prose swathed in style and atmosphere, his characters rich, unusual but always utterly believable. James Lee Burke is an exceptional writer; no qualification necessary' *Observer*

'Not since Raymond Chandler has anyone reinvented the crime and mystery genre as James Lee Burke' Jim Harrison

'One of the finest American novels I've read recently, and one that makes Burke one of the best fictional stylists currently writing in America' *City Life*

'This is prose that cuts straight to the heart, summoning a wonderful parade of damaged humanity in its wake'
Maxim Jakubowski, *Guardian*

James Lee Burke is the author of twenty-four novels, including fourteen featuring Detective Dave Robicheaux, and a volume of short stories. *The Lost Get-Back Boogie* was nominated for a Pulitzer Prize; *Black Cherry Blues* won the Edgar Award in 1989; and *Cimarron Rose*, Burke's first novel featuring Billy Bob Holland, won the 1997 Edgar Award. In 1998 *Sunset Limited* won the CWA Macallan Gold Dagger for Fiction. *Crusader's Cross* is his latest book, available in Orion hardback. James Lee Burke divides his time between Missoula, Montana, and New Iberia, Louisiana.

By James Lee Burke

DAVE ROBICHEAUX NOVELS

The Neon Rain
Heaven's Prisoners
Black Cherry Blues
A Morning for Flamingos
A Stained White Radiance
In the Electric Mist with Confederate Dead
Dixie City Jam
Burning Angel
Cadillac Jukebox
Sunset Limited
Purple Cane Road
Jolie Blon's Bounce
Last Car to Elysian Fields
Crusader's Cross

OTHER FICTION

Half of Paradise
To the Bright and Shining Sun
Lay Down My Sword and Shield
Two for Texas
The Lost Get-Back Boogie
The Convict and Other Stories
Cimarron Rose
Heartwood
Bitterroot
White Doves at Morning
In the Moon of Red Ponies

JAMES LEE BURKE

A MORNING FOR FLAMINGOS

PHOENIX

A PHOENIX PAPERBACK

First published in Great Britain in 1992
by Century
This paperback edition published in 2005
by Phoenix,
an imprint of Orion Books Ltd,
Orion House, 5 Upper St Martin's Lane,
London WC2H 9EA

3 5 7 9 10 8 6 4 2

A CIP catalogue record for this book
is available from the British Library.

ISBN-13 978-0-7538-2029-2
ISBN-10 0-7538-2029-3

Printed and bound in Great Britain by
Clays Ltd, St Ives plc

The Orion Publishing Group's policy is to use papers that
are natural, renewable and recyclable products and
made from wood grown in sustainable forests. The logging
and manufacturing processes are expected to conform to
the environmental regulations of the country of origin.

www.orionbooks.co.uk

To Martin and Jennie Bush

1

We parked the car in front of the parish jail and listened to the rain beat on the roof. The sky was black, the windows fogged with humidity, and white veins of lightning pulsated in the bank of thunderheads out on the Gulf.

'Tante Lemon's going to be waiting for you,' Lester Benoit, the driver, said. He was, like me, a plainclothes detective with the sheriff's department. He wore sideburns and a mustache, and had his hair curled and styled in Lafayette. Each year he arranged to take his vacation during the winter in Miami Beach so that he would have a year-round tan, and each year he bought whatever clothes people were wearing there. Even though he had spent his whole life in New Iberia, except for time in the service, he always looked as if he had just stepped off a plane from somewhere else.

'You don't want to see her, do you?' he said, and grinned.

'Nope.'

'We can go in the side door and bring them down the back elevator. She won't even know we've been there.'

'It's all right,' I said.

'It's not me that's got the problem. If you don't feel good about it, you should have asked off the assignment. What's the big deal, anyway?'

'It's not a big deal.'

'Then blow her off. She's an old nigger.'

'She says Tee Beau didn't do it. She says he was at her house, helping her shell crawfish, the night that guy got killed.'

'Come on, Dave. You think she's not going to lie to save her grandson?'

'Maybe.'

'You damn straight, maybe.' Then he looked off in the direction of the park on Bayou Teche. 'It's too bad the fireworks got rained on. My ex was taking the kids to it. Happens every year. I got to get out of this place.' His face looked wan in the glow of the streetlight through the rain-streaked window. His window was cracked at the top to let out his cigarette smoke.

'Let's do it,' I said.

'Give it a minute. I don't want to drive in wet clothes all the way up there.'

'It's not going to let up.'

'I'll finish my cigarette and we'll see. I don't like being wet. Hey, tell me on the square, Dave, is it delivering Tee Beau that bothers you, or do we have some other kind of concerns here?' The streetlight made shadows like rivulets of rain on his face.

'Have you ever been to one?' I asked.

'I never had to.'

'Would you go?'

'I figure the guy sitting in that chair knew the rules.'

'Would you go?'

'Yeah, I would.' He turned his head and looked boldly at my face.

'It can be an expensive experience.'

'But they all knew the rules. Right? You stuff somebody in the state of Louisiana, you get treated to some serious electroshock therapy.'

'Tell me the name of one rich man the state's burned. Or any state, for that matter.'

'Sorry. I'm not broken up about these guys. You think Jimmie Lee Boggs should have gotten life? Would you like him back around here on parole after ten and a half?'

'No, I wouldn't.'

'I didn't think so. I'll tell you another thing. If that guy tries anything on me, I'll park one in his mouth. Then I'll find his mother and describe it to her on her deathbed. How's that sound?'

'I'm going in now. You want to come?'

'She's going to be waiting,' he said, and grinned again.

She was. In a drenched print-cotton dress, sun-faded and colorless from repeated washings, that clung to her bony frame like wet tissue paper. Her mulatto hair looked like a tangle of gray-gold wire, her high-yellow skin as though it were spotted with brown dimes. She sat alone on a wood bench next to a holding cell, next to the elevator from which her grandson, Tee Beau Latiolais, whom she had raised by herself, would emerge in a few minutes with Jimmie Lee Boggs, both of them manacled in waist and leg chains. Her blue-green eyes were covered with cataracts, but they never left the side of my face.

3

She had worked in one of Hattie Fontenot's cribs on Railroad Avenue in the 1940s; then she'd spent a year in the women's penitentiary for stabbing a white man through the shoulder after he beat her up. Later she worked in a laundry and did housework for twenty dollars a week, which was the standard full-time salary for any Negro in South Louisiana, wherever he or she worked, well into the 1960s. Tante Lemon's daughter gave birth prematurely to a baby that was so small it fitted into the shoe box she hid it in before she put it in the bottom of a trash barrel. Tante Lemon heard the child's cries when she went out to use the privy the next morning. She raised Tee Beau as her own, fed him *cush-cush* with a spoon to make him strong, and tied a dime around his neck with a string to keep illness from traveling down his throat. They lived in an unpainted shack whose gallery had totally collapsed, so that the steps looked as if they led into a gaping, broken mouth, in an area people called nigger town. Each spring my father, who was a commercial trapper and fisherman, hired her to shell crawfish for him, though he could scarcely afford her meager salary. Whenever he caught mullet or gar in his nets, he dressed it and dropped it by her house.

'I ain't eating that, me,' he would say to me, as though he owed and explanation for being charitable.

I could hear the elevator coming down. A uniformed jailer at a small desk was finishing the paperwork on the transfer of the prisoners from the parish jail to Angola.

'Mr. Dave,' Tante Lemon said.

'Tell them up there they already been fed,' the jailer said.

'There ain't anything wrong with them, either. The doctor checked out both of them.'

'Mr. Dave,' she said again. Her voice was low, as though she were speaking in church.

'I can't help, Tante Lemon,' I said.

'He was at my little house. He didn't kill no redbone,' she said.

'Somebody's going to take her home,' the jailer said.

'I told all them people, Mr. Dave. They ain't listen to me. What for they gonna listen an old nigger woman worked Miz Hattie's crib? That's what they say. Old nigger *putain* lyin' for Tee Beau.'

'His lawyer's going to appeal. There are a lot of things that can be done yet,' I said. I kept waiting for the elevator doors to open.

'They gonna electrocute that boy,' she said.

'Tante Lemon, I can't do anything about it,' I said.

Her eyes wouldn't leave my face. They were small and wet and unblinking, like a bird's.

I saw Lester smiling to himself.

'A car's going to take you home,' the jailer said to her.

'What for I goin' home, me? Be home by myself in my little house?' she answered.

'You fix something hot, you get out of them wet clothes,' the jailer said. 'Then tomorrow you talk to Tee Beau's lawyer, like Mr. Dave says.'

'Mr. Dave know better,' she said. 'They gonna burn that little boy, and he ain't done nothing

5

wrong. That redbone pick on him, make fun of him in front of people, work him so hard he couldn't eat when he got home. I fix chicken and rice, everything nice, just the way he like it. He sit down all dirty at the table and stare at it, put it in his mouth like it ain't nothing but a bunch of dry bean. I tell him go wash his face and arm, then he gonna eat. But he say, "I tired, Gran'maman. I cain't eat when I tired." I say, "Tomorrow Sunday, you gonna sleep tomorrow, you, then you gonna eat." He say, "He coming' for me in the morning. We got them field to cut."

'Where everybody when that little boy need he'p?' she said. 'When that redbone roll up a newspaper and swat him like he's a cat? Where them police, them lawyer then?'

'I'll come over to your house tomorrow, Tante Lemon,' I promised.

Lester lit a cigarette and smiled up into the smoke. I heard the elevator motor stop; then the door slid open and two uniformed sheriff's deputies walked Tee Beau Latiolais and Jimmie Lee Boggs out in chains. They were dressed in street clothes for the trip up to Angola. Tee Beau wore a shiny sports coat the color of tin, baggy purple pants, and a black shirt with the collar flattened out on the coat. He was twenty-five, but he looked like a child in adult clothes, like you could pick him up around the waist as you would a pillow slip full of sticks. Unlike his grandmother's, his skin was black, his eyes brown, too big for his small face, so that he looked frightened even when he wasn't. Someone in the jail had cut his hair but had not shaved the neck, leaving a black wiry line low on the back of his neck that looked like dirt.

But Jimmie Lee Boggs was the man who caught your eye. His hair was silver, long and thin, and it hung straight back off his head like thread that had been sewn to the scalp. He had jailhouse pallor, and his eyes were elongated and spearmint green. His lips looked unnaturally red, as though they had been rouged. The curve of his neck, the profile of his head, the pink-white scalp that showed through his threadlike hair, reminded me of a mannequin's. He wore a freshly laundered T-shirt, jeans, and ankle-high black tennis shoes without socks. A package of Lucky Strikes stuck up snugly from one of his pockets. Even though his hands were manacled to the waist chain and he had to shuffle because of the short length of chain between his ankles, you could see the lean tubes of muscle move in his stomach, roll in his arms, pulse over his collarbones when he twisted his neck to look at everyone in the room. The peculiar light in his eyes was not one you wanted to get lost in.

The jailer opened a file cabinet drawer and took out two large grocery bags that were folded and stapled neatly across the top. The name 'Boggs' was written on one, 'Latiolais' on the other.

'Here's their stuff,' he said, and handed the bags to me. 'If y'all want to stay up there tonight, you can get a per diem.'

'Lookit what you send up there, you,' Tante Lemon said. 'Ain't you shamed? You put that little boy in chains, you pretend he like that other one, 'cause you conscience be bothering y'all at night.'

'I had that boy in my jail eight months, Tante Lemon, long before he got in this trouble,' the jailer

7

said. 'So don't be letting on like Tee Beau never done anything wrong.'

'For taking from Mr. Dore junkyard. For giving his *gran'maman* an old window fan ain't nobody want. That's why y'all had him in y'all's jail.'

'He stole Mr. Dore's car,' the jailer said.

'That's what *he* say,' Tante Lemon said.

'I hope I don't have to pay rent here tonight,' Lester said, and brushed cigarette ashes off his slacks by flipping his nails against the cloth.

Then Tante Lemon started to cry. Her eyes closed, and tears squeezed out of the lids as though she were sightless; her mouth trembled and jerked without shame.

'Good God,' said Lester.

'Gran'maman, I be writing,' Tee Beau said. 'I be sending letters like I right down the street.'

'I got to go to the bathroom,' said Jimmie Lee Boggs.

'Shut up,' the jailer told him.

'That boy innocent, Mr. Dave,' she said. 'You know what they gonna do. *T'connais*, you. He goin' to the Red Hat.'

'Y'all get out of here. I'll see she's all right,' the jailer said.

'Fuck, yes,' Lester said.

We went out into the dark, into the rain and the lightning that leapt across the southern sky, and locked Jimmie Lee Boggs and Tee Beau into the back of the car behind the wire-mesh screen. Then I unlocked the trunk and threw the two paper bags containing their belongings inside. At the back of the trunk, fastened to the floor with elastic rope, were a .30–06 scoped rifle in a zippered case and a twelve-gauge pump shotgun with a pistol stock. I got in the passenger's side, and we drove out of town on the back road that led through St. Martinville to Interstate 10, Baton Rouge, and Angola Pen.

The spreading oaks along the two-lane road were black and dripping with water. The rain had slackened, and when I rolled my window partly down I could smell the sugarcane and the wet earth in the fields. The ditches on both sides of the road were high with rainwater.

'I got to use the can,' Jimmie Lee Boggs said.

Neither Lester nor I answered.

'I ain't kidding you, I gotta go,' he repeated.

'You should have gone back there,' I said.

'I asked. He told me to shut up.'

'You'll have to hold it,' I said.

'What'd you come back to this stuff for?' Lester said.

'I'm into some serious debt,' I said.

'How bad?'

'Enough to lose my house and boat business.'

'I'm going to get out one of these days. But me a place in Key Largo. Then somebody else can haul the freight. Hey, Boggs, didn't the mob have enough work for you in Florida?'

'What?' Boggs said. He was leaning forward on the seat, looking out the side window.

'You didn't like Florida? You had to come all the way over here to kill somebody?' Lester said. When he smiled, the edge of his mouth looked like putty.

'What do you care?' Boggs asked him.

'I was just curious.'

Boggs was silent. His face looked strained, and he shifted his buttocks back and forth on the seat.

'How much did they pay you to do that bar owner?' Lester said.

'Nothing,' Boggs said.

'Just doing somebody a favor?' Lester continued.

'I said "nothing" because I didn't kill that guy. Look, I don't want to be rude, we got a long trip together, but I'm feeling a lot of discomfort back here.'

'We'll get you some Pepto Bismol or something up on the Interstate,' Lester said.

'I'd appreciate that, man,' Boggs said.

We went around a curve through open pasture. Tee Beau was sleeping with his head on his chest. I could hear frogs croaking in the ditches.

'What a July Fourth,' Lester said.

I stared out the window at the soaked fields. I didn't want to listen to any more of Lester's negative comments, nor tell him what was really on my mind, namely, that he was the most depressing person I had ever worked with.

'I tell you, Dave, I never thought I'd have an assignment with a cop who'd been up on a murder beef himself,' he said, yawning and widening his eyes.

'Oh?'

'You don't like to talk about it?'

'I don't care one way or the other.'

'If it's a sore spot, I'm sorry I brought it up.'

'It's not a sore spot.'

'You're kind of a touchy guy sometimes.'

The rain struck my face, and I rolled the window up again. I could see cows clumped together among the streets, a solitary, dark farmhouse set back in a sugarcane field, and up ahead an old filling station that had been there since the 1930s. The outside bay was lighted, and the rain was blowing off the eaves into the light.

'I got something bad happening inside me,' Boggs said. 'Like glass turning around.'

He was leaned forward on the seat in his chains, biting his lip, breathing rapidly through his nose. Lester looked at him, behind the mesh screen, in the rearview mirror. 'We'll get you the Pepto. You'll feel a lot better.'

'I can't wait. I'm going to mess my pants.'

Lester looked over at me.

'I mean it, I can't hold it, you guys. It ain't my fault,' Boggs said.

Lester craned his head around, and his foot went off the gas. Then he looked over at me again. I shook my head negatively.

'I don't want the guy smelling like shit all the way up to Angola,' Lester said.

'When you transport a prisoner, you transport the prisoner,' I said.

'They told me you were a hard-nose.'

'Lester—'

'We're stopping,' he said. 'I'm not cleaning up some guy's diarrhea. That don't sit right with you, I'm sorry.'

He pulled into the bay of the filling station. Inside the office a kid was reading a comic book behind an old desk. He put down the comic and walked outside. Lester got out of the car and opened his badge on him.

'We're with the sheriff's office,' he said. 'A prisoner needs to use your rest room.'

11

'What?' the kid said.

'Can we use your rest room?'

'Yeah, sure. You want any gas?'

'No.' Lester got back into the car, leaving the kid standing there, and backed the car around the side of the station, out of the light, to the men's room door.

Tee Beau was awake now, staring out into the darkness. In the headlights I could see a tree-lined coulee, with canebrakes along its banks, behind the station. Lester cut the engine, got out of the car again, unlocked the back door, and helped Boggs out into the light rain by one arm. Boggs kept breathing through his nose and letting the air out with a shudder.

'I'll unlock one hand and give you five minutes,' Lester said. 'You give me any more trouble, you can ride the rest of the way in the trunk.'

'I ain't giving you no trouble. I told them all day I was sick.'

Lester took his handcuff key out of his pocket.

'Check the rest room first,' I said.

'I've been here before. There's no window. Lay off me, Robicheaux.'

I let out my breath, opened my door, and started to get out.

'All right, all right,' Lester said. He walked Boggs to the rest room door, opened it, flipped on the light, and looked inside. 'It's a box, like I said. You want to look?'

'Check it.'

'Bullshit,' he said. He unlocked Boggs's right hand from the manacle attached to the waist chain. As soon as Boggs's hand was free, he combed his

12

hair back over his head with his fingers, looked back at the car, then walked inside the rest room with the short mincing steps that the leg chain would allow him. He clicked the bolt behind him.

This time I got out of the car.

'What's the matter with you?' Lester said.

'You're doing too many things wrong.' I came around the front of the car toward him. The headlights were still on.

'Look, I'm in charge of this assignment. You don't like the way I handle it, you write up a complaint when we get back.'

'Boggs has killed three people. He killed the bar owner with a baseball bat. Does that tell you something?'

'Yeah, that maybe you're a little bit obsessive. You think that might be the problem here?'

I unsnapped the holster on my .45 and banged on the rest room door with my fist.

'Open it up, Boggs,' I yelled.

'I'm on the toilet,' he said.

'Open the door!'

'I can't reach it. I got the shits, man. What's going on?' Boggs said.

'You're fucking unbelievable,' Lester said.

I hit the door again.

'Come on, Boggs,' I said.

'I'm going to get some cigarettes. You can do what you want to,' Lester said, and walked toward the front of the station.

I stepped back from the door, rested my palm on the butt of the .45, and kicked the door hard under the knob. It didn't give. I saw Lester turn and stare at me. I kicked it again, and this time the lock splintered out of the jamb and the door crashed back on its hinges.

My eyes saw the paper towel dispenser torn apart on the wall and the paper towels scattered all over the floor even before I saw Boggs, his knees squatted slightly in a shooting position, the links of chain crimped tightly into his body, one manacled hand frozen against his side like a bird's claw, his right arm outstretched with a nickel-plated revolver. His spearmint-green eyes were alive with excitement, and his mouth was smiling, as though we were in this joke together.

I got the .45 halfway out of my holster before he fired. The report was no louder than a firecracker, and I saw sparks from the barrel fly out into the darkness. In my mind's eye I was twisting sideways, raising my left arm in front of my face, and clearing my holster with the .45, but I do not think I was doing any of these things. Instead, I'm sure that my mouth opened wide in disbelief and fear as the round struck me high up in the chest like a fist that was wrapped in chain mail. My breath exploded out of my lungs, my knees caved, my chest burned as though someone had cored through sinew and bone with a machinist's drill. The .45 fell uselessly from my hand into the weeds, and I felt my left arm go limp, the muscles in my neck and shoulder collapsing as though all the linkage were severed. Then I was stumbling backward in the rain toward the coulee, my hand pressed over a wet hole in my shirt, my mouth opening and closing like a fish's.

Lester had a .38 strapped to his ankle. He had once told me that a cop he knew in Miami Beach carried his weapon in the same fashion. His knee came up in the air, his hand dropped towards his shoe, and in the light from the filling station front window his face looked absolutely white, frozen, beaded with raindrops, just before Jimmie Lee Boggs doubled him over with a round through the stomach.

But I wasn't thinking about Lester, nor in honesty can I say that I cared about him at that moment. Amid the pistol shots and the pop of lightning on the horizon, I heard a black medic from my outfit say, *Sucking chest wound, motherfucker. Close it, close it, close it. Chuck got to breathe through his mouth.* Then I crashed backward through a canebrake and tumbled down the slope of the coulee through the reeds and tangle of underbrush. I rolled on my back, my ears thundering with bugles and distant drums, and my breath came out of my mouth in a long sigh. The limbs of oak trees arched over the top of the coulee, and through the leaves I could see lightning flicker across the sky.

My legs were in the water, my back covered with mud, the side of my face matted with black leaves. I felt the warmness from the wound spread from under my palm into my shirt.

'Get in there, you sonofabitch,' Boggs said up in the darkness.

'Mr. Boggs,' I heard Tee Beau say.

'Get the car keys and open the trunk,' Boggs said.

'Mr. Boggs, they ain't no need to do that. That boy too scared to hurt us.'

'Shut up and get the guns out of the trunk.'

'Mr. Boggs . . .'

I heard a sound like someone being shoved hard

15

into a wall, then once again the report of the pistol, like a small, dry firecracker popping.

I swallowed and tried to roll on my side and crawl farther down the coulee. A bone-grinding, red-black pain ripped from my neck all the way down to my scrotum, and I rolled back into the ferns and the thick layer of black leaves and the mud that smelled as sour as sewage.

Then I heard the unmistakable roar of a shotgun.

'Try some Pepto Bismol for it,' Boggs said, and laughed in a way that I had never heard a human laugh before.

I slipped my palm away from my chest, put both of my hands behind me in the mud, dug the heels of my shoes into the silt bottom of the stream, and began to push myself toward a rotted log webbed with dried flotsam and morning glory vines. I could breathe all right now; my fears of a sucking chest wound had been groundless, but it seemed that all my life's energies had been siphoned out of me. I saw both Tee Beau and Boggs silhouetted on the rim of the coulee. Boggs held the pistol-grip twelve-gauge from the car trunk at port arms across his chest.

'Do it,' he said, took the nickel-plated revolver from his blue jeans pocket, and handed it to Tee Beau.

'Suh, let's get out of here.'

'You finish it.'

'He dying down there. We ain't got to do no more.'

'You don't get a free pass, boy. You're leaving here dirty as I am.'

'I cain't do it, Mr. Boggs.'

16

'Listen, you stupid nigger, you do what I tell you or you join the kid up in the can.'

In his oversized clothes Tee Beau looked like a small stick figure next to Boggs. Boggs shoved him with one hand, and Tee Beau skidded down the incline through the wet brush, the branches whipping back across his coats and pants. The pistol was flat against his thigh. He splashed through the water toward me.

I ran my tongue across my lips and tried to speak, but the words became a tangle of rusty nails in my throat.

He knelt in front of me, his face spotted with mud, his eyes round and frightened in his small face.

'Tee Beau, don't do it,' I whispered.

'He done killed that white boy in the bat'room,' he said. 'He put that shotgun up against Mr. Benoit face and blowed it off.'

'Don't do it. Please,' I said.

'Close your eyes, Mr. Dave. Don't be moving, neither.'

'What?' I said, as weakly as a man would if he were slipping forever beneath the surface of a deep, warm lake.

He cocked the pistol, and his bulging eyes stared disjointedly into mine.

Some people say that you review your whole life in that final moment. I don't believe that's true. You see the fold in a blackened leaf, mushrooms growing thickly around the damp roots of an oak tree, a bullfrog glistening darkly on a log; you hear water coursing over rocks, dripping out of the trees, you smell it blowing in a mist. Fog can lie on your tongue as sweet and wet as cotton candy, the cattails and reeds turning a silver-green more beautiful than a painting in one flicker of lightning across the sky. You think of the texture of skin, the grainy pores, the nest of veins that are like the lines in a leaf. You think of your mother's powdered breasts, the smell of milk in her clothes, the heat in her body when she held you against her; then your eyes close and your mouth opens in that last strangled protest against the cosmic accident that suddenly and unfairly is about to end your life.

He was crouched on one knee when he pulled the trigger. The pistol went off ten inches from my face, and I felt the burnt powder scald my skin, the dirt explode next to my ear. My heart twisted in my chest.

I heard Tee Beau rise to his feet and brush his knees.

'I done it, Mr. Boggs,' he said.

'Then get up here.'

'Yes suh, I'm moving.'

I remained motionless, my hands turned palm upward in the stream. The night was filled with sound: the crickets in the grass, the rumble of thunder out on the Gulf, the cry of a nutria farther up the coulee, Tee Beau laboring up through the wet brush.

Then I heard the car doors slam, the engine start, and the tires crunching over the gravel out on to the two-lane road.

It rained hard once more during the night. Just before dawn the sky cleared, and the stars were bright through the oak branches overhead. The sun came up red and hot above the tree line in the east, and the fog that clung to the bottom of the coulee was as pink as blood diffused in water. My mouth was dry, my breath foul in my own nostrils. I felt dead inside, disconnected from all the ordinary events in my life, my body trembling with spasmodic waves of shock and nausea, as though I lay once again on the side of a trail in Vietnam after a bouncing Betty had filled my head with the roar of freight trains and left me disbelieving and voiceless in the scorched grass. I heard early morning traffic on the road and car tires cutting into the gravel; then a car door opened and someone walked slowly along the side of the filling station.

'Oh Lawd God, what somebody done done,' a Negro man said.

I tried to speak, but no sound would come out of my voice box.

A small Negro boy in tattered overalls, with the straps hanging by his sides, stared down at me from the lip of the coulee. I raised my fingers off my chest and fluttered them at him. I felt one side of my mouth try to smile and the web of dried mud crack across my cheek. He backed away from the coulee and clattered through the cane, his voice ringing in the hot morning air.

2

Three months later I spent much of my day out on the gallery at home. The days were cool and warm at the same time, the way they always are during the fall in southern Louisiana, and I liked to put on a pair of khakis, a soft flannel shirt, and my loafers, and sit on the gallery and watch the gold light in my pecan trees, the hard blue ceramic texture of the sky above the marsh, the red leaves floating like rose petals on the bayou, the fishermen on my dock shaking sacks of cracked ice on their catches of *sac-à-lait* and big-mouth bass.

Sometimes after a couple of hours I would walk down through the grove of pecan trees and across the dirt road to the dock and bait shop and help Batist, the Negro man who worked for me, count the receipts, seine the dead shiners out of the aluminum bait tanks, or paint *sauce piquante* on the split chickens and links of sausage that we barbecued in an old oil drum I had cut longways with an acetylene torch and welded hinges and metal legs on. It was a good season that year, and I made a lot of money renting boats and selling bait and beer and serving barbecue lunches to the fishermen who came in at noon and sat around my Southern Bell spool tables with beach umbrellas set in the centers. But I would tire of my own business in a short while, and walk back up on the gallery and look out at the round shafts of light in the trees, and the gray squirrels that ran through the piles of leaves around the trunks.

My left shoulder and arm and upper chest didn't hurt me anymore when I moved around, or even when I turned on to my left side in my sleep. I was all right unless I picked up a lot of weight suddenly with my left hand. Sometimes I unbuttoned my shirt and fingered the round scar that was an inch and a half below my collarbone. It was the size of a dime, red, indented, rubbery to the touch. In an almost narcissistic fascination with my own mortality, I could reach over the top of my shoulder and touch the rubbery scar that had grown over the exit wound. The bullet had gone through me as clean and as straight as an arrow shaft.

On some afternoons I unfolded a card table on the gallery and took apart my guns – a double-barrel twelve-gauge, a .25-caliber hide-away Beretta, and the .45 automatic that I had brought home from Vietnam – and oiled and wiped and polished all the springs and screws and tiny mechanisms. Then I'd oil them again and run bore brushes through the barrels before I reassembled them. I liked the heavy weight of the .45 in my palm, the way the clip snugged up inside the handle, the delicate lines of my fingertips on the freshly oiled metal. One day I loaded the clip with hollow-points, walked down to the duck pond at the back of my property, eased a round into the chamber, and sighted on a broad green hyacinth leaf. But I didn't pull the trigger. I lowered the automatic, then raised it and aimed again. The afternoon was bright and warm, and the grass in my neighbor's pasture was dull green in the sunlight. I lowered the .45 a second time, released the clip from the magazine, slipped it into my back pocket, pulled back the receiver, and ejected the round in the chamber. I told myself that the pistol's report, which was a deafening one, would be unsettling to the neighbors.

I walked back to the house, put the .45 under some shirts in my dresser drawer, and took no more interest in it.

I did not handle the nights well. Sometimes after supper I took Alafair, my adopted daughter, to Vezey's in New Iberia for ice cream; later, we would drive back down the dirt road along the bayou in the waning twilight, the fireflies lighting in the sky, and I would begin to feel a nameless apprehension that seemed to have no cause. I would try to hide my self-absorption from her, but even though she was only in the second grade, she always read my moods accurately and saw through my disguises. She was a beautiful child, with a round, tan face, wide-set Indian teeth, and shiny black hair cut in bangs. When she smiled her eyes would squint almost completely shut, and you would not guess that she had witnessed a massacre in her Salvadorean village, or that I had pulled her from a pocket of air inside a crashed plane, carrying illegal refugees, out on the salt.

One evening on the way home from the ice cream parlour I could feel her eyes watching the side of my face. I looked over at her and winked. We had bought some new Curious George and Baby

Squanto Indian books, and she rode with them stacked on her knees.

'Why you always thinking about something, Dave?' she said. She wore her elastic-waisted jeans, pink tennis shoes, a USL T-shirt with the words 'Ragin' Cajuns' printed on it, and an oversized Houston Astros ball cap.

'I'm just tired today, little guy.'

'A man in Vezey's said hello to us and you didn't say anything.'

'I guess I didn't hear him.'

'You don't smile or play anymore, Dave. It's like something's always wrong.'

'I'm not that bad, am I?'

She looked straight ahead, her cap bouncing with the bumps in the road.

'Alf?' I said.

But she wouldn't turn her head or reply.

'Hey, Baby Squanto, come on.'

Then she said in a quiet voice, 'Did I do something that made you sad?'

'No, of course not. Don't ever think of a thing like that, little guy. You're my partner, right?'

But her face was morose in the purple light, her dark eyes troubled with questions she couldn't answer.

After I said her prayers with her and kissed her good-night, I read until very late, until my eyes burned and I couldn't register the words on that page and the darkness outside was alive with the cries of night birds and nutrias in the marsh. Then I watched the late show on television, drank a glass of milk and fell asleep with my head on the kitchen table. I woke during the night to the sound of

Alafair's slippered feet shuffling across the linoleum. I looked up bleary-eyed into her face. Her pajamas were covered with smiling clocks. She patted me on top of the head as she would a cat.

He waited for me in my dreams. Not Tee Beau Latiolais or Jimmie Lee Boggs but a metamorphic figure who changed his appearance every night but always managed to perform the same function. Sometimes it was ole Victor Charlie, his black pajamas glued against his body with sweat, his face strung with human feces out of a rice paddy, one bulging walleye aimed along the iron sights of a French bolt-action rifle. When he squeezed the trigger I felt the steel-jacketed bullet rip through my throat as easily as it would core a cantaloupe.

Or I would see myself down a narrow, unlighted brick passageway off Dauphine in the French Quarter. I could smell the damp stone, the mint and roses growing in the courtyard, see the shadows of the banana trees waving on the flagstones beyond the piked gate that hung open at the end of the passageway. My hand tightened on the grips of the .45; the mortar between the bricks in the wall felt like claws in my back. I worked my way up to the courtyard entrance, my breath ballooning in my chest; then suddenly the scrolled iron gate swung into my face, broke two of my fingers as if they were sticks, raked the .45 out of my hand, and knocked me backward into a pool of rainwater. An enormous black man in a child's T-shirt, in lavender slacks at least three sizes too small for him, so that his scrotum was outlined like a bag of metal washers, squatted down with a .410 shotgun pistol resting on

24

his thigh and looked at me through the bars of the gate. He was toothless, his lips purple with snuff, his eyes red-rimmed, his breath rank with funk.

'Your turn to beg, motherfucker,' he said. 'That's right, beg for your worthless shitass life.'

The he smiled, lifted the point of my chin with the shotgun barrel, and cocked the hammer.

I would awake on the couch, my T-shirt and shorts damp with perspiration, and sit in a square of moonlight on the edge of the couch, my head bent down, my jaws clenched tight to keep them from shaking.

I was given full pay during my three months' leave, and when I returned to work I was assigned to restricted duty. I stayed in the office most of the time; I interviewed witnesses for other detectives; or sometimes I investigated traffic accidents out in the parish. I did a great deal of paperwork. I was treated with the deference you often see extended to a wounded and recuperating soldier. The attitude is one of kindness, but perhaps a degree of fear is involved also, as though mortality is an infectious condition that must be treated by isolation.

My life became as bland and unremarkable as the season was soft and warm and transitory.

Then, on a windblown afternoon, with leaves flying in the air, I drove to Lafayette in my truck to see Minos P. Dautrieve, an old friend and DEA agent who was now assigned to the Presidential Task Force on Drugs.

He loved to fish, and because I didn't want to talk with him at his house, with his wife or children somewhere on the edge of the conversation, I asked him to bring his spinning rod and drive with me to the levee at Henderson Swamp.

I stopped at one of the bait and boat-rental shacks below the levee and bought two poor-boy shrimp sandwiches and a long-necked bottle of Jax for him and a Dr Pepper for me. We walked down to a grassy place on the bank, across from a row of willow islands that acted as a barrier between the channel along the levee and the swamp itself, which was actually an enormous wetlands area of bays, canals, bayous, oil platforms, and flooded stands of cypress and willow trees. He flipped his Rapala out to the edge of the willow pads that grew on the opposite side of the channel.

Minos had been All-American honorable mention when he played forward for LSU, and he still wore his hair in a college-boy crew cut, mowed so close that the scalp glowed. He was as lean, flat-stomached, and tapered-looking as he had been when sports-writers named him Dr. Dunkenstein. He had been a first lieutenant with army intelligence in Vietnam, and although he was often flippant and cynical and defensive about his role as a government agent, he had a good heart and a hard-nosed sense about right and wrong that sometimes got him in trouble with his own bureaucracy.

I sat down on the incline and tore a long-bladed stem of grass along the spine. I told him about the strange sense of ennui that characterized my days. 'It's like being in the middle of a dead zone. It's like suddenly there's no sound, like all movement has stopped.'

'It'll pass,' he said.

26

'It doesn't feel like it.'

'You got two Hearts in 'Nam. You came out of it all right, didn't you?'

'That was different. The first wound was superficial. The second time I didn't see it coming. There's a difference when you see it coming.'

'I never got hurt, so maybe you're asking the wrong guy. But I've got a feeling that something else is bothering you.'

I dropped the torn grass blade between my knees and wiped my fingers on my pants.

'I feel like I begged,' I said.

'I don't understand. You begged Boggs before he shot you?'

'No, when Tee Beau climbed down into the coulee and cocked the .38 in my face.' I had to swallow when I said it.

'It sounds to me like you did just fine. What were you supposed to do? You had a round through your chest, you had to lie there in the dark with your own thoughts while a couple of guys talked about killing you, then you had to depend on the mercy of a black kid who'd already been sentenced to the electric chair. I don't think I would have come out of that altogether intact. In fact, I know I wouldn't.'

He flipped his lure out again and retrieved it in a zigzag motion just below the water's surface. Then he set the rod down on the bank, took our sandwiches and drinks out of the paper bag, and sat down beside me.

'Listen, podna,' he said. 'You're a brave man. You proved that a long time ago. Stop trying to convince yourself that you're not. I think what we should be talking about here is nailing Boggs. Like

27

cooling out his action, dig it, like blowing up his shit. How'd he get the gun in the can, anyway?'

'He had a girlfriend in Lafayette, a dancer. She blew town the same day he escaped, but she left her fingerprints all over the towel dispenser.'

'Where do y'all think he is now?'

'Who knows? He left the car in Algiers. Maybe he went back to Florida.'

'How about the black kid?'

'Disappeared. I thought he'd show up by now. He's never been anywhere, and he's always lived with his grandmother.'

'Catch him and he might give you a lead on Boggs.'

'He might be dead, too.'

Minos opened the bottle of Jax with his pocketknife, put the cap inside the paper bag, and drank out of the bottle, staring out at the long, flat expanse of gray water and dead cypress. The sun was red and low on the western horizon.

'I think it's time to put your transmission into gear and start hunting these guys down,' he said. 'The rules of the game are kick ass and take names.'

I didn't say anything.

'It's pretty damn boring to be a spectator in your own life. What do you think?' he said.

'Nothing.'

'Bullshit. What do you think?' He hit me in the arm with his elbow.

I let out my breath.

'I'll give it some thought,' I said.

'You want any help from our office, you've got it.'

'All right, Minos.'

'If the black kid's alive, I bet you nail him in a week.'

'Okay.'

'You know Boggs'll show up, too. A guy like that can't get through a day without smearing shit on the furniture somewhere.'

'I think I'm getting your drift.'

'All right, I'm crowding the plate a little bit. But I don't want to see you sitting on your hands anymore. The lowlifes are the losers. They get up every morning knowing that fact. Let's don't ever let them think they're wrong, partner.'

He smiled and handed me a poor-boy sandwich. It felt thick and soft in my hand. Across the channel I could see the ridged and knobby head of an alligator, like a wet, brown rock, among the lily pads.

The next day I read all the paperwork on Tee Beau Latiolais and talked to the prosecutor's office and the detective who did the investigation and made the arrest. Nobody seemed to have any doubt about Tee Beau's guilt. He had worked for a redbone named Hipolyte Broussard, a migrant-labor contractor who had ferried his crews on rickety buses from northern Arizona to Dade County, Florida. I remembered him. He was a strange-looking man who had moved about in that nether society of people of color in southern Louisiana – blacks, quadroons, octoroons, and redbones. You would see him unloading his workers at dawn in the fields during the sugarcane harvest, and at night he would be in a Negro bar or poolroom on the south side of town or out in the parish, where he paid off the laborers or lent them money at high interest rates at a table in back. Like all redbones, people who are a mixture of Negro, white, and Indian blood, he had skin the color of burnt brick, and his eyes were turquoise. His arms and long legs were as thin as pipe cleaners, and he wore sideburns, a rust-colored pencil mustache, and a lacquered straw hat at a jaunty angle on his head. He worked his crews hard, and he had as many contracts with corporate farms as he wanted. I had heard stories that workers, or even a whole family, who gave him trouble might be put off the bus at night in the middle of nowhere.

Nobody doubted why Tee Beau had done it, either. In fact, people were sympathetic with his apparent motivation. For one reason or another, Hipolyte Broussard had made Tee Beau's life as miserable as he could. It was the way in which Tee Beau had killed him that had caused the judge to sentence Tee Beau to the electric chair.

It was misting slightly when I drove down the dirt road into the community of Negro shacks out in the parish where Tante Lemon now lived. The shacks were gray and paintless, the galleries sagging, the privies knocked together from tar paper, scrap lumber, and roofing tin. Chickens pecked in the dirt yards, the ditches were littered with garbage, the air reeked of somebody cooking cracklins outside in an iron kettle, which produces an eye-watering stench like sewage. On the corner was a clapboard juke joint, with tape crisscrossed on the cracked windows, and because it was Friday afternoon the oyster-shell parking lot was already full of cars, and the roar of the jukebox inside was so loud it vibrated the front window.

Tante Lemon's house was raised off the ground on short brick columns, and a yellow dog on a rope had dug a depression under the edge of the house from which he looked up at me and flopped his tail in the dirt. Flies buzzed back in the damp shadows beneath the raised floor. I knocked on the screen door, then saw her ironing at a board in the corner of her small living room. She stopped her work, picked up a tin can, held it to her lips, and spit snuff in it.

'They think they send you, I'm gonna tell where that little boy at?' she said. 'I ain't seen him, I ain't talk with him, I don't even know Tee Beau alive. That's what y'all done to us, Mr. Dave. Don't be coming round here pretend you our friend, no.'

'Will you let me in, Tante Lemon?'

'I done tole them po-licemens, I tell you, I ain't seem him, me, and I ain't he'ping you, me.'

'Listen, Tante Lemon, I don't want to hurt Tee Beau. He saved my life. It's the white man I want. But they're going to catch Tee Beau sooner or later. Wouldn't you rather I find him first, so nobody hurts him?'

She walked to the screen and opened it. Her dress was wash-faded almost colorless, and it flapped on her body and withered breasts as shapelessly as rag.

'You going lie now 'cause I an old nigger?' she said. 'You catch that boy, they gonna carry him up to the Red Hat, they gonna strap him down, put that tin cap on his little head, cover up his face with cloth so they ain't got to look his eyes, let all them people watch my little boy suffer, watch the electricity burn up his body. I was on Camp I, Mr.

31

Dave, when they use to keep womens there. I seen them take a white man to the Red Hat. They had to pull him along the ground from the car, pull him along like a dog wrapped up in chains. Then all them people sat down like they was at the ballpark, them, and watch that man die.'

She raised the tin can to her lips and spit snuff in it again, then picked up her iron and began pressing a starched white shirt. She smelled of dry sweat, Copenhagen, and the heat rising from the ironing board. The walls of her house had been pasted with pages from magazines, then overlaid with mismatched strips of water-streaked wallpaper. The floor was covered with a rug whose thread had split like crimped straw, and the few piece of furniture she owned looked as though they'd been carted home a piece at a time from the junkyard where Tee Beau used to work.

I sat down on a straight-backed chair next to her ironing board.

'I can't promise you anything,' I said, 'but if I find Tee Beau, I'll try to help him. Maybe we can get the governor to commute his sentence. Tee Beau saved the life of a police officer. That could mean a lot, Tante Lemon.'

'The life of that pimp mean a lot.'

'What?'

'Hipolyte Broussard a pimp, and he was gonna make Tee Beau do it, too.'

'I never heard that Broussard was involved with prostitution.'

'White people hear what they want to hear.'

'I didn't see anything like that in the case record, either. Who'd you tell this to?'

'I ain't tole nobody. Ain't nobody ax me.'

'Where was he pimping, Tante Lemon?'

'Out of the juke, there on the four-corner,' she said, and nodded her head toward the outside of the house. 'Out in them camps, where them farm worker stay at.'

'And he wanted Tee Beau to do it, too?'

'He make Tee Beau drive them girls from the juke down to the camp. Tee Beau say, "I cain't do that no more, Hipolyte." Hipolyte say, "You gonna do it, 'cause you don't, I gonna tell your P.O. you been stealing from me and you going back to jail." And it don't matter Tee Beau do what he say or not. Hipolyte keep making him feel awful all the time, sticking his thumb in that little boy seat, in front of all them people, shame him till he come home and cry. If that man ain't dead now, I go kill him myself, me.'

'Tante Lemon, why didn't you tell this to somebody?'

'I tole you, they ain't ax me. You think them people in that courtroom care what an old nigger woman say?'

'You didn't tell anybody because you thought it would hurt Tee Beau, that people would be sure he did it.'

It started raining outside. The hinged flap on the side window was raised with a stick, and in the gray light her skin had the color of a dull penny. She mashed the iron up and down on the shirt she was ironing.

'I can tell lots of things 'bout that juke up the four-corner, 'bout the *traiteur* woman run that place with Hipolyte, 'bout them crib they got there. Ain't

33

nobody interested, Mr. Dave. Don't be telling me they are, no. Just like when I up in Camp I in Angola. On the Red Hat gang they run them boys up and down the levee with they wheelbarrow, beat them every day with the Black Betty, shoot them and bury them right there in the Miss'sippi levee. Everybody knowed it, nobody care. Ain't nobody care about Tee Beau or what I got to say now.'

'You should have talked to somebody. They didn't give Tee Beau the chair because he killed Hipolyte. It was the way he did it.'

'Tee Beau in this house, shelling crawfish. Right here,' she said, and tapped her finger on the ironing board.

'All right. But somebody drove the bus off the jack on top of Hipolyte. Tee Beau's fingerprints were all over the steering wheel. His muddy shoe prints were all over the floor pedals. Nobody else's. Then while Hipolyte was lying under the brake drum with his back broken, somebody stuffed an oil rag in his mouth so he could spend two hours strangling to death.'

'It wasn't long enough.'

'Where is Tee Beau?'

'I ain't gonna tell you no more. Waste of time,' she said, took a cigarette from a pack on the ironing board, and lit it. She blew the smoke out in the humid air. 'You a white man. Colored folk ain't never gonna be your bidness. You come round now 'cause you need Tee Beau catch that white trash shot you. You just see a little colored boy can he'p you now. But you cain't be knowing what he really like, how he hurt inside, how much he love his *gran'mamam*, how much he care for Dorothea and

34

what he willing to do for that little girl. You don't be knowing none of these things, Mr. Dave.'

'Who's Dorothea?'

'Go up the juke, ax her who she is. Ax her about Hipolyte, about what Tee Beau do for her. You, that's gonna take him up to the Red Hat.'

I said good-bye to her, but she didn't bother to answer. It was raining hard when I stepped off the gallery, and drops of mud danced in the dirt yard. Down the street at the four-corners, the clapboard facade of the juke joint glistened in the gray light, and the scroll of neon over the door, which read BIG MAMA GOULA'S, looked like purple smoke in the rain that blew back off the eaves.

The inside was crowded with Negroes, the air thick with cigarette smoke, the smell of dried sweat, muscat, talcum powder, chitlins, gumbo, flat beer, and bathroom disinfectant. The jukebox was deafening, and the pool players rifled the balls into side pockets, shouting and slamming the rack down on the table's slate surface. Beyond the dance floor a zydeco band with an accordion, washboard, thimbles, and an electric bass was setting up on a small stage surrounded by orange lights and chicken wire. Behind the musicians a huge window fan sucked the cigarette smoke out into the rain, and their clothes fluttered in the breeze like bird's feathers. Two deep at the bar, the customers ate *boudin* and pickled hog's feet off paper plates, drank long-necked Jax and wine *spotioti*, a mixture of muscat and whiskey that can fry your head for a week.

I stood at the end of the bar, saw the eyes flick

momentarily sideways, then heard the conversations resume as though I were not there. I waited for the bartender to reach that moment when he would decide to recognize me. He walked on the duckboards to within three feet of me and began lifting handfuls of beer bottles between his fingers from a cardboard carton, fitting them down into the ice bin. There was a thin, dead cigar in his mouth.

'What you want, man?' he asked, without looking up.

'I'm Detective Dave Robicheaux with the sheriff's department,' I said, and opened by badge in my palm.

'What you want?' His eyes looked at me for the first time. They were sullen and flecked with tiny red veins.

'I'd like to talk to Dorothea.'

'She's working the tables. She's real busy now.'

'I only want a couple of minutes of her time. Call her over, please.'

'Look, man, this ain't the place. You understand what I'm talking about?'

'Not really.'

He raised up from his work and put his hands flat on the bar.

'That's her out yonder by the band,' he said. 'You want to go out there and get her? That what you want?'

'Ask her to come over here, please.'

'Listen, I ain't did you nothing. Why you giving me this truck?'

The men next to me had stopped talking now and were smoking their cigarettes casually and

36

looking at their own reflections in the bar mirror. One man wore a lavender porkpie hat with a feather in the brim. His sports coat hung heavy on one side.

'Look, man, you got a car outside?' the bartender asked.

'Yes.'

'Go sit in it. I'll be sending her,' he said, then his voice changed. 'Why you be bothering that girl? She ain't did nothing.'

'I know she hasn't.'

'Then why you bothering her?' he asked.

Before I turned to go outside, I saw a big black woman in a purple dress looking at me from the far end of the duckboards. Her hands were on her hips, her chin pointed upward; she took the cigarette out of her mouth and blew smoke in my direction, her eyes never leaving my face. In the dim light I thought I saw blue tattoos scrolled on the top of her breasts.

The rain clattered on the roof of my car and streamed down the windows. At the back of the juke joint, beyond the oyster-shell parking lot covered with flattened beer cans, were two battered house trailers. Two men who looked like Latins, in denim work clothes and straw hats, drove up in a pickup truck and knocked at one of the trailers, their bodies pressed up against the door to stay out of the rain. A black woman opened the inside door and spoke to them through the screen. They got back in their truck and left. I saw one of them look back through the rear window as they pulled on to the dirt road.

37

Five minutes later the bartender appeared in the front door of the juke joint with a small Negro girl at his side and pointed at my car. She ran across the parking lot toward me, with a newspaper spread over her head. When I pushed open the passenger door she jumped inside. She wore black fishnet stockings, a short black waitress's skirt, and a loose white blouse that exposed her lace bra, but she looked both too young and too small for the job she did, and the type of clothes that she wore. It was her hair that caught your attention, black and thick and brushed in soft swirls around her head, almost like a helmet that made her toy face seem even smaller than it was. She was frightened and would not look at me directly.

'You know I'm a police officer?' I said.

'Yes suh.'

'Tee Beau saved my life, so I don't want to see him hurt. The man I'm after is named Jimmie Lee Boggs. He killed two people and took Tee Beau with him when he escaped. You know all that, don't you?'

'Yes suh, I knows that.'

'You don't have to call me sir. If Tee Beau can help me find this man Boggs, maybe I can help Tee Beau.'

She nodded her head. Her hands were motionless on top of the wet newspaper in her lap.

'Did he tell you where Boggs dropped him off?' I said.

'Suh?' Her eyes cut sideways at me, then looked straight ahead again.

'When you talked to him, did he say anything about Jimmie Lee Boggs?'

38

'I ain't talked to Tee Beau.'

'I bet you have,' I said, and smiled.

'No suh, I ain't. Nobody know where Tee Beau at. Tante Lemon don't know. Ain't nobody know.'

'I see. Look here, Dorothea, I'm going to give you a card. It has my phone number on it. When you talk to Tee Beau, you give him this number. You tell him I appreciate what he did for me, that I want to help him. He can call me collect from a pay phone. I won't know where he's living. All I want to do is find Jimmie Lee Boggs.'

She took the card in her small hand. She looked out at the rain, her eyes quiet with thought.

'How you gonna he'p him?' she said.

'We can get his sentence commuted. That means he won't go to the electric chair. Maybe he can even get a new trial. The jury didn't hear everything they should have; did they?'

'What you mean?'

'About Hipolyte Broussard. Was he a pimp?'

'Yes suh.'

'Did he try to make Tee Beau a pimp, too?'

'He make him drive the bus with the girls out to the camp.'

'What else did Hipolyte do?'

'Suh?'

'Did Hipolyte do something to you?'

Again her eyes cut sideways, then looked straight ahead. I could see her nostrils quiver when she breathed.

'You don't have to tell me if you don't want to,' I said. 'But maybe Tee Beau had a good reason to kill Hipolyte. Maybe other people might think so, too.'

She squeezed her fingers and looked down at her lap.

'He say I got to get on the bus,' she said.

'Who?'

'Hipolyte. He say I got to go out to the camp. Tee Beau say I ain't going, even if Hipolyte hit him and knock him down in the dirt. Hipolyte say I going or I ain't working here no more.'

'So that's why he killed Hipolyte?'

'I ain't said that. I ain't said that at all. You ax me what Hipolyte done to me.'

I looked out at the trailers behind the parking lot.

'Is somebody bothering you now, Dorothea?' I said. 'Does anybody try to make you do something you don't want to?'

'Gros Mama's good to me.'

'Does she make you do something you don't want to?'

'I wait the table, I pass the mop on the floor 'fore I go home. She don't let no mens bother me. She pass for me in the morning, carry me to work, tell me not be worrying all the time 'bout Tee Beau, he gonna be all right, he coming back one day. Gros Mama know.'

'How does she know that?'

'She a *traiteur*. She got power. That's why Hipolyte scared of her. He got the *gris-gris*. That many you looking for, Jimmie Lee Boggs? You ain't got to worry about him, no. He got a *gris-gris*, too. He gonna die, that one.'

'Wait a minute, Dorothea. You knew Boggs?'

'I seen him with Hipolyte, back yonder by that trailer. Right there. Gros Mama say they both got the *gris-gris*, they carry it in them just like a worm. Suh?'

40

'What?'

'Suh?'

'What is it? And you really don't need to call me sir.'

'I wants to ax you something.' She looked at me full in the face for the first time. Her lipstick was on crooked. 'You ain't lying? You can really he'p Tee Beau?'

'I can try. If he'll let me. Do you know where he is, Dorothea?'

'Gros Mama want me back inside now. Friday a real busy day.'

'If you talk to Tee Beau, tell him I said thank you.'

'I got to be going now.'

'Wait a minute. I have an umbrella,' I said.

I popped it open in the rain and walked her to the entrance of the juke joint. Then she walked hurriedly past the men staring at her from the bar, toward her station by the dance floor.

I had promised to take Alafair to the open-air restaurant at Cypremort Point for bluepoint crabs, a weekly ritual whose aftermath made the waitresses cringe: Alafair, in a white bib with a big red crawfish on it, went about disassembling the crabs with wood mallet and nutcrackers and such clumsy intensity that the plank table had to be washed down later with a hose. I tried never to disappoint her, or see her hurt any more than she had already been hurt by the drowning of her real mother in the crashed plane, and the death of Annie, my second wife. But since I had been shot by Jimmie Lee Boggs, I had become an ineffectual caretaker in my own home rather than a parent, and I had no idea when I would put everything back in the proper box and see the worry and uncertainty go out of Alafair's eyes. And I knew absolutely that that moment would not come of its own accord.

So I drove down to a café on the blacktop, called the house, and asked Clarise, my mulatto house-keeper and baby-sitter, to give Alafair her supper and to stay with her until I got home. I talked with Alafair and told her I would take her out for ice cream later and we would go to Cypremort Point for crabs the next night. I sat at the counter and ate a plate of red beans, rice, and breaded pork chops, and drank coffee until over an hour had passed. Then I headed back to the juke joint.

It had stopped raining now, and the air was clear and cool, the sky dark except for a lighted band of purple clouds low on the western horizon. I drove through the parking lot to the back of the building, the flattened beer cans and wet oyster shells crunching under my tires, and through the big fan humming in the back wall I could hear the zydeco band pounding it out:

> 'Mo mange bien, mo bois bon vin,
> Ça pas coute moi à rien.
> Ma fille aime gumbo filé
> Mo l'aime ma fille aussi.'

I parked by one of the trailers and walked up on the wood steps. Back under a solitary spreading oak tree was the pickup truck I had seen earlier: only one man was in the cab now. The trailer was made out of tin and had been covered with thick layers of green paint. Curtains were pulled across the windows, but a light was on inside. The inner door was closed and the screen was latched. I tapped on the screen with my knuckles and looked back over my shoulder at the man in the truck. He looked away from me.

'Sheriff's department,' I said, and tapped again.

There was no answer, but I heard movement inside.

'Open up,' I said.

Still no answer. I grasped the handle to the screen door firmly and jerked the latch out of the jamb, then opened the inner door, which was unlocked, and stepped into the trailer.

The musky, thick odor of marijuana struck at my face like a fist. The woman whom I had seen at the trailer door earlier lay on a narrow bed in a pink bra and pink panties, her head reclining on a pillow, one arm propped casually behind her head, her free hand holding a joint over an ashtray on a small nightstand. She put the joint to her lips, looked me straight in the face, and took a long, deep hit, ventilating the edges of the paper, until the ash was a bright red coal in the gloom of the trailer.

But the dark-skinned man in denims and work boots, his straw hat clenched against his thigh, his belt buckle still hanging down over his fly, was obviously terrified. His eyes were riveted on the badge in my palm.

'It's not a bust, partner. Rest easy,' I said.

He continued to stare wide-eyed at me. His hands were square with calluses, his fingernails half-mooned with dirt.

'Do you speak English?' I said. Then to the woman, 'Does your friend speak English?'

'You do it the same way in Mexican or English, honey,' she said.

'It's time for you to take off, partner,' I said.

But he didn't understand. I folded up my badge and slipped it in my back pocket.

'You can go now. We don't need you for anything. There's no problem. *No problema*. Your friend is waiting for you,' I said.

I took him gently by the arm and opened the door for him.

'*Adios*,' I said.

This time he realized what he was being offered and he was gone into the darkness like a shot. I closed the door behind him.

'You're a very cool lady,' I said.

She took a slow, easy hit on the reefer and let the smoke curl out of her mouth into her nose.

'I guess I just don't scare you too much,' I said.

She flexed herself on the bed and drew one knee up before her. Her toenails were painted red.

'You gonna do what you gonna do, ain't you?' she said.

'Possession can be serious stuff in Louisiana.'

'Honey, if you was interested in 'resting me, you wouldn't be tapping on no do'.'

'You're pretty hip, too.'

'Why don't you tell me what you want, sweetheart? Somebody tole you the black berry got the sweet juice?'

'Was Hipolyte Broussard your pimp?'

'That's a bad word. Like it mean I doing something I ain't suppose to.'

44

I turned a straight-backed chair around backward and straddled it.

'Let's understand something,' I said. 'I don't care what y'all do here. I'm after a white man named Jimmie Lee Boggs. I'll do just about anything to find him. I feel that way about him because he shot me. Are we communicating here?'

She smiled lazily in the smoke.

'So you the one?' she said.

'That's right. And let's get rid of this distraction, too.' I took the roach out of her fingers and mashed it out in the ashtray. 'Did you know Boggs?'

'I seen him.'

'Where?'

'He come see Hipolyte.'

'Why?'

'Where you been, honey? You ever see black folks who ain't got to give part their money to white folks? You ain't dumb. You just pretend, you. I think you just here to see me.' She smiled again and stretched both her arms over her head.

'Did Boggs come see Gros Mama Goula?'

'That white trash mess with Gros Mama, snakes be crawling out his grave.'

I heard the screen open on the spring; then the inside door raked back on the buckled linoleum floor, and the black woman in the purple dress with the scrolled blue tattoos on the tops of her breasts stood in the doorway, one hand on her hip, a flowered kerchief curled in her fingers.

'You taking up too much of people's time,' she said. 'You got jelly roll on your mind, or you think bothering my womens gonna clean that man outta your head?'

45

'What?' I said.

She told the woman on the bed to dress and get up to the juke and help wait tables. She picked up the ashtray with the roach in it and threw it outside into the darkness.

'Wait a minute, what did you say?' I said.

She ignored me.

'And tell that drunk nigger giving Al trouble when I be back up there his skinny ass better be gone,' she said to the other woman, who buttoned her jeans, pulled on her blouse, and went out the door.

Gros Mama Goula's face was big and hard-boned, like a man's, her eyes deep-set and dark, so that they had a cavernous quality under the broad forehead and thick brows. I had heard stories about her from other Negroes, the juju woman who could blow the fire out of a burn; stop bleeding by pressing her palm against a wound; charm worms out of a child's stomach; cause a witch to invade the marriage bed, straddle the husband, and fornicate with him until his eyes crossed and he would remain forever discontent with his wife.

'What did you say?' I repeated.

'Po-licemens after jelly roll just like everybody else. You want it, you come ax me first, don't be bothering my womens. That ain't what on your mind, though. You got Jimmie Lee Boggs crawling round in your head. Jelly roll ain't gonna get him out you. He lying there, waiting.'

'Is this supposed to impress me?'

She opened a cabinet over the stove, took out a jelly glass and a pint bottle of rum, poured herself three fingers, sat down at a small breakfast table,

46

and lit a cigarette. She drank down the rum, inhaled from the cigarette, blew smoke out over her hand, and studied her knuckles as though I were not there.

'What you want?' she said.

'For openers take a break on the *traiteur* routine.'

'What you mean?'

'You talked with Dorothea. You knew I was looking for Boggs. You'd seen my picture in the newspaper, or you figured out I was one of the men he shot.'

'Think what you want. I ain't got the problem.'

'What I think is you're operating a place of prostitution.'

She smoked and flicked her ashes and waited for me to go on.

'I don't bother you?' I said.

'You want to carry me up to the jail, that's your bidness. They's people pay my bond make sure I stay open.'

'Was Jimmie Lee Boggs cutting into Hipolyte's and your action?'

'Darlin', they ain't nobody cutting into my action.'

'I don't believe you, Gros Mama. There's not a hot-pillow house in South Louisiana that doesn't have to piece off its action to New Orleans.'

She poured rum into her glass again, then as an afterthought looked at me and pointed her finger at the bottle.

'No thanks,' I said.

She screwed the top slowly onto the bottle.

'Lookie here,' she said. 'You don't care 'bout them dagos in New Orleans, 'bout what some

47

niggers be doing down here on Saturday night. You want that man 'cause he hurt you, 'cause he walking round in your sleep at night. You wake up tired in the morning, cain't open and close your hands on the side the bed. You dragging a big chain all day long. Food don't taste no good, womens just something for other mens. You can tell the whole round world I lying, but me and you knows better.'

I stared at her woodenly. She continued to smoke idly.

'I ain't seen him since they 'rested him for killing that man with the ball bat,' she said. 'He in New Orleans, though.'

'How do you know?'

'He gonna die over there. In a black room, with lightning jumping all over it. Don't mess with it, darlin'. Come down see Gros Mama when you wake up with that bad feeling. She make you right,' she said, and squared her shoulders so that the tattoos on her breasts stretched like a spiderweb.

3

The next morning Alafair and I raked and burned leaves under the pecan trees in my front yard. It was a perfect blue-gold autumn day, and the smoke from the fire hung in the spangled sunlight and drifted out across the bayou into the cypress trees. A little over two years earlier my wife, Annie, and I had been seining for shrimp just the other side of Marsh Island when we saw a twin-engine plane trailing a column of thick black smoke across the sky. It pancaked into a trough, dipped one wing into a wave, and cartwheeled like a child's stick toy across the water. While Annie called the Coast Guard on the emergency channel, I went over the side with an air tank and weight belt and swam down into the greenish-yellow light to the plane, which had come to rest upside down in a trench. Through the window, among the drowned bodies undulating in their seats, I saw Alafair kicking her legs and fighting to keep her head afloat inside a wobbling envelope of trapped air. Her small mouth looked like a guppy's above the waterline.

Later, Annie and I would find the bruise marks

on her legs where her mother had held her up in the air pocket while she herself lost her life.

I gave Alafair my mother's name, and after Annie's death I legally adopted her. But even now I still knew little of the Central American world which she had fled, except that memories of it had given her nightmares for a long time and she thought of manual labor almost as play. She loved to work in the yard with me. She held the rake handle midway down and scoured the ground bare with the tines, her elastic-waisted jeans grimed at the knees, her face hot and bright with her work. She wore her yellow T-shirt with a smiling purple whale and the words 'Baby Orca' embossed on it, but it was too small for her now and her arms looked fat and round in the sleeves.

It was too good a day to dwell on Jimmie Lee Boggs and Gros Mama Goula and a lot of mojo claptrap, so Alafair and I took the jugboat and headed out Southwest Pass onto the salt. It was called a jugboat because it had been used by a marine seismograph company to lay out and recover the long rubber-coated cables and instruments, or 'jugs', that recorded the vibrations off the substrata after an explosion was detonated in the drill hole. It was narrow and long, built for speed, with a low draft, a big Chrysler engine, two screws, and the windowed pilot's cab flush on the stern. I had outfitted it with gear boxes, ice bins, a small galley, a bait well, winches for my trawling nets, iron rod-and-reel sockets for trolling. In the middle of the deck I bolted down a telephone-company spool table, with a collapsible Cinzano umbrella set in the center hole.

The day was warm, the ground swells long and gentle and rolling, so that when they crested the wave broke into a thin froth and blew in the wind. I kept the bow into the wind and idled through the swells while Alafair set the rods into the sockets, spun out the lines behind us so the lures bounced in our wake, clicked on the drags, and threw chum overboard as if she were flinging shot. High up against the blue dome of sky, brown pelicans drifted in formation on the wind stream. Then suddenly their wings would collapse, cock into their sides like fins, and they would plummet with the speed of an aerial bomb into the water and rise from the foam with a menhaden or flying fish dripping from their pouched beak.

In the middle of a long green trough I saw a greasy slick on the water and smelled the fecund odor of speckled or white trout in a big school. I cut the engine, threw the anchor, and let the jugboat swing back against the tension in the rope. We reeled in our lines and rigged them with heavy teardrop weights, bait hooks, and big corks. Alafair's two-handed cast sent a lead weight and hook singing past my ear.

The clouds in the west looked like strips of flame above the green horizon when we headed back through the Pass into Vermilion Bay. The ice bin was loaded with gaff-top catfish and speckled trout, gutted and stiff and laid out in cold rows, their mouths hooked open, their eyes black and shiny as glass. Alafair sat on my lap and steered us between the buoys into the channel; when I touched her head with my chin I could feel the sun's heat in her hair.

'Let's take some to Batist tonight,' she said.

'That's a good idea, little guy.'

She twisted her head around and grinned up at me.

'Then maybe rent a movie,' she said.

'You got it, Alf.'

'Buy some *boudin* and fix some Kool-Aid, too.'

'That's actually been on my mind all day.'

'All right, big guy.'

We were happy and tired when we drove down the dirt road under the oaks toward my house on the bayou. Our clothes were flecked with fish blood and membrane, our skin salty and dry from the wind and the sun. It had been a fine day. I was determined that it would remain so, even though I saw Minos Dautrieve's car parked by my gallery and Minos sitting on my front step.

Alafair rinsed the fish in the sink while Minos and I went out in the backyard and sat at my redwood picnic table under the mimosa tree. The moon was up, and I could see my neighbor's sugarcane in the field.

'I've got a proposal for you,' he said.

'What's that, Minos?'

'You know I'm on that Presidential Task Force on Drugs?'

'Yeah.'

'It's an election year, and everybody wants to stomp the shit out of the drug dealers. Never mind the fact that we've had our budgets cut for years. But that's all right, it's all rock 'n' roll, anyway. We'll cripple up as many lowlifes as we can and let somebody else worry about the rest, right?'

'Minos –'

'Okay, take it easy. Have you tried to turn up that black kid?'

'It's all dead-end stuff. His grandmother and his girlfriend probably know where he is, but they're not saying. I ended up last night talking with a *traiteur* woman named Big Mama Goula in a hot-pillow joint. That's a long way from Jimmie Lee Boggs.'

'Look, I think your life's been too dull. So I talked with some people on the task force, then I talked with the Iberia sheriff. We want to put you inside the mob.'

'What?'

'You're the perfect guy.'

'Are you out of your mind?'

'Hear me out.'

'No. I went back with the sheriff's department to pay off some big debts. I got shot. You think I want to go undercover now?'

'That's why you're the perfect guy, Dave. It wouldn't be undercover. You resign from the department, we set you up in New Orleans, give you a lot of money to flash around the lowlifes. Then we put out the word with a couple of our snitches that you were encouraged to resign, you're a burnout, maybe you've been on a pad.'

I was shaking my head, but he kept talking.

'There's a new player in New Orleans we want to nail real bad. His name's Anthony Cardo, also known as Tony C. and Tony the Cutter. No, he's not a shank artist. He's supposed to have a schlong that's a foot and a half long, the Johnny Wad of the Mafia. He grew up across the river in Algiers, but he's got operations in Miami and Fort Lauderdale. In fact, we think he's a linchpin between the dope traffic in South Florida and southern Louisiana.'

'I'm not interested.'

'Look, it'd be a three- or four-week scam. If it doesn't work, we'll mark it off.'

'It won't work.'

'Why not?'

'They won't buy a cop who just turned in his badge.'

'Yeah, they will. They'll buy you,' he said, and tapped his finger at the air.

'I have a feeling you're about to say something else complimentary.'

'Let's look at your record, fair and square, podna. You were almost fired from the force in New Orleans, you have an alcoholic history, you've been in your own drunk tank, you were up on a murder charge, for God's sakes. All right, it was a frame, and that situation with the New Orleans P.D. was a rotten shake, too, but like I told you when I first met you, it makes socko reading material. How about your old Homicide partner, what's his name?'

'Cletus Purcel.'

'He didn't have any trouble going to work for the wiseguys, did he? They bought him, toenails to hairline.'

'He's clean now. He owns a club on Decatur.'

'That's right. But he still knows the greaseballs. They come in his place.'

'It's a free country.'

'You've got the conduit into the mob, Dave. They'll buy it.'

'Not interested.'

'It's no more complicated than a simple sting.'

'I told you you're talking to the wrong guy, Minos.'

'There's another factor. We think Jimmie Lee Boggs might be back in New Orleans.'

'Why?'

'A telephone tap. Last week one of Tony Cardo's people was talking about bringing in a mechanic from Florida to take care of a guy who held back twenty thou on a sale. Then yesterday somebody did this black street dealer with a baseball bat in Louis Armstrong Park. Sound familiar?'

'Why would he go back to a state where he's already been sentenced to the chair?'

'It doesn't make any difference where he is. There're warrants on him in three other states, and the FBI's after him as an interstate fugitive. Number two, he'll go where Tony Cardo tells him to go.'

'I'm not up to it. You'll have to get somebody else.'

'That's it, huh?'

'Yep.'

He looked at me reflectively in the moonlight. I could see his scalp glisten through his thin crew cut.

'How you feeling?' he said.

'Fine.'

'You're a good cop, Dave. The best.'

After he was gone, I sat by myself in the yard awhile and tried to put my thoughts into separate envelopes. Then I gave it up and went inside to eat supper with Alafair at the kitchen table.

So the days went by and I watched the leaves fall and my neighbor harvest his sugarcane, which was now thick and gold and purple in the fields. Each evening I jogged three miles down the dirt road to the drawbridge on the bayou, the air like a cool burn on my skin, and as the sun set over the bare field behind my house I did sit-ups and stomach crunches in my backyard, curled a fifty-pound dumbbell with my right arm, a ten-pound bar with my left, and sat down weary and glazed with sweat in the damp grass. I could feel my body mending, the muscles tightening and responding in my upper chest and neck the way they had before a bullet had torn through the linkage and collapsed it like a broken spiderweb.

But to be honest, the real purpose in my physical regimen was to induce as much fatigue in my body as possible. Morpheus' gifts used to come to me in bottles, Beam and black Jack Daniel's, straight up with a frosted schooner of Jax on the side, while I watched the rain pour down in the neon glow outside the window of an all-night bar not far from the Huey Long Bridge. In a half hour I could kick open a furnace door and fling into the flames all the snakes and squeaking bats that lived inside me. Except the next morning they would writhe with new life in the ashes and come back home, stinking and hungry.

Now I tried to contend with my own unconscious, and the dreams it brought, with a weight set, a pair of Adidas shoes, and running shorts.

Then one evening, a week after Minos had appeared again, a pickup truck with two cracked front windows, crumpled fenders, and a bumper that hung down like a broken mouth bounced through the depressions in my drive, the tailgate slamming on the chain, the rust-gutted muffler roaring like a stock-car racer. Tante Lemon's head barely extended above the steering wheel; her chin was pointed upward, her small hands pinched on the wheel, her frosted eyes pinpoints of concern as she tried to maneuver through the trunks of the pecan trees. Dorothea sat next to her, one hand propped against the dashboard.

'She wanta tell you something,' Tante Lemon said.

'Come in,' I said, and I opened the truck door for her.

'We ain't got to do that,' she said.

'Yeah, you do,' I said.

They both followed me up onto the gallery. I opened the screen door. I wondered how many times Tante Lemon had walked through a white person's front door. Once inside, neither of them would sit until I told them to.

'What is it?' I said.

'Ax her,' Tante Lemon said.

I looked at Dorothea. She wore an orange polyester dress and a straw purse on a strap, but her black pumps were scuffed and dusty.

'Tee Beau say maybe he can find out where that man's at,' she said.

'You talked to him?'

She looked at her hands in her lap.

'You got to promise somet'ing, Mr. Dave,' she said. 'Tee Beau say you a good man. Tante Lemon say your daddy good to her, too. It ain't right if you try to trick Tee Beau, no.'

'What do you mean?'

'You tole me Tee Beau can call you collect. From

a pay phone. But you can find out where he's at that way, cain't you?'

'You mean trace the call?'

'That's right. I seen them do that on TV. You gonna do that to Tee Beau, suh?' she said, and looked down at her lap again.

'If he'll call me, I'll promise not to do that, Dorothea. Look, I can't tell Tee Beau what to do, but isn't it better that he talk to somebody like me, who knows something about his case, who owes him a debt, than let some other cops hunt him down as an escaped killer?'

'Tee Beau say that man mean all the way through. He tell Tee Beau anybody stop them and Tee Beau open his mouth, he shoot everybody there and he shoot Tee Beau first.'

'Where does he think Boggs is?'

'He say he keep talking about the Italians, how they owe him a lot of money, how they gonna take care of him, how if Tee Beau smart he stay in New Orleans and sell dope. All the time Tee Beau sitting in back, scared that man gonna find out he ain't killed you in the coulee.'

'Tell him to call me at home. I'll write down my number.'

'He gonna find out where that man at first.'

'No, he shouldn't do that.'

'That little boy got courage,' Tante Lemon said. 'People ain't never see that in him. All they see is a little throwaway baby in a shoe box, him. Like when he took Mr. Dore car. He ain't stole it. Our truck was broke and I didn't have no way to go to the Charity in New Orleans. Me going blind, couldn't see to light my stove in the morning. He come flying

58

round the corner in Mr. Dore car, couldn't even drive, smash right over the church mailbox. Policemens come out and put handcuffs on him, shove him in their car with their stick like he's a raccoon. Ain't nobody ever ax why he done it.'

'You tell him I said to stay away from Boggs. That's not his job.'

'That ain't what you said before,' Tante Lemon said.

'I didn't tell him to go looking for Boggs.'

'No suh, you say Tee Beau he'p you find that man, you he'p Tee Beau,' Dorothea said. 'That's what you tell me at the juke, out there in your car, out there in the rain. When I tell that to Tee Beau I say I don't knows what to think. He say Mr. Dave a white man, but he don't never lie.'

Then both of them looked at me silently in the half-light of my living room. Tante Lemon's frosted turquoise eyes were fixed on me with the lidless glare of a bird's.

A therapist once told me that everyone has a dream box in his head. He said that sometimes an event provides us with a rusty key to it that we can well do without. Jimmie Lee Boggs had turned all the tumblers in the lock, and I discovered that, like a perverse nocturnal demiurge, he had taken my ten months in Vietnam from me, reactivated every fearful moment I had lived through, and written himself into the script as a player.

The sun is hot in the sky but I cannot see it through the thick canopy of trees overhead. The light is diffused a yellow-green through the sweating vegetation, as though

I am looking at it through water. The trunks of the banyan trees are striped with moisture; the blades of elephant grass, which can leave your skin covered with paper-thin cuts, are beaded with wet pinpoints of light. I lie flat on my chest in the grass, and the air is so humid and superheated I cannot keep the sweat out of my eyes – my forearm only rubs more sweat and dirt into them. I can feel ants crawling inside my shirt and belt, and ahead of me, where the elephant grass slopes down to a coulee, a gray cloud of mosquitoes hovers over a dead log, and a red centipede, as thick as a pencil and six inches long, is wending his way across the humus.

I can smell the sour odor of mud, stagnant water in the coulee, the foul reek of fear from my own armpits. An eighteen-year-old kid nicknamed Doo-Doo, from West Memphis, Arkansas, lies next to me, his bare chest strung with bandoliers, a green sweat-soaked towel draped from under the back of his pot.

His ankle is broken, and he keeps looking back at it and the boot that he has worked halfway off his foot. His sock looks like rotted cheesecloth. The whites of his eyes are filled with ruptured blood veins.

'They got Martinez's blooker. Don't go out there, Lieutenant. They waiting for you in the tree line,' he says.

'They'll bang him up in a tree.'

'He at the bottom of the ditch. You cain't get him out. They waiting for you, Lieutenant. I seen them.'

The rivulets of sweat leaking out of his pot and running down his face and shoulders look like lines of clear plastic against his black skin.

I crawl on my stomach through the grass with the barrel of the .45 lifted just above the mud. The underside of my body is slick with green-black ooze; my elbows, knees, and boots make sucking sounds with each movement forward. My face is alive with cuts and mosquitoes. Behind me I bear Doo-Doo easing a clip into his rifle.

The grass thins at the edge of the coulee, and down the incline Martinez lies crucified in a half inch of water, his flak jacket blown off his chest, his face white with concussion, his dented pot twenty yards down from him. He has long eyelashes like a girl's, and they keep fluttering as he looks up at me; his mouth opens and closes as though he's trying to clear his ears.

The ground on the other side of the coulee is flat and clear for thirty yards back to a line of rubber trees. The sunlight here is bright and hazy, and I shield my eyes with my hand and try to look deep into the shadows of the rubber trees. The air is breathless, the reeds and elephant ears along the bank absolutely still. I drop over the lip of the coulee and slide erect down the embankment with my boot heels dug into the mud.

Martinez tries to speak, but I see the sucking chest wound now and the torn, wet cloth of his undershirt that flutters in the cavity from the release of air. He sounds like a man strangling in his own saliva.

I try to lift him on my shoulders and hold one of his arms and legs in front of me, but my knee folds and we both go down in a pool of muddy water that's hotter than the air. Then I see them walk out of the rubber trees against the sun. They look no bigger than children. Their black pajamas stick wetly to their bodies; their faces are skeletal and filled with teeth. One of them squats down and aims Martinez's blooker at me. A man behind him shakes cigarettes out of a pack of Lucky Strikes for his friends. They are all laughing.

61

My .45 lies somewhere in the clouded water, my boots are locked in mud. I hear Doo-Doo firing, but it makes no difference at this point. I stare at my executioner, my body painted with the tropical stink of his country, an unformed prayer wheezing like sand from my throat. The short, fat barrel of the grenade launcher recoils upward in his hands with a deep-throated roar, and a moment later I'm caught in an envelope of flame and I feel a pain in my chest like jagged iron twisting its way through tendon and bone.

Then I am on all fours, like a dog, vomiting blood on my hands, and in the smoke and the smell of burnt powder I stare up the embankment at where the small men in pajamas should be but are not. Instead, Jimmie Lee Boggs takes his package of Lucky Strikes from his blue jeans pocket and lights one. His mannequinlike head is perfectly still as he puffs on his cigarette and lets the smoke drift from his lips. Then he flips the butt in an arc out on the coulee, works his way down the embankment, and finds my .45 in the water.

He works the receiver and knocks the barrel clean of mud on his jeans. He casually points it behind my ear, lets the iron sight bite into my scalp.

'You thought the zips were going to get you, but I'm the one can make you cry,' he says.

I woke up with the sheets twisted across my chest, my body hot in the cold square of moonlight that shone through the window. Outside, the pecan trees were black against the sky. I lay awake until dawn, when the light became gray, then pink, in the flooded cypress on the far side of the bayou. Then I tried to sleep again, but it was no use. I helped Batist open up the bait shop, and at eight o'clock I drove to work at the sheriff's office and began pro-

cessing traffic accident reports, my eyes weak with
fatigue.

That afternoon, four days after Tante Lemon and
Dorothea's visit, I drove to Minos Dautrieve's
house in Lafayette. He lived in the old part of town
on the north side, a neighborhood of Victorian
homes, deep lawns, enormous live oak trees, iron
tethering posts, gazebos, screened galleries, and
cascading leaves. He had grown up in a shotgun
farmhouse outside of Abbeville, but I always
suspected that inside his cynicism he had a jaded
reverence for the ways of late-nineteenth-century
southern gentility.

We sat on cushioned wood lawn chairs in his
backyard and drank lemonade amid the golden
light and the leaves that scratched across the flagstones, or floated in an old stone well that he had
turned into a goldfish pond.

'You already talked to the sheriff?' he asked.

'He says it's between me and you. I'll be on lend-
lease to the Presidential Task Force, but my salary
will still come from the department. Evidently everybody thinks this task force is big stuff right now.'

'You're not impressed?'

'Who cares what I think?'

'Come on, you don't believe we're winning the
war on drugs?' He was smiling. He had to squint
against the yellow orb of sun that shone through the
oak limbs overhead.

'The head of the DEA says the contras deal
cocaine. Reagan and the Congress give them guns
and money. It's hard to put all that in the same
basket and be serious about it,' I said.

He stopped smiling.

'But there's one difference,' he said. 'No matter what those guys in Washington do, we still send the lowlifes up the road and we trash their operation everywhere we can.'

'All right.'

'I'm not making my point very well, though.'

'Yes, you are. Look, I respect your agency, I appreciate its problems.'

'Respect's not enough. When you work for the federal government, you have to obey its rules. There's no area there for negotiation.'

'This whole business was your idea, Minos.'

'It's a good idea, too. But let's look at your odometer again. Sometimes you've had a way of doing things on your own.'

'Maybe that's a matter of perception.'

'You remember that guy you busted with a pool cue in Breaux Bridge? They had to use a mop to clean up the blood. And the guy you cut in half through an attic floor in New Orleans? I won't mention a couple of other incidents.'

'I never dealt the play. You know that.'

'I can see you've had a lot of regret about it, too.'

'I'm just not interested in the past anymore.'

'There are some people who aren't as confident in you as I am.'

'Then let them do it.'

He smiled again.

'That happens to be what I told them,' he said. 'It didn't light up the room with goodwill. But seriously, Dave, we can't have Wyatt Earp on the payroll.'

'You're the skipper. If I do something that causes

problems for your office, you cut me loose. What's the big deal?'

'You know, I think you have another potential. Maybe in scholarship. Like reducing the encyclopedia to a simple declarative sentence.'

I set my empty glass on a table. The wafer of sun was low in the sky now, the air cooler, the leaves in the goldfish pond dark and sodden. A neighbor was barbecuing, and smoke drifted over the garden wall into the yard. I leaned forward in the chair, one hand pinched around my wrist.

'I think your concern is misplaced,' I said. 'When I got hurt the second time in Vietnam, it was a million-dollar wound. I was out of it. I didn't have to prove anything, because there was no place to prove it. This one's different. It's ongoing, and I don't know if I'll measure up. I don't know if you have the right man.'

I saw his eyes move over my face.

'You're going to do fine,' he said.

I didn't answer.

'Like I said, it's not much more complicated than a simple sting,' he continued. 'We take it a step at a time and see where it leads. If it starts to get nasty, we pull you out. That has nothing to do with you. We don't want any of our people hurt. It's not worth it. We figure the shitbags all take a fall sooner or later.

'Look, this is the way it's going to work. We've got an apartment for you on Ursulines in the Quarter, and the word's going to be out on the street that you're fired and dirty. There are five or six dealers around there you can approach to make a buy. Nothing real big right now, four or five keys,

65

maybe a fifty-thousand-dollar buy. They're not going to trust you. They'll jerk you around, give you a lot of bullshit probably, maybe test you in some way. But these are low-level, greedy guys who are also dumb, and they get a hard-on when they see money. You set up the score, we let it go through, then we move up to bigger things.'

'Where's all this money coming from?'

'It's confiscated from drug deals. Don't worry, we'll get it back. Anyway, once these guys are convinced you're the real article, you tell them you want to reinvest your profits. Then we offer them some serious gelt. They don't want the action, you tell them you can make the score in Houston. Tony Cardo hates the guy who runs the action out of Houston. The word is he screwed Tony's wife in a bathroom stall at the Castaways in Miami. We're talking about a real class bunch here. The goal, though, is to get Cardo involved in the deal. He's a weird fucking guy.'

I had to laugh.

'What's your idea of normal?' I asked.

'No, this guy's special. He not only looks weird, he's deeply fucked up in the head. Maybe it's his background. His mother used to shampoo corpses for funeral homes.'

'What?'

'That's how she made her money. She washed the hair of corpses for a mortician. Finally she bought her own funeral parlor in Algiers. Tony C. must not have liked it, though, because he put it up for sale two days after he inherited it.'

'What if I run across Jimmie Lee Boggs?'

'You let us handle him. We'll figure out a way to

have him picked up without compromising you.'

'There's one other thing. Tee Beau Latiolais, the black kid who escaped with Boggs, he's in New Orleans. He told his girlfriend he's going to try to find Boggs for me.'

'Why does he want to do that?'

'I sent word to him that I'd help him if he'd help me. I didn't mean for him to go looking for Boggs, though.'

'You worry too much. It's just a sting. Hey, you're going back to New Orleans.'

4

I took Alafair to stay at the home of my cousin Tutta, a retired schoolteacher in New Iberia. It wasn't easy. I carried her suitcase and her paper bag of Curious George and Baby Squanto books and coloring materials up onto the gingerbread porch and sat down with her in the swing. The sun was bright on the lawn. Bumblebees hummed over the hibiscus and the pale blue hydrangeas in the flower beds.

'It's not going to be for long, little guy,' I said. 'I'm going to call you almost every night, and Tutta will take you out to feed your horse. If I can, I'll come back on a weekend.'

She looked out blankly at the dew shining on the grass.

'It's a business trip, Alafair. It's just something I have to do.'

'You said we wouldn't leave New Iberia again. You said you didn't like New Orleans anymore, that it was full of dope and bad people.'

'That doesn't mean we have to be afraid of those things, does it? Come on, we're not going to let a short trip get us down, are we? Guys like us are too tough for that.'

Her face was sullen. I took off her Astros cap and set it sideways on her head, then looked down into her face.

'Trust me on this one, Alf,' I said. My cousin came out on the porch. I squeezed Alafair against me. Her body felt hard and unyielding. 'Okay, little guy?'

Her eyes were blinking, and I touched her face with my hand.

'Hey, you remember what my father used to do when he had a problem?' I asked. 'He'd grin right in its face, then give the old thumbs-up sign. He'd say, "You mess with us coonass, we gonna spit right in yo' mouth."'

She looked up at me and smiled faintly. My cousin held the screen for her.

'Dave?' Alafair said.

'Yes?'

'When you come back, it's gonna be like it was?'

'What do you mean?'

'Playing and joking, like we always did. You always coming home full of fun.'

'You bet. I just have to clear up some problems, that's all.'

'I can go with you. I can cook meals, I can wash clothes in the machine.'

'Not this time, Alf.'

Tutta took Alafair's hand in her own.

'Dave, those bad people, they're not gonna hurt you again, are they?' Alafair said.

'You remember what Batist did when that gator got inside his fishnet and tore it up?' I said.

She thought, then grinned broadly.

'That's right,' I said. 'He grabbed the gator by its tail, swung it around in the air, and threw it all the way over the levee. Well, that's the way we handle the bad guys when they give us trouble.'

I hugged her again and kissed her forehead.

'Good-bye, little guy,' I said.

''Bye, Dave.'

Her eyes were starting to film, and I walked down to the picket gate before I turned and glanced back at her. She stood in the open screen door, one of her hands in Tutta's, her ball cap low on her ears. She looked back at me from under the bill of her cap and raised her thumb in the air.

I left Batist to manage the bait shop and boat dock, and on Halloween I moved into my apartment on Ursulines in the Quarter. Most people identify the Quarter with the antiques stores on Royal, the sidewalk artists around Jackson Square, and the strip joints and T-shirt shops on Bourbon Street, but it has a residential and community life of its own: a Catholic elementary school, a city park, small grocery stores with screen doors, wood floors, ceiling fans, display coolers loaded with cheeses, sausages, and skinned catfish, and bins of plums and bananas set out on the sidewalk under the colonnade.

My apartment was inside a walled courtyard that you entered through an iron gate and a domed brick walkway. The flower beds were thick with blooming azalea and camellia and untrimmed banana trees, and the people who lived in the second-story apartments had placed coffee cans of begonias and hung baskets of impatiens along the balcony.

My place was on the first floor, and it had a bedroom, a small kitchen, a bath with a shower, and a living room. Like those of most residences in the Quarter, its walls were marked with all the historical attempts of its owners to adapt to technological change. The gas lamps had been removed and plastered over at the turn of the century; bricks had been torn out of the walls to replumb and rewire the kitchen and the bath; big hand-twist electric switches stuck out of the plaster but turned on no light.

I opened the windows and began to hang my clothes in the closet. Maybe I should have felt good to be back in New Orleans, where I had been a policeman for fourteen years in the First District, but it felt strange to be alone in a rented apartment, with the late-afternoon light cold and yellow on the banana trees outside. Or maybe it was simply a matter of age. Solitude and the years did not go well with me, and even though I had lived over a half century, I had concluded that I was one of those people who would never know with any certainty who they were, that my thoughts about myself would always be question marks; my only identity would remain the reflection that I saw in the eyes of others.

I could feel myself slipping inside that dark alcoholic envelope of depression and regret that for long periods had been characteristic of my adult life. I finished putting my shirts, underwear, and socks in the dresser drawers, stripped down to my skivvies, and did ten one-arm chins on an iron pipe in the kitchen, forty leg lifts, and fifty stomach crunches, and got into the shower and turned the water on so hot that my skin turned red and grainy through my suntan.

I dried off and combed my hair in the mirror. I had lost fifteen pounds since Boggs had shot me; my stomach was flat, the love handles around my waist had almost disappeared, the scar tissue where a bouncing Betty had gotten me in Vietnam looked like a spray of small gray arrow points that had been slipped under the skin on my right thigh and side. I still had my father's thick black hair and mustache, except for the white patch above my ear, and if I didn't pay attention to the lines in my neck and around my eyes and the black-peppery flecks of skin cancer on my arms, I could still pretend it was only the bottom of the fifth.

Question: Where do you score a few grams of coke in New Orleans?

Answer: Almost anywhere you want to.

But where do you score a thousand grams, a kilo? The question becomes more complicated. Minos had accused me of being simplistic. Later I would wonder when he had last been on the street with his own clientele.

It was dusk when I got to the address on Esplanade on the edge of the Quarter; the air was crisp, the dry palm fronds on the neutral ground clattered in the breeze, and costumed Negro children with jack-o'-lanterns ran in groups from one high, lighted gallery to the next. The man I was looking for lived in a garage apartment behind a columned one-story wood house on the corner, which like many New Orleans antebellum homes was built up high above the lawn because of floods. But the wood doors on the drive were padlocked, and the iron gate that gave on to the side yard wouldn't open either. I could see a man working under an automobile in the drive, with a mechanic's lamp attached to an extension cord.

I shook the gate against the iron fastenings in the brick wall. The man slid out from under the car on a creeper. A lighted cigar lay on the cement by his head. One eye squinted at me like a fist.

'What do you want?' he said.

'I'm looking for Lionel Comeaux.'

'What do you want?'

'Are you Lionel Comeaux?'

'Yeah, what do you want?'

'Can I come in?'

'The latch is inside, at the top of the gate,' he said, and picked up a crescent wrench off the cement to begin working under the car again.

I entered the yard and walked through flower beds filled with elephant ears and caladium and waited for him to slide back from under the car again. He didn't, so I had to squat down to talk to him. 'I want to make a buy.'

'Buy what?' he said, blinking at the rust that fell out of the car frame into his eyes. He wore jeans and a purple and gold LSU jersey with the sleeves cut off at the shoulders. His arms were big and covered with tan, and he had a deep red U.S. Navy tattoo on one bicep. His head was square, his dark hair crew cut. He chewed gum, and there were lumps of cartilage behind his ears.

'I want some pure stuff, no cut, a good price,' I said. 'I hear you're the guy who can help me.'

'Pure what? What are you talking about, buddy?'

'What the fuck do you think I'm talking about?'

He stopped working, removed a piece of grit from his eyelashes with this thumb, and looked at me. The backs of his hands were shiny with grease.

'Who sent you here?' he said.

'Some people in Lafayette.'

'Who?'

'People I do business with. What do you care?'

'I care, man. What's your name?'

'Dave Robicheaux.'

He pushed the creeper out from under the car and raised himself up on one elbow. He was maybe twenty-five and had the neck and shoulder tendons of a weight lifter.

'You're talking about dope, right? Skag, reefer, stuff like that?' he said. He picked up his cigar off the cement and puffed it alight.

'I'm talking about cocaine, podna. Ten thou a key. I can take five keys off you.'

'Cocaine?' he said.

'That's right.'

'That's interesting. But number one, I'm not your podna, because I don't know who you are. Number two, I don't know where you got my name or this address, but you've got the wrong information, wrong person, wrong house.'

'You see Tony Cardo?'

'Who?'

'Look, I don't mean to offend you, but the bozo routine is wearing thin. You tell Cardo there's some oil people in Lafayette with a lot of money to invest. He doesn't want the business, that's fine. You don't want to pass on the information, that's fine. We can get what we need in Houston. You know where

74

Clete's Club is?'

'No.'

'You know where Joe Burda's Golden Star is on Decatur?'

'Yeah.'

'It's two doors up from there. If you want to do some business, leave word at the bar.'

'Make sure the gate latches on your way out,' he said.

The next two people whose names and addresses Minos had given me were equally unproductive. One was a bar owner who was in jail in Baton Rouge, and the other, a wrestling promoter, had died of AIDS.

At eleven that night I walked down Bourbon in the roar of noise from the bars and strip joints, amid the Halloween revelers, the midwestern conventioneers, breathless, red-faced college kids who spilled beer from their paper cups down the front of their clothes, and the Negro street dancers whose clip-on taps rang like horse-shoes on the cement. Bourbon is closed to automobile traffic, so that the street itself is like an open-air zoo, but by and large it's a harmless one. The girls still take off their clothes on the runways and hookers work out of taxicabs in the early morning hours. Occasionally a cop will cool out a drunk with a baton in a side-street bar, and the burlesque spielers in candy-striped vests and straw boaters can conjure up visions right out of adolescent masturbation; but ultimately Bourbon offers the appearance of sleaze to the tourists with the implicit understanding that it contains no real threat of injury to them.

In fact, the man I wanted to find ran a T-shirt and souvenir shop, and he was as innocuous in dress and manner as an ice cream salesman. He walked out from behind a curtain in back after his clerk told him I wanted to talk to him, and his oval face was pink and shining, his thin red hair combed back with water, his mouth wide with a grin, his neck powdered with talcum. He wore a white suit and a silver silk shirt, and his appearance gave every indication of a harmless, happy fat man – except that on second glance you noticed that his chest was as broad as his stomach, that he wore gold chains around his neck, that his eyes took your inventory and did not smile with his mouth.

'I know you,' he said, and shook his finger playfully at me. 'You're a police officer. No, you used to be one, right here in the Quarter.'

'That's right.'

'You were a lieutenant.'

'That's right.'

'You probably don't remember me, but I used to see you and your partner over at the Acme. You used to come in at lunch for oysters. What's his name? He's got a club here now.'

'Cletus Purcel.'

'Yeah. I was in his place the other day. Real nice. I think he's going to make it.'

'Could I talk to you in private?'

He looked at the ruby-studded gold watch on his wrist.

'Sure thing,' he said, and held back the curtain for me.

His office was a small, cluttered room in the back, with a desk, three chairs, and old jazz posters

76

on the brick walls. He sat in the swivel chair behind the desk and tapped the bottom of a poster with his finger.

'See that name there?' he said. 'You got to look close, but that's me, Uncle Ray Fontenot. I played trombone right down the street at Sharky Bonnano's Dream Room. You remember him?'

'Sure.'

'You remember those two colored guys used to tap-dance on the stage there, Pork Chops and Kidney Beans?'

'I want to score five kilos of uncut coke. You deliver good stuff at the right price, we'll be doing more business later.'

He peeled the cellophane off a package of Picayune cigarettes.

'Not too many ex-cops come in here with that kind of statement,' he said. He had never stopped smiling.

'Forget the ex-cop business. It all spends.'

'Oh, don't misunderstand me. I'm not knocking a man trying to make a little money. But your information's dated. That's what I'm trying to say.'

'How's that?'

He tilted back in the swivel chair, his silver shirt tight across his broad chest and stomach, his eyes bright and squinted with goodwill.

'I always had problems with weight and high blood pressure,' he said. 'I smoked reefer every night to keep my blood pressure down, then I'd go out and eat a whole pizza by myself. I got on prescription diet pills, then I started using some stuff that was a little more serious. Finally I was in the business myself, you know what I mean? So

77

whoever gave you my name wasn't all wrong. But I bottomed out and went into treatment a year ago. The only problem I've got now is I eat all the time.'

'You're in a twelve-step program?'

'What?'

'You're out of the business?'

'That's about it.'

'Tell me, when you give a guy like Tony C. the deep six, what do you do? Just drop around one day and say, "I bottomed out, Tony. I'm out of the business, see you around, you don't like it, fuck you"?'

This time the words bit into some nerve endings behind that pink and smiling face. He lit his cigarette and blew smoke at an upward angle into the air.

'I've never met the gentleman,' he said, his eyes crinkling again.

'I see. Sorry to have wasted your time. I'll run along now, Mr. Fontenot. Say, the next time you give somebody that treatment shuck, you might find out what a twelve-step program is.'

He tipped his ashes into an ashtray and looked pleasantly into his cigarette smoke without seeing anything.

'Tell Tony C. his distribution in southwestern Louisiana is lousy,' I said. 'I can double or triple it. But I've got nothing to prove. There's some guys in Texas who want to branch out.'

'Then maybe that's who you should deal with.'

'They've got a bad reputation. But maybe you're right. If I meet Tony C., I'll tell him what you said.'

'Now, wait a minute . . .'

'I don't blame you for bullshitting me, Mr.

Fontenot, but if you get serious, leave a message for me at Clete's Club. I'll be back in touch.'

I walked back through the T-shirt shop and out into the neon lights and cacophony of jazz and rock bands on Bourbon Street.

I was tired, unshaved, weary of the people I had been with, my ears thick with the sound of trumpets and trombones and electric guitars, yet I did not want to return to the apartment and be alone. I walked to the Café du Monde for coffee and *beignets*, but it had already closed. So I sat on an iron bench in front of the cathedral in Jackson Square and watched the moon rise in the sky. The air was heavy with the smell of camellias, and the magnolia and banana trees that grew along the piked fence behind me made shifting patterns of shadow and light on the cement. A wind came up off the river, and it started to mist; then a shower clattered across the banana leaves in the square and blew in a spray under the lighted colonnades. I walked home on a quiet street, away from the noise of the tourists, keeping close under the scrolled iron balconies to avoid the rain.

It was warm and muggy the next morning, as it can be in southern Louisiana well into the Christmas season, and I had breakfast and read the *Times-Picayune* at the Café du Monde before the crowds of tourists came in, then walked across the square past the sidewalk artists and went inside the cathedral briefly because it was All Saints' Day. Later, I found two more of the contacts Minos had given me. One was a bail bondsman who told me to get out of his office, and the other was a woman who ran an occult bookstore that smelled of soiled cat litter. Her face was white with makeup, her eyes stenciled with purple eyeliner, her cigarette breath devastating. For fifteen minutes I pretended to examine her racks of books while she carried on a conversation with her customers about telepathic communication with UFOs and a hole in the dimension that exists in the middle of the Bermuda Triangle and operates like a drain in an enormous sink. Finally I bought a book on cats and left.

I called New Iberia that night to check on Alafair, and the next morning I walked over to Clete's Club on Decatur, across from the French Market. For years Clete had been my partner in the First District. He'd learned his law enforcement methods from an uncle who had walked a beat in the Irish Channel – 'Bust 'em or smoke 'em,' Clete always said – and had literally terrorized the lowlifes in the First. All you had to do was mention to a pimp or house creep or jackroller that Cletus Purcel would like to interview him, and he would be on the next bus or plane to Miami. Then Clete got into debt to the shylocks, ruined his marriage with whores and his stomach with booze and aspirin, and finally went on a pad and took ten thousand dollars from some drug dealers and right-wing crazies to get rid of a federal witness.

Later he would run house security at a casino in Nevada and become the bodyguard for a midlevel Mafia character and ex-con by the name of Sally Dio. But eventually what I thought of as Clete's most essential characteristics – his courage and his loyalty to an old friend – had their way, and he managed to walk away reasonably intact from all the wreckage in his life.

He was at the back of the bar, loading the stainless steel cooler with bottles of long-necked Jax. He looked up and smiled when he saw me. His body always looked too big for his clothes. He loved pizza, poor-boy sandwiches, deep-fried shrimp and oysters, dirty rice, *beignets*, ice cream, which he would eat with a tablespoon by the half gallon. He was convinced that he could control his weight by pumping iron every other night in his garage, and limit his ulcer damage by smoking Lucky Strikes through a cigarette filter and drinking his scotch with milk.

'What's happening, Streak?' he said. 'I had a feeling, you'd be by.'

'How's that?'

'I'm hearing weird stuff about you, mon.'

'Did somebody leave a message for me?'

'Nope.'

'Then what did you hear?'

He stood erect from his work, flexed the stiffness out of his back, and grinned at me. His skin was ruddy, his hair sandy and combed straight back on his head, his green eyes intelligent and full of humor. A scar that was the color and texture of a bicycle tire patch ran down through one eyebrow and across the bridge of his nose.

'How about you spring for some oysters and I'll fix you a drink?' he said.

'I don't have time.'

'Yeah, you do.' Then he turned to a Negro who was sweeping between the tables by the dance floor. 'Emory, go down to Joe Burda's and get us a couple of dozen on the half shell.'

The Negro went out, and Clete fixed me a tall glass of shaved ice, 7-Up, Collins mix, candied cherries, and orange slices. He poured a cup of coffee for himself behind the bar, then came around and sat down beside me. The club was empty, the front door open; the light outside was bright under the colonnade.

'What the fuck are you up to, Streak?' he said.

'I've got an apartment over on Ursulines. I haven't bounced back too well since that guy put a hole in me.'

'You like listening to drunks break bottles out in the street all night?'

'It's not bad.'

'I bet. How many queers are in your building?'

'Lay off it, Clete.'

'Then tell me why I'm hearing these weird stories.'

'I don't know what you've heard.'

'That an ex-Homicide roach is trying to score five keys of coke. That he got canned from the Iberia Parish Sheriff's Department because he was taking juice. That he's floating Tony C.'s name around town.'

'Word spreads.'

'Among some people I'd stay away from, the kind we used to mash into the cement.'

'The kind you used to mash.'

'I'm not kidding you, partner. I heard this bullshit from three different guys.'

'Who?'

'I can't control who drinks at my bar. There're some connected guys come in here. They know I used to work for the Dio family out in Vegas and

Tahoe, so they're always inviting me back to their booth. You've got to see it, Dave, to appreciate it. About six of them, all guys, cram into the vinyl booth back there on Saturday night. They always sit so all of them can look out at the dance floor and flash their bucks and shake hands with everybody like they're celebrities. I'm talking about guys who couldn't put spaghetti on a plate without a diagram.'

'These are Cardo's people?'

'One way or another. He pieces off a lot of his action so all the greaseballs stay happy. You ever meet him?'

'No.'

'One of his broads lives in the Pontabla. He brings her in sometimes for a drink. He looks like somebody slammed a door on his head.'

'When does he come in?'

'He's not a regular.'

'What's the woman's name?'

'Who knows? I got a proposition for you, though.'

Emory, the black barman, brought in a tin tray loaded with oysters on the half shell, slice of lemon, and a bottle of Tabasco sauce. I gave him six dollars for the restaurant bill and a dollar for himself. He went into the back of the club and began stacking cartons of empty beer bottles in a storage room.

'Let me in on it,' Clete said. There was a bead of light in his green eyes.

'On what?'

'The sting, mon.' He seasoned one of the oysters, squeezed lemon on it, cupped the shell in his hand, and let the muscle slide down his throat. He smiled and the juice ran down the corner of his mouth. 'I figure it's probably a DEA gig. They've got the gelt, they can afford another player.'

I didn't say anything.

'Here's what you tell them,' he said. 'I can cover your back, I know most of the dealers on a first-name basis. I can open doors. Right now you've probably got a couple of street snitches doing your p.r.'

'You don't buy my cover?'

'Are you kidding?' He started laughing.

'I thought it was pretty good.'

'It is, for anybody who doesn't know you. But you're talking to ole Cletus here, so save the shuck for the lowlifes and the melt-downs. I ain't putting you on, mon, I'd love to get back in it. I'm thinking of opening up a P.I. office in the Quarter. A lot of it is running down bond jumpers and doing bullshit for attorneys, but so what? I can keep my hand in, carry a piece again, make life more interesting for some of the shitbags.'

'Call up the DEA in Lafayette. Tell them what you told me.'

'Wouldn't that be something, me and you working together again? You remember when we blew up Julio Segura's shit in the back of his Caddy?'

I looked out at the sunlight under the colonnade.

'Hey, I don't feel bad about smoking a pimp and drug dealer,' he said. 'I think it's a mainline perk of the business. There's nothing like the smell of cordite to clear up your sinuses.'

'You almost got us killed.'

'Who's perfect? But let's be serious a minute,

mon.' He pushed at an oyster with his fork. There were deep acne scars on the back of his red neck. His big shoulders were bent, and this shirt was stretched tight across the wide expanse of his back. 'I don't know what kind of info you're operating on, but this is what I hear. Cardo's out for the big score. Florida's already locked up, so is Texas. So he wants to control the Louisiana coast. He's got some nasty types working for him, too, guys who paint the ceiling when they do a job on somebody. You don't want him to think you're a competitor. Look, Dave, they say he's different from the other greaseballs. He's not predictable, he does strange stuff that nobody can figure out.

'The last time he brought his broad in here, a Marine gunnery sergeant sat on the stool next to him. Cardo says, "Give me and the lady another Collins and give the gunny what he wants." Then they start talking about Vietnam and Cherry Alley in Tokyo. This is in front of his broad, can you dig it? All the time I'm washing glasses about two feet away, so Cardo stops talking and says to me, "You got a question about something?"

'"What" I say.

'"You look like you're getting an earful. You got a question?" he says.

'"You're only in the crotch one," I say.

'"You cracking wise or something?" he says.

'"I'm not doing anything. It's a Marine Corps expression. I was in the corps myself," I say.

'He starts grinning and points both fingers to his chest and says, "You think you got to tell me what it means?" and his broad starts making these clicking, no-no sounds with her mouth. "Come on, you explaining to me what the fuck that means?" he says. "Somebody appointed you to explain these things to other people?"

'So I said, "No, I'm just telling you to enjoy your drink," and I walked back to my office. It was about that time I started thinking about changing my line of work.'

'Have you heard of a guy named Jimmie Lee Boggs?'

'A contract man, out of Florida?'

'That's the one.'

'What about him?'

'He's the guy who put a hole in me. Somebody told me he might be back in New Orleans.'

Clete smiled.

'That's the bait they used to get you into the sting, huh?' he said. 'They saw you coming, Streak. That guy's long gone now.'

'Maybe.'

'Get me in on it, mon.'

'I don't call the shots on this one, Cletus. Here's my telephone number and address. But don't give them to anyone, okay? Just keep any messages I get and I'll check back with you.'

'You need somebody to watch your back. Don't trust the feds to do it. You heard it first from ole Clete.'

'I don't know if any of this is going anywhere, anyway,' I said. 'A few more days of this and I might be back in New Iberia.'

He put a matchstick in his mouth. His hands were big and square and callused around the edges, the nails chewed back to the quick.

'Don't underestimate their potential,' he said.

'Most of them wouldn't make good bars of soap. But turn your back on them and they'll take your eyes out.'

That afternoon I talked to another of Minos's contacts, a Negro bartender on Magazine. His head was bald and waxed, and he wore gray muttonchop sideburns that looked as though they were artificially affixed to his face. He was as passive, docile, and uncurious about me as if I had been selling burial insurance. His eyelids were leaded, and his head kept nodding up and down while I talked. He told me: 'See, I ain't in the bidness no more myself. I had a bunch of trouble 'cause of it, had to go out of town for a little while, know what I mean? But somebody came in want the action, I'll tell them you in town. You want another 7-Up?'

'No, this is fine.'

'How about some hard-boiled eggs?'

'No, I'm fine.'

'I got to go in the kitchen and start my stove now.'

'Thanks for your time. You were up at Angola?'

'Where's that at?' he said. His eyes looked speculatively out into space.

The next morning I walked over to the Café du Monde again and had coffee at one of the outside tables. Across the street the spires of the cathedral looked brilliant in the sunlight, and the wind off the river ruffled the banana trees and palm fronds along the black iron piked fence that bordered the park inside Jackson Square. I finished reading the paper, then walked back to the apartment and called

87

Clete's bar for messages. There were none. I called Minos's office in Lafayette.

'Don't be discouraged,' he said.

'I think maybe I'm not cut out for this.'

'Why?'

'I was a Homicide cop. I never worked Vice or Narcotics.'

'It's a different kind of gig, isn't it?'

'Look, busting them is one thing. Pretending to be like them is another.'

'Have a few laughs with it.'

'It's not funny, Minos. You got me into this stuff, and it's not paying off. I've got another problem, too – the reliability of your information.'

'Oh?'

'I find out that people are either dead, or in jail, or they're crazy and run bookstores that smell like cat shit.'

'If our information was perfect, these guys wouldn't be on the street. We get it from snitches and cons cutting deals and wiretaps on pathological liars. You know that.'

'I struck out.'

'You don't think any of these people are dealing now?'

'Maybe a couple of them. But they didn't buy my act.'

'It's like throwing chum overboard to a school of barracuda. They just have to smell the blood.'

'How about another metaphor?'

'Just hang in there. It takes time.'

'I'm ready to pull the plug.'

'Give it two more days.'

'All right. Then that's it, Minos.'

'Now, I want to pick a bone with you about this guy Purcel.'

I had to wince a little on that one.

'He called you?' I asked.

'He called the office. The call finally got referred to me. He said he was calling at your suggestion.'

'He figured out the scam. I didn't tell him anything he didn't already know.'

'He's got some idea he should go undercover for the DEA.'

'Maybe it's not a bad idea,' I said.

'Are you serious? He's got a rap sheet that's longer than some cons'. He was charged with a murder, he worked for the mob, the National Transportation Safety Board thinks maybe he caused a plane crash that killed a bunch of greaseballs.'

'Clete's had a checkered career.'

'It's not going to include working for the DEA.'

'What do you hear on Boggs?'

'Nothing. Look, I'm coming over to New Orleans for the next three weeks. After today call me at the office there. I'll be staying at the Orleans Guest House on St. Charles.'

'Think about putting Purcel on the payroll. He knows more about the lowlifes than any cop in New Orleans.'

'Yeah, not many ex-cops can produce letters of reference from the Mafia. You really come up with some good ones, Dave.'

That afternoon a message *was* left for me at Clete's bar. But it was not what I was expecting. It was written in ballpoint in a careful hand on a flattened paper napkin, and it read:

Dear Dave,

I was surprised to learn that you were back in New Orleans. I had heard that you had returned to New Iberia to live. I was surprised to hear some other things, too. But maybe life has changed a lot for both of us. I'd love to see you again. I've thought about you many times over the years. Call or come by if you feel like it. I live in the Garden District. It's a long way from Bayou Teche, huh, cher?

Your old friend,
Bootsie Mouton Giacano

Her telephone number and street address were written at the bottom.

Sometimes the heart can sink with a sense of mortality and loss as abrupt as opening a door to a shop filled with whirring clocks.

5

If her name is Bootsie Mouton and it sends you back to 1957 and the best summer of your life. It was after my sophomore year at Southwestern Louisiana Institute, and my brother and I worked all summer on an offshore seismograph rig to buy a 1946 canary-yellow Ford convertible that we waxed and rubbed with rags until it had a glow like soft butter. One night at a dance out on Spanish Lake I saw her standing by herself under the oak trees by the water's edge, the light from Japanese lanterns flickering on her honey-colored hair, her moist brow and olive skin, the lavender dress she wore with a spray of white flowers pinned above the breast. She kept lifting her hair off her neck in the warm breeze that blew across the water, and pulling at the straps of her dress with her thumb.

'Would you like to dance?' I said.

'I can't. I have a fresh sunburn. We went crabbing at Cypremort Point today.'

'Do you want a drink or a beer or a Coke or something?'

'Somebody went to get one for me.'

'Who?'

'The boy I came with.'

'Who's that?'

She looked at me quizzically. Her eyes were dark, her mouth parted and red in the shadows.

'A boy from Lake Charles,' she said.

'I don't see anybody from Lake Charles here. What kind of drink do you like?'

'A vodka Collins.'

'Don't move. I'll be right back,' I said.

She lived on the lake, out by the little town of Burke, which was composed mostly of Negro tenant farmers. I told her that I wanted to come out to her house, that night, after her date dropped her off. I was insistent, aggressive, rude, I suppose, but I didn't care. She was the most beautiful girl I had ever met. Finally her date got angry and petulant and left with a group headed for Slick's Club in St. Martinville, and I drove her home down the blacktop highway between the sugarcane fields, the breeze drowsy with the scent of jasmine and magnolia and blooming four-o'-clocks, the moss-hung oaks and cypress etched against the moon out on the lake.

Two weeks later we lost our virginity together. A man always remembers several details about that initial experience, if he has it with someone he loves. I recall the warmness of the evening, the washed-out lilac color of the sky, the rainwater dripping out of the cypress trees on to the motionless surface of the lake, the banks of scarlet clouds in the west that glowed like fire through the cracks in the boathouse wall. But the image that will always remain in my mind was her face in that final heart-twisting moment. Her eyes closed, her lips parted silently, and then she looked up at me like an opening flower and cupped my face in her hands as she would a child's.

It should never have ended. But it did, and for no reason that I could ever explain to her. Nor could I explain it to my father, a priest in whom I trusted, or myself. Even though I was only twenty years old I began to experience bone-grinding periods of depression and guilt that seemed to have no legitimate cause or origin. When they came upon me it was as though the sun had suddenly become a black cinder, and had gone over the rim of the earth for the last time. I hurt her, pushed her away from me, wouldn't return her telephone calls or answer a poignant and self-blaming note she left on our front screen. Even today I'm hard put to explain my behavior. But I felt somehow that it was intrinsically bad, that anyone who could love me didn't know who I really was, and that eventually I would make that person bad, too.

It was not a rational state of mind. A psychologist would probably say that my problem was related to my mother's running off with a *bourré* dealer from Morgan City when I was a child, or the fact that my father sometimes brawled in bars and got locked up in the parish jail. I don't know if theories like that would be correct or not. But at the time there was no way I could think myself out of my own dark thoughts, and I became convinced that the happy times with Bootsie had simply been part of the summer's rain-spangled illusion, as transient and mutable as the season had been warm and fleeting.

When she would not be dissuaded, I took out another girl, a carhop from up north who wore hair rollers in public and always seemed to have sweat rings under her arms. I took her to a lawn party given by Bootsie's aunt and uncle on Bayou Teche, where she got drunk and called the waiter a nigger.

Later that night I got into a fistfight at Slick's, tore the fenders off my car on the drawbridge over the Teche, and woke up in the morning handcuffed to the bottom of the iron ladder on the Breaux Bridge water tower, because it was during Crawfish Festival and the small city jail was already full. As I looked up at the white sun, smelled the hot weeds around me, and swallowed the bile in my throat, I didn't realize that I had just made the initial departure on a long alcoholic odyssey.

Then the years passed and I would not see her again until I came home from the war. In the meantime I committed myself totally to charcoal-filtered bourbon in a four-inch glass, with a sweating Jax on the side, and finally I didn't care about anything.

Now she lived on Camp Street in the Garden District. Her married name was Giacano, the same as that of the most notorious Mafia family in New Orleans. I told myself that I should put her note away and save it for another time, when I could afford a futile pursuit of the past. But I seldom listen to my own advice, and that evening I rode the old iron streetcar down St. Charles under the long canopy of spreading oaks, past yards filled with camellias and magnolia trees, sidewalks cracked by oak roots, without having called first, and found myself on Camp in front of a narrow two-story white-painted brick home with twin chimneys, a gallery, and garden walls that enclosed huge clumps of banana trees and dripped with purple bugle vine.

She answered the door in a one-piece orange bathing suit and an open terry cloth robe, and explained with a flush that she had been dipping leaves out of the pool in back. Her Cajun accent had been softened by the years in New Orleans, and she was heavier now, wider in the hips, larger in the breasts, thicker across the thighs. She brushed the gray straight up in her honey-colored hair, so that it looked as though it had been powdered there. But Bootsie was still good to look at. Her skin was smooth and still tanned from the summer, her hair cut short like a girl's and etched on the neck with a razor. Her smile was as genuine and happy as it had been thirty years before.

We walked through her house and onto the patio and sat at a glass-topped table by the pool. She brought out a tray of coffee and milk and pecan pie. The water in the pool was dark and glazed with the evening light, and small islands of oak leaves floated against the tile sides. She had been widowed twice, she told me. Her first husband, an oil-field helicopter pilot, had flown a crew out to a rig south of Morgan City, then hit a guy wire and crashed right on top of the quarter boat. Five years later she had met her second husband, Ralph Giacano, in Biloxi.

'Have you heard of him?' she asked.

'Yes,' I said, and tried to keep my eyes veiled.

'He told me he had a degree in accounting and owned half of a vending machine company. He didn't have a degree, but he did own part of a company,' she said.

I tried to look pleasant and show no recognition.

95

'I found out some of the other things he was involved in after we were married,' she said. 'Last year somebody killed him and his girlfriend in the parking lot of the Hialeah racetrack. Poor Ralph. He always said the Colombians wouldn't bother him, he was just a small-business man.'

'I'm sorry, Bootsie.'

'Don't be. I spent two years feeling sorry for Ralph while he mortgaged this house, which was mine from my first marriage, and spent the money in Miami and Las Vegas. So now I own his half of the vending machine business. You know who owns the other half?'

'The Giacanos were always a tight family.'

'I guess I can't surprise you with very much.'

'Ralph's uncle was a guy named Didi Gee. He's dead now, but three years ago he hired a contract killer to shoot my brother. Jimmie's doing okay now, but for a while I thought I was going to lose him.'

'I didn't know.'

'Maybe it's time to get away from your in-laws.'

'When you sell to the Giacanos, it's twenty cents on the dollar, Dave. Nobody else is lining up to buy into their business, either.'

'Get away from them, Bootsie.'

Her eyes glanced into mine. There was a curious bead of light in them.

'I don't understand this,' she said.

'What?'

'You're telling me to get away from them. Then I'm hearing this strange story about you.'

I looked away from her.

'You hear a lot of bullshit in the streets,' I said.

'This is from my in-laws, Dave. They work for Tony Cardo.'

I didn't answer and tried to grin good-naturedly. Her eyes peeled the skin off my face.

'They say you're dirty. Don't they have a wonderful vocabulary?' she said.

I pushed at a piece of piecrust on my plate with my fork.

'They say you want to deal,' she said.

'You have to make up your own mind about people.'

'I *know* you, Dave Robicheaux. I don't care what you've done in your life, this stuff isn't you.'

'Then ignore what they say, Bootsie, and stay out of it.'

'I'm worried about you. I work with these people. You can't believe how they think, what they're capable of doing.'

'Oh yes I can.'

'Then what are you doing?'

'Be my friend on this. Don't mix in it, and don't worry too much about what you hear.'

Her face was lighted with the late sun's glow over the garden wall. She raised her chin slightly, the way she always did when she was angry.

'Dave, you left me. Do you think you should be telling me what to do now?'

'I guess not.'

'I survive among these animals because I have to. It isn't fun. I'm on my own, and that isn't fun, either. But I handle it.'

'I guess you do.'

'Why didn't you marry me?' she said. Her eyes were hot and bright.

'You'd have married a drunk. It wouldn't have been a good life, believe me.'

'You don't know that. You don't know that at all.'

'Yes, I do. I became a full-blown lush. I tried to kill my first wife's lover at a lawn party out by Lake Pontchartrain.'

'Maybe that's what he deserved.'

'I tried to kill him because I had become morally insane.'

'I don't care what you did later in your life. Why'd you close me out, Dave?'

I let my hands hang between my knees.

'Because I was dumb,' I said.

'It's that simple?'

'No, it's not. But how about suffice it to say that I made a terrible mistake, that I've had regret about it all these years.'

Her legs were crossed, her arms motionless on the sides of the cushioned iron chair, her face composed now in the tea-colored light. The top of her terry cloth robe was loose, and I could see her breasts rise and fall quietly with her breathing.

'I do have to go,' I said.

'Are you coming back?'

'If you'd like to see me again, I'd surely like to see you.'

'I'm not moving out of town, *cher*.' Then her face became soft and she said, 'But, Dave, I've learned one thing with middle age. I don't try to correct yesterday's mistakes in the present. I mark them off. I truly mark them off. A person hurts me only once.'

'No one could ever say they were unsure where you stood on an issue, Boots.'

She smiled without answering, then walked me to the front door, put her palms on my shoulders, and kissed me on the cheek. It was an appropriate and kind gesture and would not have meant much in itself, but then she looked into my face and touched my cheek with her fingertips, as though she were saying good-bye to someone forever, and I felt my loins thicken and my heart turn to water.

It was almost dark when I got off the streetcar at the corner of St. Charles and Canal and went into the Pearl and had a poor-boy sandwich filled with oysters, shrimp, sliced tomatoes, shredded lettuce, and *sauce piquante*. Then I walked to my apartment and paused momentarily outside my door while I found my key. The people upstairs were partying out on the balcony, and one of them accidentally kicked a coffee can of geraniums into the courtyard. But in spite of the noise I thought I heard someone inside my apartment. I put my hand on the .25-caliber Beretta in my coat pocket, unlocked the door, and let it swing all the way back against the wall on its hinges.

Lionel Comeaux, the man I'd found working under his car on the creeper, was in the kitchen, pulling the pots and pans out of the cabinet and placing them on the table. The jolly fat man who called himself Uncle Ray Fontenot and said he used to play trombone at Sharky's Dream Room had emptied the drawers in the bedroom and had laid all my hangered clothes across the bed. My .45 lay on top of a neatly folded shirt. Both of them looked at me with flat, empty expressions, as though I were the intruder.

The fat man, Fontenot, wore a beige suit and a cream turtleneck shirt. I saw his eyes study my face and my right hand; then he smiled and opened his palms in front of him.

'It's just business, Mr. Robicheaux,' he said. 'Don't take it personal. We've treated your things with respect.'

'How'd you get in?'

'It's a simple lock,' he said.

'You've got some damn nerve,' I said.

'Close the door. There's people out there,' Lionel, the man in the kitchen, said. He wore Adidas running shoes, blue jeans with no belt, a gold pullover sweater with the sleeves pushed up over his thick, sun-browned arms.

I could hear my own breathing in the silence.

'Lionel's right,' Fontenot said. 'We don't need an audience here, do we? Getting mad isn't going to make us any money, either, is it?'

I took my hand out of my coat pocket and opened and closed it at my side.

'Come in, come in,' Fontenot said. 'Look, we're putting your things back. There's no harm done.'

'You toss my place and call it no harm?' I said. I pushed the door shut behind me.

'You knew somebody would check you out. Don't make it a big deal,' the younger man said in the kitchen. He lit a dead cigar in his mouth and squatted down and started replacing the pots and pans in the cabinets next to the stove.

'I don't like people smoking in my apartment,' I said.

He turned his head at me and paused in his work. The red Navy tattoo on his flexed bicep was ringed with blue stars. He was balanced on the ball of one foot, the cigar between his fingers, a tooth working on a bloodless spot on his lower lip. Fontenot walked out of the other room.

'Put out the smoke, Lionel,' he said quietly. His eyes crinkled at the corners. 'Go on, put it out. We're in the man's home.'

'I don't think it's smart dealing with him. I said it then, I'll say it in front of him,' Lionel said. He wet the cigar under the tap and dropped it in a garbage bag.

'The man's money is as good as the next person's,' Fontenot said.

'You were a cop,' Lionel said to me. 'That's a problem for me. No insult meant.'

'You creeped my apartment. That's a problem for me.'

'Lionel had a bad experience a few years back,' Fontenot said. 'His name doesn't make campus bells ring for you?'

'No.'

'Second-string quarterback for LSU,' Fontenot said. 'Until he sold some whites on the half shell to the wrong people. I think if Lionel had been first-string, he wouldn't have had to spend a year in Angola. It's made him distrustful.'

'Get off it, Ray.'

'The man needs to understand,' Fontenot said. 'Look, Mr. Robicheaux, we're short on protocol, but we don't rip each other off. We establish some rules, some trust, then we all make money. Get his bank, Lionel.'

Lionel opened a cabinet next to the stove, squatted down, and reached his hand deep inside. I heard the adhesive tape tear loose from the top of the cabinet behind the drawer. He threw the brown envelope, with tape hanging off each end, for me to catch.

'We want you to understand something else, too,' Fontenot said. 'We're not here because of some fifty-thou deal. That's toilet paper in this town. But the gentleman we work for is interested in you. You're a lucky man.'

'Tony C. is interested?'

'Who?' He smiled.

'Five keys, ten thou a key, no laxative, no vitamin B twelve,' I said.

'Twelve thou, my friend,' Fontenot said.

'Bullshit. New Orleans is white with it.'

'Ten thou is the discount price. You get that down the line,' Fontenot said.

'Then go fuck yourself.'

'Who do you think you are, man?' Lionel said.

'The guy whose place you just creeped.'

'Let's split,' he said.

I looked at Fontenot.

'What I can't seem to convey is that you guys are not the only market around. Ask Cardo who he wants running the action in Southwest Louisiana. Ask him who punched his wife in a bathroom stall in the Castaways in Miami.'

'There're some people I wouldn't try to turn dials on, Mr. Robicheaux,' Fontenot said.

'You're the one holding up the deal. Give me what I want and we're in business.'

'You can come in at eleven thou,' he said.

'It's got to be ten.'

'Listen to this guy,' Lionel said.

'The money's not mine. I've got to give an accounting to other people.'

'I can relate to that. We'll call you,' Fontenot said.

'When?'

'About this time tomorrow. Do you have a car?'

'I have a pickup truck.'

He nodded reflectively; then his mouth split in a grin and I could see each of his teeth like worn, wide-set pearls in his gums.

'How big a grudge can a man like you carry?' he asked.

'What?'

'Nothing,' he said, and shook all over when he laughed, his narrowed eyes twinkling with a liquid glee.

The next morning I was walking down Chartres towards the French Market for breakfast when a black man on a white pizza-delivery scooter went roaring past me. I didn't pay attention to him, but then he came roaring by again. He wore an oversized white uniform, splattered with pizza sauce, sunglasses that were as dark as a welder's, and a white paper hat mashed down to his ears. He turned his scooter at the end of the block and disappeared, and I headed through Jackson Square toward the Café du Monde. I waited for the green light at Decatur; then I heard the scooter come rattling and coughing around the corner. The driver braked to the curb and grinned at me, his thin body jiggling from the engine's vibration.

'Tee Beau!' I said.

'Wait for me on the bench. I gotta park my machine, me.'

He pulled out into the traffic again, drove past the line of horse-and-carriages in front of the square, and disappeared past the old Jax brewery. Five minutes later I saw him coming on foot back down Decatur, his hat hammered down to the level of his sunglasses. He sat beside me on a sunlit bench next to the pike fence that bordered the park area inside the square.

'You ain't gonna turn me in, are you, Mr. Dave?' he said.

'What are you doing?'

'Working at the pizza place. Looking out for Jimmie Lee Boggs, too. You ain't gonna turn me in, now, are you?'

'You're putting me in a rough spot, Tee Beau.'

'I got your promise. Dorothea and Gran'maman done tole me, Mr. Dave.'

'I didn't see you. Get out of New Orleans.'

'Ain't got no place else to go. Except back to New Iberia. Except to the Red Hat. I got a lot to tell you 'bout Jimmie Lee Boggs. He here.'

'In New Orleans?'

'He left but he come back. I seen him. Two nights ago. Right over yonder.' He pointed diagonally across the square. 'I been watching.'

'Wait a minute. You saw him by the Pontabla Apartments?'

'Listen, this what happen, Mr. Dave. After he killed that policeman and that white boy, he drove us all the way to Algiers, with lightning jumping all over the sky. He made me sit in back, with chains on, like he a po-liceman and I his prisoner, in case anybody stops us. He had the radio on, and I was 'fraid he gonna find out I didn't shoot you, drive out in that marsh, kill me like he done them poor people in the filling station. All the time he was talking, telling me 'bout what he gonna do, how he got a place in the Glades in Florida, where he say – now this is what he say, I don't use them kind of words – where he say the hoot owls fucks the jackrabbits, where he gonna hole up, then come back to New Orleans and make them dagos give him a lot of money.

'Just befo' we got to town he called somebody from a filling station. I could hear him talking, and he said something 'bout the Pontabla. I heard him say it. He don't be paying me no mind, no, 'cause he say I just a stupid nigger. That's the way he talk all the time I chained up there in the backseat.'

'Tee Beau, are you sure it was Boggs? It's hard to believe you found him when half the cops in Louisiana can't.'

'I found you, ain't I? He don't look the same now, Mr. Dave. But it's him. His hair short and black now, he puts glasses, too. But it's Jimmie Lee Boggs. I followed him in my car to make sure.'

'Where'd you get a car?'

'I borrowed it.'

'You borrowed it?'

'Then I put it back.'

'I see.'

'I followed him out to the Airline Highway. To a boxing place. No, it ain't that. They put on gloves, but they kick with the feet, too. What they call that?'

'Full-contact karate.'

'I looked inside, me. Phew, it stink in there. Jimmie Lee Boggs in long sweatpants kicking at some man in the ring. His skin white and hard, shining with sweat. I got to swallow when I look at him, Mr. Dave. That man make me that afraid.'

'You did fine, Tee Beau. But I want to ask something of you. You leave Jimmie Lee Boggs for other people. Don't have anything more to do with this.'

'You gonna get me a new trial?'

'I'll try. But we have to do it a step at a time, partner.'

His hands were folded in his lap, and he was bent forward on the bench. His small face looked like a squirrel's with sunglasses on it. Wiry rings of hair grew across the back of his neck.

'I got bad dreams at night. 'Bout the Red Hat, 'bout they be strapping me down in that chair with that black hood on my face,' he said.

'You killed Hipolyte Broussard, though, didn't you, Tee Beau?'

His breath clicked in his throat.

'I done part of it. But the part I done was an accident. I swear it, 'fore God, Mr. Dave. Hipolyte kept cussing me, tole me all the bad things he gonna do to me, do to Dorothea, tole me I got jelly in my ears, me, that I cain't do nothing right, that I better stomp on the brake when he say, take my foot off when he say. He under there clanking and banging and calling me mo' names, saying "Stomp now, stomp now."

'So that what I done. I close my eyes and hit on that brake, and I hit on it and hit on it and pretend it be Hipolyte's face, that I smashing it like a big eggshell, me. Then I feel the bus rock and that jack break like a stick, and I know Hipolyte under the wheel now, I hear him screaming and flopping

106

around in the mud. But I scared, Mr. Dave, I be running, run past the shed, down the road past Hipolyte's house, down past the cane field. When I turn round he look like a turtle on its back, caught under that big iron wheel. But I keep on going, I run plumb back to Gran'maman's house, she be shucking crawfish, say, "You go wash, Tee Beau, put on your clean clothes, you, sit down with your *gran'mamam* and don't tell them policemens nothing, you."'

'Why was Hipolyte always deviling you?' I said.

He didn't answer.

'Was it because he wanted you to pimp for him? Or make Dorothea get on the bus when he drove the girls out to the camp?'

'Yes suh.'

'But Dorothea said Gros Mama Goula wouldn't let men bother her.'

'Yes suh, that's right.'

'That Hipolyte was afraid of Gros Mama, that she could put a *gris-gris* on him.'

'Yes suh.'

'Then Dorothea was safe, really?'

'What you saying, Mr. Dave?'

'Dorothea wasn't your main problem with Hipolyte.'

He looked out at the shadows of the palm fronds on the pavement.

'It was something else,' I said. 'Maybe not just the pimping. Maybe something even worse than that, Tee Beau.'

I could not see his eyes behind the dark glasses, but I saw him swallow.

'What was it?' I said.

'For why you want to study on that?' he said. 'It gonna get me a new trial? It gonna make all them white people believe I ain't knock that bus on Hipolyte, I ain't stuff a dirty rag down his mouth? I ain't talking about it no mo', Mr. Dave.'

'You'll need to at some point.'

He looked small inside his white delivery uniform. The sleeves almost covered his folded hands.

'Hipolyte was selling dope for Jimmie Lee Boggs. That ain't all they was doing, either. They send some of them girls to Florida, to Arizona, anywhere Hipolyte take the bus. Them girls never come back. They families ain't ever find out where they at. All I ever done was taken Mr. Dore car, taken an old junk fan out his yard, but people be wanting to kill me. I tired of it, Mr. Dave. I tired of feeling bad about myself all the time, too.'

I took a piece of paper from my wallet and wrote on it.

'Here's my address and phone number, Tee Beau,' I said. 'Here's the address and number of a bar where you can leave messages, too. Call me if I can help you with anything. Do you have enough money?'

'Yes suh.'

'Don't look for Boggs anymore. You've done enough. Okay?'

'Yes suh. You want to know where I'm staying at?'

'I don't want to know. Give me your word you won't borrow any more cars.'

He didn't bother to reply. He looked down between his knees and tapped the soles of his shoes on the pavement. Then he said, 'You think I ever gonna get out of this?'

'I don't know.'

'Gros Mama tell Dorothea that Jimmie Lee Boggs gonna die in a black box full of sparks. She say you go in there with him, you gonna die, too.'

'Gros Mama's a juju con woman.'

'She put the *gris-gris* on Hipolyte. When he in the coffin, his mouth snap open and a black worm thick as my thumb crawl out on his chin. It ain't no lie, Mr. Dave.'

I had breakfast at the Café du Monde, then walked back to the apartment to call Minos at the DEA office. Before I could, the phone rang. It was Ray Fontenot.

'Your offer's accepted,' he said.

'Ten thou a key, not cut?'

'What I just said, Mr. Robicheaux.' Then he told me to meet him that afternoon in the parking lot of a bar just the other side of the Huey Long Bridge.

'You want me to make the buy in the parking lot of a bar?' I asked.

'We start it from there. Quit sweating it. You're gonna be rich,' he said, and hung up.

I called Minos.

'It's on at five today,' I said.

'Where?'

I told him about the bar.

'We'll have somebody inside, somebody outside taking pictures with a telephoto lens,' he said. 'But you won't know who they are, so you won't need to look at them. This is what's going to happen, Dave. They'll take you somewhere in their car, or you'll follow them in your truck. At some point they'll probably check you for a wire. We'll have a loose tail on you, but we're not going to get too close and blow it. So when you make the buy, you're pretty much on your own. Are you nervous?'

'A little.'

'Carry your piece. They'll expect that. Look, you've handled it fine so far. The deal's not going to sour. They want you in.'

'This morning I heard that Jimmie Lee Boggs is in town.'

'Where?'

'Somebody saw him around the Pontabla Apartments two nights ago. It makes sense. Tony Cardo's girlfriend lives there. The same night, he was at a full-contact karate place out on the Airline.'

'Who told you all this?'

'A guy I know.'

'Which guy?'

'Just a guy in the street.'

'What are you hiding here, Dave?'

'Are you going to check out the karate club, or do you want me to do it?'

'We'll handle it.'

'His hair's dyed black and cut short now, and he may be wearing glasses.'

'Who's the guy in the street?'

'Forget it, Minos.'

'You never change.'

'What if the deal goes sour today?'

'Then get the fuck out of there.'

'You don't want me to bust them?'

'You walk out of it. We don't borrow people from other agencies to get them hurt.'

'One other thing I didn't mention to you. This

guy Fontenot knows I've got a grudge against Boggs. I get the feeling he'd like to see me go up against him.'

'You know what a yard bitch is in the joint? That's Uncle Ray Fontenot, a fat dipshit who gets off watching the swinging dicks carve on each other. Call me after the score and we'll take the dope off you.'

I *was* nervous. My palms were moist. I walked about aimlessly in the apartment, I burned a pan on the stove. Finally I put on my gym shorts, running shoes, and a sweatshirt, jogged along the levee by the river, and circled back on Esplanade. I showered, changed into a fresh pair of khakis and a long-sleeved denim shirt. Then I fastened the holster of the Beretta to my ankle, dropped the .45 automatic in the right-hand pocket of my army field jacket, slipped the brown envelope with the fifty one-thousand bills in it into the left pocket, buttoned the flap, and backed my pickup out of the garage. The sky had turned a solid gray from horizon to horizon, the wind was blowing hard off the Gulf, and I could smell rain in the air. My palms left damp prints on the steering wheel.

Rain began to tumble out of the dome of sky through the girders when I crossed the Mississippi on the Huey Long. The river was wide and yellow far below, and froth was blowing off the bows of the oil barges. The willows along the banks were bent in the wind. As my tires whirred down the long metal-grid incline on the far side, I saw the low, flat-topped brick nightclub set back among oak trees on the left-hand side of old Highway 90. Jax and Dixie neon signs glowed in the rain-streaked windows, and when I crunched on to the oyster shells in the parking lot I saw Ray Fontenot, Lionel Comeaux, and a redheaded woman in a new blue Buick.

The woman was in back, and Fontenot was in the passenger seat and had the door partly open and one leg extended out on the shells in the light rain.

'Park your truck and get in,' he said.

'Where we going?'

'Not far. You'll see. Get in.'

I turned off the ignition, locked my truck, and got into the backseat next to the woman. She wore Levi's, an open leather jacket, and a yellow T-shirt without a bra, so that you could see her nipples against the cloth. The air inside the car was heavy and close with the drowsy smell of reefer.

'Great place to be toking up,' I said.

'What do you care?' Lionel said.

'I care when I'm in your car,' I said.

'Don't worry about it. You won't be long,' he said.

'What?'

He started the engine, drove the Buick behind the nightclub, and parked it under a spreading oak.

'What's the game?' I said.

'Show-and-tell,' he said, got out of the car, walked around, and opened my door. 'Step outside, please.'

'We do the same thing with everybody. Then everybody's comfortable, everybody's relaxed with everybody else,' Fontenot said.

'I'm not relaxed. Who's the girl?' I asked.

'Do I look like a girl to you?' she said. Her eyes were green, the whites tinged red from the reefer hits.

'Who is she?' I said to Fontenot.

'This is Kim. She's a friend, a nice person,' he said.

'I'm not fond of standing out here in the rain. You want to step outside, please,' Lionel said. He spoke with his face turned at an angle from me, as though he were addressing a lamppost.

'What's she doing here?' I said.

'Certain people like her. She goes where she wants. Let's get on with the business at hand, sir,' Fontenot said.

'Boy, talk about a personality problem. Who's he been doing business with?' Kim said. Her red hair was looped over one ear. When she saw me looking at her, she pointed her chin up in the air and lifted her hair off the back of her neck.

'He's just a careful man. He doesn't mean anything by it,' Fontenot said. 'But let's not delay any longer, Mr. Robicheaux.'

I stepped outside and let Lionel work his hands up and down my body. He pulled my shirt out of my trousers, patted under my arms, slipped his hands down my spine, felt my pockets and along my legs.

'You think you're going to need all that fire-power?' he asked.

'It's an old habit,' I said.

Fontenot was looking at Lionel's face.

'He's cool,' Lionel said.

'Time to open the candy store,' Fontenot said.

Lionel got back in the Buick and backed it up to where my truck was parked. I glanced again at the girl. She wore no makeup, and her face was hard and shiny. Pretty but hard. She looked like she had

113

a hard body. Her hands were big and knuckled like those on a cannery worker.

'You got something on your mind?' she said.

'Not a thing,' I said.

'Good, because I'm not into eye fucking,' she said.

'Eye fucking?' I said.

Fontenot was grinning from the front seat. He was always grinning, his teeth set like pieces of corn in his gums.

'I have to end your fun now,' he said. 'I'll hop in your truck with you, Mr. Robicheaux, and we'll be on our way.'

We headed south of the city into St. Charles Parish. Gray clouds tumbled across the sky in the fading light, and white streaks of lightning trembled on the horizon beyond Lake Salvador. The Buick was a quarter mile ahead of us on the tar-surfaced road.

'I need to take a leak,' Fontenot said.

I stopped next to an irrigation ditch between two dry rice fields, and he got out and urinated into the weeds. I could hear him passing gas softly. His beige sports jacket, with brown suede pockets, was spotted with rain. He smiled at me in the wind as he zipped up his pants, then got back in the truck, took a woman's compact from his coat pocket, and gingerly scraped some white powder from it with the blade of his penknife. He lifted the knife to one nostril, then the other, snorting as though he were clearing his nasal passages, widening his eyes, crimping his lips as though they were chapped. Then he licked the flat of the blade with his tongue.

'You want a taste?' he said.

114

'I never took it up.'

'You think you could take up Kim?'

'I just wonder what she's doing here, that's all.'

'She works in one of Tony's clubs. I suspect he probes her recesses. I know that's what Lionel would like to do.'

'You know Tony now?'

'You're in the business now, my friend. It's a nice one to be in. Lots of good things to be had. You want to meet him?'

'It doesn't matter to me, as long as I get what I want.'

'What is it you want?' There were tiny saliva bubbles between his teeth when he grinned.

'One big score, then maybe I piece off the action and buy a couple of businesses in Lafayette and Lake Charles.'

'Ah, you're a Rotary man at heart. But in the meantime, how about all the broads you want, your own plane to fly down to the islands in, lobster and steak every night at the track? You don't think about those things?'

'I have simple tastes.'

'How about squaring a debt?' he asked.

'With who?'

'Everybody's got a debt to square. Winning's a lot more fun when you get to watch somebody else lose.'

'I never gave it much thought.'

'Oh, I bet.'

'Fontenot, that's the second time you've given me the impression you know something about me that I don't.'

'You used to be a cop. That's not the best

115

recommendation. We had to do some homework, stick our finger into a nasty place or two.'

'Okay . . .'

'I'd be mad at somebody who put a hole in me and left me to die in a ditch.'

'You're right. Do you know where he is?'

'I stay away from some people.'

'Then you don't need to be worrying about it anymore.'

'Of course.'

We crossed a bayou on a wooden bridge and drove across a flooded area of saw grass and dead cypress. Blue herons stood in the shallows, and mud hens were nesting up against the reeds out of the wind. In the distance I could see the hard tin outline of a sugar mill. Fontenot opened the compact, balanced some coke on the tip of his knife blade, and took another hit. His face was an oval pie of satisfaction.

'Are you interested in politics?' he asked.

'Not particularly.'

'Tony is. He writes letters to newspapers. He's a patriot.' He smiled to himself, and his eyes were bright as he looked out at the rain through the front window.

'I thought the mustaches stayed out of politics,' I said.

'Bad word for our friends.'

'Why does he write letters?'

'He was a Marine in Vietnam. He likes to take about "nape."'

Then Fontenot changed his voice, his eyes glittering happily. '"Five acres of fucking nape climbing up a hill. They smelled like cats burned up

116

in an incinerator. Fucking nape, man."' He started giggling.

'I think you'd better not put any more shit up your nose.'

'Indeed you are a Rotary man.'

We passed a gray, paintless general store under a spreading oak tree at a four-corners, then drove through a harvested sugarcane field that was covered with stubble and followed a bayou through a wooded area. The bayou was dented with rain, and I could see lights in fishing shacks set back on stilts in the trees. We came out into open fields, and it began to rain harder. It was almost completely dark now.

'There.' Fontenot pointed at a small wood house with a gallery at the end of a dirt road in the middle of a field.

'This is it?'

'This is it.'

'You guys can really pick them.'

'You should be impressed. It's a historic place. You remember when a union man from up north tried to organize the plantation workers around here back in the fifties? He was crucified on the barn wall behind that little house. The barn's not there anymore, but that's where it happened. For some reason the state chamber of commerce hasn't put that on any of its brochures.'

'Look, I want to get my moods and get out of here. How much longer is this going to take?'

'Kim'll fix some sandwiches. We'll have some supper.'

'Forget the supper, Fontenot. I'm tired.'

'You're an intense man.'

117

'You're making things too complicated.'

'It's your first time out. We make the rules.'

'Fuck your rules. On any kind of score, you get in and out of it as fast as you can. The more people in on it, the more chance you take a fall. You went out on a score holding. That's affected my confidence level here.'

'If you'll look around you, you'll notice that you can see for a mile in any direction. You can hear a car or a plane long before they get here. I think we'll keep doing things our way. Kim's sandwiches are a treat. Kim's a treat. Think about it. You didn't see her flex her stuff when you looked at her? Maybe she'd like you to probe her recesses.'

His lips were purple and moist in the glow of the dashboard.

I followed the Buick down the dirt road to the house. We all went inside, and Lionel turned on the lights. Kim carried a grocery bag into the kitchen, and Lionel started a fire of sticks and wadded-up newspaper in the fireplace.

'Where are my goods?' I said.

'They're being delivered. Be patient,' Fontenot said.

'Delivered? What is this?' I said.

'A guy can always find another store if he doesn't like the way we do it,' Lionel said. He was squatted down in front of the fireplace, and he waved a newspaper back and forth on the flames.

'You've got too many people involved in this,' I said.

'He's an expert all right,' Lionel said without turning his head.

'When's the delivery going to be here?' I said.

'In minutes, in minutes,' Fontenot said.

I sat by myself at the window while the three of them ate ham and cheese sandwiches at a table in the center of the room. The house had no insulation, except the water-streaked and cracked wallpaper, and the yellow flames crawling up the stone chimney did little to break the chill in the room. The sky was black outside, and the rain slanted across the window. When they finished eating, Kim cleaned up the table and Lionel went into the back of the house. Fontenot opened the compact and took another hit on the blade of his penknife.

'I have to use the bathroom,' I said.

He wet his lips and smiled at me.

I walked down a short hallway, opened a closet door, passed a bedroom that was stacked with hay bales, and opened the last door in the hall. Lionel sat on the side of a brass bed, his left arm tied off with his belt, the syringe mounted on a thick purple vein. A lighted candle and a cook spoon with a curdled handle lay on a nightstand next to the bed. He had just taken the hit, and his head was tilted back, his mouth open, his jaws slack as though he were in the midst of orgasm. The flame from the candle flickered on the muscular contours of his body. His breath went in and out with the crush, his eyes trying to focus on me and gain control of his situation again.

He set the syringe down, popped loose the belt on his arm, and straightened his back.

'What the fuck do you want, man?' he said hoarsely.

'I was looking for the bathroom.'

'It's a privy. Out back, where a privy is.'

I closed the door on him, went out into the rain, then walked back through the kitchen. Kim was leaning against the drainboard, looking down at the floor. She had taken off her leather jacket to make the sandwiches, and her breasts were stiff against her T-shirt.

'Is it always this much fun?' I said.

'Always,' she said.

Fifteen minutes later came in the form of a Latin man with a black bandanna tied down on his head, beige zoot pants, a canary-yellow shirt unbuttoned to his navel, a soft pad of chest hair on which a gold St. Christopher's medal rested, a leather sports coat that folded and creased as smoothly as warm tallow. He carried a cardboard box wrapped in a black plastic garbage bag. He set the box on the table and removed five individual packages wrapped in butcher paper, opened a single-bladed knife, and handed it to me. I cut through the butcher paper on one of the packages and punched through the clear plastic bag inside. I rubbed the white granules between my fingers, then wiped my fingers clean on the paper.

'You don't want a taste?' he said.

'I trust you.'

'You trust me?' he said.

'Yeah.'

He looked at Fontenot.

'Mr. Robicheaux doesn't have certain vices,' Fontenot said.

'It's good shit, man. Like Ray ordered, no cut,' the Latin man said. The hollows of both his cheeks were sprayed with tiny acne scars like needle marks. 'Where's Lionel at?'

'He's a little noddy right now. Must be the weather,' Fontenot said.

I took the brown envelope with the money out of my left pocket and put it in Fontenot's hand. He counted the bills out on his thigh.

'All the stiff and green. It can make the ashes in an old man's furnace glow anew,' he said.

The Latin man looked furtively toward the kitchen, where Kim sat at the table, a cup of coffee balanced on her fingers, her eyes staring listlessly out the window into the darkness.

'Jennifer and Carmen are at the bar on the blacktop,' he said.

'I don't see why they should be left alone,' Fontenot said.

The Latin nodded his head at the kitchen, his face a question mark.

'She's an extraordinary girl. Maybe she can ride back with Mr. Robicheaux,' Fontenot said.

I put the five kilos of cocaine back in the cardboard box and wrapped the black garbage bag tightly around it. I lifted it on to my shoulder.

'The next time you guys cut a deal, why not do it in the Greyhound bus depot?' I said.

'Oh, that's good,' Fontenot said.

I walked outside to my truck, set the box on the floor, and started the engine. The Latin man came out the front door, got in a TransAm, turned around in a circle, his headlights bouncing up into my face, and headed down the dirt road in the rain. Through the living room window I could see the girl speaking heatedly to Fontenot.

I went back up on the gallery and opened the door.

'You want to go with me, Red?' I said.

'Red?' she said.

'Kim.'

'Why not?' she said.

She was quiet for a long time in the truck. The rain slackened, and the moon rose among the strips of black cloud. When we crossed the flooded section of saw grass and dead cypress the light reflected off the canals and small bays like quicksilver. I cracked my window, and the wind smelled of rain and moss and wet leaves.

'You were really a cop?' she said.

'Off and on.'

'Why'd you give it up?'

'It gave me up.'

'They say you were taking juice.'

'Sometimes you get some bad press.'

'What do you think about that back there?' she said.

'I think they're going to do time.'

'Have you?'

'What?'

'Done time.'

'I was in the bag a little while in Lafayette,' I said.

'What for?'

'Murder.'

She turned her head and looked at me directly for the first time since she had gotten in the truck.

'I was cleared. I didn't have anything to do with it,' I said.

'You don't add up.'

'Why's that?'

'They could have taken you off tonight. You

should have known that.'

'I don't figure them for it.'

'What a laugh. You sure you were a cop?'

'They work for Tony Cardo, right? They're not going to burn his customers. Are they?'

I could feel her eyes roving on the side of my face.

'The raghead who brought your kilos . . .'

'Yes?'

'He and Lionel did a guy with a piece of piano wire. Stop up there at the filling station. I have to pee.'

I parked under a dripping oak tree while she went inside. She came back out and got in the truck, and I drove back on to the blacktop. It had stopped raining completely now; the moon was bright in the sky, and when the wind blew through the flooded saw grass and cypress, the light clicked on the water like silvery dimes.

'Why does everything down here smell like mold and leaking sewage?' she said.

'Maybe because there's a lot of mold and leaking sewage here.'

For the first time she smiled.

'Who'd they do?' I said.

'Did I say that? I talk funny when my bladder's full.'

She tied up her hair with a bandanna and looked out the window.

'You know Jimmie Lee Boggs?' I asked.

'The television minister in Baton Rouge?'

'A guy like Lionel doesn't bother me, but Boggs is special.'

'What's it to me?'

'Nothing. I gave you a ride.'

123

'Expensive ride.'

'You're a tough lady.'

'You look like a nice guy. I don't know what the fuck you're doing dealing dope, but you're an amateur. Do you know where South Carrollton runs into the levee?'

'Yes.'

'That's where I live. If that's out of your way, I can take the streetcar.'

'I'll drive you home. Do you live with someone?'

'You mean do I live with a guy. Sure, Tony C. is interested in broads who live with guys. You're something else.'

She closed her eyes and went to sleep with the nape of her neck against the back of the seat, her calves resting across the box of cocaine. Her nose had a bump on the bridge like a Roman's. Her face shone with the luminescence of bone in the moon glow.

Later, I drove down South Carrollton to the river and woke her up at the end of the street.

'You're home,' I said.

She rubbed her face with her hand and opened and closed her mouth.

'I'd invite you in for a drink, but I have to be at the club at seven in the morning. The liquor man comes tomorrow. He screws Tony on the bottle count if I'm not there.'

'It's all right.'

She popped open the door and put one leg out on the street. She was poised against the streetlight, her bandanna tied across the crown of her head as in a photograph of a 1940s aircraft worker.

'Watch your buns, hotshot. Or go back on the

bayou where you belong,' she said.

Then she was gone.

When I got back to the apartment I called Minos at the guesthouse on St. Charles. I told him the buy had gone all right.

'We were only about a mile away. You didn't see us?' he said.

'No.'

'You stopped at a filling station on the way back. You had a girl with you.'

'You guys are pretty good. You know anything about the girl? Her first name is Kim.'

'No. What about her?'

'She seems too smart for the company she keeps.'

'If she's with Tony C.'s crowd, she's somebody's punch.'

'I don't read her like that.'

'A broad's a broad to those guys. They don't keep them around because they have Phi Beta Kappa keys.'

'She said Lionel and the Latin guy who made the delivery killed somebody with a piece of piano wire.'

'I haven't heard that one. But Lionel's got the potential. He was on the boxing team in Angola. They say he did some real damage to a couple of guys.'

'Thanks for telling me, Minos.'

'An agent'll pick up the coke about eight-thirty in the morning. He'll look like a geek, but he's one of ours.'

'I don't want to make this a permanent job. Let's up the ante now.'

'It went well tonight. Be patient. Let things take their own course.'

'Those guys are dipshits and addicts. The mule talked like a pimp. We're not going to get anywhere dealing with them. Let me take a deal straight to Cardo, something that'll make him hungry.'

'Like what?'

'Can you shake loose five hundred thou?'

'Maybe. But you may still end up dealing with the dipshits.'

'No, I'm going to offer him something he doesn't have. But you've got to give me some more help. Get Purcel in on the sting.'

'No.'

'He's a good man.'

'It's out of the question.'

'Minos, I'm by myself in this thing. I want somebody covering my back.'

'What are you going to offer Cardo besides the buy?'

'Deal Purcel in and we'll talk about it.'

'We don't negotiate at this phase of the operation, Dave.'

'We do.'

'I think you're beat,' he said. 'I think you need to get some sleep. We'll talk in the morning.'

'It's not going to change. Clete backs my play or it's up the spout.'

'Good night,' he said. His voice was tired. I didn't answer, and he hung up.

Sleep. It was the most natural and inevitable condition of the human metabolism, I thought, as I sat on the edge of my bed in the dark that night. We can abstain from sex and thrive on the thorns of our desire, deny ourselves water in the desert, keep silent on the torturer's rack, and fast unto the death; but eventually sleep has its way with us.

But if you are a drunk, or a recovering drunk, or what some people innocently call a recovered drunk, that most natural of human state seldom comes to you on your terms. And you cannot explain why one night you will sleep until morning without dreaming while the next you will sit alone in a square of moonlight, your palms damp on your thighs, your breath loud in your chest. No more than you can explain why one day you're anointed with magic. You get high on the weather, you have a lock on the perfecta in the ninth race; then the next morning you're on a dry drunk that fills the day with monstrous shapes prized out of memory with a dung fork.

I could hear revelers out in the street, glass breaking, a beer can rolling across the cement. What was my real fear, or theirs? I suspected mortality more than anything else. You do not wish to go gently into that good night. You rage against it, leave your shining bits of anger for a street sweeper to find in the early morning light, kneel by your bed in the moon glow, the scarlet beads of your rosary twisted around your fist.

But as always, just before dawn, the tiger goes back in his cage and sleeps, and something hot and awful rises from your body and blows away like ash in the wind. And maybe the next day is not so bad after all.

6

The next morning was Saturday. I got up early and, after the DEA agent picked up the coke, invited Bootsie for breakfast at a restaurant on St. Charles. When I picked her up at her house on Camp, she had on dark slacks, gray pumps, a white silk blouse that hung over her waist, and a pearl necklace. Her face was fresh and cheerful with the morning, and the dark and light swirls and streaks of gray in her thick hair, which she'd had cut since I had visited her, gave her an elegance that you seldom see in maturing Acadian women.

I opened the door of the pickup and helped her in. The air was balmy, the street full of blowing leaves, the trees in the yards filled with the sounds of blue jays and mockingbirds.

'I hope you don't mind riding down St. Charles in a pickup,' I said.

'Darlin', I don't mind riding anywhere with you,' she said, with the innocent flirtatious gaiety that's characteristic of New Orleans, and that allows you to never feel awkward or embarrassed with a woman.

'Bootsie, you look absolutely great.'

'Thank you,' she said, moving her lips without sound, a smile in her eyes.

The restaurant had a domed, glassed-in porch, but it was warm enough to eat at the tables outside. The sunlight looked like bright smoke in the oak trees overhead; the air smelled of green bamboo, gardenias, the camellias that bloomed in yards all along the street, the occasional hot scorch of the old green streetcar that rattled down the esplanade, or what the people in New Orleans call the neutral ground. We ate hot, fresh-baked bread with honey and marmalade, and the Negro waiter poured the coffee and milk from two long-spouted copper pots.

I touched Bootsie on the top of her hand.

'I'm going back to New Iberia for the weekend,' I said. 'I have an adopted daughter there.'

'Yes?'

'Do you ever go home?'

'Not really. My parents are passed away. Sometimes I feel strange back there. New Iberia never changes. But I have, and it hasn't all been for the good.'

'Hey, not beating up on ourselves today, Boots.'

'It's funny looking back at the past, isn't it? That night you asked me to dance under the trees on Spanish Lake, I remember it like a photograph. My back was on fire with sunburn. You brought me a vodka Collins, then a handful of aspirin. I thought how kind you were, but then you wouldn't go away.'

'I see. I was the one who put everything in motion.'

'What are you talking about?' Her eyes were smiling again.

'You remember what you did with that vodka

Collins? You took the cherry out and bit it between your teeth and kept chewing it while you looked into my eyes. You knew I wasn't going to leave you alone after that.'

'I did that? It must have been your imagination.'

'Come back with me today. I still live in my father's old house,' I said. Then I added, 'We have a guest room.'

'What are you trying to start, hon?'

'I'm in the one-day-at-a-time club. Tomorrow takes care of itself. I've got three tickets to the LSU-Ole Miss game tonight. We'll take Alafair with us and have crawfish at Mulate's, then go on up to Baton Rouge.'

She didn't answer for a moment; then she said, 'I'm flattered you want me to meet your daughter, but do you think maybe you're trying to fix yesterday's mistakes?'

'No,' I said, and felt my throat color.

'Because if your conscience bothers you, or if you feel that somehow you need to make amends to me, I want you to stop now.'

'It's not that way.'

'Which way is it, then?'

'It's a beautiful day. It's going to be a fine weekend. Why not take a chance on it?'

'You made a choice for both of us thirty years ago, Dave. I didn't have a chance to participate in it. Since then, most of my choices have turned out to be bad ones.'

'Boots, I'll never intentionally hurt you again.'

'We get hurt worse by the people whom we care about. And they seldom mean to do it. That's what makes it so painful, kiddo.'

'At any point you wish, you just say, "Let's go home, Dave. Let's not try to be kids again." It'll end right there.'

'People make lots of promises in the daylight.'

This time I simply looked back across the table at her. Her hair was so thick and lovely. I wanted to reach over and touch it.

'Are you sure this is what you want?' she said finally.

'I can't think of anything better in the whole world,' I said.

I dropped her off at her house, went back to the apartment and packed, left a message for Minos on his answering machine; then two hours later she and I were on our way across the Atchafalaya Basin, on a perfect blue and gold fall day, the wind blowing across the bays and saw grass and dead cypress, the elevated highway like a long white conduit into the past.

You never forget an LSU-Ole Miss game: the tiers upon tiers of seats filled with people, the haze around the banks of lights in the sky, the thunder of marching bands on the field, cheerleaders tumbling like acrobats, Confederate flags waving wildly in the crowd, Mike the Tiger in his cage riding stiff-legged around the track, the coeds with mums pinned on their sweaters, their breath sweet with bourbon and Coca-Cola – then, suddenly, one hundred thousand people rising to their feet in one deafening roar as LUS's team pours on to the field in their gold and purple and white uniforms that shine with light and seem tighter on their bodies than their very muscles.

131

Alafair fell asleep between us on the way back home, and I carried her into her bedroom and tucked her in. Then I heated some *boudin*, and Bootsie and I ate it at the kitchen table. Her face was sleepy with the long day, and she smiled and tried to stay attentive while I talked, but her eyes kept shutting lazily and finally her hand slipped off the side of the table.

'I think it's time you went to sleep,' I said.

'I'm sorry. I'm so tired. It's been a wonderful day, Dave.'

'It'll be an even better one tomorrow.'

'I know,' she said.

'Good night.'

'Good night. I'm sorry to be so tired.'

'It's all right. You're supposed to be tired. I'll see you tomorrow.'

She went into the back bedroom, and I could see the light for a few minutes under her door. I turned on the television set in the living room and lay down on the couch. Her light went off, and I stared at a late show starring a famous actor who had been deferred from service during the Vietnam War because he had been the sole support of his mother. I didn't blame the actor for his deferment, but I didn't have to watch him, either. I turned off the set and lay back down on the couch with my arm over my eyes. I heard the scream of nutria out in the marsh, the sound of night birds out in the bare sugarcane fields behind my property, the occasional thump of pecans falling to the ground in the front yard.

It *had* been a fine day. Why did I always expect more out of the day than perhaps I had earned?

A few minutes later I heard her click on the bedside lamp; then she opened the door and stood framed against the light. She didn't speak. Her face was dark with shadow, her body outlined against her white nightgown, her short-cropped hair diffused with light.

I went into the room with her, and she closed the door as though it were her house rather than mine. She clicked off the lamp, smoothed the pillows, pulled back the covers, then touched my face with her hand, kissing me on the mouth, lightly at first, then her mouth opening and wet, her face changing the angle, her tongue inside me, her eyes opening and shutting but always focusing on mine as though I might somehow elude the moment she was creating for both of us.

She worked her nightgown over her head and lay down partially on her side with her knees close together, her palm behind her head, and waited for me. When I lay down beside her, she stretched out against me, breathing on my neck and chest, rubbing her hair against my face as though she were a cat. I kissed her eyes and mouth and breasts, and felt the smoothness of her stomach and thighs and the contours of her lips. I brushed her hair with my palm, stroked the stiffness of it where it was tapered at the back of her head, smelled the expensive and delicate perfume behind her ears.

Then she took me in her hand, her thighs widening, and placed me inside her. Her lips parted, her eyes closed and opened, and she slipped her arms low on my back and tucked her face under my chin. She didn't speak while she made love. Her concentration and body heat were so intense, the

133

movement of her hands and thighs and stomach so directed and encompassing, the hoarse, regular sounds in my ear so natural and heart-swelling, that I knew she too was back thirty years before on the float cushions in my father's boathouse, the lavender sky streaked with fire through the cracks, the shrimp boat knocking against the pilings, the raindrops dripping like lead shot out of the cypress into the bay.

But on Monday Alafair was back with my cousin Tutta, Bootsie was at work at her vending machine company, and I was talking with Minos in his room at the guesthouse on St. Charles about New Orleans flake and people who gave you reason to think twice that toxic waste had been dumped in the human gene pool.

He stood at the ceiling-high window with a coffee cup in his hand, looking down on the courtyard behind the guesthouse. Banana trees and bamboo grew along the back brick wall, and on the other side of the wall there were garbage cans in the alley. Minos had on tan slacks and a yellow golf shirt with an alligator on it. As always, his scalp gleamed through his close-cropped hair and his jaws looked as though he had just shaved.

'I understand, they're dangerous. You don't have to convince me of that,' he said. 'But it comes with the territory. I don't think the situation will improve because we make Purcel a player.'

'You don't have anybody inside. So we bring him in with me. Give the guy a break. He has a lot of qualities.'

'He worked for the mob, for Christ's sake.'

'I think he took some of them off the board, too.'

'That's the last kind of cowboy bullshit we want in this operation.'

'What's it going to be, partner?'

'We did some homework over the weekend. Purcel has some bad debts around town. One of them is to a loan company owned by the grease-balls. He's also got a reputation for parking his swizzle stick in anything that looks vaguely female.'

'In or out?' I asked.

He bit a corner of his lip and continued to look down into the courtyard. He seemed almost as tall as the window.

'The money comes out of the snitch fund,' he said. 'You can tell him whatever you want to. But he's not an employee of the DEA. Nor its representative.'

'How much?'

'Two hundred a week.'

'That's an insult.'

'Too bad.'

'Listen, Minos, let's stop messing around. You give the guy five hundred a week, treat him with some respect, or I'm going to walk out of this.'

'I'll talk to somebody about it later.'

'No, make the call now.'

I saw him take a breath, his finger tap on his thigh.

'All right, you've got my word,' he said.

'He was a good cop till he had marital trouble and got on the sauce. He'll do fine. You'll see.'

'I hope so. Because if he doesn't, somebody's going to feed your butt through the paper shredder an inch at a time.'

'You really know how to say it, Minos.'

He picked up a towel from the bathroom floor and started buffing one of his loafers on top of a wood chair.

'Where'd this broad, Kim, the one at the score, tell you she was from?'

'She didn't.'

'Hmmm.'

'What is it?'

'We checked her out. Her last name's Dollinger. She's an assistant manager at one of Cardo's clubs on the Airline Highway. She hit town about six months ago. She tells people she worked at a lounge in North Houston, some dump on Jensen Drive. We made a couple of calls. They never heard of her.'

'She said something. About everything down here smelling like mold and leaking sewage. I don't think she's from Houston.'

'Those kinds of broads make up their own dossiers. I've got something else on my mind that's giving me the start of a migraine, Dave.'

I waited for him to go on.

'Bootsie Giacano,' he said.

'I had a feeling you'd say that. Do you have a tail on me?'

'It wouldn't be a bad idea, but we don't.'

'A tap on her phone?'

'What do you think? She was married to Ralph Giacano. Her business partners are mainline greaseballs.'

'She can't get out from under them.'

'Always the humanist. Look, Dave, what you do with your private life is your business. But if you compromise the operation, it's ours.' He sat on the wood chair and threw the towel back on to the bathroom floor. 'Look, I'm your friend. I got you into this stuff. You think I want to see you hurt?'

'I won't get hurt because of her.'

'You don't know that. Are you sleeping with her?'

'I'm going to be on my way now.'

'She'll know you're running a sting. She tips the greaseballs, it doesn't matter how, in some innocent way, we're going to pull you out of Lake Pontchartrain.'

'It's not going to happen.'

His eyes were level, unblinking, and they stared straight into mine.

'It did two years ago,' he said. 'To a local narc N.O.P.D. got inside. They threw his body off the causeway. A .22 Magnum through the mouth, one under the chin, one through the temple. They didn't weight him down either. They wanted to send a floating telegram.'

'You can get the five hundred thou?'

'Yep.'

'I'm going to try to set up a meet with Cardo. I'll call you.'

'Let some time go by, Dave. Let them feel more confident about you.'

'You said it yourself, these guys love money. How do they put it, "Money talks and bullshit walks"? I'm going to play out the hand. If they buy it, fine. If not, I'm going back home.'

He pulled on his ear and made a snuffing sound in his nose.

'What I'm saying is we don't know everything

137

we'd like to know about Cardo. He messes around in politics, sends money to right-wing crazies, stuff like that. He was shooting off his mouth around town about bringing Oliver North to New Orleans. He thinks he's a big intellectual because he's got a degree from a junior college in Miami.'

'So?'

'So he's hard to read. We know there're some guys in Miami and Chicago who think maybe he shouldn't be running things here, that maybe he's crazy or he keeps his brains in that schlong he's so proud of. Figure it out, Dave. What kind of guy would keep Jimmie Lee Boggs around?'

'You're worrying too much, Minos.'

'Because I've been doing this stuff a long time. I told you it was a simple sting. That's what it should be. But you don't hear me when I say things to you, and I'm bothered by that.'

I left by the back entrance and walked down the alley to the side street where my truck was parked. I could hear the streetcar clattering down the tracks on St. Charles. The sky was a hard blue, the noon sun bright overhead, and gray squirrels raced each other around the trunks of the oak trees on the street. Now all I had to do was find a way inside the insular and peculiar world of Anthony Cardo.

'You just fucking do it, mon,' Clete said that same day as we ate lunch at the bar in the Golden Star on Decatur. 'The guy lives in a house, right, not the Vatican. We're talking about a bucket of shit, mon, not the pope. You don't get a number and wait when you deal with a bucket of shit, do you?'

He took an enormous bite of his oyster loaf

sandwich. His face was ruddy and cheerful, his crushed porkpie hat down low over his eyes, his sports coat as tight as a sausage skin on his broad back. His cigarette burned in an ashtray, and by his elbow was a Bloody Mary with a celery stalk in it.

'Call up the cocksucker and tell him we're coming out,' he said.

'It's not that easy, Cletus.'

'I don't see the problem.' His cheek was as big as a baseball with unchewed food. We were alone at the bar. The walls were covered with the framed and autographed photos of movie stars.

'He has an unlisted number. Minos gave it to me, but I don't have a way to explain to Cardo how I got it. I asked Fontenot for it, and he wouldn't give it to me. He said he had to clear it with Cardo first.'

'Fontenot's the tub, the one with the T-shirt shop on Bourbon?'

'That's the man.'

'He wants to control access to the piggy bank, huh?'

'Something like that.'

'Stay here.'

'Where are you going?'

'Remain cool and copacetic, my mellow man. I'll be back before you finish your gumbo.'

'Wait a minute, Clete.'

But he was out the door. Fifteen minutes later he was back, his green eyes smiling under the short brim of his hat. He dropped a slip of paper with Cardo's phone number on it next to my plate.

'What did you do to him?' I asked.

'Hey, come on, Fontenot's a reasonable guy. I just explained that you and I are in partnership now.

He liked the idea. That's right, I ain't putting you on.'

'Clete, if we get into Cardo's, you've got to take your transmission out of overdrive.'

'Trust me, mon.' the fingers of his big hands were spread out like banana peels on top of the bar. He grinned at me, squinted his eyes, and clicked his teeth together. 'You're looking at a model of restraint, I worked Vice, remember. I know these fuckers. They'll love having me on board.'

It was easier than I thought. I called Cardo's house, a maid answered, then Cardo was on the line. He was polite, even expansive. The accent was typical New Orleans Italian, which sounded like both Flatbush and the Irish Channel.

'I've heard a lot about you,' he said. 'I've been looking forward to meeting you. You play tennis?'

'I'm afraid not.'

'You like to watch tennis?'

'Sure.'

'Where are you now?'

'At the Golden Star, across from the French Market.'

'Can you come out in an hour? We'll have some drinks, I'll hit the ball a little bit, we'll talk.'

'Sure. I'd like that. Can you give me your address?'

He gave me directions to a neighborhood out by Lake Pontchartrain.

'How'd you get this number?' he asked.

'It came from Ray.'

'That's strange. Ray usually doesn't give it out.'

The receiver was quiet a moment.

'You haven't been bouncing my help around, have you?' he said; then he laughed. 'Don't worry about it. Ray needs a little excitement. Cleans the fat out of his veins. You didn't hurt him, though, did you?'

'I didn't do anything to him. I'd like to bring along a friend of mine. He's going into business with me.'

'That's fine with me. We'll be expecting you. Say, you know that newsstand a few doors down from you? Pick me up a copy of the *Atlantic*, will you? My subscription didn't come.'

'Sure thing, Mr. Cardo.'

'Hey, it's Tony or Tony C. or Tony some-other-things, but nobody calls me Mr. Cardo. Do I sound like a Mr. Cardo to you?'

'I'm looking forward to it. We'll see you in an hour,' I said.

I hung up the phone and looked at Clete at the bar.

'The *Atlantic*?' I said.

'What?'

'This guy's a beaut.'

His home was a short distance from the lake. The immense, sloping lawn was shaded by live oaks, and the one-story house was long and white with a wide marble porch, a three-car garage, and a gingerbread gazebo in a side yard that was planted with blooming citrus trees and camellias. The swimming pool had a colonnade built on to one side, like a Roman porch, and behind the pool was a screened-in clay tennis court, and I could see a trim, suntanned man in white shorts and a polo shirt *whocking* balls at a machine that fired them automatically over the net.

'The mustaches know how to live, don't they?'

141

Clete said, his tie askew, one arm back on the seat, flipping ashes out the window of the truck.

'Play it cool on the remarks.'

'Ease up. There're only two rules when you deal with these guys. Don't mess with their broads and don't steal from them. These guys just aren't complicated. What would a guy like Tony Cardo do if he couldn't deal dope? He'd probably be running a fruit stand. You think a greaseball like that could honestly earn a joint like this?'

'I'll do most of the talking today, all right, Clete?'

'You've got a lot of anxiety over nothing, mon. But it's your gig. What do I know?' He flipped his cigarette in an arc into a flower bed.

A negro man in a white jacket and black pants walked out the side door of the house and stood on the edge of the drive while we got out of the truck.

'Mr. Cardo want y'all come out by the pool,' he said. 'He be with y'all in a minute.' He couldn't keep his eyes from glancing sideways at the truck.

'You like it? Dave might part with it for the right price,' Clete said.

'Mr. Cardo ax you gentlemens if you want a drink,' the Negro said.

'Give me a double black Jack on ice,' Clete said. 'What do you want, Dave?'

'Nothing.'

'You got a bathroom?' Clete said to the Negro.

'Yes suh, follow me inside.'

I sat in a beach chair under the colonnade by the side of the pool. The bottom of the pool was inset with a mosaic mermaid that glittered with chips of light. The suntanned man on the court was hitting the ball with this back to me, but I felt that he was

142

aware I was watching him through the myrtle trees that grew along the screens. He stayed on the balls of his feet, the muscles in his brown calves and thighs taught and glazed with perspiration, his forehand shot a white blur across the net.

Clete came out of the side of the house with a highball glass in his hand and sat down heavily in a beach chair next to me.

'You ought to see the can,' he said. 'It looks like a pink whorehouse. Erotic art all over the wallpaper, a toilet seat inlaid with silver dollars. The colored guy went in after me and started cleaning the toilet with a brush. Should I take that personally?'

'Probably.'

'Thanks.'

The man on the tennis court turned off the ball machine and walked across the close-clipped lawn towards us, zipping up the case on his racket. He was truly a strange-looking man. His head was long and narrow, his ears tiny and pressed tightly against the scalp as though part of them had been surgically pared away. His hair grew in gray and black ringlets that were tapered on the back of his neck like the flange of a helmet. His smile exposed his long white teeth, and his chest hair was black and slick with perspiration.

'Tony Cardo,' he said, his hand outstretched like a greeter's in a restaurant.

'It's nice to see you, Tony,' I said. 'This is a friend of mine, Clete Purcel.'

'What's happening, Tony?' Clete said, rising up enough from the beach chair to shake hands.

'I remember you from somewhere,' Cardo said to him.

'You drink vodka Collins,' Clete said.

Cardo pursed his lips together in the shape of a tiny butterfly.

'You're a bartender in the Quarter,' he said.

'I own the bar.'

'You were in the corps.'

'That's right.'

'We had some words or something.'

'No, I don't have words with people.'

'Yeah, we did. Something about the corps. No, something about "the crotch", right?'

'You got me. I don't argue with people.'

'Who's arguing? But you said something, almost like getting in a guy's face. Then you walked away. I was buying a drink for the gunny.'

Clete shrugged his shoulders.

'It must be somebody else. I just remember you drink vodka Collins, that's all,' he said.

'Hey, don't sweat it. You're a diplomat. That's good. It means you're a good businessman.'

'I got no beef with anybody, Tony.'

'I like that,' Cardo said.

'Clete was my Homicide partner a few years ago,' I said. I watched Cardo's face.

'What made you change careers?' His eyes smiled as though he were looking at a private conclusion inside himself. The black houseman brought out a tray with a Collins and bowl of chilled shrimp on it and set it on a circular redwood table next to Cardo's chair.

'A little trouble in the department, nothing big,' Clete said. 'I went down to the tropics for a while to get my priorities straight. Then I got into casino security out in Vegas and Tahoe for Sally Dio.'

144

'Yeah, Sally Dee out of Galveston,' Cardo said. 'His plane smacked into a mountain out in Montana or somewhere.'

'Yeah, it was too bad. He was a great guy to work for,' Clete said.

'I always heard he was a prick,' Cardo said.

'Well, some people had that opinion, too,' Clete said.

'You're not drinking anything, Dave?'

'No thanks. Can we talk some business, Tony?'

'Put on some swimsuits. Let's take a dip,' he said.

'It's a little cool, isn't it?' I said.

'I keep the water at eighty-two degrees. You'll love it. There're some suits over there in the cottage,' he insisted.

He went into his own house to change, and Clete and I walked across the lawn to a small white stucco cottage that was surrounded with palm and banana trees.

'He's one slick motherfucker. You won't get a wire into this place, partner,' Clete said.

Inside the cottage we found a cardboard box full of men's and women's bathing suits on top of the bar. Clete started rooting through them and found only one pair that wasn't too small for him, an enormous pair of red boxer trunks with a white elastic band.

'I bet these belong to that blimp who runs the T-shirt shop,' he said. He looked at my face. 'It's not funny, Dave. These guys pass around VD like a family heirloom.' He went into the bedroom, found a safety pin in a drawer, and began undressing by the bar.

'He really put you under the microscope,' I said.

'They're all the same, mon. They love to peel back your skin.'

'What do you think all that Marine Corps stuff is about?'

'Who cares? Figuring out the greaseballs is like putting your hand in an unflushed toilet.'

I laid my clothes across the back of a couch and slipped on a pair of trunks. Clete poured a glass of Jack Daniel's at the bar and looked at my chest.

'That's where Boggs popped you, huh?' he said. 'Does it give you much trouble?'

'I'm still weak on the left side. Sometimes it throbs a little in the morning.'

'What else?'

'What do you mean "what else"?'

'Don't try to put on your old partner. You remember when that kid planted a couple of .22 rounds in me? I had the nightly sweats for a long time, mon.'

'It comes and goes.'

'Like hell it does.' Then he took a drink and smiled at me. His faced looked as big and hard-ribbed as a grinning pumpkin under his porkpie hat. 'But don't worry. Before this is over, we're going to cook Jimmie Lee Boggs's hash, I mean sling some serious shit on the walls. You wait and see, ole Streak.'

He winked at me and walked duck-footed to the door, with his drink in his hand, his red trunks askew on his hips, lighting a cigarette.

'You think he's got any broads around?' he said.

I took the copy of the *Atlantic* out of my pocket and followed him to the pool.

Tony Cardo hit the water in a long, flat dive and swam with deep strokes to the diving board, blowing water out his nose, then made an underwater turn and pushed off the tiled side and swam into the shallow end. He raked the water out of his eyes and curly hair and spit into the trough that surrounded the pool.

'That's a nasty scar on your chest, Dave,' he said.

'A nasty guy put it there.'

'Yeah, I heard about that.'

'He works for you.'

'That's not exactly true, Dave. He used to work for some people I do business with. He doesn't now. I don't know where he is. I heard Florida.'

'I wouldn't want a guy like that to blindside me, Tony.'

'You're an up-front guy. But you got no worries on that. Not in this town.'

'The people I represent like the quality of your product, they like the way you do business. They've given me a half million to work with. I want the same quality goods, same price on the key. Can we do some business today?'

'You cut right to it, don't you?'

'You're a serious man, you have a serious reputation.'

'You're talking a big score.'

'That's why I'm dealing with you. The word is that the Houston people are undependable.'

'The problem I got sometimes is access, Dave. Or what you might call transportation. The product's out there, but there're a lot of nautical factors involved here, you know what I mean? Something happens to the product out on the salt,

147

a lot of people lose money, a lot of people get real mad.'

'That's the other thing I want to talk to you about. I grew up in the wetlands. I know every bayou and channel from Sabine Pass over to Barataria. I can get it through for you, and on a regular basis.'

'I bet you can,' he said.

But his attention was no longer on me. His arms were folded on top of the trough, and he was looking across the blue-green expanse of lawn and trees at the front porch of his house, where a blond woman in a red dress and a hat was counting the suitcases the houseman was bringing inside. A moment later one of the gatemen walked up the drive and backed a restored 1940s Lincoln Convertible out of the garage. It had wire wheels, a deep maroon finish, and an immaculate white top. The gateman and the Negro put the woman's luggage in the trunk. She never glanced in our direction.

'What do you think of my car?' he said finally.

'It looks great.'

'Yeah. That's what I think.' But his eyes were still concentrated on the woman. 'You married?'

'Not now.'

He continued to stare as she got into the Lincoln and the gateman drove her down the long driveway towards the street. Then his eyes clicked back to mine.

'Hey, let me ask you something else. Because I like you. I like the way you talk,' he said. 'What's your attitude about dealing in the product?'

'I don't understand.'

'You're an educated man. I want to know what an educated man thinks about dealing in the product.'

'I never saw anybody chop up lines because somebody forced him to.'

'I think that's an intelligent attitude. But I want you to understand something else, Dave. I got lots of businesses. Vending and video machines, a restaurant, nightclubs, half of a trucking company, real estate development out by Chalmette, some investments in Miami. This other stuff comes and goes. Five years from now the in thing might be huffing used cat litter. There's always a bunch of bozos around with money. Why fight the fashion?'

His eyes looked at the empty drive and the front gage that was closed once again.

'Excuse me,' he said, and raised himself out of the pool, walked dripping to the redwood table, and punched one button on the phone. He put his little finger in one of his tiny ears and shook water out of it. At the end of the drive I saw the other gateman walk to a box that was inset in the stucco wall.

'Tommy, get some people over here, call up the catering service,' he said. 'I got some guests here, I want to entertain them right . . . Don't ask me who, I don't give a shit, get them over here.'

He hung up the phone and looked at me.

'I live in a place that costs a million bucks, and half the time it's like being the only guy in the fucking Superdome,' he said.

'Before your friends get here, can we agree on a deal of some kind, Tony?' I said.

'There's some people I bring out here like I order lawn furniture. There's other people I invite because I respect their experience and what's in their heads. Don't hurt my feelings,' he said.

His guests arrived like actors who played only one role, their smiles welded in place, their eyes aglitter with the moment. They were people without accents or origins, as though they had lived on the edge of a party all their lives. But besides their good looks and their late-season suntans, their most singular common denominator was their carefree trust in the walled-in tropical opulence that surrounded them. They smoked dope by the pool, snorted lines off a mirror in the guest cottage, ate chicken and mayonnaise sandwiches from the caterer's tray, with never a sideways glance at gatemen who wore shoulder holsters or a thick-bodied, silent man in cutoffs who waxed an Oldsmobile in the driveway with such a mean energy that his jailhouse tattoos danced like snakes on his naked back.

Even Clete quickly fell into the ambience, his arms spread out on the tile trough in the deep end, his pale blue canvas hat low on his brow, a twenty-year-old girl hovering within the crook of his arm. Her mouth was red and cold from the whiskey sour she sipped from a glass in one hand, and she laughed at everything he said and balanced herself by cupping his shoulder whenever she started to float away from the pool's edge. I could see her knee rake against his thigh.

The air was becoming cooler now, and I treaded water to stay warm. It was impossible to get Cardo alone. He sat at the redwood table in a white terry cloth robe, one leg crossed on his knee, smoking a Pall Mall in a gold cigarette holder, while four of his guests sat around him and smiled brightly into his words. I hung from the diving board by one arm and began to think it was better to mark the day off.

'How do you like being in the life?' a voice said behind me.

She sat on the diving board mat in a light green dress covered with tiny pink flowers. She had tucked her red hair up into a green beret, but one side of it had fallen down on her neck. Her lipstick was bright red, and she wore too much of it, but when she parted her mouth and looked directly at me, she disturbed me and made me keenly aware that there is no safety for the male in either age or pride.

'What's happening, Kim?' I said.

'What's happening with you, hotshot?'

'Like you say, enjoying the life. You don't want to swim?'

'I think I'll pass. Two nights ago they were screwing in here.'

'I beg your pardon?'

'You heard me. On a rubber raft, with the lights on. What a bunch.'

I lifted myself out of the pool and walked to the guest cottage to shower and dress. I heard her laugh behind me. When I came back out she was sitting on a cushioned, scrolled iron chair with her legs crossed. I sat down on the dry mat on the back edge of the diving board.

'You're a case,' she said.

'How's that?' I said, looking toward the shallow end, where Tony was tapping a beach ball back and forth with two girls.

'You make me think of a cat that's trying to like sitting on a hot stove,' she said.

151

'Where did you say you're from?'

'I didn't.'

'I need to talk to Tony alone. It's hard to do.'

'You're still out for the big score, huh, hotshot?'

'How about cutting me a little slack?'

'All you want, babe.'

'Are you his girl?'

She looked away from me at the trees in the yard, her face cool and sculpted, her hair thick and dark red where it was pinned up on the back of her neck. She touched at an area between her teeth with her little fingernail, then glanced back into my face. Her eyes looked directly into mine, but they were impossible to read.

'What?' I asked her.

Still she didn't answer, and instead continued to stare into my face. I took a breath.

'I think I need to get something to eat,' I said.

'If you want to see Tony alone, he'll be going up to the house soon to check on his little boy. He always does.'

'His little boy?'

'It's the reason his wife's always taking off. She can't handle it.'

'What are you talking about?'

'Do yourself a favor and go home, Robicheaux.'

She stood up, tucked her hair under her beret, and walked off alone toward the tennis court. A moment later I saw her leaning on her arms against the wire mesh, looking at nothing, her face wan and empty in the shadow of the myrtle bushes.

She was right about Tony Cardo, though. Ten minutes later, when I was about to signal Clete that it was time to hang it up, Cardo excused himself from his guests and walked across his lawn to a glassed-in sun porch at the back of his house. I went to the side door of the house and knocked. The Negro houseman answered, a polishing cloth in his hand.

'I'd like to see Mr. Cardo,' I said.

'He be out directly.'

'I'd like to see him inside, please.'

'Just a moment, suh,' he said, and walked into the back of the house. Then he returned and unlatched the screen. 'Mr. Cardo want you to wait in the library.'

I followed the houseman through a huge, gleaming kitchen, a living room furnished with French antiques and hung with a chandelier the size of a beach umbrella, into a pine-paneled study whose shelves were filled with encyclopedias, sets of science and popular history books, novels from book clubs, and plastic-bound collections of classics, the kind that are printed on low-grade paper and advertised on cable TV stations. The chairs and couch were red leather, the big glass-topped mahogany desk one that would perhaps befit Leo Tolstoy.

Tony slid open the far door and stepped inside in his terry cloth robe and sandals. Before he closed the door again, I looked out on the sun porch and saw the back of a wheelchair framed against a lighted television screen. The floor around the chair was strewn with toys and stuffed animals.

'I didn't give you your magazine,' I said, and took the copy of the *Atlantic* out of my pocket and handed it to him.

'Hey, thanks, Dave. I appreciate it.'

'I have to go, too. I just wanted to tell you I'd like to do business with you, but I have to have something firm. Like this afternoon, Tony.'

'I want you to understand something, and I don't want you to take offense. The house is a family place, I don't do business in it. Call Ray Fontenot tomorrow. We'll work something out. You got my word on it.'

'All right.'

'Your face looks a little cloudy.'

'I don't trust Fontenot. I don't know that you should, either.'

'Serious charge. What'd he do?'

'He's an addict and he looks after his own butt.'

'They all do.'

'Thanks for having us out.'

'Wait a minute, don't run off. I heard you were in 'Nam.'

'Ten months, before it got real hot.'

'Those scars on your thigh, you got hit?'

'A bouncing Betty on a trail. It was a dumb place to be at night.'

'Sit down a second. Come on, you're not in that big a hurry. Then you got to go back to the States?'

'Sure. A million-dollar wound.'

'In the corps, unless you get the big one, you got to earn two Hearts before you skate.'

'You were hit?'

'Right in the butt. A zip up in a tree, maybe three hundred yards out.'

I looked at my watch. I didn't want to talk more about the war, but it was obvious that he did. His eyes wandered over my face, as though he were

154

searching for a piece of knowledge there that had eluded him in his own life. Then because I had to say something, I asked him a question that produced a strange consequence.

'What was your outfit?'

'Third Battalion, Seventh Regiment, First Marine Division,' he said, and smiled.

'Oh yeah, you guys were around Chu Lai.'

The skin of his face tightened.

'How do you know that?' he said.

'I was there,' I said, confused.

'You were in Chu Lai?' The skin around his eyes and nostrils was white.

'No, I mean I was in Vietnam. I knew some Marines who were around Chu Lai, that's all.'

'Who were these guys?'

'I don't even remember their names, Tony.'

'I just wondered.'

'Are you all right, partner?'

He widened his eyes and breathed air up through his nose.

'It was a fucking meat grinder, man,' he said.

'Maybe it's time to give it the deep six.'

'What?'

'We didn't ask to get sent over there. A time comes when we stop dragging the monsters around.'

'You saying I did something over there?'

'If you didn't, you saw it done.'

He looked at me for a long moment, his mouth a tight line.

'You're an unusual man,' he said.

'I don't think so.'

'One day just kick the door shut on Shitsville?'

155

'You already lived it. Why watch the replay the rest of your life?'

'Some guys say the war's never over.'

'It is for me.'

'No dreams?'

I didn't answer.

'That's what I thought,' he said. His body was deep in a leather chair. He smiled crookedly at me.

But my strange afternoon at Tony C.'s was not over. When Clete and I waked out to my truck, I noticed that my wallet was gone. I looked into the guest cottage and out by the pool, then realized that it had probably fallen out of my pocket when I was sitting in the library. The black man let me in the side of the house again. This time the sliding door of the library that gave on to the sun porch was open, and I saw Tony dressing a little boy in the wheelchair surrounded by a litter of toys. He did not see me, not at first. The little boy might have been seven or eight. His face was handsome and bright, but his head rested on his shoulders as though he had no neck, his legs were too short for his truncated body, and his back was deformed terribly. His hair was brown and wet, and Tony Cardo parted and combed it and leaned over and kissed him on the brow. Then his eyes glanced up into my face.

'I'm sorry. I dropped my wallet in the chair,' I said.

He walked to the door and slid it shut.

That night it rained. It ran off the roof, the gutters, the balconies, clattered on the palm fronds and

156

banana trees, spun like a vortex of wet light inside the courtyard. Lightning cracked across the sky and rattled the windows, and I slept with a pillow crimped across my head. I did not hear the lock pick in the door nor the handle turn when the bolt clicked free of the jamb. Instead, I felt a drop in the room's temperature, and smelled leaves and rain. I raised up on one elbow and looked into the face of Tony Cardo, who leaned forward on a straight-backed chair by the side of my bed. One of his gatemen stood behind him, dripping water on the floor.

'How scared you ever been?' he said. His narrow, elongated face looked white in the glow of the electric light that shone through the window from the courtyard.

'What?' My hand went toward the drawer of the nightstand.

'No,' he said, took my wrist, and pushed my arm back on the bed.

'What are you—'

'How scared you ever been?' he repeated. His eyes were absolutely black and glazed with light, as though they had no pupils.

I was sitting straight up now. The front door was halfway open, and leaves and mist were blowing inside the living room.

'Listen, Tony—'

'It was after you got hit, wasn't it? When you had to lie in the dark by yourself and think about it.'

I couldn't smell alcohol on him. Then I looked again at his eyes, the lidless intensity, the heat that was like a match burning inside of black glass.

'Admit it,' he said.

157

'I was scared every minute I was over there. Who cares? You're speeding, Tony.'

Then I saw him raise the revolver from between his thighs.

'You know how to overcome it?' he said.

I looked at the gateman. His face was empty of expression, beaded with raindrops.

'You confront the dragon,' Tony said.

'Ease up, partner. This isn't your style.'

'What the fuck you know about my style?'

'I didn't do it to you. I don't have anything to do with your life. You're talking to the wrong guy.'

'You're the right guy. You know you're the right guy.'

'Everybody was afraid over there. It's just human. What's the matter with you?'

'You buy that? I say fuck you. You stare it in the face. Can you stare it in the face?'

His mouth looked purple in the glow from the window. His ears were like tiny white cauliflowers pressed against his scalp.

'I think you're loaded Tony. I think we're talking black beauties here. I'm not going to help you with this bullshit. Go fuck yourself.'

I could see his thin nostrils quiver as he breathed. He rested the revolver on the top of his right thigh. Then he said, 'This is how you do it, my man.'

He flipped out the cylinder from the frame and ejected six .38 cartridges into his palm. He clinked them all into his coat pocket except one. He fitted it into a chamber and snapped the cylinder back into place.

'Tony, pull the plug on this before it goes any further. It's not worth it,' I said.

He set the hammer on half cock, spun the cylinder twice, then brought the hammer all the way back with his thumb and fitted the barrel's opening under his chin. The skin of his face became as stiff and gray as cardboard, his eyes focused on a distant thought somewhere behind my ear. Then he pulled the trigger.

'Jesus Christ, Tony,' I heard the gateman say, his breath rushing out of his chest.

Tony put an unlit cigarette in his mouth, opened the cylinder again, and fitted the five rounds from his pocket back into the chambers.

'It wasn't even close, two chambers away from the firing pin,' he said. 'Don't ever let me see pity in your face when you look at me and my little boy again.'

A solitary drop of water fell out of his hair and spotted the unlit cigarette in his mouth.

7

The next morning the streets in the Quarter were thick with mist, and I could hear the foghorns of tugs and oil barges out on the river. I had coffee and *beignets* at a table inside the Café du Monde; then the sun broke out of the clouds and Jackson Square looked bright and wet and green after the night's rain. I walked over to Ray Fontenot's T-shirt shop on Bourbon and found him practicing his trombone in a small weed-grown, rubble-strewn courtyard in back. He wore a purple turtleneck sweater, gray slacks, and shades, even though there was little sunlight in the enclosure. He was not a gelatinous man. The rings of fat across his stomach looked hard, the kind your fist would do little harm to.

My conversation with him did not go well.

'So we're agreed on everything,' he said. 'You'll bring your boat over from Morgan City, and we'll take a little tarpon-fishing trip out on the salt. By the way, what's your boat doing in Morgan City if you live in New Iberia?'

'I just had the engine overhauled.'

'That's good. And you'll have all the money?'

'That's right.'

'Because we want lots of product for all the little boys and girls. It's what keeps everybody's genitalia humming. Like little nests of bees.'

'Day after tomorrow, two A.M. at Cocodrie. Dress warm. It'll be cold out there,' I said, and started to leave.

'Thank you, kind sir. But there's one change.'

He drained the spittle out of his trombone slide on to the weeds at his feet.

'What's that?' I said.

'Your friend Purcel is not going with us.'

'He's my business partner. He's in.'

'Not on this trip.'

'Why not?'

'He hasn't quite learned how to behave. Besides, we don't need him.'

'Listen, Fontenot, if Clete gave you a bad time over Tony's phone number, that's a personal beef you work out on your own. This is business.'

'He no play-a, he no go-a.'

'What does Tony say?'

'I make the deals for Tony, I make the terms. When you talk to me, it's just like you're talking to Tony.'

'You mind if I make a call?'

'I wouldn't have it any other way, good sir.' He took off his sunglasses and smiled. His eyes were flat and dead and looked as if they belonged in another face.

I used the telephone in Fontenot's office. I could hear him blowing into his trombone.

'Hey, good morning. How you doing today?' Tony Cardo said.

'I'm fine.'

'Sure?'

'I'm just fine, Tony.'

'You don't have a hard-on about last night?'

'You've got your own point of view about things. I don't want to intrude upon it.'

'I got strong emotions. About family stuff. I get a little weird sometimes. You got to bear with me.'

'I respect your feelings, Tony.'

'You don't rattle, do you?'

'Morning and night, podna. I've got a problem here. Ray doesn't want my friend along on the tarpon trip.'

'That's too bad.'

'I think my friend should be able to go.'

'I can't interfere, Dave. It's Ray's call.'

'He's got his nose bent out of joint over a personal affront. It's not the way a pro does things.'

'Indulge the man.'

'He's a fat shit, Tony.'

'Hey, catch a big fish for me. And I want you out to dinner this weekend. Bring your buddy, too. I like him.'

He hung up the phone. Ray Fontenot stood in the doorway to the courtyard, his eyes filled with merriment, his tongue thick and pink on his teeth.

At noon I went to Clete's to pick him up for lunch. We drove in his car to a Fat Albert's off St. Charles and ordered paper plates of red beans and dirty rice with lengths of sausage. It was warm enough to eat outside, and we sat at a green-painted picnic table under a live oak whose roots had lifted up the slabs of sidewalk and cracked the edge of the parking lot. Out on St. Charles I saw the old iron streetcar rattle

162

past the palm trees on the esplanade.

I told Clete about my conversation that morning with Fontenot. He chewed quietly without speaking, his green eyes thoughtful. I waited for him to say something. He didn't.

'Anyway, he says you're out, and Cardo backed him up.'

He wiped the juice from his sausage off his mouth with a paper napkin, then sucked on the corner of his lip.

'I'd be careful,' he said.

'What are you thinking?'

'He's up to something.'

'I think he just doesn't like you. What did you do to him to get Cardo's phone number?'

'Nothing.'

'Clete?'

'I told him I wasn't leaving till I got the number. I made a little noise in front of his customers. I didn't touch him.'

'It surprises you he doesn't want to see you again?'

'What if I have another talk with him?'

'That's out. The deal has to go through.'

'I'm worried about you, mon. You're not seeing things straight. You're doing the grunt work for the DEA, they take the glory. There's something else to think about, too. How's a drug buy out on the salt going to put Cardo away?'

'I've got to get next to him with a wire.'

'Why not get a Pap smear while you're at it?' He lit a cigarette and blew smoke off into the dappled sunlight. 'We used to call the FBI "Fart, Barf, and Itch", remember? Why do you think these DEA

163

cocksuckers are any different? If you ask me, this deal down at Cocodrie stinks.'

There was no point in arguing. I also felt that he was more disappointed in being cut out of the sting than anything else. But his eyes continued to wander over my face while he smoked.

'For God's sakes, what is it?' I said.

'I don't know if you need this right now, but a colored kid was in the bar looking for you this morning. He wouldn't give his name, but I have an idea who he is.'

'Oh?'

'That kid from New Iberia you were taking up to Angola with Jimmie Lee Boggs.'

'What did he say?'

'"Tell Mr. Dave I seen Jimmie Lee yesterday on Bourbon."' Clete continued to look at my face. 'I'm right, that's the kid who got loose from you?'

'Yes.'

'You're in contact with him?'

'More or less.'

'Are you out of your mind?'

'Does he look like a dangerous and violent man to you? You think I ought to send him to the chair?'

'I think you ought to watch out for your own butt once in a while.'

'What else did he say?'

'Nothing. A weird kid. If a black ant wore a pizza uniform, that's what it'd look like. You really think he saw Boggs?'

'I don't know.'

'Why would Boggs be walking around on Bourbon?'

'I don't know, Clete.'

164

'Come on, don't look so disturbed. The kid's probably imaginative.' Then he pressed his lips together in a tight line. 'Listen, Dave, keep your attitudes simple about this guy. You see him, you smoke him. No warning, no talk, you just blow his fucking head off. Case closed.'

I didn't finish my plate. I rolled it up, dropped it in a trash barrel, then sat back down at the wood table under the tree. Clete kept pushing a ring around on his index finger while his eyes studied me.

'You think you lost your guts?' he said.

'No.'

'Like Boggs has got the Indian sign on you or something?'

'I'm cool. Don't worry about it.'

'You bothered because you want to do this guy?'

'No.'

'You listen to me. It's a perk when you get a chance to grease a guy like that. You take him off at the neck and the world applauds.' But he saw his words were having no effect. 'What happened in that coulee?'

'I thought my clock had run out. I don't think I behaved very well. I always thought I would do better.'

'Nobody handles it well. They cry, they call out for their mother. It's a bad moment. It's supposed to be.'

'You don't feel the same about yourself later.'

He picked at the calluses on his hands, his eyes downcast.

'My noble, grieving mon,' he said.

'Look, Clete, I appreciate—'

165

'You know what I think all this is about? You want to drink. Whenever I went out on the edge of the envelope, I'd mellow out with some skull-fuck *muta* and JD on the rocks. You can't drink anymore, so you walk around with this ongoing horror show inside you.'

'How about we put the cork in the five-and-dime psychology? Look, I think Cardo's heavy into crank.'

'He's a speed freak?'

'He came into my apartment in the middle of the night and snapped a revolver under his chin.'

Clete grinned, shook his head, and rolled a matchstick across his teeth.

'What's funny?' I said.

'This is the guy you're going to get next to with a wire? And you worry about Boggs or whether you still got your guts? Streak, you're a pistol.'

I talked with Minos Dautrieve that afternoon and made arrangements to have my converted jugboat moved from Morgan City to a commercial dock at Cocodrie, near Terrebonne Bay. Over the phone I sensed a fine wire of anxiety in Minos's voice.

'What is it?' I said.

'It bothers me they don't want Purcel with you.'

'He got in Fontenot's face. Clete has a way of scaring the hell out of people he doesn't like.'

'Maybe.'

'Are you worried about the half a million.'

'I'm worried about you. But some other people are having misgivings about the operation. It's a big expenditure. Cardo's not getting brought into things the way he should.'

166

'I can't help that.'

'They're thinking about their own butts. They don't want to get burned. But that's not your problem. The Coast Guard's going to track the mother boat and nail it after you're gone. So the government'll get its money back. I don't know why these guys are sweating. They piss me off.'

'Run Cardo's military record for me.'

'What for?'

'Something about Vietnam is eating his lunch.'

'What's new about that?'

'I think he's a complex man. You didn't tell me about his son.'

'Yeah, that's a sad case.'

'Evidently he really looks after him.'

The phone was silent a moment.

'Cardo's a drug dealer, and his hired shitheads kill people. Anything else is irrelevant. It's important to understand that, Dave.'

'I'm just saying you can't dismiss the guy as a geek.'

'Right. He hires them instead. Like Jimmie Lee Boggs. Get your head on straight. I'll be back with you later. Carry your piece out there on the salt. I want your ass back home safe on this one.'

He hung up the phone.

That night I wanted to take Bootsie out for supper, but she had to work late at her office, and when she finally finished it was after ten o'clock. So I read a book in bed and went to sleep sometime after midnight with the light on and a pillow over my head.

The twilight is purple and the willow trees along the

banks of the Mississippi are filled with fireflies when they take the black kid out of the van and walk him inside the Red Hat House in a waist chain. His hair has been shaved down to the scalp and his ears look abnormally large on the sides of his head. The wind is blowing off the river, ruffling the corn and stalks of sugarcane in the fields, but his face is dripping with sweat as though he's been locked inside an iron box. He smokes an unfiltered cigarette without being able to take it from his lips, because his hands are manacles at his sides. Before they go inside the squat, off-white concrete building, a gun-bull takes the cigarette out of the boys' mouth and flips it into a pool of rainwater, where it is suddenly extinguished.

Inside, I sit on one of the wood benches with the other witnesses – television and newspaper reporters, a medical examiner, a Negro preacher, and the parents of the girl the convict shot to death in a filling station robbery. They're Cajuns from New Iberia. They sit rigidly and without expression, their eyes never quite focusing on the boy while he is being strapped arm and leg to the electric chair. The woman keeps twisting a handkerchief in her fingers; finally her husband wipes his hand across his mouth and puts a cigarette between his lips, but he looks at the gun-bull and doesn't light it. Through the barred window the tip of the setting sun is crimson above the green line of willow trees on the river.

Then suddenly the boy begins fighting. It's the moment that no one wants, that embarrasses and shames. His terror has eaten through the Thorazine he's been fed all day, and he gets a foot loose and kicks wildly at a guard. But the guard is a professional and knows how to grab the ankle and calf and use his weight to press the leg firmly back against the oak chair and

168

buckle the leather strap quickly across the shinbone.

The heat and humidity inside the room are almost unbearable. I can smell my own odor and the sweat in the clothes of the people around me. The mother of the murdered girl is looking at the floor now with one white knuckle pressed against her teeth. No one speaks, and I hear the boy's breath sucking in and out of his throat. His eyes are bloodshot and wide, his mouth quivering, and his neck so swollen with fear and blood that it looks as rigid as a fire hydrant. Before the cloth hood and metal skullcap go down over his head he stares straight into my face. An unanswered expectation bulges from his eyes.

I nailed him in New Orleans, busted him in a Negro hot-pillow joint off Magazine, took a .32 automatic and a straight razor off him and dropped them in a toilet bowl while a half dozen of his friends watched, threatened, and finally did nothing. Later I escorted him back to Iberia Parish for trial. For some reason he has asked me to be here in the Red Hat House. I think he is a borderline psychotic or retarded, or perhaps he has simply melted down his head with cocaine. But I'm convinced that in these last few moments he believes I can wave a wand over his circle of torment, pop the straps and buckles loose from his body, and lead him back outside into the wind, the ruffling sugarcane, the smell of distant rain.

When the voltage hits him his body leaps against the straps, stiffens, trembles violently with a life of its own, like that of a man having a seizure. A curl of smoke rises from under the facecloth. They hit him again, and we can hear the leather straining against the oak arms and legs of the chair. The smell is like the electric scorch of a streetcar, like the smell of hair burning in a barbershop *trash barrel. A newsman next to me puts his hand-kerchief in his mouth and begins gagging.*

Later I'm in a bar one mile down the road from Angola Penitentiary. The bar is in a remote and thickly wooded area, and the few people who drink in there either work at the penitentiary or in a piney-woods sawmill nearby. It's a joyless place where personal and economic failure and institutional cruelty are not made embarrassing by comparisons with the outside world. The light in the bar is hard and yellow, the wood floor scorched with cigarette and cigar burns.

Dry lightning leaps outside the window and turns the oak trees white. I order a schooner of Jax and a shot of Jim Beam. I lower the jigger into the schooner, release it, and watch it slide down the side of the glass to the bottom. The sour mash rises in a cloud and turns the beer from gold to amber, and I cup the schooner with my fingers and drink it empty with one long swallow.

'You were up at the Red Hat tonight?' the bartender asks. He's a barrel-chested man, with gray hair curling over his shirt lapels. A blue chain is tattooed around his thick neck.

'Yes.'

'What's a guy think in those last few seconds?'

'He begs.'

'I wouldn't do that. Would you?'

I don't answer.

'Would you?' he says again.

I tell him to hit me again. He refills my schooner and pours another shot of Beam on the side.

I empty the jigger into the beer and raise the schooner to my mouth. In the bar mirror the cloud of whiskey floating in beer is the color of blood that has dried in the sun, that has been burned with an electric arc. I can feel

170

the glass begin to boil in my hands. Lightning explodes in the shell parking lot outside, illuminating the battered cars and pickup trucks and racist bumper stickers. The air is filled with a wet sulfurous smell; my ears ring with a sound that is like a scream muffled under a black cloth.

It was two in the morning when I awoke from the dream and sat listlessly on the side of the bed. What did the dream mean? Was it simply a replay of the electrocution that I had in fact witnessed when I was a newly promoted detective with the New Orleans Police Department? Old-timers at AA would probably say it had to do with fear, which they believe is the cause of all the problems of alcoholics. Fear of mortality, fear that we'll drink again, fear of the self's dark potential. And for an alcoholic, *fear* is the acronym for Fuck Everything And Run. Clete had had his hand on it. I had loved bars and bust-head whiskey with the adoration and simple trust of a man kneeling before a votive shrine. That kind of emotional faith and addiction dies no less easily than one's religion.

The phone rang at one the next afternoon. It was Kim Dollinger.

'I want to talk to you,' she said.

'Go ahead.'

'No, come down to your buddy's place. I'll buy you a drink.'

'What is it you want to tell me?'

'What's the matter, your social calendar all full?'

'No, I just—'

'Then come on over, hotshot.'

'I'm not up to nicknames today. My name is

Dave. To tell you the truth, Kim, you sound like you got started a little early today.'

'Then buy me a cup of coffee. You have that paternal quality. Are you coming or not?'

Ten minutes later I was at Clete's Club. Clete and his black helper were filling the beer coolers, and she was at the far end of the bar. She wore black stockings, a denim skirt, and a sleeveless orange sweater, and she had had her hair cut so that it was short and thick on her pale neck.

'I want to tell you something before you leave,' Clete said to me as I passed him.

'What is it?'

'Later, noble mon.'

I sat on the stool next to Kim. She had a gin gimlet wrapped in a napkin in front of her.

'You want one?' she asked.

'No, thanks.'

'You don't go to a whorehouse to play the jukebox, do you?'

'I joined the Dr Pepper crowd a few years ago.'

'Too much. You want to be in the candy business, but you don't touch the juice?'

'How about holding it down?'

'You sure you're not just a big put-on?'

'What do you mean?'

'I think somebody shook up your puzzle box, that's what I mean.'

'How about I buy you some gumbo?'

'I think you're weird. Do people in the bayou country grow up weird and think they can make big money in the city dealing with somebody like Ray Fontenot? Are you that dumb?'

'What is it you want to tell me, Kim?'

'I don't know what I want to tell you.' She looked away into space. The green and purple neon tubing on the bar mirror glowed on her face. 'You don't listen to people. Back there where you come from, don't you have something better going than this stuff in New Orleans? You want to risk it for a score with a bunch of dipshits who wouldn't take a leak on you if you were burning?'

'Why all this concern for me?'

'Because you didn't try to put moves on me. Because there're things about you that are nice. Also, because I think you're a fish.'

'I look like a fish?'

'I *know* you're a fish, hon.'

She finished her gimlet and signaled the black barman for another. He took her glass away and filled a fresh one from the blender. The color in her green eyes deepened when she sipped from the glass.

'Is there something I should know, Kim?' I asked.

'You're a big boy. Make up your own mind. Look at the flamingos.'

'What?'

'Painted on the edge of the mirror. The pink flamingos. When I was a little girl we lived in Miami. My father was the guy who took care of the flamingos at the Hialeah racetrack. Before the seventh race he'd chase them with a broom in the center ground and make them fly high above the stands. That was his job. He thought it was a real important job.'

She drank again from her glass and closed and opened her eyes slowly. Her mouth was bright red.

'I see,' I said.

'One morning he took me to work with him and told me to sit on this wood bench by the finish line while he picked up paper from the track with a stick that had a nail in it. But I wandered out in the center ground and started feeding the flamingos. There was a bucket of ground-up shrimp by the lake, and I was throwing handfuls of it at these big, beautiful pink birds. I didn't see or hear him come up behind me. My hair was long then, and he twisted it in his hand and jerked it against my scalp like you'd snap a rope. He pulled me back to the bench and told me if I cried any more I'd get it again when I got home.

'Then this horse trainer walked up and shook his finger at my father and said, "Don't hurt that little girl, Bill. She didn't mean no harm." He picked me up in his arms like my father wasn't there and carried me to his car. "She don't belong out here. I'm going to take her to the zoo. You go on about your work," he said. "I'll bring her back to your trailer later. Don't be giving me any trouble about it, either, Bill."

'He drove me down to Crandon Park to see the flamingos. He said my father wouldn't hurt me anymore, not as long as he was around. Then he bought me some ice cream and parked the car in some palmettos and sat me in his lap. Then he unbuttoned my blouse. I've always thought of it as my morning for flamingos.'

'That's a bad story, Kim.'

'You learn early or you learn late. What difference does it make?'

'Are you really that hard?'

'No, I just like hanging around people like Ray

174

and Lionel and the raghead for kicks. You'll see. It's a great life.'

She finished her drink, went to the women's room, and came back. I could smell mints on her breath. The Negro barman started to pour her another gimlet from the blender but she shook her head negatively. Somebody had put an old recording of 'Please Don't Leave Me' by Fats Domino on the jukebox.

'Dance with me,' she said.

It was dark and the vinyl booths were empty at the back of the dance floor. She felt light and small in my arms, and her head rested against my chest. I felt her hair touch my cheek.

'Look, Kim, let me buy you some gumbo at the Golden Star,' I said.

She didn't answer. I could feel her stomach and breasts against me, and I was becoming increasingly uncomfortable.

'Hey,' I said, and looked at her and smiled. 'I'm an over-the-hill guy who doesn't deserve the kindness of a pretty young woman.'

'Tony lets me use his beach house in Biloxi. Come with me there today.'

'It sounds like a good way to end up in an oil barrel.'

'He won't hurt you. He likes you. I don't think Tony's going to be around much longer, anyway.'

'Why not?'

'People in Miami and Houston want him out of the way. He keeps breaking all their rules. Sometimes I feel sorry for him. Will you come with me?'

'I'm involved, Kim. You're sure a big temptation, though.'

Her feet stopped moving and her hand rested on my arm. She looked out at the light from the opened front door. A lock of her hair hung down on one eyebrow. Her face had the same wan expression on it that I had seen when she had been staring out at Tony Cardo's empty tennis court. Then she touched my throat with her fingers.'

'So long, hotcakes. Don't think too bad of me,' she said.

She left me on the dance floor, picked up her purse from the bar, and walked through the brilliant square of light at the front on to Decatur Street. Clete parted the window blinds with his fingers and squinted out on to the street.

'Yep, there he goes,' he said.

'Who?'

'Nate Baxter, my man.'

'Nate Baxter?'

'Yeah, I didn't think you'd forget him. The one genuine sonofabitch from the First District. I saw him watching her from under the colonnade across the street when she came in. A car just picked him up when she left.'

'Why's a guy from Internal Affairs interested in Kim Dollinger?'

'He's not in Internal Affairs anymore. He's Vice. The perfect guy for it, too. A prick from the crown of his head to the soles of his feet. What's going on, Dave?'

'I don't know.'

'Some sting. Half the city of New Orleans seems to be in on it. Listen, get out of that gig at Cocodrie. I've got a real bad feeling on this one.'

'Those are the ones you skate through. You buy

it when you've got your pot off and you're reading a newspaper. You know that.' I winked at him.

'Save the Little Orphan Annie routine for somebody else, Streak. When my ovaries start tingling, I listen to them. Anytime you see that buttwipe Baxter, it's bad news. You can count on it.'

Back at the apartment I called the commercial dock at Cocodrie to check on my jugboat, then called Minos at his office to confirm the pickup of the half million.

'Our special-delivery man will be there with your bus locker key in about two hours,' he said. 'Did you know a half-million dollars in hundred-dollar bills weighs exactly eleven pounds?'

'No, I didn't know that.'

'Don't drop it overboard. As I mentioned before, some of my colleagues are a little anxious about this one.'

'I'm tired of hearing about your colleagues' problems.'

'Your voice sounds funny.'

'I've been doing push-ups. I'm still out of breath.'

'Yeah?'

'Sure. I'm all right.'

'When I was undercover I'd wake up with my heart racing. I'd smoke a pack of cigarettes before noon sometimes.'

'My ears keep popping, like I've been on an airplane.'

'Dave, you can throw it in anytime you want, and nobody will think less of you for it.'

'I'm copacetic. Don't sweat it.'

'Remember, we're never going to be too far away.'

Then I told him about Nate Baxter's surveillance of Kim Dollinger.

'They're interested in Cardo, too,' he said. 'They're probably keeping some strings on his entourage.'

'Why her? She's no dealer.'

'I'll check. They're supposed to coordinate with us, anyway. Have you got some kind of personal involvement with this guy Baxter?'

'He tried to get me fired from the department when he was in Internal Affairs.'

'So?'

'It didn't end there. I split his lip in the squad room, in front of about twenty-five cops.'

'Dave, you never disappoint me,' he said.

I rode the streetcar down St. Charles to Bootsie's house that evening, and the wind through the open window was cool and smelled of old brick, wet moss, and moldy pecan husks. But I couldn't concentrate on anything except my anxieties about the buy out on the salt and my questions, which I could not successfully bury, about Bootsie's involvement with the mob. How did an intelligent and educated woman from a small Bayou Teche town like New Iberia marry a member of the Giacano family? I tried to imagine what he must have looked like. Most of the Giacanos were built like piano movers, notorious for their animal energies, their enormous appetites and bovine behavior in restaurants, their emotionalism and violence. Their weddings and funerals were covered by local television stations with the same sense of mirth and expectation that people might have when visiting an amusement park.

The image just wouldn't fit.

But the image of her first husband sure did. He was a helicopter and pontoon plane pilot for Sinclair Oil Company, and I remembered him most for his suntanned, blond good looks and the confident, unblinking light in his blue eyes. In fact, I could never quite forget the night I met him, at a dance at the Frederic Hotel in New Iberia, right after I had been released from an army hospital. I was on a cane then. It was 1965, when the war was just heating up for other people, and it felt funny to go to a dance by myself and to discover that I was alone in more ways than one, that I was already used up and discarded by a war that waited in a vague piece of neocolonial geography for other boys whose French names could have belonged to Legionnaires.

Then through the potted palm fronds and marble columns, I saw her in a pink organdy dress, dancing with him in her stocking feet. Her face was flushed from the champagne punch, and strands of her hair stuck damply to her skin like wisps of honey. They walked toward the punch table, where I was standing, and I saw her gaze focusing on me as though I had stepped unexpectedly off a bus into the middle of her life. Then I realized she was drunk.

She started blowing air up into her face to get her hair out of her eyes.

'Well!' she said.

'Hello, Boots,' I said.

'Well!' she repeated, and blew a web of hair out of her eyes again. 'John, this is Dave Robicheaux. It looks like Dave has come back to visit New Iberia. What a wonderful event. Maybe he can come to our wedding.'

He smiled with his white teeth when he shook hands. His eyes went back and forth between us, and I could see the recognition grow in them.

'It's nice to meet you, Dave. The wedding is Saturday at St. Peter's,' he said. 'Please come if you feel like it.'

'Thank you,' I said. And I cleared my throat so they wouldn't see me swallow.

Bootsie blew more gusts of air up into her face and her eyes became brighter, as though a generator were gaining momentum inside her.

'I could have told you I was pregnant. That would have blown your mind, wouldn't it?' she said.

'What?' I felt my mouth hang open, because in New Iberia at that time it was unthinkable to talk like that in a public place.

'But that would have seriously screwed you up,' she said. 'You would have ended up a family guy with kiddies and you couldn't go off to war, then come home and stand around on a cane like an F. Scott Fitzgerald character. The pose is perfect, Dave. You look so absolutely sad and wounded. We wouldn't rob you of it for anything.'

'I think you're being pretty rotten,' I said.

'Hold on, now,' her fiancé said.

'No, rotten is when you put it in without a rubber because you're really promising that person you're going to marry her, then you leave her like she's

180

yesterday's backseat hand job.'

The band had stopped playing, and her words carried out to the edge of the dance floor. People stared at us with their smiles suddenly frozen on their faces. Bootsie's eyes were watery and shining, and there were beads of perspiration on her upper lip. In the silence I could feel the skin of my face tighten and flex against the bone.

When I woke in the morning a note folded inside an envelope was stuck in my screen door. It read:

I'm sick and trembling with a hangover this morning, and I guess I deserve it. I'm sorry for what I said to you last night. I shouldn't apologize to you, but I do anyway. But tell me this, Dave, please please please tell me this, why did you push me away, why did you destroy it for both of us, why did you ruin everything we'd shared together that summer, tell me in the name of suffering God why you did it, Dave.

Love,
Bootsie

P.S. On second thought it's probably better that you don't answer this note. I'm going to be married to John, and the past is past, right? If I say that enough it'll finally be true. I hope you have a good life. I really mean that even though I think you were a bastard.

But as she said, the past was the past, and after we had dinner, we washed the dishes, put them away, and went upstairs to her bedroom. It was misting outside, and the sky was a soft gray, the sun a low red ball on the western horizon. The long strips of pink cloud above the trees reminded me of flamingo wings.

I took off my shirt, then sat on the side of the bed to remove my shoes. She sat next to me in only her bra and a half-slip and put her hand on my back.

'Your skin's hot,' she said.

'It happens when I'm with a certain lady,' I said, and tried to smile.

'No, your muscles are tight as iron. What is it, Dave?'

'I just have a couple of things on my mind right now.'

'There's a big buy going down, isn't there?'

'Why do you think that?'

'I always know. I hear people talking on the phone, a lot of money gets transferred around. Dave, are you still a cop?'

'No questions tonight, Boots.'

'They'll catch on to you eventually. What you don't understand is that the narcs who get inside the organization are like them. You're not. It's a matter of time before they'll see that.'

'Let's not talk about it anymore.'

'All right, if that's what you want. But at some point you'll have to confide in me. If not now, later. You know that, Dave.'

I touched her lips with my fingers.

'It's going to rain,' I said. 'Remember when we used to go to my father's boathouse in the rain?'

She laid her cheek against my bare shoulder and rested her hand lightly on my arm. I finished undressing, and she pulled her slip up over her thighs and sat on top of me. I felt myself go deeply inside her, felt her heat and wetness spread across

182

my loins. Her face became round and pale in concentration. She made love with the confidence and knowledge of an older woman, and when she came she pressed my palm hard against her breast as though she were forcing me to share the whirrings of her heart.

It was dark outside, and the rain was slanting against the French windows. An oak tree raked wetly against the side of the house. She lay inside my arm, with her hand on my stomach, and I could smell the rose-scented shampoo in her hair and taste the thin film of perspiration on her forehead.

Then, as though determined to pass on all my anxieties and fears to someone else, as though I had to hurt her again as I had many years before, I asked her the question that had bothered me since I'd first gone to her house on Camp Street.

'Why don't you get out from under them?'

'I told you why.'

'You said you didn't know your husband was in the mob when you married him. I never knew one of them who wasn't obvious, Boots.'

'I wasn't very careful, I guess.'

'Bootsie, you *had* to know.'

'He was good-looking and well-mannered. He said he had a degree from Tulane. He smiled all the time. He was fun to be around, Dave.'

'All those game-room machines you distribute are made by a Mafia front in Chicago. You're into it big-time, old pal.'

Her hand left my stomach, and she sat up on the side of the bed and looked out at the wet treetops. Then she walked barefoot in her bra and half-slip to a cabinet above a small desk, her hips creasing softly. I could see the dark outline of her sex through her slip.

'I'm going to have a glass of cream sherry,' she said. 'You don't mind, do you? It helps me to sleep sometimes. I always have trouble sleeping when it thunders. It's a silly way to be.'

She kept her face turned toward the French windows, but I could see the wet shine on her cheeks.

8

It was black and raining hard when I guided the jugboat from the dock down the canal toward open water. The boat was built to float high up in the water, but the tide was out, the canal was shallow, and yellow mud and tangles of dead hyacinths boiled up under the propeller. The long expanses of saw grass on each side of us were bent in the rain.

Ray Fontenot and Lionel Comeaux both wore yellow raincoats with hoods and sat hunched forward in their chairs by my small butane stove, which held a pot of coffee. The weather had turned cold, and their faces were morose and irritable. When we hit open water I pushed the throttle forward and felt the engine surge and the bow lift into the waves. The coastline became gray and indistinct and then dropped behind us altogether. In the distance I could see a gas flare burning on an offshore oil well.

'Turn off your running lights,' Lionel said.

'There's a fogbank up there.'

'I don't care. Turn off your lights.'

'Look, if you're worried about the Coast Guard, it monitors the traffic by radar. You don't become visible by turning off your lights.'

He got up from his chair, walked to my instrument board, and clicked off the two toggle switches that controlled the red and green running lights on the stern and bow. I pulled the throttle back to idle and cut the ignition. Suddenly it was quiet except for the rain against the roof and the glass. The jugboat pitched in one trough and then slid over the top of a black wave into another; the coffeepot crashed on the floor.

'These are the rules, partner. There's one skipper on a boat,' I said. 'You're looking at him. If that doesn't sit right with you, we'll turn it around here.'

'We've made this run a dozen times. You don't advertise,' Lionel said.

'What's the matter with you?' I said. 'The best way to attract attention is to do something stupid like run without lights.'

'It's your first time out. I'm trying to be helpful.'

'What's it going to be, Fontenot?'

'Much ado about nothing,' he said from his chair. 'Let him have his lights, Lionel.'

I hit the starter and pushed the throttle open again. We hit a cresting wave in a shower of foam and then flattened out in a long trough. The water was black and rolling and hammered with raindrops. Then the fogbank slipped over the bow and the pilothouse, as cold and damp on the skin as a gray, wet glove.

'What's Tony going to get out of the score?' I asked Ray Fontenot.

'What do you mean?'

'It's my buy, my stash. What's the profit for him?'

'He gets a cut from the Colombians. The action gets pieced off all the way back to Bogotá.'

186

'Where's your piece come in?'

'We're doing it as a favor.'

'No kidding?' I said.

'We like you.' He smiled from under his yellow rain hood.

Lionel rubbed the moisture off the window glass with his palm.

'There it is,' he said.

A shrimp boat with its wheelhouse lighted rose in the swell, then slipped down below a long, sliding wave.

'How do we make the exchange?' I said.

'I'll take the money on board and come back with the stash,' Lionel said.

'They're shy?' I said.

'You don't want to meet them,' Fontenot said. 'They're not a nice group, our garlic-scented friends. They seem to like Lionel, though. The colored woman who cooks for them likes him very much. Lionel had a big change of luck at the track after he met her.'

'You ought to get laid more, Ray. You wouldn't have all these cute things to say,' Lionel said.

I saw the shrimp boat drift to the top of the swell again. Its white paint was peeling, its scuppers dripping with rust. Lionel had taken off his raincoat and was putting on a life jacket.

'You should appreciate Lionel's efforts on your behalf,' Fontenot said.

'Forget the appreciation. Just put it hard against the tires and keep it there till I'm on the ladder,' Lionel said.

He laced the life jacket under his chin, then slipped a rope through the aluminum suitcase that

187

contained the money and tied it crossways on his chest.

'I go between the hulls and you're out a half mil,' he said.

'We can make the exchange without you getting on their boat,' I said. 'There's a thirty-foot coil of rope in that forward gear box. Tie it on to the suitcase, throw the other end on the shrimper, and we'll get the stash back the same way.'

'I gotta check it.'

'We'll check it when it's on board.'

'You don't inspect the goods after the fact when you deal with spics,' he said.

'Let's not have discord on the Melody Ranch, boys and girls,' Fontenot said. 'Lionel's an old pro at this, Mr. Robicheaux. He's not going to drop your money.'

'I'm going in on the swell,' I said. 'Get ready.'

Two deckhands came out of the wheelhouse and stood by the gunwales in the rain and wind. They were unshaved, and their black hair and beards dripped with water. I came in on the lee side of the shrimper, gunning the engine in the trough, and bumped against the row of tires that were hung along the hull. Lionel grabbed the rope ladder, pushed himself with one foot off the handrail of the jugboat, and scampered on board the shrimper, the aluminum suitcase banging across the gunwale with him.

'What are you going to do with all your money, Mr. Robicheaux?' Fontenot said. He had a lit cigarette cupped on his knee, and he was looking out indifferently at the glaze of light from the shrimp boat on the water.

'Why is it I get the feeling you're not interested in

the questions you ask other people?' I said.

'Oh, forgive me, good sir, if I ever convey that impression. That would be a terrible sense to give someone, wouldn't it?'

'I'm going back through Atchafalaya Bay, not to Cocodrie. I can put you guys ashore at several places. You tell me where.'

'Not to Cocodrie? But our car is there,' he said. And he said it in a whimsical manner, his eyes still fascinated with the patches of yellow light on the waves.

'I think it's smart to off-load in a different spot. I told Tony I've got the access he needs, a couple of bayous nobody uses except in a pirogue.'

'I'm sure he'll be intrigued.'

I looked at the side of his face in the glow of the instrument lights. Then I saw the color in his eyes brighten and the corner of his mouth twitch in a grin when he realized that I was staring at him.

'Excuse me if I don't bubble up at the perfection of it all,' he said. 'I'm afraid it's my fate to simply be an old mule. But Tony will love a tour through the bayous. You two can talk about "nape."'

I continued to stare at him.

'What are you wondering, kind sir?' he said.

'Why he keeps you guys around.'

'We don't measure up, do we? Listen, you lovely boy, we take the risks but Tony gets the big end of the candy cane. Some might think he's done very well by us. Would you like to jump between boats like Lionel just did? I don't think Tony would.'

'My impression is the guy can handle the action.'

'Oh, you must tell him that. He loves that kind of big-dick talk.'

'I don't know what's bugging you, Fontenot, but I think this is our last run together,' I said.

'You can never tell,' he said, and grinned again and puffed on his cigarette in the luminescence of the instrument panel.

Ten minutes passed, and I kept the jugboat steady in the trough so it wouldn't slam up against the hull of the shrimper. Through the rain I could see the silhouettes of several people in the wheel-house. Then I saw Lionel talking, but his face was turned toward the front glass, not toward the people around him. I squinted hard through the rain.

'He's talking on the shortwave,' I said.

'Who?'

'Lionel. What's going on, Fontenot?'

'Nothing.'

'Don't tell me that. Why's the man on the radio?'

'I don't know. You think he's calling the Coast Guard? Use your judgment, sir.'

'Fontenot, if you guys—'

'I'm not up to any more words of assurance tonight, Mr. Robicheaux. I don't believe you belong in our business, to tell you the truth. It isn't the Rotary Club. It isn't made up of nice people. I've grown a bit weary of you wrinkling your nose at us.'

The two deckhands carried two wooden crates out of the forward hatch and set them inside a cargo net that was slung from a boom. Lionel stepped out of the wheelhouse and waved for me to bring the jugboat alongside again. I waited until the shrimper dipped into the trough, then bumped up against the row of tires. When both boats rose with the swell, Lionel sprang from the shrimper on to my deck. His jeans and denim shirt and canvas life preserver were dark with rain.

One of the deckhands operated the motor on the boom and swung the cargo net out over the jugboat, letting the net collapse in a tangle, with the two crates inside, on the deck. Lionel pulled the crates free, and I put the engine in reverse and backed away from the side of the shrimper. The empty cargo net swung out in open space and cut through the tops of the waves.

I shifted the engine forward again and turned the bow toward the southern horizon.

'I'm going to help him stow it,' I said. 'Hold the wheel and keep it pointed into the waves. The throttle's set, so you don't need to touch it.'

'Really, now?' Fontenot said.

Outside, the rain was cold and stung my face and hands, and the waves broke hard on the bow and blew back across the deck in a salty spray. I unlocked the forward gear box and lifted one of the wooden crates inside. It was heavy, and the sides were stamped with the name of a South American cannery. Lionel swung the second crate up on the edge of the gear box.

'What were you doing on the radio?' I said.

'What?' He wore long underwear buttoned at the throat under his denim shirt, but he was shivering with the cold.

'You heard me.'

'I wasn't on the radio.'

'You had the mike in your hand, partner.'

He wiped the water out of his eyes, then focused on my face again.

'Maybe I got a weather report. Maybe I moved it to pick up my coffee cup. Maybe you need glasses.'

He dropped the crate on top of the first one. 'It doesn't matter. Tony C. cut you in as a favor. If you want to know, the weight and quality are right. You got a sweet deal, man. I don't think you deserve it.'

He flipped the top of the gear box shut and walked away toward the pilothouse, balancing himself against the roll of the deck.

It had stopped raining, but the fog was thick and white on the water and I could hardly see the bow of the jugboat.

'This stuff will probably start to lift with first light,' I said. 'When we come out of it, I'm going to turn northwest for Atchafalaya Bay. Where do you guys want to go ashore?'

Lionel was looking out into the fog through the front glass. His eyes were narrowed and red-rimmed with fatigue.

'Where do y'all want me to put you off?' I repeated.

We passed a shut-down oil platform. The waves were black and streaked with oil as they slid through the steel pilings.

Still neither Lionel nor Fontenot answered me. Then I heard a boat engine out in the fog before I saw its running lights. Fontenot looked up from his cup of coffee. I turned to port, away from the sound of the engine, just as the hull of a thirty-foot white cabin cruiser came out of the fogbank. I could see the silhouette of a solitary figure at the wheel. I turned to look again at Lionel and Fontenot, as though all the frames in a strip of film negatives had suddenly made sense, and I guess my right hand was already moving toward the .25-caliber Beretta strapped to my ankle, but it was too late. Lionel had taken a nine-millimeter automatic from the canvas carry-on bag at his foot, and he placed the iron sight hard behind my ear. His free hand went down my right leg and pulled the Beretta from its holster.

'Cut the engine,' he said.

I didn't move.

'It's not a time for thought,' he said.

I heard his thumb cock the hammer. I turned off the ignition switch, and we drifted sideways with the waves and dipped down breathlessly into a trough.

'Oops,' Fontenot said, and his mouth made an O inside the yellow hood of his raincoat.

'Go forward and throw out the anchor, Ray,' Lionel said. 'We'll swing tight against the rope, and he can come around and tie on the stern.'

'I think we're doing it the hard way,' Fontenot said.

'It's the way he wants it. I ain't arguing with him.'

'The tropics beckon, Lionel. We don't want to waste time out here.'

'Tell him that. The guy's got a hard-on about our man here. It's like talking to a vacant lot.'

Fontenot got up from his chair and made his way along the deck, holding on to the rail. His yellow raincoat glistened in the turning fog. I heard the clank of the chain and the X-shaped welded pieces of railroad track that I used for an anchor as he pitched them off the bow. The jugboat swung with the incoming tide toward the coast and straightened against the anchor rope. The cabin cruiser idled past us, then turned in a circle and came up astern. It was a Larson, built for speed and comfort, its paint as white and flawless as enamel.

'I want you to know something before all this goes down,' Lionel said.

I started to turn my head towards him. He nudged the automatic against my ear.

'No, keep your eyes straight ahead,' he said. 'I want you to know it's not personal. I don't like ex-cops, I don't think they should have ever let you in on a buy, but that's got nothing to do with this. We've been somebody's fuck for too long, it's time we got what's ours. You just came along at a real bad time.'

I heard the engine of the cabin cruiser die; then somebody threw a knotted rope from the bow on to the roof of the jugboat's pilothouse.

'That other thing,' he said, 'that other thing I didn't have anything to do with.'

From the direction of his voice I could tell that he was now looking toward the stern.

'What other thing?' I said.

Then his voice came back toward the side of my face: 'Are you kidding, man? You were taking the guy up to Angola to fry. What do you think a guy like that feels about you? I'm sorry for you, man, but I got nothing to do with it.'

I didn't care about the pistol behind my ear now. I turned woodenly in the pilot's seat and looked up at the bobbing, moored bow of the cabin cruiser. As Tee Beau had said, Jimmie Lee Boggs had cut his hair short and dyed it black, but every other detail about him was as though he had walked out of a familiar dream: the mannequinlike head, the pallid skin, the lips that looked like they were rouged, the spearmint-green eyes with a strange light in them.

He wore rubber-soled canvas shoes, dungarees, a

194

heavy blue wool shirt with wide gray suspenders, and when he stepped from the cabin cruiser on to the back rail of the jugboat and grabbed Ray Fontenot's hand, his forearm corded with muscle and his stomach looked as flat and hard as boiler plate.

He put one hand on the edge of the pilothouse's roof and leaned over me. Salt spray dripped from his face, and I could smell snuff on his breath.

'Been thinking of me?' he asked.

'I thought maybe you couldn't find us,' Fontenot said. 'It's thick out there.'

'Lionel told me on the radio y'all would be coming past an oil platform,' Boggs said. 'I just lay south of the rig and listened for your engine. This thing sounds like a garbage truck.'

Then Boggs looked down at me again. I still sat in the pilot's seat. His wrists looked as thick as sticks of firewood.

'This guy give you any trouble?' he said.

'Not really,' Fontenot said. He had removed his raincoat and was putting on a life jacket.

'You guys get the stuff on board. I'll take care of it here,' Boggs said. He took the nine-millimeter from Lionel's hand.

Fontenot cleared his throat. 'We wonder if you . . . if we really need to do that, Jimmie Lee,' he said.

'You got a problem with it?' Boggs said.

'The man isn't likely to call the law,' Fontenot said.

'You got that right,' Boggs said.

'I don't see the percentage,' Fontenot said. 'Right now we're simply transferring some product. Why complicate it?'

'I ain't telling you what to think, Jimmie Lee,' Lionel said, 'but the guy's not going to do anything. He's a fired cop, a drunk. He tries to make any trouble later, you can have him hit for five hundred bucks.'

'I don't pay to clip a guy. Besides, you did a guy with a piano wire, Lionel. Why you giving me this bullshit?'

'I got out of it, too. I don't want to go that route anymore,' Lionel said. 'Look, he's an amateur. You let the amateurs slide, Jimmie Lee. You whack out an amateur, their families make a lot of trouble.'

Lionel blew out his breath. The fog was white and so thick you could lose your hand in it as it rolled off the water and across the deck.

'I don't want to have to lose my piece. I just bought it,' he said.

'Get the coke on board and bring me the shotgun. It's clipped under the forward hatch,' Boggs said.

'You guys got to deal with Tony,' I said to Lionel and Fontenot.

'Good try, prick, but Tony's history. He just don't know it yet,' Boggs said.

'Sorry, Mr. Robicheaux,' Fontenot said. Then he looked at Lionel and said, 'See no evil.'

The two of them started up the deck toward the forward gear box, where the two crates of cocaine were stowed. I was sweating heavily inside my clothes, and my breath was coming irregularly in my chest. The jugboat dipped in the ground swell, and the barrel of the automatic touched the side of my head like a kiss.

'I'll say it once, and you guys can believe it or not,' I said. The front glass of the pilothouse was pushed ajar, and they could hear me out on the deck. 'I'm still a cop. I'm undercover for the DEA. We're on Coast Guard radar right now.'

I saw Lionel and Fontenot stop and turn around. The fog drifted across their bodies like strips of torn cotton. They started back toward the pilothouse.

'It's all a sting,' I said. 'Minos Dautrieve's been running it from the start. You know who Minos Dautrieve is, right?'

Boggs's fingers laced in my hair; then he slammed my head forward on the instrument panel. I felt the skin split above my right eye, and the blood and the salt water leaked down across my eyelid.

'Hold on, listen to him,' Fontenot said.

'You guys rattle too easy,' Boggs said.

'Dautrieve's a narc out of Lafayette,' Lionel said.

'So he knows that,' Boggs said.

'Clete Purcel is DEA undercover, too,' I said. 'You clip me, he'll even the score. Ask anybody in New Orleans. Check out what he did to Julio Segura.'

Boggs held the automatic by the barrel and raked it across my mouth as though he were wielding a hammer. My bottom lip burst against my teeth, and a socket of pain raced deep into my throat and up into my nose. I leaned forward on the wheel with my mouth open, as though my jaws had become unhinged, while a long string of blood and saliva dripped between my legs.

'This deal's going sour,' Lionel said.

'There's nothing wrong with the deal. Stop acting like a cunt,' Boggs said.

'I ain't going back to Angola,' Lionel said. 'I ain't going down for snuffing a cop, either.'

'This guy's shark food. Count on it. He don't

have to be the only one to go over the gunwale, either. You getting my drift?' Boggs said.

'You got nothing to lose, Jimmie Lee. We do,' Lionel said.

'You got a lot to lose, man. It's important you understand that,' Boggs said. He had shifted the barrel of the automatic so that it now hovered between me and Lionel.

'We just wanted to hear a little more of what Mr. Robicheaux had to say,' Fontenot said.

'I'll show you what he's going to say,' Boggs said, and he knotted my shirt in his fist at the back of my neck, pulled me erect, and pushed the barrel of the automatic hard into my spine. 'He's gonna say "please," and he's gonna say, "I'll pay you money," and he's gonna say, "Mr. Boggs, I'll do anything you want if you don't hurt me."'

He pushed me ahead of him on the deck, his clenched hand trembling with energy, then stomped on my leg just above the calf, as though he were breaking a slat, and knocked me to my knees. He let the automatic swing loosely over the back of my neck. In the reflection of the running lights the blood from my mouth looked purple on the backs of my hands. My ears were filled with sound: the waves bursting against the bow and hissing back along the hull, Jimmie Lee Boggs's heated breathing, a buoy clanging somewhere beyond the oil platform, a thick, obscene noise like wet cellophane crackling when I tried to swallow.

'Lionel, you got two minutes to load the stash and come back with my shotgun,' Boggs said. 'Don't fuck up my morning.'

'We'll transfer the goods. There's no problem,

198

Jimmie Lee,' Fontenot said.

'I didn't think there was,' Boggs said.

Out of the corner of my vision I could see Fontenot and Lionel carrying the crates back to Boggs's boat. Their rubber-soled shoes squeaked on the deck.

'I'll hand it up to you,' I heard Fontenot say.

'Why don't you take swimming lessons, go to the Y?' Lionel said.

'You know why I like a shotgun?' Boggs asked me. His dungarees were bell-bottomed and dark with water above his white socks.

'No hands, no face,' he said. 'Think of a broken cherry pie.'

The jugboat dropped off the edge of a big wave and slapped hard against the water. Then I heard someone behind me.

'Here it is,' Lionel said.

'Thank you, my man,' Boggs said.

'What do you want to do with his boat?' Lionel said.

'I'll open the cocks and down she goes.'

'Hurry all this up, it's gonna be light.'

'Just get the fat man on board and let me worry about the rest of it.'

Lionel walked away toward the stern, and I saw Boggs's feet and legs move in front of me. I heard him rack a shell into the chamber of a shotgun.

'Would you look up here so I could have your attention a minute?' he said.

I raised my head slowly, my eyes traveling over his thighs, which were tensed against the roll of the deck, his flat stomach under his gray suspenders, his sawed-off pump shotgun with a stock that had been

199

wood-rasped into a pistol grip, his red mouth crimped in expectation, as though he had just sucked on a salted lime. My split eye throbbed, blood and saliva ran off my lip, my pulse roared in my ears.

'Boggs . . . ,' I said.

He didn't answer.

'Boggs . . .'

I opened my mouth to let it drain. I spit on myself.

'Boggs . . .'

'What?' he said.

'You'd fuck up a wet dream. Shoot and be done with it.'

I saw his eyes narrow. They were liquid and rheumy, like a lizard's, the whites flecked almost entirely red with broken blood veins. His right hand, wrapped around the trigger guard, was white and ridged with bone. The edges of his eyes trembled with anger. His tongue tasted his lip, and he looked like a man whose sexual satisfaction was about to be denied him.

'We gotta go, Jimmie Lee,' Lionel said from the stern.

But Boggs's attention had shifted. He stared out into the fog, the shotgun at port arms, his dyed, threadlike hair wet and stuck against his scalp like a duck's feathers. Then I saw and heard it, too: the glow of running lights in the fog, the drone of a big engine, of boat screws that cut a deep trough in the water.

Suddenly no one was interested in me. I raised up slowly from all fours and sat back on my heels. Lionel had been trying to push Fontenot's huge weight up on to the bow of the cabin cruiser, but they were both frozen now on the stern of the jugboat. Fontenot's neck looked like a turtle's inside his life jacket.

The electric arc of a searchlight burst through the fog. It was hot and white and blinding to the eyes, and now the jugboat and the green, white-capping waves had the strange luminescence of objects lighted by a pistol flare.

A man's voice boomed through a bullhorn across the water: 'This is the New Orleans Police Department. You're under arrest. Put down your weapons and lace your hands on your head.'

Lionel's arm went up, and he aimed the nine-millimeter across the roof of the pilothouse.

'No!' Fontenot shouted. Then he shouted it again, 'No!' His face was round and soft and full of disbelief.

But it was too late. Lionel and Boggs were both shooting now, the muzzle flashes from their guns almost lost in the searchlight's hot glare. I could hear the brass hulls from Lionel's pistol clinking on the pilothouse roof. Then the searchlight glass shattered and almost simultaneously two kneeling figures on the bow of the police boat, bill caps turned backwards on their heads, began firing M-16 rifles on full automatic.

They blew wood divots out of the deck and pilothouse, exploded my instrument panel, rang metal-jacketed bullets off the deck rails, gear boxes, pots and pans and stove in the galley, scissored through the tin side of a bait well, and trapped Ray Fontenot helplessly against the back rail of the jugboat.

He tried to crouch down behind the corner of the pilothouse, his mouth wide and pink with words that no one could hear. His fists were balled, his wrists crossed in an X in front of his eyes; then the bullets danced across his life jacket, split the canvas like dry blisters popping, and his throat and great heaving chest erupted with red flowers. His mouth hung open as though he had swallowed a chicken bone.

I lay flat on the deck, my arms folded across the crown of my skull. Boggs was hunkered down behind the iron gear box that had held the crates of cocaine, and the M-16 rounds whanged off the top and the sides and sparked in the darkness. But he didn't wince. He kept firing, pumping the empty shell casings out on the deck, his body small and constricted with muscle like a rifleman's. His shotgun must have been loaded with double-aughts or deer slugs, because I could hear the damage to the police boat, the glass breaking, the hard slap of heavy shot across wood surfaces.

Then the police boat veered back into the fog, turning into its own wake, but not before one of the kneeling figures on the bow emptied his clip and bit into the auxiliary gasoline drum welded against the jugboat's deck rail. The gasoline gushed across the deck and drained into the engine well. I don't know what ignited it – a spark jumping off a metal surface, shorted wiring, or an exploded starter battery – but suddenly the deck was flaming, the gas drum was ringed with fire; then it blew with a *whoompth*, like a large furnace kicking on deep in the bowels of a tenement building.

I crawled across the deck, squeezed under the bottom rail, and rolled over the side. I could not see the police boat now, but before I dropped into the water I saw Jimmie Lee Boggs running for the stern, his hard, lean body silhouetted among the flames. Lionel was on his knees by the pilothouse, his hand pressed against a hemorrhaging wound in the center of his throat. His shoulders shook and convulsed as though he were trying to expel a piece of angle iron from his chest. He tried to catch Boggs's dungarees with his fingers as Boggs went past him. The back of Lionel's hand was scarlet and shining in the fire's light. But Boggs pulled the mooring line free, jumped from the stern rail on to the bow of his boat, and in seconds started the engine, opened the throttle full-out, and spun on the back of a breaking wave into the fog.

I treaded water and drifted away from the jugboat. It was burning brightly now, from bow to stern, and when the anchor rope burned through, it floated sideways in the swell, and a big wave broke against the pilothouse and turned to steam. The water was cold and smelled of oil and gas. In the distance I could hear the thinning sound of Boggs's cabin cruiser and the police boat in pursuit. I tried to save my strength and float on my back, but each time I rose with a wave, the water broke across my mouth and nose, and I had to right my head and churn with my hands and feet again.

The tide was coming in, and I couldn't swim against it to the oil platform. The Coast Guard was out there somewhere, but it had probably become occupied with the shrimper. The jugboat was only a red glow in the fog now. I heard another *whoompth*, a sound like boiling water, a rush of air bubbles, the hiss of steam rising from heated metal; then the glow died, and the fogbank was absolutely white.

A few minutes later it began to rain again. The

rain danced on the water, drummed on my head, beat in my ears. So this is how your death comes, I thought. You don't buy it with the enemies of your dreams – the black-clad toy men whose breath, even in your sleep, stunk of fish; a psychotic killer of children who tried to push an ice pick behind your ear; the Vegas hit man who handcuffed you to a drainpipe, taped your mouth, and spoke compassionately to you about the means of your execution while you stared helplessly at the white threads of light in his vacuous blue yes. Instead, you slip down into a cold green envelope beneath the roll and pitch of the waves; you drift and bump across the sandy Gulf floor, your clothes stringing bubbles to the surface, your eyes a feast for crabs and eels.

Then the fog began to flatten the water and break up into turning wisps and wraiths that hovered just above the waves, and the eastern sky went gray. A soft rose-colored light broke on the horizon, and I saw the quarter moon for the first time that night. Fifty yards away a round shape, like the back of an enormous seagoing turtle, floated in the swell. I swam to it, one long stroke at a time, breathing sideways, blowing water out of my nose, until finally my hand struck the life jacket that was wrapped around the chest of Ray Fontenot.

I had to roll him over to get to the laces. His body was strung with kelp, his skin blistered with burns and streaked with oil, his sightless eyes poached in his head. I jerked the jacket free and put my arms through the openings and felt the tension and ball of pain go out of my lower back as I was suddenly made weightless, bobbing along in a cresting wave that swept me toward the Louisiana shore.

For a short time I fell asleep, then awoke to the sound of sea gulls, the shadows of pelicans gliding by overhead, the heavy, fecund smell that speckled trout make when they school up, the early sun like a red wafer over the long green roll of the Gulf.

Five minutes later I heard an outboard engine, and I tried to wave my arms above the waves. Then he saw me and turned his engine so that he made a wide circle and approached me with the waves at his stern. It was a bass boat, a long, aluminum, flat-bottomed boat designed for freshwater fishing, not for weather or being any distance from land. The man sitting at an angle in the stern, with the throttle of the Evinrude in his hand, wore Marine Corps utility pants, a gold and purple LSU jersey with Mike the Tiger on the front, a pale blue porkpie hat mashed down on his big head.

He cut the engine, drifted into me, then reached down and grabbed me by the back of the lifejacket. His face was round and flushed red with windburn and the strain of lifting me.

'What's happening, Streak?' Cletus said.

I lay in the bottom of his boat, my skin numb and dead to the touch and wrinkled with water-soak. I could see the coastline, the tide breaking across a sandbar, and white cranes rising from a cypress swamp.

You went out after me in this? I wanted to say. But I was breathless with cold and the words wouldn't come.

'How you like civil service with the DEA?' he said above the engine's roar. 'Those babies really know how to take care of you, don't they? Yes, indeedy, they do.'

205

9

Through my hospital room windows I could see the tops of oak trees, a pink two-story house with iron grillwork across the street, palm fronds on the esplanade, and, where the side street fed into St. Charles, the big green iron streetcar when it passed. My room was white, and the sunlight was bright above the oak trees outside.

My right eye was crimped partly shut by the tape that covered the stitches in my eyebrow. There were four stitches in my lip, and they felt like a large plastic insect when I moved my tongue across them. I slept through most of the morning, and at noon I ate a lunch of mashed potatoes, baked chicken, early peas, and Jell-O, and fell asleep again. Two hours later I was awakened by Minos's phone call.

'What happened out there?' he said.

I told him.

'How'd you know which hospital I was in?' I asked.

'Your buddy Clete called me. Look, I'm sorry about this, Dave. I really am. There's always a risk in undercover work, but we usually do a better job of protecting our people.'

'How did New Orleans Vice get in on it?'

'I don't know. I talked to this character Nate Baxter. He's a nasty sonofabitch, isn't he?'

'You got it.'

'He stonewalled me, said he couldn't talk to me without clearance, said he wasn't even sure who I was.'

'Did you mention my name?'

'Of course not.'

'Don't tell him anything about our operation. He'll divulge it or use it in some way for his own ends. In the meantime call his superiors.'

'I already have a call in. But I appreciate you telling me how to do these things.'

'You sound a little irritable this afternoon.'

'Your busted head and the loss of your boat weren't the only problems that developed out there.'

'Wait a minute. They got Boggs, didn't they?'

'No.'

'What?'

'Boggs got away. With fifty keys of pure flake.'

'I can't believe it.'

'Evidently he went between two sandbars and they went over the top of one. At least that's what the Coast Guards says. Our man Baxter has no comment.'

'You got the shrimper, didn't you?'

'We got the shrimper. But no dope. No money, either. They dumped it all overboard.' I could almost hear him swallow when he said it.

'It all went for nothing?'

'That's what a few people have been telling me today.'

'What about my boat?'

'We'll see what we can do.'

'Listen, Minos, it'll take me thirty thousand dollars to replace it.'

'People down here are not sympathetic to my point of view right now. A half-million dollars of DEA money is at this moment bouncing along the bottom of the Gulf.'

'Your friends have an interesting attitude about personal responsibility.'

'Nobody here wants to spend the rest of his career in western Nebraska. But it happens. Give me a little time.'

'I mean it, Minos. That's a big part of my livelihood that went down out there. I want it back.'

'You made your point.'

'One other thing. Boggs said something about Cardo's being history. Is there a whack out on him or something?'

'It's funny you say that. We heard rumours like that from both Houston and Miami in just the last two days.'

A nurse came in to take my temperature, and I started to say good-bye to Minos.

'How close did it get out there, Dave?' he said.

'Down to the wire.'

'Are you all right?'

'It's just a few stitches. They're keeping me a day or so because I got some water in my lungs. Sometimes that can cause pneumonia.'

'No. I mean are you all right?'

'I'm fine.' And I looked out at the sunlight on the trees and realized that I meant it.

'I think we're going to pull you out of the sting. It went out of control. It wasn't anybody's fault, it just happens. But you've done enough. I'll be back with you tonight.'

After he hung up and the nurse had taken my temperature, I used the bathroom, then walked to the window and looked down the side street towards St. Charles. The streetcar rattled down the esplanade under the massive canopy of oak trees, the wood seats filled with Negroes and working-class white people. Down below, the gutters were full of pink and blue camellias from the previous night's rain, and the wet stone was streaked with color like dye washed out of paper flowers.

Ten minutes later Clete walked through the door with a pizza in a flat box, a can of Jax in one coat pocket, and a Dr Pepper in the other. His porkpie hat was tilted down on his forehead. He sat on the side of my bed and flipped open the top of the box, his intelligent green eyes smiling at me.

'Hospital food usually tastes like a cross between spit and baby pabulum,' he said. 'So I brought you a dynamite combo of anchovies, sausage, pepperoni, and double cheese. How do you like it, my noble mon?'

'How about some peanut brittle? It goes great with stitches in the mouth, too.'

He ate a huge wedge and popped open the can of Jax, drank it half-empty, then picked up another wedge and started chewing, smiling all the time. There were flecks of pizza sauce on his mouth and shirt.

'The next time, I cover your butt from Jump Street,' he said.

'All right.'

'The feds don't send out my old partner on any more Lone Ranger jobs.'

'Okay, Clete.'

'Because you can't depend on these white-collar dickheads.'

'I got your drift.'

'Did that pencil pusher call you yet?'

'Minos?'

'Yeah.'

'About ten minutes ago.'

'His sting has turned to shit. He's not too happy. I told him they took a hell of a risk with a guy they recruited from outside their agency. He didn't seem to like that.'

'Minos is all right. How do you think New Orleans got in on it?'

'Maybe a wiretap, maybe a snitch. Who cares? They saved your tokus, didn't they?'

'Not intentionally. You remember what it was like when somebody opened up on you with an M-16?'

'Maybe we ought to 'front Nate Baxter about it. Sometimes he comes into my club after work. I've always thought his head would make a good toilet brush.'

He continued to study my face.

'What are you thinking about?' he asked.

'It wasn't a tap. The DEA would know about a tap. Somebody dropped the dime on the buy.'

'Who knew about it?'

'Cardo . . . Fontenot . . . Lionel . . . obviously Boggs . . .'

'Why you got that big wrinkle between your eyes, Streak?'

'I'm involved with somebody. She knew about it, too.'

'That's great. Why don't you run an ad in the *Times-Picayune* the next time out?'

'I didn't tell her. She picked up on it somewhere else.'

'What's her name?'

'Bootsie Giacano.'

'Oh, man, I don't believe it. You're in the sack with one of the Giacanos?'

'She's an old friend from New Iberia. She married into the family.'

'Probably like one of Charlie Manson's people, just a casual member of the family.'

'Knock it off, Clete.'

He grinned and squinted at me.

'The other one that bothers me is Kim Dollinger,' I said. 'She was trying to tell me something in your club. I thought she was just bombed.'

'She is one tough badass broad, isn't she? I'd like to get to know her a lot better.'

'I get the feeling you're not too serious about any of this.'

'Why should I be? The whole sting was put together by clowns, if you ask me. They almost got you killed out there. I don't like federal farts doing that to my podjo.'

'I think you need to broaden your attitudes, Clete.'

He opened my can of Dr Pepper, poured it in a glass with ice, set a glass straw in it, and put it in my hand.

'Drink your pop,' he said. 'Hey, you know who I got the pizza from?'

'Don't tell me.'

'You got it, mon. That strange, buglike colored kid. He works in that pizza joint right around the corner from the Pearl. Hey, mon, it's time to get out of this G-man bullshit. Let them clean up their own mess for a while. If you still want to square the beef with Boggs, you and I'll do it together. With no forms to fill out, either. You know what I mean?'

'I'll let you know.'

'Something happened out there, didn't it?' he said.

'What do you mean?'

'The dragon went away.'

'Something like that.'

'It's a rush, isn't it?'

I nodded and looked out the window at the tops of the trees moving in the sunlight.

'Yeah, a real high,' he said. 'Maybe one a guy doesn't always want to turn loose of. Almost as good as a glass of black Jack on ice with a Tuborg to chase it home. Think about it, Dave. The time to go is right after you hit the daily double.'

He folded the pizza box shut and looked directly into my face. His weight made a big dent on the side of the bed. His face was as flat and round as a cake pan.

Later, I phoned New Iberia to check on Alafair, then I called Bootsie to apologize for the things that I had said to her. I hadn't changed my mind about her – if she was involved with the mob in New Orleans, she had become a willing victim – but what right did I have to judge her and wound her again after all these years? It was a difficult conversation

212

because I knew her phone was tapped and I did not want her to compromise herself. But I did apologize.

'It's all right, *cher*,' she said. 'I haven't told you everything. Sometime I will.'

I was silent.

'You came to some conclusions that most people would,' she said.

'Can you come up here?'

'Anytime for you, darlin'.'

'Not today, though. Tomorrow morning. I've got the bed spins now. I guess I had a big drop in body temperature out there. I don't look too good, either.'

'I'll drop by around nine.'

'Boots?' I said.

'What?'

'Boots?' And I wanted to ask her if she knew how it had gone sour on the salt.

'Yes?'

'I always loved you. All these years. I never forgot that summer of 1957.'

'I didn't either, Dave. Who could? You get one like that in a lifetime.'

That evening I ate supper from the tray on my bed and watched the light fade above the trees and the roofs of houses. Then it was dark, and when people turned on their porch lights I could see the black outlines of the palms and philodendron and stands of bamboo in their front yards, and then the iron streetcar clattering by on the St. Charles esplanade, the closed windows filled with the purple and green neon glow from the Katz and Bezthof drugstore on the corner.

213

I fell asleep and dreamed that I was sliding down a wave into a great slate-green trough; the horizon was tilted, the sky a dirty veil of gray like incinerator smoke. My ears were filled with the hiss of water and wind humming in a seashell. My legs were atrophied, bloodless with cold, but I knew there were makos and hammerheads turning below me in the depths, and they could find feeling and extract a torrent of color from skin that had puckered as white as a fish's belly.

I *felt* him at the side of my bed and opened by eyes on the pillow as though someone had clapped his hands close to my face.

'Hey, it's just me,' Tony Cardo said, smiling. 'I don't want to give you a coronary, too.'

I pushed myself up on my arms and licked the dry welt of stitches on my lip.

'You must have some mean dreams,' he said.

He wore a striped brown suit, a pale yellow shirt with French cuffs and a dark brown knit necktie, a fedora tilted on his head, wing-tip shoes that were spit-shined to the soft gleam of melted plastic. The man with jailhouse tattoos I had seen waxing Tony's Oldsmobile stood behind Tony, his hand folded patiently in front of him, his expressionless eyes never quite meeting mine, his bristle-flecked cannonball head motionless as though he were listening for something.

'I feel bad about what happened to you out there, Dave,' Tony said. 'You saw it coming, didn't you, and I didn't listen to you. You're a smart man.'

'Not smart enough, Tony. I walked into it. I lost my boat out there, too.'

'I know all about it.'

214

'How?'

'The people on the other end. They had to dump a lot of inventory overboard. Your money with it. It was a bad night for business.'

'It was a bad night in a lot of ways, Tony.'

'You mean Lionel and Ray buying it? I never thought those two would try to rip me off. But you have to deal with a lot of untrustworthy types in this business, Dave.'

'You know all about the rip-off, then? You know about Jimmie Lee Boggs?'

'A guy like Boggs has one talent. You probably met one or two like him in 'Nam. He'd take out a water buffalo or spook a farmer out of a rice field so he could drop him. Anything to stay busy. But he's not too bright about anything else. The word's already out, he wants to lay off fifty keys of pure product.'

'Where is he?'

'Here, Miami, Houston. It's all Motel Eight to a guy like that.'

'Do you know why they tried to take you off?' I said.

He sucked in his cheeks, and his mouth became small and button-shaped. The man behind him flexed his shoulders as though he had a neck ache.

'You're telling me something?' Tony said. His eyes were bright, amused.

'Like you said, you didn't think Lionel or Fontenot had it in them.'

'I didn't put it that way, but all right . . .'

'Boggs is a psychopath, but he's a pro. He doesn't make moves without somebody's permission,' I said.

215

Tony's eyes were dark and friendly, his lashes as long as a girl's.

'Go on, Dave,' he said.

'I'm saying these guys are piranhas. They don't attack until they smell blood in the water.'

'I look like I'm bleeding?' he said, and smiled with the corner of his mouth.

'I'd watch my back.'

'Listen to this guy. He gets beat up, he almost drowns, he loses his boat and money, and he worries about somebody else.'

'Take it for what it's worth, Tony. I think they've got a whack out on you.'

'What do you think, Jess?' he said to the man with the cannonball head.

'I think they'd better not fucking try,' the man said.

'See,' Tony said. 'This is New Orleans. We don't worry about some gumballs in Miami or Houston. They want to get ugly, we take it into their backyard.'

'Lionel used the shortwave on the shrimper to call Boggs. Did they tell you that?'

I saw the pause come into his eyes.

'No, I didn't know that,' he said.

'Maybe they didn't speak English. Or maybe they didn't have any way of knowing he was setting up a rip-off.'

'What you're saying, Davie, is they probably didn't care.'

'Maybe.'

'You're a good guy, Dave, but you're still a newbie. There's two ways you run the business – you don't get greedy, you piece off the action, you

216

treat people fair. Then your conscience is clear, you got respect in your community, people trust you. Then when somebody else breaks the rules, gets greedy, tries to put a lock on your action, you blow up their shit. You don't fuck around when you do it, either. It's like a free-fire zone. Nobody likes it, but the only thing that counts is who walks out of the smoke.'

I got up to go to the bathroom. The floor felt as though it were receding under my feet.

'You still got the deck pitching under you, huh?' Tony said.

'Yeah.'

'Well, you're coming home with us, anyway. You'll sleep better there. I got a good cook, too, fix you some gumbo and dirty rice. How's that, podna?'

'What?'

'You're staying at my place. I already signed you out and paid your bill.'

'You can't sign me out.'

'You know how much I donate to this place each year? What's the matter, you like the smell of bedpans?'

Just then one of his gatemen came through the door with two ambulance attendants pushing a gurney.

'Now wait a minute, Tony,' I said.

'I got a nice room waiting for you. With cable TV, books, magazines, you want a broad to turn the pages for you, you got that, too. Like I told you before, I'm a sensitive man about friendship. Don't be hurting my feelings.'

Then the two attendants and his hired hoods

went about packaging me up as though I were a piece of damaged china. I started to protest again as they placed their hands gently on my arms, and gray worms danced before my eyes. But Tony put a finger to his pursed lips and said, almost in a private whisper, 'Hey, guys like us already got our tickets punched. It's all a free lunch now. You're in the magic kingdom, Dave.'

So that's how to the dark tower I came.

Early the next morning Tony, his little boy, and I had breakfast in the glass-enclosed breakfast room, which had a wonderful view of Tony's myrtle-lined tennis court, oak and lemon and lime trees, and blue lawn wet with mist. The back door gave on to a wheelchair ramp that led down to the driveway.

'The bus picks up Paul right here at the door,' Tony said. 'They're going on a field trip today, to an ice factory, to learn how ice is made.'

'It's the gifted class. We get to go on a field trip every Friday,' Paul said. He smiled when he talked. He wore a purple sweater and gray corduroy pants and sat on top of cushions in his wheelchair so he could reach the table adequately. His brown hair had been cut recently, and it was combed with a part that was as exact as a ruler's edge. 'My daddy says you were in the war, too.'

'That's right.'

'You think a war's ever going to come here?' he said.

'No, this is a good place, Paul,' I said. 'We don't worry about things like that. I bet you're going to have a good time at the ice factory.'

'Do you have any little boys or girls?' Paul said.

'A little girl, about your age. Her name's Alafair.'

'What's she like to do?'

'She has a horse. She likes to feed him apples and ride him when she comes home from school.'

'A horse?' he said.

'Yeah, we call him Tex because we bought him over in Texas.'

'Boy.'

He had a genuinely sweet face, with no recognition in it of his own limitations.

'Maybe we'll go riding with Dave and his daughter one day,' Tony said.

'That'd be fine,' I said.

'There's a couple of bridle paths here, or sometimes I take Paul on trips over by Iberia Parish,' Tony said. 'Maybe we'll drive over, take you guys out to eat, go out for a boat ride, something like that,' he said.

'Yeah, that's a good idea, Tony.'

'I hear the bus,' Paul said.

His father hooked his canvas book bag, which had a lunch kit strapped on to it, on the back of the chair and wheeled him down the ramp to the waiting bus. The driver lowered a special platform from the back of the bus, and he and Tony fixed the wheels of Paul's chair to it. Before the driver raised the platform, Tony leaned down and hugged his son, pressed his head against his chest, and kissed his hair.

He came back in and sat down at the table. He wore white tennis slacks and a thick white sweater with blue piping on it.

'You have a fine little podna there,' I said.

'You'd better believe it. How'd you sleep last night?'

219

'Good.'

'You like my home?'

'It's beautiful.'

'I wish my mom had lived to see it. We lived in Algiers and the Irish Channel. We had colored people living next door and across the street from us. You know what my mom used to do for a living?'

I shook my head no.

'She washed the hair of corpses. She'd come home, and I could smell it on her. Not just the chemicals. That same smell when you pop a body bag. Not as strong, but that same smell. Man, I used to hate it. I think that's why she always talked about lemon and lime trees back in Sicily. She said on her father's farm there was this old Norman tower made out of rocks, and lemon and lime trees grew all around it. When it was real hot she and her sisters would play inside the rocks where it was cool, and they could smell the lemons and limes on the wind.'

Two men walked into the kitchen, their faces full of sleep, and began clattering around in the cabinets.

'Where's the cereal bowls at?' one of them said. He was dark and thin; he wore slippers and his print shirt was unbuttoned and hung half out of his slacks, but he hadn't forgotten to put on his shoulder holster.

'Right-hand side,' Tony said. 'Look, you guys, there's eggs and bacon in the warmer out in the dining room. There's extra coffee there, too.'

They shuffled around in the kitchen and didn't reply. Then they went out into the dining room.

These were only two of eight hired men I had seen in the house since the night before. They had slept on couches, in the attic, the television den, and guest cottage, and had taken turns walking around on the grounds and driveway during the night.

'They're good boys, just not too sophisticated,' Tony said. 'Do they make you uncomfortable?'

'No.'

'A couple of them made you.'

I looked at him blankly.

'They can spot a cop,' he said. 'I told them you're all right, though. You're all right, aren't you, Dave?'

His eyes took on that strange, self-amused light again.

'You have to be the judge of that, Tony.'

'I think you're a solid guy. You know what a solid con is?'

'Yes.'

'You're that kind of guy. You've got character.'

'Maybe you don't know everything about me.'

'Maybe I know more than you think,' he said, and winked.

I didn't know his game, or even if he was playing one, but I didn't like meeting his eyes. I took a bite of my soft-boiled eggs and looked out at the mist in the citrus trees.

'Where's the contract coming from?' I said.

'There's one guy in Houston that wants me out bad. Two or three in Miami. Maybe they got permission from Chicago, maybe they're acting on their own, I don't know. You heard stories about me, Dave, about some stuff I do, waving the flag around, bullshit like that?'

'I guess I have.'

'That I been breaking one of the big rules, getting mixed up in politics, focusing attention on the organization?'

'That's what you hear sometimes.'

'Let me tell you about a guy used to live in Plantation, Florida. You remember the name Johnny——? This guy went back to the days of Bugsy Siegel, I mean he survived gang wars for forty years. But Johnny and a couple of other guys thought they could jerk the CIA around. They told some CIA people they could whack out Castro for the government, like do a patriotic act and maybe get the casinos open in Havana again. So the CIA buys it, and the word is out that our guys are going to clip Castro. Maybe they even sent a couple of kamikaze gumballs to do it, but the bottom line is that Castro looks pretty healthy today. In other words, it looks like it was a scam to pump juice and influence out of the government. So the commission in Chicago tells these guys that what they're doing is stupid and they'd fucking better knock it off. But Johnny doesn't listen. So one day a couple of guys invite him fishing out in Biscayne Bay, except they put one in his ear, cut his legs off, and stuff him inside an oil barrel.

'They weighted the barrel down with chains, and shoved an ice pick in Johnny's stomach to break the gas bag. Nobody would have ever seen him again, but they screwed it up. They missed the wall of his stomach, and he floated the barrel up.

'It makes a good story, doesn't it, about what happens when a guy decides to get political?'

'I've heard it before.'

'Then maybe you also know it's bullshit. Johnny

got clipped because of money. It's always money, Dave. Those guys in Miami and Houston want to take over the action on the Louisiana coast. There's four or five other guys in New Orleans they'll have to cut in, guys who are anybody's cornhorn, but the word is I'm definitely not going to be a player.' He smiled and put a dripping spoonful of cereal in his mouth. 'There's supposed to be some real talent in town right now. I hear it's a twenty-five-thou contract.'

'Maybe it's a good time to take the family on a vacation to the islands,' I said.

'They don't hurt families. We don't do that to each other. Not even these guys, Dave.' But I saw the cloud slide across his face. He looked out at the lawn and rubbed his finger against his temple.

'I need to use your phone,' I said. 'A lady was coming up to see me at the hospital this morning.'

'Who is she?' he asked, and smiled again.

'Bootsie Giacano.'

'No kidding? You got good taste. She's a class broad, I mean lady. You gotta excuse my vocabulary. I went to college, but most of the time you wouldn't know it.'

'You know her?'

'Sure. I own part of her business. She's nice. I like her.'

I used the phone in the kitchen and told Bootsie where I was and that I would see her later.

'You're where?' she said.

I cleared my throat and told her again I was at Tony's. I could hear her breathing into the mouthpiece of the receiver.

'I won't ask you any more questions,' she said.

'I'm sure you know what you're doing, Dave. You know what you're doing, don't you?'

'Sure,' I said, then, 'I'll call you tonight. Everything's fine, kiddo.'

'Yeah, sure it is,' she said, and hung up.

I sat back down with Tony just as his wife came into the kitchen in a blue house robe and slippers, her face dull with sleep, her hair in pink foam-rubber curlers. She didn't speak. She filled a coffee cup from the electric pot on the Formica counter, shook two aspirins from a bottle and set them by the side of her saucer, and sat at the kitchen table with her back to us, smoking silently while she drank her coffee. The backs of her hands were coarse and heavily veined, and her nails, long and bright red, made clicking sounds when she picked up her coffee cup.

'Clara, this is Dave Robicheaux. He stayed with us last night,' Tony said.

Again she didn't speak. Her blond hair was dark close to her scalp. I could see nicotine stains on her fingers, dried makeup around the corners of her mouth, her thin whitened nostrils when she breathed.

'Dave and I were talking about taking Paul for a horse ride,' Tony said.

She blew smoke up against the window glass and flicked her ashes in her saucer.

'I think maybe everybody was making a little too much noise last night,' Tony said.

'May I speak to you alone, please?' she said.

'Uh-oh,' he said.

'I'd like to see your tennis court. I'll be outside,' I said.

'Yeah, we'll hit some balls. Tell Jess to load up the ball machine,' he said, but he didn't hide the embarrassment in his face well.

I walked down the wheelchair ramp and across the damp, spongy Saint Augustine grass toward the court. The sun was pale and yellow above the myrtle trees, the canvas windscreens were streaked with water, and the fog blew off the lake in wisps and glistened on the waxy green surface of the citrus leaves. I could hear her voice behind me: 'They can stay in the cottage . . . I don't want them all over my house . . . Did you see the bathroom this morning . . . You wouldn't have this trouble if you were reasonable, if you didn't have to be the big war hero . . . Everyone's tired of it, Tony, they've made allowances for a long time, they're not going to go on doing it forever . . . Maybe you're not going to like this, but I think they've been fair, I think you're acting crazy . . . Go ahead, eat some more of that stuff. It's only eight o'clock in the morning. That'll fix 'em in Miami.'

They went at it for ten minutes. I didn't find Jess, so I began to load the automatic ball machine myself. When Tony came out of the house with an oversized tennis racket across his shoulder, he was grinning as though he were serenely in charge of the morning, but his eyes had a black, electrical gaze in them, the skin of his face was stretched tight against the bone, and I could see the pulse jumping in his neck as though he had been running wind sprints.

'I love Indian summer in Louisiana. I love the morning,' he said.

'It's been a pretty fall.'

'Fucking A,' he said, clicked on the ball machine

225

with a remote control button, and stationed himself like a gladiator behind the baseline.

I sat on a bench and watched while the machine hummed, then *thropped* balls across the net, and Tony slammed them back with a fierce energy that left skid marks in the soft green clay.

'It's funny how many people can want a piece out of your ass,' he said. 'Wives, broads, cops, lawyers, these guys I pay to keep me alive. You rent their loyalty by the day. I can name two hundred people in this city I've made rich. Even a psychotic piece of shit like Jimmie Lee Boggs. Can you dig it, when I first met that guy he was doing five-hundred-dollar hits for a couple of Jews out of Miami. Even after he escaped from you, his big score was going to be to blackmail some colored woman in New Iberia. Now he's got a half-million bucks of product.'

'What colored woman?' I said.

'I don't know, he was going to move in on a hot-pillow joint or something. That's Jimmie Lee's idea of the big score.'

'Wait a minute, Tony. This is important. Do you remember the name of the woman?'

'It was French. It was Mama something.' He hit the ball long, into the canvas windscreen. 'To tell you the truth, I'm not real interested in talking about colored whorehouses.'

'I have to ask you anyway. What'd he have on her?'

'Maybe we're not communicating too well here,' he said, and slapped one ball hard against the tape and whanged another off the ball machine itself.

'Maybe he knows something that might keep a kid out of the electric chair.'

'It's got something to do with snuffing a redbone.

226

What the fuck do I know about redbones? I got a problem here, I hear you talking about some colored woman, about keeping a kid out of the electric chair, about a cathouse in New Iberia, but I don't hear you talking about the half million your people put up. That bothers me a little bit, Dave.'

'There's nothing I can do about what happened out on the salt.'

'Yeah? How about the guys who lost their money? Are they cool?'

'They're oil people. They're not in the business. They're not going to do anything about it.'

'You must know a different class of people than me, then. Because the people I've known will do anything because of money. But you're telling me these guys are different?'

'It's just something I'll have to handle myself, Tony.'

'Yeah, if I was you, I'd handle it. I'd really handle it.' He lowered his racket and looked at me, a dark light in his eyes. A ball whizzed past him and bounced off the windscreen behind him. He removed his sweater, wiped the sweat off his face with it, and threw it to the side of the court.

Then a strange transformation took place in him. The tautness of his face, the hard, black shine in his eyes, the rigidity of the muscles in his body, suddenly left him like air rushing out of a balloon. His skin grew ashen, sweat ran out of his hair, he began swallowing deep in his throat, and his lungs labored for air.

'What is it, partner?' I said.

'Nothing.'

I took him by the arm and walked him to the

227

bench. His arm felt flaccid and weak in my hand. He propped the racket on the clay and leaned his head down on it. Sweat dripped off the lobes of his tiny ears.

'You want me to take you to a doctor?' I said.

'No.'

'You want me to get your wife?'

'No. It's going to pass.'

I picked up the sweater and blotted his hair and the back of his neck with it, then draped it over his shoulders. He began to breathe more regularly; then he pinched the bridge of his nose and held his head back in the cool air as though he had a nose-bleed.

'I think you need to talk to somebody,' I said. 'I think you're dealing with something that's going to eat your lunch.'

He folded his arm on top of his perpendicular racket and rested his head on his arm.

'What are you gonna do, a kid needs a mother. It's all a pile of shit, man,' he said. 'All of it.'

When I went back to my room, which gave on to a side yard that contained a swing set and a solitary moss-hung oak tree, my clothes from my apartment were laid out neatly on the tester bed. Even my .45, with the spare clip and box of shells, lay on top of a folded flannel shirt. I went to look for Tony, but he was in the shower. I walked out the front door and down the long, tree-lined drive to the front gate, where Jess sat in a chair, wearing a blue jumpsuit. It was zippered only halfway up his chest, and I could see the leather straps of his shoulder holster against his T-shirt.

'Where's the closest drugstore?' I said.

'What do you need?'

'Some razor blades.'

'It's five blocks, down by the lake. We'll send a car.'

'I need the walk. I still feel like I've got rapture of the deep.'

'What?'

'How about opening up?' I said.

He unlocked the chain and slid back the gate wide enough so that I could step out on the street. I walked past the rows of banked lawns and oleander-lined piked fences to a thoroughfare and a tan stucco and red-tiled shopping center that looked as if it had been torn out of the ground in southern California and dropped in the middle of New Orleans. I used a pay phone outside a drugstore to call Minos.

'You pulled it off, Dave. You're across the moat and inside the castle,' he said before I explained.

'How'd you know where I was?'

'Everybody who goes in that gate is on videotape. How do you like it with the spaghetti-and-meatball crowd?'

'I'm not sure.'

'I told you, didn't I, Cardo's head was in the blender too long.'

'Minos, you guys are all turning the screws on this guy, and, to tell you the truth, I'm not sure why.'

'What are you talking about?'

'He's just one guy. What about these guys in Miami and Houston who've got a contract out on him? The odds are Tony's going to lose.'

229

'Let us worry about Houston and Miami. You want in or out, Dave?'

'I haven't made up my mind.'

'You'd damn well better.'

'I want Boggs.'

'You're in the right place, then. He'll be back. He's not a guy who leaves loose ends. Besides, we hear it's an open contract. It's the perfect opportunity for him.'

'Did you find out who dropped the dime on the buy?'

'Baxter said he couldn't compromise his informant.'

'He's not going to share a bust with a federal agency.'

'Forget about that guy. Look, Washington called yesterday with some information about Cardo's military record. He got a Silver Star for going after a point man who stepped on a mine.'

'He didn't tell me that.'

'After he was wounded, he got moved back to Chu Lai for the last four months of his tour.'

'Why was he moved back to Chu Lai?'

'How should I know?'

'There's something not right. The Marines were real hard-nosed about keeping a guy in his platoon until he had a million-dollar wound or two Purple Hearts.'

'Maybe he had some pull. Listen, Dave, don't get involved with the guy's psychology. Eventually we're going to punch his ticket. You'll probably be there when it happens. Or you'll be in court testifying against him. All this *semper fi* bullshit won't have anything to do with it. You want a lesson from Vietnam? Don't think about the guy who's in your sights.'

'You always cut right to the bone, Minos.'

'I didn't invent the rules. By the way, we have that house under twenty-four-hour surveillance. If it turns to shit inside, throw a lamp or a chair through a window. In the meantime, think about how far you want to take it. Nobody'll blame you if you decide to go back to New Iberia.'

It was cool under the stucco colonnade, and red leaves were blowing out of a heavily wooded lot across the street.

'Dave, are you still there?' he asked.

'Yeah . . . I'll try to call you back tonight or tomorrow. Talk to you later, Minos.'

I hung up the phone and wondered if Minos would tell the lion tamer that he could put down his whip and chair and walk out of the lions' cage whenever he wished. I went inside the drugstore, bought a package of razor blades, and came out just as Tony and Jess pulled to the curb in the maroon Lincoln convertible.

10

Tony was in the passenger's seat. He reached over the backseat and popped open the back door for me. He had changed into loafers, a rust-colored sports shirt, pleated tan slacks, a cardigan, and a yellow Panama hat.

'You could have taken the car, Dave. You didn't have to walk,' he said.

'It's a good day for it.'

'How do you like my hat?'

'It looks sharp.'

'I got a collection of them. Hey, Jess, go inside and get me a copy of *Harper's*,' he said.

'What?' Jess said.

'Get me a copy of *Life*.'

'Sure, Tony,' Jess said, cut the engine, and went inside the drugstore.

Tony smiled at me across the back of the seat. The Lincoln had a rolled leather interior, a fold-out bar, a wooden dashboard with black instrument panels.

'Jess has an IQ of minus eight, but he'd eat thumbtacks with a spoon if I told him to,' he said. Then the smile went out of his face. 'I'm sorry you had to hear that stuff between me and Clara. In particular I'm sorry you had to hear that about me being a war hero. Because I never told anybody I was a hero. I knew some guys who were, but I wasn't one of them.'

'Who was, Tony? Did you ever read a story by Ernest Hemingway called "A Soldier's Home"? It's about a World War I Marine who comes back home and discovers that people only want to hear stories about German women chained to machine guns. The truth is that he was afraid all the time he was over there and it took everything in him just to get by. However, he learns that's not a story anyone is interested in.'

'Yeah. Ernest Hemingway. I like his books. I read a bunch of them in college.'

'Look, on another subject, Tony. I'm not sure your wife is ready for houseguests right now.'

He puffed out his cheeks.

'I invite people to my home. I tell them if they should leave,' he said. 'You're my guest. You don't want to stay, that's your business.'

'I appreciate your hospitality, Tony.'

'So we're going back home now and get you changed, then we're taking Kim out to the yacht club for a little lunch and some golf. How's that grab you?'

'Fine.'

'You like Kim?'

'Sure.'

'How much?'

'She's a pretty girl.'

'She ain't pretty, man. She's fucking beautiful.' His eyes were dancing with light. 'She told me she got drunk and came on to you.'

'She told you that?'

'What's the big deal? She's human. You're a good-looking guy. But you don't look too comfortable right now.' He laughed out loud.

'What can I say?'

'Nothing. You're too serious. It's all comedy, man. The bottom line is we all get to be dead for a real long time. It's a cluster fuck no matter how you cut it.'

We drove back to his house, and I changed into a pair of gray slacks, a charcoal shirt, and a candy-striped necktie, loaded two bags of golf clubs into the Lincoln, and with a white stretch Caddy limousine full of Tony's hoods behind us, we picked up Kim Dollinger and headed for the country club out by the lake.

We filled two tables in the dining room. I couldn't tell if the attention we drew was because of my bandaged head, Tony's hoods, whose dead eyes and toneless voices made the waiters' heads nod rapidly, or the way Kim filled out her gray knit dress. But each time I took a bite from my shrimp cocktail and tried to chew on the side of my mouth that wasn't injured, I saw the furtive glances from the other tables, the curiosity, the titillation of being next to people who suddenly step off a movie screen.

And Tony must have read my thoughts.

'Watch this,' he said, and motioned the maître d' over. 'Give everybody in the bar and dining room a glass of champagne, Michel.'

'It's not necessary, Mr. Cardo.'

'Yeah, it is.'

'Some of our members don't drink, Mr. Cardo.'

234

'Then give them a dessert. Put it on my bill.'

Tony wiped his small mouth with a napkin. The maître d' was a tall, pale man who looked as if he were about to be pushed out an airplane door.

'Hey, they don't want it, that's okay,' Tony said. 'Lighten up, Michel.'

'Very good, sir.' The maître d' assembled his waiters and sent them to the bar for trays of glasses and towel-wrapped bottles of champagne.

'That was mean,' Kim said.

'I didn't come here to be treated like a bug,' Tony said.

We finished lunch and walked outside into the cool afternoon sunlight and the rattle of the palms in the wind off the lake. The lake was murky green and capping, and the few sailboats that were out were tacking hard in the wind, the canvas popping, their glistening bows slapping into the water. Tony and most of his entourage loaded themselves into golf carts for nine holes, and Kim and I sat on a wood bench by the practice green while Jess made long putts back and forth across the clipped grass without ever hitting the cup.

She wore a gray pillbox hat with a net veil folded back on top of it. She didn't look at me and instead gazed off at the rolling fairways, the sand traps and greens, the moss-hung oaks by the tees. The wind was strong enough to make her eyes tear, but in profile she looked as cool and regal and un-perturbed as a sculptor's model. Behind her, the long, rambling club building, with its glass-domed porches, was achingly white against the blue of the sky.

'Maybe we should go inside,' I said.

'It's fine, thanks.'

'Do you think it's smart to jerk a guy like Tony around?'

She crossed her legs and raised her chin.

'He's got a burner turned on in his head. I wouldn't mess with his male pride,' I said.

'Is there something wrong with the way I look? I wish you'd stop staring at me.'

'I think you've got a guilty conscience, Kim.'

'Oh you do?'

'Did you drop the dime on us?'

She watched Jess putt across the green. The red flag on the pin flapped above his head in the distance. Finally the ball clunked into the cup. My eyes never left the side of her face. She pulled her dress tight over her knee. Her hips and stomach looked as smooth as water going over stone.

'Somebody told the Man. It wasn't Lionel or Fontenot,' I said.

'Do you think Tony would be taking me out for lunch if he thought I was a snitch?'

I think only Tony knows what goes on in Tony's head. I think he likes to live on the outer edge of his envelope. Eating black speed is like sliding down the edge of a barber's razor.'

'Why do you keep saying these things to me? I have nothing to tell you.'

'Do you know a Vice cop named Nate Baxter?'

I could see the color in her cheeks.

'Why should I know—,' she began.

'He was following you the day you were in Clete's place. This guy's a lieutenant. Why's he interested in you, Kim?'

Her eyes were wet, and her lip began to tremble.

'All right, come on now,' I said.

'You're a shit.'

Jess had stopped putting and was looking at us. The gray hair on his chest grew like wire out of his golf shirt.

'Maybe I'm just a little worried about you,' I said.

'Leave me alone. Please do that for me.'

'I'll buy you a drink instead.'

'No, you stay away from me.'

'Listen to me, Kim—'

She picked up her purse and walked in her high heels across the lawn toward the club. Her calves looked hard and waxed below the hem of her knit dress. Jess walked off the green with the putter hanging loosely at his side.

'What's wrong with her?' he said.

'I guess I don't know how to talk to younger women very well.'

'She's a weird broad. I don't trust her.'

'Why not?'

'She don't ask for anything. A broad who don't ask you for anything has got a different kind of hustle going. Tony don't see it.' He twirled the putter like a baton in his fingers.

I found her sitting on a tall chair-backed stool in the bar. The bar was done in mahogany and teakwood, with brass-framed round mirrors and barometers on the walls and copper kettles full of ferns hung in the windows that looked out over the yacht basin. Her eyes were clear now, and her hands lay quietly on the polished black surface of the bar, her fingers touching the sides of a Manhattan glass. She nibbled at the orange slice; then her face tightened

237

when she saw me walk into the periphery of her vision.

I ordered a cup of coffee from the bartender.

'What do I have to say? Don't you know how to let someone alone?' she said.

'I think you need a friend.'

'And you're it. What a laugh.'

'I know Baxter. If you've got a deal going with him, he'll burn you.'

I saw her swallow, either with anger or fear.

'What is the matter with you? Are you trying to get me killed?' she said.

'Get on a plane, Kim. L.A.'s great this time of year. I'll get some money for you.'

She looked straight ahead and breathed hard, way down in her chest.

'You're a cop,' she said.

'Ex.'

'Now.'

'You'd better check out my record. Cops with my kind of mileage are the kind they shove out the side door.'

'I can't afford you. I'm going to ask you one more time, get away from me.'

'You're a nice girl. You don't deserve the fall you're headed for.'

She started to speak again, but her words caught in her throat as though she had swallowed a large bubble of air. Then she sipped from her Manhattan, straightened her back, and signaled the bartender.

'This man is annoying me,' she said.

He was young, and his eyes glanced nervously at me and then back at her.

'Did you hear me?' she said.

'Yes.'

'Would you tell him to leave, please?' she said.

'Sir, this lady is making a request,' the bartender said. He wore a long-sleeved white shirt and a black bow tie, and his hair was blond and oiled.

'Yeah, I heard, podna. I don't know where else I should go, though.'

'Would you tell him to get the fuck out of the bar?' she said.

'Miss, please don't use that language.'

'I ordered a drink. I didn't ask to have a dildo sit next to me while I drank it. Tell him to get out.'

'Miss, please.'

'What does it take to get through to you?' she said.

Other people had stopped eating and drinking and were looking at us.

'Sir, would you mind—,' the bartender said.

'No. I don't mind,' I said. 'Where should I go?'

'Try Bumfuck, Kansas,' she said.

'Miss, I'll have to ask you to leave, too.'

'Is that right?' she said. 'Would you page Mr. Cardo out on the golf course and tell him that? I would appreciate it if you would tell him that.'

'You're Mr. Cardo's guest?' the bartender said. His face was bloodless.

'Don't sweat it, partner. We're leaving,' I said.

'Is that what we're doing? Is that what you think we're doing? I don't think we're doing that at all,' she said, and shattered her highball glass on the liquor bottles behind the bar.

The bar area and dining room were silent. Her gray pillbox hat was askew on top of her forehead, and a lock of red hair hung down in one eye. The

239

bartender stood on the duckboards and stared wide-eyed at Jess, who had just thrust open the outer glass doors to the bar, the putter still in his hand, his face pushed out of shape like white rubber.

We were driving away from the lakefront, on Orleans Avenue, past City Park. Tony had the window down and was turned in his seat, looking back at me and Kim, and his black and gray hair blew like tiny springs in the wind.

'What were you guys doing?' he said. He tried to hold a grin on his face.

'I was trying to have a drink,' Kim said.

'Some fucking way to get the bartender's attention,' Jess said.

'I'm sorry about that back there,' I said to Tony.

'I can't believe it, eighty-sixed out of my own club,' he said. 'You know what it took for me to get a membership in that place?'

'You want me to go back and talk with somebody about it later?' Jess said.

'What's the matter with you? It's a country club. You can't come crashing into the bar with a golf club in your hand,' Tony said.

'I thought they were in trouble,' Jess said.

'So you had to knock a waiter down?'

'I didn't see him. What the fuck, Tony. Why you reaming me? I didn't start that stuff.'

'I think you ought to consider who you invite out to lunch,' Kim said.

'I think I ought to get a new life. Am I the only person that's sane in this car?' Tony said.

'It's my fault. I'm sorry about it,' I said.

'How gallant,' Kim said.

240

'All right, all right. I'll try to square it. It's just a club, anyway, right? Jesus Christ,' Tony said, and blew out his breath.

We could see golfers out on the fairways in City Park and children on horseback beyond a grove of oak trees. Jess looked in the rearview mirror and changed lanes. Then he looked in the rearview mirror again, accelerated, and passed two cars. I saw his eyes go back into the mirror.

'We've got some guys behind us,' he said.

'What guys?' Tony said.

'Two guys in a Plymouth. Behind the limo.'

'Can you make 'em?' Tony said.

'No.'

'They look like talent?'

'I don't know. What d'you want to do, Tony?'

'Pull into the park and stop.'

'You want to do that?' Jess said, looking sideways at him.

'They'll cut and run. Watch. Come on, the day's starting to improve.'

'Bad place if it goes down, Tony. Everybody gets pissed when it goes down in a public place,' Jess said.

'Hey, is it our fault? Now, turn in here. Let's have some fun with these guys.'

Kim was looking backward out the window. Tony reached over the seat and touched her on the knee, then winked at her and grinned.

'Tony, I don't need this shit,' she said.

'Will you guys mellow out? Why is everybody trying to drive me nuts today?' he said. Then he slapped open the glove box and took out a chrome-plated .45 automatic.

The white limo followed us into the park. We drove along the side of a grassy lake and stopped under a spreading oak tree. The dry leaves under it blew in the wind and clicked and tumbled across the grass. Jess reached under the seat and took out a double-barrel .410 shotgun pistol wrapped inside a paper bag. He rolled down his window and held the shotgun pistol below the level of the window jamb.

When the Plymouth turned in after us, Tony put the .45 in his right-hand coat pocket and stepped out on the cement, smiling across the top of the car as though he were welcoming guests.

'What a day,' Kim said.

'Hey, give it a break,' Jess said, without turning his head.

The Plymouth followed along the grassy lake, passed the limo, and stopped abreast of us. The man in the passenger's seat hung his badge out the window, then stepped out in the sunlight.

Nate Baxter had changed little since I had last seen him. He still wore two-tone shoes and sports clothes, but as his styled blond hair had receded he had grown a narrow line of reddish beard along his jawbones and chin. He had worked for CID in the army, and as an investigator for Internal Affairs in the New Orleans Police Department he had combined a love of military stupidity with a talent for dismembering the wounded and the vulnerable.

Jess looked straight ahead, lowered the shotgun pistol between his legs, and pushed it back under the seat.

'Put your hands on top of the car, Tony,' Baxter said.

'You're kidding?' Tony said.

'You see me smiling?' Baxter said.

'I don't think this is cool, Lieutenant,' Tony said, his hands now resting casually on the waxed maroon hood of the Lincoln. 'We've been out for some golf. We're not looking to complicate anybody's day.'

'Go tell that limo full of meatballs to get out of here,' Baxter said to his partner, who was now standing behind him. Then he turned back towards Jess and said, 'Get out of the car, Ornella.'

'Why the roust, Lieutenant?' Tony said.

'Close your mouth, Tony. Did you hear what I said, Ornella?'

Jess got out of the car with his palms turned outward, his brow furrowed above his close-set eyes. He set his hands on the convertible roof.

The white limo made a U-turn behind us and drove slowly out of the park, its black-tinted windows hot with sunlight. Baxter's partner came back and stood next to him. He was a muscular, crew-cut man, with a grained, red complexion, who wore shades and a pale blond mustache. Like Baxter, he carried a revolver under his tweed sports jacket in a clip-on belt holster. But in his face, even with his shades on, I could see a question mark about what Baxter was doing.

'Shake them down,' Baxter said.

'Come on, Lieutenant, give it a rest. This is bullshit,' Tony said.

'I look like bullshit to you?' Baxter said.

'We don't make trouble for you guys. It's a chickenshit roust. You know it is.'

Baxter nodded impatiently to his partner.

'I got a piece in my coat pocket. You want the sonofabitch, take it. What the fuck's with you, Baxter?' Tony said.

'Easy, Tony. We don't have a big problem here,' Baxter's partner said, his hands gentle on Tony's back and sides. 'No, no, look straight ahead. Come on, man, you're a pro.'

Then, like a dentist who had just pulled a tooth, he held up Tony's chrome-plated automatic in the sunlight.

'I got a permit for it,' Tony said.

'You want to produce it?' Baxter said.

'It's at home. But I got one. You know I got one.'

'Good. Your lawyer can bring it down to your arraignment,' Baxter said.

His partner pulled Tony's arms behind him, cuffed his wrists, and sat him down on the curb. Then he ran his hands down Jess's sides, back, stomach, and legs. He rose up and shook his head at Baxter.

'Under the seat,' Baxter said.

His partner leaned into the car, worked his hand around under the seat, and pulled out the shotgun pistol. He snapped open the breech and removed the two slender .410 shells and dropped them in his pocket.

'You're under arrest for possession of an illegal firearm, Ornella,' Baxter said.

'You got to have cause to get in the car, Lieutenant,' Jess said.

'You took some law courses up at Angola?' Baxter said.

'You got to have cause,' Jess said.

Baxter's partner cuffed him and led him over to

244

the curb. Two squad cars, the backup that Baxter
had probably called for, turned into the park.
Baxter opened the back door of the convertible and
told me to step out.

'It looks like you finally found your element,' he
said.

'It must be a dull day, Nate.'

'How do you like working for the greaseballs?'

'You ought to brush up on your procedure.
Probably talk a little bit with your partner. He
seems to know what he's doing.'

'No kidding?'

'Nobody here was serious. Otherwise you might
have gotten your hash cooked, Nate.'

'I'm probably just lucky you were along to cool
things out,' he said, put a filter-tipped cigarette
between his teeth at an upward angle, and lit it with
a Zippo lighter. He snapped the lighter shut and
blew smoke out into the sunlight. Then he said, 'I
like your threads. They're elegant.'

'Get to it, Nate. You're wasting a lot of people's
time.'

'No, I mean it. You're stylish. I remember you
when you smelled like an unflushed toilet with
booze poured in it.' He rubbed his fingers up and
down the edge of my coat lapel. Then he touched
my tie, put one finger under it, drew it slowly from
my chest and let it drop.

I looked away at the grassy lake and the way the
wind made the light break on the water. The golfers
on the other side of the lake had stopped their game
and were watching us.

'You like the pockets in that shirt?' And his two
fingers slid down inside the cloth, so that I could

245

feel them against the nipple.

'Don't do that, Nate.'

'It's got a nice feel to it. It pays to buy a quality shirt.'

I could see the peppery grain of his skin along the edge of his beard, a piece of yellow mucus in the corner of his eye, the pucker in his mouth that almost made me smile. His fingers felt as thick and obscene as sausages inside my pocket.

I raised my hand and pushed his arm slowly away from me.

'That's not smart,' he said quietly, and reached his hand toward me again.

I put the flat of my hand against his forearm and moved it away from me as you would press back a slowly yielding spring. He smiled and took a puff of the filter tip of his cigarette, his lips making a soft popping sound.

'Bust him. Interference with an officer in the performance of his duty,' he said to his partner. Then to me, 'I'll ask them to process you right into the population so you can eat mainline tonight.'

'Fuck you, Baxter. We'll make bail in two hours,' Tony said as a uniformed cop raised him to his feet.

'It's Friday afternoon, Tony,' Baxter said. 'Next arraignment is Monday morning.'

'What about the broad?' his partner said.

'Tell her to take a cab. Tow his car and tear it apart.'

'Nate, we might be on shaky ground here,' the partner said.

'Not with this bunch,' Baxter said.

A few minutes later I sat handcuffed next to Tony behind the wire-mesh screen of a squad car.

Through the window I could see Kim walking hurriedly out of the park toward the avenue, her face as white as bone.

Tony, Jess and I were put in a holding cell a short distance from the drunk tank. Because it was a holding cell, it had no toilet or running water and contained only an iron bench that was bolted to one wall. The bars of the door had been repainted so many times the layers of white paint formed a shell around the metal. The walls were grimed with handprints and scuff marks from people's shoes, covered with scratched drawings of genitalia and names that had been scorched into the paint with butane cigarette lighters. The heat was turned up and the cell was hot. Someone in the drunk tank began screaming and was taken out by two uniformed cops.

Tony paced up and down, took off his rust-colored sports shirt, then worked his T-shirt over his head and used it to wipe his skin.

'What's the drill with this guy? Somebody tell me what the fucking drill is,' he said.

'It's Baxter. He's a bad cop. He can't make his case, so he finds something he can do,' I said.

'We ain't sitting in this shithole three days. That's out,' he said.

'Your lawyer had better know a judge, then.'

'You got it,' Tony said.

'I got to use the toilet,' Jess said.

'Hey, you hear that?' Tony shouted through the bars. 'We got a man in here needs to use the toilet.'

His olive skin glistened with perspiration, and he kept biting his lower lip. By the time we were booked and moved up to the general population, on the second floor, his hands trembled and he couldn't drink enough water. I sat next to him on the edge of an iron bunk that hung from wall chains. His back was running with sweat now. He leaned forward on his thighs and ran his hand through his wet hair.

'Lockup is at eight o'clock,' I said. 'Let's go down to the shower.'

'I'm cool,' he answered.

'You'll feel better after a shower.'

'Don't worry about me. I'm solid, man.' He gripped the edge of the bunk and shuddered as though he had malaria. 'Did anybody make you?'

'I don't think so. I've been out of New Orleans too long now.'

'Anybody make you, get in your face, tell them we're tight.'

'All right, Tony.'

'There's guys in here who'll do an ex-cop, Dave. That's not a shuck.'

'I think you just figured out Nate Baxter.'

'Yeah, well, I'm going to square it with that cat. The word is he's getting freebies from French Quarter street whores. I know one who's got AIDS. I'm going to fix it so she gets in the sack with him.'

Then he bent over and squeezed his palm across the back of his neck and said, 'Oh man, the tiger's got me.'

I stood him up and walked him by the arm down to the shower. Inmates lounging in the open doors of their cells or sitting on the big water pipe against the corridor wall looked at him with the curiosity and reverence of their kind – prisoners in a parish or city jail – when they were in the actual proximity of a mainline con or Mafia don. Some rose to their feet, offered to help, made an extravagant show of sympathy.

'He just got hold of some bad food,' I said.

'Yeah, it's rotten, Tony,' one man said.

'A roach crawled out of the grist one time, man. That's no shit,' another said.

'We got a stinger and some canned goods. You're welcome to it, Tony,' a third said.

Tony stood naked under the shower with his hands propped against the tiles. The water boiled his scalp white and sluiced over his olive skin and the knotted muscles in his back. In one pale buttock was a puckered red scar just above the colon. He held his face into the rush of hot water and opened and closed his small mouth like a guppy. When he turned off the faucets he breathed deeply through his nose, as though he were inhaling the morning air, and wiped his face slick with his palm.

'That's a little better,' he said.

Two men farther down the shower were staring at his phallus.

'You guys got a problem with your gender or something?' he said.

'Sorry, Tony. We don't mean anything,' one man said.

'Then act decent,' he said.

'Sure, Tony. Everybody's glad to have you here. No, I mean, we're sorry you're busted—'

'Get out of here,' Tony said.

'Sure, anything you want. We—' then the man lost his words, and he and his friends walked quickly out of the shower with their towels wrapped around their hips.

'That's what nobody understands about a jail. It's full of degenerates,' Tony said.

I walked with him back to our cell. Through the corridor window I could see downtown New Orleans and the glow of the city against the clouds. He put on his slacks and shirt and lay down barefoot on the bunk across from me. He folded his arm behind his head. Water dripped out of his hair on to the striped mattress.

'I'm supposed to take Paul to a soccer game tomorrow afternoon,' he said.

'He'll understand,' I said.

'That's not the way it works with kids. You're either there for them or you're not there.'

He let out a long breath and stared at the ceiling. Somebody down the corridor shouted, 'Lockup, five minutes.'

'How do I get out of it, man?' he said.

'What?'

'I'm addicted. Big-time. On the spike. I got blood pressure you could cook an egg with.'

'Maybe you should think about a treatment program.'

'One of those thirty-day hospital jobs? What about Paul? What about my fucking wife?'

'What about her?'

'She never dresses him or plays with him. She won't take him shopping with her or to a show. But I kick her out, she'll sue for custody. That's her big edge. And, man, does she work it. I should have used that psycho Boggs to whack her out. Her and that prick over in Houston.'

'Who?'

'She makes it with one of the Dio crowd from Houston. They meet in Miami. That's why she's always flying over there. Come on, man. You read a lot of books. What would you do?'

'You're trying to deal with all the monsters at the same time. Start with the addiction.'

'I tried. Out at the V.A. I think I'm in it for the whole ride.'

'There're ways out, Tony.'

'Yeah, and you can scrub the stink out of shit, too. You came home okay, Dave. I blew it.'

He turned on his side and faced the wall. When I spoke to him again, he did not answer.

The daytime noise level in any jail is grinding and ceaseless, particularly on a Saturday morning. I woke to the clanging of cell doors, shoes thudding on spiral metal stairs, cleaning crews scraping buckets across the cement floors, shower water drumming on the tile walls, radios tuned to a dozen different stations, someone cracking wind into a toilet bowl or roaring out a belch from the bottom of his bowels, inmate shouting from the windows to friends on the other side of the razor wire that bordered the street – a dirty, iron-tinged, cacophonous mix that echoed down the long concrete corridor with such an ear-numbing intensity that the individual voice was lost in it.

We lined up when the trusties wheeled in the steam carts loaded with grits, sausage, black coffee, and white bread, and later Tony and I played checkers on a homemade board in our cell. Then, because we had nothing else to do, we followed Jess down to the weight room at the end of the corridor.

The weather was warm and sunny, so the solitary barred window high up on the wall was open, but the room reeked of the men clanking barbells up and down on the cement. They were stripped to the waist, or wore only their Jockey undershorts or cutoff sweatpants, their bodies laced with rivulets of sweat. They had bulging scrotums, necks like tree stumps, shoulders you could break a two-by-four across. Some of the Negroes were as black as paint, the Caucasians so white their skin had a shine to it. And they all seemed to contain a reservoir of rut and power and ruthless energy that made you shudder when you considered the fact that soon they would be back on the street.

Their tattoos were a marvel: spiders in purple webs stretched across the shoulder blades, serpents twined around biceps and forearms, beret-capped skulls, hearts impaled on knives, swastikas clutched in eagle claws, green dragons blowing fire across loins, Confederate flags, lily-wrapped crucifixes, and the face of Christ with beads of blood upon his tortured brow.

For a moment we almost had trouble. A tall white man with a black goatee, wearing only a jockstrap and tennis shoes, sat against the wall and wiped his chest and stomach with a tattered gray towel. His eyes focused on my face and stayed there; then he said, 'I know that guy. He's a cop.'

The clanking of the barbells stopped. The room was absolutely quiet.

Then a big black man, with a nylon stocking crimped on his head, set down his weights and said to me, 'What about it, Home?'

'I look like heat? Take a look at my charge sheet,' I said.

'No, we don't look at nothing. This guy came in with me,' Tony said. He looked down at the tall white man sitting on the floor with his knees splayed open. 'You saying I brought a cop in with me?'

The man's eyes met Tony's, then became close-set and focused on nothing.

'He looked like a guy I used to see around,' he said. 'Some other guy.'

The room remained quiet. I could hear traffic out on the street. Everyone was watching Tony.

'So don't worry about it,' he said. He laughed, pulled the towel from the man's hand, and rubbed the man's head with it. 'Hey, what's with this crazy guy? Y'all made him weird or is that the way they come in from Jump Street these days?'

The man grinned sheepishly; then everyone was laughing, clanging the barbells again, grabbing themselves, nodding to one another in admiration of Tony's intelligence and wit or whatever quality it was that allowed him to charm a snake back into a basket.

Tony walked past me out the door, his smile welded on his face, and nudged me in the side with his thumb. We walked side by side back toward our cell. He kept his face straight. He whistled a disjointed tune and then said, 'Do you know who that guy was?'

'No, I don't remember him.'

'He did a snitch with an ice pick in Angola for twenty bucks. Let's play a lot of checkers today, hang around the cell, talk about books, you get my drift?'

'You're a piece of work, Tony.'
'What I am is too old for this shit.'

But our worries about the group in the weight room were unnecessary. Tony's lawyer had us sprung by noon, all charges dropped. Nate Baxter had not had probable cause to stop and search us, Tony's lawyer had produced the permit for Tony's pistol, and the charge against me – interfering with an officer in the performance of his duty – was a manufactured one that the prosecutor's office wouldn't waste time on. The only loser was Jess, who had his .410 shotgun pistol confiscated.

We picked up the Lincoln at the car pound and Tony treated us to lunch at an outdoor café on St. Charles. It was a lovely fall day, seventy-five degrees, perhaps, with a soft wind out of the south that lifted the moss in the oak trees along the avenue. A Negro was selling snow cones, which people in New Orleans call snowballs, out of a white cart, with a canvas umbrella over it, on the esplanade. The dry fronds of a thick-trunked palm tree covered his white uniform with shifting patterns of etched lines. I heard the streetcar tracks begin to hum, then farther up the avenue I saw the streetcar wobbling down the esplanade in a smoky cone of light and shadow created by the canopy of oaks.

'When we were kids we used to put pennies on the tracks and flatten them out to the size of half-dollars,' Tony said, wiping the tomato sauce from his shrimp off his mouth with a napkin. 'They'd still be hot in your hand when you picked them up.'

'That's not all you done when you were a kid,'

Jess said. 'You remember when you and your cousins found them arms behind the Tulane medical school?' Jess looked at me. 'That's right. They got this whole pile of arms that was supposed to be burned in the incinerator. Except Tony and his cousins put them on crushed ice in a beer cooler and got on the streetcar with them when all the coloreds were just getting off work. They waited until it was wall-to-wall people, then they hung a half dozen of these arms from the hand straps. People were screaming all over the car, trampling each other to get out the door, climbing out the windows at thirty miles an hour. One big fat guy crashed right on top of the snowball stand.'

'Hey, don't tell Dave that stuff. He's going to think I'm a ghoul or something,' Tony said.

'Tony used to flush M-80s down the commode at the Catholic school,' Jess said. 'See, the fire would burn down through the center of the fuse. They'd get way back in the plumbing before they'd explode, then anybody taking a dump would get douched with pot water.'

People at the other tables turned and stared at us, openmouthed.

'You finished eating, Jess?' Tony said.

'I'm going to get some pecan pie,' Jess said.

'How about bringing the car around? I've got to get home,' Tony said.

'What'd I do this time?'

'Nothing, Jess. You're fine.'

'You make me feel like I ought to be in a plastic bubble or something. I was just telling a story.'

'It's okay, Jess. Just get the car,' Tony said. Then after Jess was gone, he said to me. 'What am I going to do? He's the one loyal guy I got. When it comes to protecting me, you could bust a chair across his face and he wouldn't blink.'

A few minutes later Jess came around the corner in the convertible and waited for us in front of the restaurant. Leaves blew under the wire wheels.

'You guys drop me by my apartment so I can get my truck,' I said. 'I'll be back out to your house a little later.'

Tony grinned, 'I bet you're off to see Bootsie. Tell her hello for me,' he said.

His presumption that Bootsie should have been uppermost in my mind was right – but she wasn't. After they left me at my apartment on Ursulines I called Minos at the guesthouse.

'I'm sorry you had to spend a night in the bag. How was it?' he said.

'What do you think?' Through the window I could see my neighbor's bluetick dog urinating against a banana tree in the flower bed.

'Look, I've got some news about Boggs, some of which I don't understand. An informant told our Lafayette office that Boggs was in New Iberia two days ago. What would he be doing in New Iberia?'

'Where'd your snitch see him?'

'In a black neighborhood, out in the parish. Why would Boggs be in a black neighborhood?'

'Tony said Boggs told him he was going to blackmail a Negro woman who owned a hot-pillow joint. It had something to do with the murder of a redbone. I think the redbone was a migrant-labor contractor named Hipolyte Broussard. But Boggs told all this to Cardo before he ripped off the coke

256

out on the salt. I don't know why he'd be interested in some minor-league blackmail when he's holding a half-million dollars' worth of cocaine.'

'I don't either. Anyway, we have some other information, too. We've got some taps on the greaseballs over in Houston. It's not an open contract on Cardo anymore. Boggs has got the hit. It's fifty grand, a big-money whack even for these guys. But they want it to go down in the next week.'

'Why the hurry?'

'They're afraid of him. Tony C. isn't one to take prisoners. One guy on the tape says it might have to be a slop shot. Have you heard that one before?'

'Yes.'

'There're no innocent bystanders. His wife, his kid, anybody around him, they're all targets if necessary. Dave, if Boggs *was* in New Iberia, do you think it has something to do with you?'

'Why?'

'Who has more reason to want you off the board? It's turned around on him. I bet he gets up thinking about you in the morning.'

'Maybe.'

'Look, I want to push this stuff to a head. Can you get a wire into Cardo's house?'

'I think so.'

'Either you can or you can't, Dave.'

'I can try, Minos.'

'Once again I'm getting a strong impression here of a lack of enthusiasm.'

'What do you expect? I'm a hired Judas goat. You want me to tell you I like it?'

He paused a moment; then he said in an even voice, 'We hear a big load of coke is going to hit

257

town in three or four days. A lot of it is going to end up as crack in the welfare projects.'

I looked out the window into the courtyard, where my neighbor was trying to leash his dog in the flower bed.

'Are you there?'

'Yeah,' I said.

'You know the scene. A human life isn't worth a stick of chewing gum in those places. All thanks to Tony C. and his friends.'

'How do you want to work it?'

'Find out his connections with the shipment. Then we'll wire you. All we need is a statement that he's in on the buy or the distribution.'

'All right.'

'You sound like you've got something else on your mind.'

'It's Kim Dollinger. I think somebody's got her out there twisting in the wind.'

'Why?'

'She was terrified when we got busted yesterday.'

'Who's she afraid of?'

'Tony, Nate Baxter, you guys. How should I know?'

'It's not us. You want us to pick her up?'

'She's a hard-nosed girl. She won't cooperate. Baxter let her walk. Why would he let *her* walk when he rousted the rest of us? It was a good opportunity to squeeze her.'

'From what I hear about this guy, he's about as complicated as an empty closet. Save yourself a lot of grief and don't make a mystery out of morons.'

'If I only had that clarity of line, Minos.'

'Work on it. It'll come with time.'

After I hung up, I shaved, showered, and changed into a pair of clean gray slacks, a maroon shirt, combed my hair in the mirror, put a touch of Vaseline on the hard knot of stitches in my lip and head, and buffed my loafers.

I tried to keep my mind blank and not think about the care I was putting into my appearance.

Then I drove down St. Charles to South Carrollton and parked my pickup truck in front of the nineteenth-century building by the levee where Kim Dollinger lived.

Her apartment was on the second floor, and there was a hand-twist bell on the door. I had to ring it twice before she answered, a towel in her hand, her neck spotted with water. She wore jeans, tan sandals, and a white peasant blouse with a pink ribbon threaded through the top. The front of her blouse hung straight down from her breasts.

'Oh boy,' she said.

'May I come in?'

She blotted the water on her neck and looked into my face.

'I'm getting ready to go to work,' she said.

Her back window was open, and I smelled the draft that blew out into the hall.

'That's not all you've been doing,' I said.

'Look—'

'Come on, I just got out of the bag. You can't offer me a cup of coffee?'

She stood back from the door for me to enter. I heard her close it behind me. Through the open window I could see the green of the levee and the wide, flat expanse of the Mississippi and the sandy

259

bank and willow trees on the far side. The living room looked furnished from a secondhand store. Off to the side was a small kitchen with bright yellow linoleum. She sat down at a breakfast table that was located between the kitchen and living room. The legs of the table and chairs were chrome and had rusty scratches on them that looked like dismembered parts of insects.

'Kim, I'm not telling you what to do, but if you've already got the dragons after you, reefer just makes the problem a lot worse,' I said.

She crumpled the towel on the tabletop. Her eyes looked out into space.

'What is it that you want?' she said.

'To talk with you on the square, with no bullshit.'

'That's it? Nothing else?'

'That's right.'

'You wouldn't like to ball me while you're at it, would you?'

'Cut the badass act, Kim. It's a drag.'

'I tried to talk with you. You wouldn't hear me.'

'I can get you out of this.'

'You?'

'That's right.'

'A guy with a mouthful of stitches.'

'I'm tired of being your dartboard. You'd better listen when a friend is talking to you.'

She put the heel of her hand against her forehead. Her skin reddened from the pressure. She crossed her legs and breathed through her mouth. There were patches of color in her throat and cheeks. She made me think of someone who might have been wrapped in invisible rope.

'Have you ever been down?' I said.

'Have I what?' Her mouth hung open.

'Have you ever done time?'

'No.'

'Are you sure?'

'I said no.'

'Have you been in custody?'

'You stop talking to me like this. Why are you saying these things to me?' Her voice started to break.

'Because somebody is turning the screws on you. I suspect it's Nate Baxter. He's a sonofabitch, Kim, and I know what he's capable of.'

She pushed the heel of her hand along her hairline.

'What does Tony know?' she said.

'I couldn't guess. Do you sleep with him?' My eyes shifted away from her face, and I didn't want to hear her answer.

'I used to. When he wanted me to, anyway. He doesn't want to anymore. It's the speed. It's messed him up.'

I glanced back at her face again. Her eyes met mine, then they looked away. There was a tingling in my throat, like a heated wire trembling against a nerve.

'Did somebody make you sleep with him?' I said.

'You don't have the right to ask me these things.'

'If Nate Baxter is behind this, he's going to have the worst experience of his life.'

'There's nothing you can do. It involves somebody else. Oh God, where's my stash?' she said.

She got up from the table, took a clear, sealed plastic bag of reefer from a kitchen drawer, sat back down, and began to roll a joint from a sheaf of

261

ZigZag cigarette papers. Her eyes were narrowed with concentration, but her fingers began to shake and strands of reefer fell from both sides of the paper. Then she gave it up, rested her elbows on the table, and pressed a knuckle from each hand against her temples.

I picked up the plastic bag, splayed it open, dropped the papers inside, raked the loose strands of reefer into it, and walked down a short hallway to the bathroom.

'What are you doing?' she said.

I emptied the bag into the toilet and flushed it. Then I dropped the bag into a kitchen garbage sack. When I turned around she was standing a foot from me. Her hair hung on her forehead, and she had accidentally smeared her lipstick.

'Why did you do that?' she said.

'You don't need it.'

'I don't need it?'

'No.'

'Tony says it's all a cluster fuck.'

'He's wrong.'

Her eyes were green and moist and they looked directly into mine. I could hear the wetness in her throat when she swallowed. The top of her pink-ribboned peasant blouse was crooked on her shoulders.

'There's always a way out of trouble,' I said. 'You just have to trust your friends once in a while.'

I touched her on the upper arm with my palm. I meant it in a protective and friendly way. Yes, I know that was the way I meant it. I could see the freckles on her shoulders, feel her breath on my face. She stepped close to me, and my arms were on her back, my hands lightly touching the coolness of her skin, the thickness of her hair. She rubbed her face under my chin, and I felt a shudder go through her body like tension leaving a metal spring.

Then she remained motionless in my arms, her breath small and regular against my chest. In the distance, I could see the hard, stiff outline of the Huey Long Bridge against a bank of purple rain clouds.

11

After I left Kim's, I drove into the French Quarter
and tried to find a place to park close by Clete's
nightclub. But it was Saturday afternoon, the
Quarter was crowded with tourists, and I had to
park off Elysian Fields and walk back down Decatur
to the club. A noisy crowd was at the bar, and a five-
piece band was blaring out 'Rampart Street Parade'
by the dance floor.

'Take a walk with me,' I said to Clete, who was
behind the bar in a pair of gray slacks and a green
Tulane sweatshirt.

'It's a little busy right now, Streak.'

'It's important.'

We crossed the street and walked down to the
Café du Monde, where I ordered *beignets* through
the takeout window.

'Beautiful day,' I said.

'I'm not kidding, Dave, I've got a bar to run.
What is it?'

'Come on,' I said. We walked over the top of the
levee and out on to the gentle green slope that led
down to the river. On the far side of the river was
the shabby outline of Algiers. 'I need a cover story.'

His eyes went up and down my shirt.

'What are you talking about?' he said.

'Minos is going to put a wire on me. I need to make Tony talk about a big drug delivery that's about to go down. I have to have some way of bringing it up.'

'You might need a cover story about something else,' he said, and reached out and removed a long strand of red hair from my shirtfront. 'Brush up against somebody in the streetcar, did you?'

'Let's keep to the subject.'

'Have you lost your mind?'

'Lay off it, Clete.'

'I told you one of the cardinal rules when you get involved with the greaseballs: Don't mess with their broads.'

'Have you heard anything about a big delivery?'

'I bet she's one hot item, though, isn't she?'

'I need your help. Will you cut out the bullshit.'

He took a *beignet* out of the napkin in my hand and bit off half of it. His green eyes were thoughtful as he looked out at the river.

'I hear crack prices are up in the Iberville welfare project, which means the supply is down,' he said. 'But next week everybody is going to have all the rock they can smoke. That's the word, anyway. What's the DEA say?'

'Same thing.'

'That crack is some mean shit. You ever watch them huff that stuff? They remind me of somebody having a seizure.'

'You know I'm staying out at Cardo's?'

'I called Dautrieve. He told me. Why is it that guy makes me feel like anthrax?'

'Boggs has been given a contract on Cardo.'

'And you're living with him? That's great, Streak. Maybe you ought to look into some real estate buys on the San Andreas fault.'

'I'm going to play it one more week, then I'm out.'

'I think you're *in*. The operative word there, mon, is *in*. Bootsie Giacano wasn't dangerous enough. You had to get in the sack with Cardo's main punch.'

'That's not the way it is. Don't talk about her that way, either, Clete.'

'Excuse me. It's my lack of couth. We're talking the parochial school sodality here. Dave, you'd better get your head on straight. You live among these people, you start to believe they're like us. They're not, mon. When it comes down to saving their own ass, they'd sell their mothers to a puppy farm.'

'Boggs has been in New Iberia. I think he's got me on his dance card. I'd rather deal with him in New Orleans than around Alafair.'

'I think you're being used. I think you should forget Cardo and these DEA jerk-offs and you and I should go after Boggs and blow out his candle. What do you care if Cardo sells dope? You shut him down, the price on the street goes up. The dealers come out ahead any way you cut it. Look, most of the dope has gone back to the slums, anyway. That's where it started, that's where it's going to stay. Then one day the poor dumb bastards will get tired of watching their own kind get hauled away in body bags.'

'I was in jail last night. Nate Baxter roused Tony and me and his driver. Can you get to somebody in the First District, find out what Baxter's doing?'

266

'In jail?'

'That's right.'

'You remind me of these kids with their crack pipes. It takes a guy like me twenty years to go to hell. They can do it in six months. But, Streak, you've got a talent for fucking up your life in weeks.'

'Will you see what you can find out about Baxter?'

'A cop who blew the country with a murder warrant on him? I'm your liaison person?'

He put the rest of the *beignet* in his mouth and laughed while he rubbed his palm clean with his napkin.

I walked back to my truck in the cooling shadows and drove down Canal to the corner of St. Charles, where Clete had seen Tee Beau Latiolais working in a pizza place. Young black men lounged in front of the liquor stores and arcades, their bodies striped with the purple and pink neon glow from the windows. I found Tee Beau in the back of a long, narrow café, his white paper hat pulled down to his eyebrows, so that he seemed to be staring at me from under a visor.

'Take a break. I need to talk to you, Tee Beau,' I said.

His eyes were peculiar, melancholy, as though he were witnessing a bad fate for a friend that the friend was not aware of.

'What is it?' I said.

He didn't answer. He wiped his hands on his apron and put on a pair of sunglasses. We walked around the corner to the Pearl and sat at the bar. A white man farther down the bar was shucking oysters with a fierce energy on a sideboard. Tee

Beau ordered a Falstaff and kept looking at me out of the side of his eye.

'You know, Tee Beau, I don't think sunglasses in the evening are the best kind of disguise.'

'Why you want to see me, Mr. Dave?'

'I heard Jimmie Lee Boggs has been in New Iberia. I'd like to find out why. Can you talk to Dorothea?'

'I ain't got to. Talked to her last night. She didn't say nothing about seeing Jimmie Lee. But she tole me what Gros Mama Goula say about you, Mr. Dave.'

'Oh?'

'You got the *gris-gris.* she say you been messin' where you ain't suppose to be messin'. You ain't listen to nobody.'

'Listen, Tee Beau, Gros Mama is a big black gasbag. She jerks your people around with a lot of superstition that goes back to the islands, back to the slave days.'

But my words meant nothing to him.

'I made you this, Mr. Dave. I was gonna come find you.'

'I appreciate it, but—'

'You put it on your ankle, you.'

I made no offer to take the perforated dime and the piece of red string looped through it from his hand. He dropped them in my shirt pocket.

'You white, you been to colletch, you don't believe,' he said. 'But I seen things. A man that had snakes crawl all over his grave. They was fat as my wrist. Couldn't keep them off the grave with poison or a shotgun. You stick a hayfork in them, shake them off in a fire, they be back the next morning,

268

smelling like they been lying in hot ash.

'A woman name Miz Gold, 'cause her skin was gold, she taken a man away from Gros Mama, then come in Gros Mama's juke with him, wearing a pink silk dress, carrying a pink umbrella, laughing about Gros Mama's tattoos and saying she ain't nothing but a nigger *putain* that does what white mens tells her. The next day Miz Gold woke up with hair all over her face. Just like a monkey. She do everything to get rid of it, Mr. Dave, pull it out of her skin with pliers till blood run down her neck. But it didn't do no good. That woman so ugly nobody go near her, no white peoples hire her. She used to go up and down the alley, picking rags out of my *gran'maman*'s trash can.'

'Okay, Tee Beau, I'll keep it all in mind.'

'No, you ain't. In one way you like most white folks, Mr. Dave. You don't hear what a black man saying to you.'

He upended his bottle of Falstaff and looked at me over the top of his glasses.

The evening air was cool and moist, purple with shadow, when I walked back to my truck. I saw a car parked overtime at a meter. I broke the red string off the perforated dime that Tee Beau had given me, slipped the dime into the meter, and twisted the handle. In front of the liquor store two Negro men in bright print shirts and lacquered porkpie hats were snapping their fingers to the music on a boom box. One of them smiled at me for no reason, his teeth a brilliant flash of gold.

I didn't go back to Tony's right away. Instead, I parked by Jackson Square and sat on a stone bench

269

in front of St. Louis Cathedral and watched people leaving Saturday evening Mass. My head was filled with confused thoughts, like a clatter of birds' wings inside a cage. I used a pay phone on the corner to call Bootsie, but she wasn't home. The square was dark now, the myrtle and banana trees etched in the light from the Café du Monde, and there was a chill in the wind off the river. After the cathedral had emptied, I went inside and knelt in a back pew. A tiny red light, like a drop of electrified blood, glowed at the top of a confessional box, which meant that a priest was inside.

Many people are currently enamored with Cajun culture, but they know little of its darker side: organized dogfights and cockfights, the casual attitude toward the sexual exploitation of Negro women, the environmental ignorance that has allowed the draining and industrial poisoning of the wetlands. Also, few outsiders understand the violent feelings that Cajun people have about the nature of fidelity, and human possession.

When I was twenty I worked as a welder's helper with my father on a pipeline outside of a little town north of the Atchafalaya Basin. Someone discovered that a married woman in the town was having an affair with the priest. A mob came for her at night, in a caravan of cars, and took her from her home and drove her to an empty field next to the church. They formed a circle around her, and while she cried and begged they beat her black and blue with hairbrushes. Simultaneously someone phoned her husband at his job in Baton Rouge and told him of his wife's infidelity. He was killed driving home that night in a rainstorm.

Some might simply explain it as redneck bigotry, but I think it is much more complex than that. In the minds of rural Acadian people the priest is the representative of God, and they will not share him or Him. Their violence seldom has to do with money. Instead, it can reach a murderous intensity within minutes over a betrayed trust, a lie, a wrong against a family member. Their sense of loyalty is atavistic and irrational, their sense of loss at its compromise as painful and unexpected, no matter how many times it happens, as a lesion across the heart.

I went inside the confessional. The priest slid back the small wooden door behind the screen, and I could see the gray outline of his head. His voice was that of an elderly man, and I also discovered that he was hard of hearing. I tried to explain to him the nature of my problem, but he only became more confused.

'I'm an undercover police officer, Father. My work requires that I betray some people. These are bad people, I suppose, or what they do is bad, but I don't feel good about it.'

'I don't understand.'

'I'm lying to people. I pretend to be something I'm not. I feel I'm making an enormous deception out of my life.'

'Because you want to arrest these people?'

'I'm a drunk. I belong to AA. Honesty is supposed to be everything in our program.'

'You're drunk? Now?'

I tried again.

'I've become romantically involved with a woman. She's an old friend from my hometown. I hurt her many years ago. I think I'm going to hurt her again.'

He was quiet. He had a cold and he sniffed into a handkerchief.

'I don't understand what you're telling me,' he said.

'I was shot last summer, Father. I almost died. As a result I developed great fears about myself. To overcome them I became involved in an undercover sting. Now I think maybe other people might have to pay the price for my problem – the woman from my hometown, a man with a crippled child, a young woman I was with today, one I feel an attraction to when I shouldn't.'

His head was bent forward. His handkerchief was crumpled in his hand.

'Can you just tell me the number of the commandments you've broken and the number of times?' he asked. 'That's all we really need to do right now.'

He waited, and it was obvious that his need for understanding, at least in that moment, was as great as mine.

Sunday morning Tony and I took Paul horseback riding on the farm of one of Tony's mobster friends down in Plaquemines Parish. Tony had dressed Paul in a brown corduroy coat and trousers, with a tan suede bill cap, and he balanced Paul in front of him on the saddle while we walked our horses along the edge of a barbed-wire-fenced hardpan field a hundred yards from the Gulf. The grass in the field was pale green, and white egrets picked in the dry cow flop. The few palm trees along the narrow stretch of beach were yellowed with blight, and they clattered and straightened in the wind that was blowing hard off the water. Behind us, parked by a tight grove of oak trees, were the Lincoln and the white Cadillac limousine. Jess and Tony's other bodyguards and gunmen were drinking canned beer and eating fried chicken out of paper buckets in the sunshine and entertaining themselves by popping their pistols at sea gulls out on a sandspit. Tony wore a white cashmere jacket, a safari hat, and riding breeches tucked inside his knee-high leather boots.

He kept wetting his lips in the wind. His skin was stretched tight around his eyes.

'How do I look?' he said.

'Good.'

'I mean how do *I* look?' He turned his face toward me and looked into my eyes.

'You look fine, Tony.'

'It's been two days since I put anything in the tank. It's got butterflies fluttering around in my head.'

'What tank, Daddy?' Paul said.

'I'm trying to get on a diet and get my blood pressure down. That's all, son,' Tony said.

'What butterflies?' Paul said.

'When I don't eat what I want, the butterflies start flitting around me. Big purple and yellow ones. Boy, do I got 'em today. Listen to those guys shooting back there. You go out to a quiet spot in the country, they turn it into a war zone.'

'Who's trying to hurt us, Daddy?' Paul asked.

'Nobody. Who told you that?'

'Jess. He said some bad man wants to hurt us.'

'Jess isn't too bright sometimes, son. He imagines things. Don't pay attention to him.' Tony looked back over his shoulder at the grove of oak trees, where his hired men lounged around the automobile fenders in sport clothes and shoulder holsters. His eyes were dark, and he rubbed his tongue hard against the back of his teeth. Then he took a deep breath through his nose.

'Paul and me have got a place down in Mexico, don't we, Paul?' he said. 'It's not much, thirty acres outside of Guadalajara, but it's got a fishing pond, a bunch of goats and chickens and stuff like that, doesn't it, Paul? It's quiet, too. Nobody bothers us there, either.'

'My mother says it's full of snakes. She won't go there anymore.'

'Which means there's no shopping mall where she can spend three or four hundred bucks a day. You ever been down there, Dave?'

'No.'

'If I could ever get some things straightened out here in the right way, I might want to move down there. If you're a gringo, you've got to pay off a few of the local greasers, but after that, they treat you okay.'

'Can we go eat now, Dad?'

'Sure,' Tony said. 'You want to eat, Dave?'

'That's a good idea.'

We could heard the flat popping sound of the pistols in the wind. We would see the smoke first, then hear the report carried to us across the flattened grass.

'Those guys and their guns. What a pain in the ass,' Tony said.

'You said not to use bad words, Daddy,' Paul said.

Tony smiled and popped up the bill of his little boy's cap.

'You got me there. But what do you do with a bunch like that? Not one of them could rub two thoughts together on his best day.' Then Tony twisted in the saddle and lifted his finger at me. In the chill sunlight his face looked as though it had been boiled empty of all heat and coherence. 'I've got to talk with you, man,' he said.

We tethered our horses in the oak grove, and Tony put Paul in his wheelchair and fixed him a paper plate of fried chicken and potato salad. Then he picked up a half-filled bucket of chicken, tossed it at me, and climbed over the barbed-wire fence out on to the beach. I followed him out on to the damp gray sand.

'I got something bugging the fuck out of me,' he said. 'I got to get rid of it, or I'm gonna shoot up again. I get back on the spike, I'm gonna end. I've got no illusions about that.'

'Maybe it's time to unload, Tony.'

'I already did. It didn't do any good. It just made it worse.'

'Then you're holding on to it for some reason.'

'That's what you think, huh?' He had a half-eaten drumstick in his hand. He flung it hard at a sea gull that was hovering above the waves. The water was dark green and full of kelp. 'Try this. I went to a psychiatrist, a ninety-buck-an-hour Tulane fruit, in a peppermint-stripe shirt with one of these round white collars. You dig the type I'm talking about? A guy about six and a half feet long, except he's made out of marshmallows. So I told him finally about some stuff back there in Vietnam, and he starts to make fun of me. With this simpering voice, like psychiatrists use when they got no answers for the problem. He says, 'Ah, I see, you're the big brave warrior who can't have weaknesses like everybody else. Tony's the superstud, the macho man from Mother Green's killing machine. Tony's not going to let anyone know he's human, too. Why, that'd be a disappointment to the whole human race.'

'Then he stretches his legs out and looks me in the eye like he's just taken my soul out of my chest with a pair of tweezers. So I say, "Doc, you're one clever guy. But there're certain things you don't say to certain guys unless you've gotten your own ticket punched a couple of times. I've got the feeling you're short on dues. And when you're short on dues and you run off at the mouth with the wrong people, you ought to expect certain consequences. What that means is you get the shit stomped out of you."'

Tony sat down on a beached cypress tree that was white with rot. The sand was littered with jellyfish that had been left behind by the tide. Their air sacs were pink and blue and translucent, their stingers coated with grit.

'So he stops smiling,' Tony said. 'In fact, his mouth is looking a little rubbery, like he just stopped sucking on a doorknob. I say, "But don't sweat it, Doc, because I don't beat up on fruits. But if you ever talk to me like that again, or you talk to other shrinks about me, or you put any of this dog shit in your files, somebody's gonna pull you out of Lake Pontchartrain with some of your parts missing."'

Tony breathed the salt wind through his nose, then popped the air sac of a jellyfish with the tip of his boot.

'Yeah, I guess that really solved your problem,' I said.

'You cracking wise with me, Dave?'

'I just don't know what I can tell you. Or what you want from me.'

'Tell me how come I don't get any relief.'

'I never figured out all my own problems. I'm probably the wrong guy to talk to, Tony.'

'You're the right guy.'

'I think you want forgiveness. From somebody who counts. The psychiatrist didn't count because he hadn't paid any dues.'

'Who's gonna hand out this forgiveness?'

'It'll have to come from somebody who's important to you. God, a priest, somebody whose experience you respect. Finally yourself, Tony. A psychiatrist with any brains would have told you that.'

'A guy like me is going to a priest?' He grinned and scraped out long divots in the sand with his boot heel. In the quiet I could hear the hiss of the waves as they receded from the beach. Then he cocked his eye and looked up at me from under the brim of his safari hat. 'Hey, don't be offended. You know stuff. You know more than any shrink.'

'You inflate my value, Tony.'

'No, I don't. You're one all-together, copacetic motherfucker, Robicheaux.'

His head nodded up and down, one eye

squinting at me as though he were fixing me inside telescopic sights.

'You've got the wrong man,' I said.

That evening Tony and Paul and I ate supper by candlelight in his dining room. We had boiled early potatoes, string beans cooked with mushrooms, and lamb glazed with a sauce made from orange marmalade; the burgundy that Tony drank must have cost fifty dollars a bottle. The tablecloth was Irish linen; in the center was a crystal bowl of water filled with floating camellias. The dessert was a choice of chocolate mousse or French vanilla ice cream or both.

Later, while Tony and his son watched television, I strolled through the grounds behind the house in the twilight. The Saint Augustine grass was thick and stiff under my feet, the flower beds absolutely weedless, the dead banana leaves and palm fronds trimmed back daily so that everything in Tony's yard looked green and full of bloom, regardless of the season.

But what was life like for most people in New Orleans that year? I asked myself. Or what had become of the city itself in the last five years?

Even a tourist could answer those questions. The bottom had dropped out of the oil market and the economy was worse than it had been anytime since the Depression. Cardboard boxes and sacks of raw garbage sat on the sidewalks for days, humming with flies; derelicts and bag ladies rooted in trash cans on Canal for food. The homicide rate had reached an average of one murder a day. If your automobile was burglarized, or all its windows smashed out with bricks, you probably would not be able to get a policeman at the scene for an hour and a half. The St. Louis Cemetery off Basin, which had always been one of the city's most interesting tourist attractions, was now so dangerous that you could enter it only on a group tour conducted by an off-duty police officer. The welfare projects – the St. Bernard, the St. Thomas, the Iberville off Canal, or, the worst of them all, the Desire – were spread throughout the city, and within them was everything bad that human society could produce: rats, cockroaches, incest, rape, child molestation, narcotics, and sadistic street gangs. Black teenagers armed with nine-millimeter pistols and semi-automatic assault rifles made large profits trafficking in crack, and they would kill absolutely anyone who tried to stop them. A black leader in the Desire project announced publicly that he was going to run the drug dealers out of the neighborhood. Two days later he was gunned down by a pair of fifteen-year-old kids, and while he lay bleeding on the sidewalk they broke his ribs with a baseball bat.

I sat on a stone bench by Tony's clay tennis court and watched the twilight fade in the stillness. The western sky was the dull gray color of scraped bone. One of the gatemen turned on the flood lamps that were anchored in the oak trees along the outer walls, and the fish ponds, the birdbaths, the alabaster statues on the lawn, seemed to glow with a humid, electric aura as though the coming of the night had no application to Tony's world.

I could see him through the glassed-in sun porch, watching television with Paul, his face laughing at a joke told by a comedian. I wondered if Tony ever

279

thought about life in New Orleans's welfare projects or that army of teenage crack addicts who cooked their brains for breakfast. I thought he probably did not.

I called Bootsie twice that evening. She wasn't home either time, but the next morning I was up early and caught her at six. Her voice was warm and full of sleep.

'I've been trying to get hold of you,' I said.

'I've been out of town.'

'Where?'

'Over at Houston. At Baylor.'

'At the hospital?'

'Yes.'

'What were you doing at Baylor?'

'Oh, it's nothing.'

'Boots?'

'Yes?'

'What are you holding out on me?'

'Don't worry about it, hon. When am I going to see you?'

'Can I come by now?' I said.

'Mmmm, what'd you have in mind?'

I suddenly realized that I didn't have an honest answer to her question.

'Because I have to go to work, hon,' she said.

'I just wanted to see you, to talk to you.'

'Is something wrong?'

'No, not really,' I said. 'Look, Boots, I have to go over to the apartment in a little bit and pick up some things. Your office is only a few blocks away. Can you come by for a few minutes? I'll fix breakfast for us.'

'I'll try,' she said. 'Dave, what is it?'

I took a breath.

'People just need to talk sometimes. This is one of them,' I said.

'Yes, I think it is,' she said.

I gave her my address on Ursulines.

'Dave?' she said.

'Yes.'

'I don't get hurt easily anymore. If that's what we're talking about.'

'We're not talking about that at all,' I said.

After I hung up the phone I looked out the window at the early sun shining through the trees in Tony's yard, the wind ruffling on his fish ponds, the flapping of the dew-soaked canvas screens on his tennis court. But I took no joy in the new morning.

I drove into the center of the city and parked my truck in the garage on Ursulines, then went through the domed brick archway into the courtyard. The flagstones were streaked with water, and I could smell coffee and bacon from someone's apartment. Upstairs on the balcony a fat woman in a print dress was sweeping dust out through the grillwork into the sunlight.

I had my keys in my hand before I noticed the soft white gashes, in the shape of a screwdriver head, between the door and jamb of my apartment. I slipped my .45 out of the back of my trousers, let it hang loosely at my side, pushed the sprung door back on its hinges with my foot, and stepped inside.

My eyes would not encompass or accept the interior of the apartment all at once, in the way that your mind rejects the appearance of your car after a street gang has worked it over with curbstones. A large bullfrog was nailed to the back of the door. Its puffed white belly was split by the force of the nail, its legs hung down limply, and its wide flat mouth stretched open as though it were waiting for a fly.

The ceiling, the walls, the cheap furniture, were dotted with blood as though it had been slung there in patterns. Above the kitchen doorway, painted redly into the plaster, were the words YOU ARE DED. The blood had run in strings down the plaster and dripped into the linoleum.

But my bedroom was untouched, and I thought I had seen the worst of it until I looked into the bathroom. The toilet lid was closed, but blood and water had swelled over the lip and streamed down the white porcelain, too thick and dark for the dilution that should have taken place. Written with a ballpoint pen on a damp sheet of lined paper that lay on the toilet lid were the words DONT FLUSH. MY BABY IS INSIDE.

I stuck the .45 through the back of my belt and started to raise the lid, then withdrew my hand. Don't rattle, I thought. They didn't do it, they didn't do *that*.

I went into the kitchen, tore off a section of paper towel, folded it in a neat square, and went back into the bathroom to lift the toilet lid. My neighbor's bluetick dog floated in the purple water, one eye of his severed head staring up at me, his entrails bulging out of the slit that ran from his testicles to a flap of skin on his neck.

I dropped the bloody piece of paper towel in the wastebasket, turned around, and saw Bootsie frozen in the doorway, her hand pinched to her mouth, her cheeks discolored, her pulse leaping in her neck.

12

She sat alone in the bedroom while I talked to two uniformed cops who had been called by the apartment owner. A black man from the city health department dipped the dog's remains out of the toilet with a fishnet, while my neighbors stared through the open front door of the apartment. I told the cops a second time that I had no idea who had done it.

One of them wrote on his clipboard. There were red marks on his nose where he had taken off his sunglasses, and his sky-blue shirt was stretched tightly across his muscular chest.

'You think maybe somebody just doesn't like you?' he asked.

'Could be,' I said.

'You're not in a cult, are you?' He grinned at the corner of his mouth.

'No, I don't know much about cults.'

He put his ballpoint pen in his shirt pocket.

'Well, there're a lot of spaced-out dopers around these days. Maybe that's all there was to it,' he said. 'I'd get some better locks, though.'

'Thank y'all for coming out.'

'Mr. Robicheaux, you say you used to be a police officer?'

'That's right.'

'You never heard about a nailed-up frog before?'

I cleared my throat and looked away from his eyes.

'Maybe I heard something. It's a little vague.'

He smiled to himself, then wrote out a number on a piece of paper and handed it to me.

'Here's the report number in case you or the owner needs it for an insurance claim. Call us if we can help you in any way,' he said.

They left and closed the door behind them. There's a cop who won't have to write traffic tickets too long, I thought.

Back in the bedroom Bootsie sat on the side of my bed, her hands folded in her lap. Her cotton dress was covered with gray and pink flowers.

'I'm sorry you had to arrive in the middle of all this,' I said.

'Dave, that officer was talking about a cult. Do you know people like that?'

'It wasn't done by cultists. He knew it, too.'

'What?'

'I'm supposed to think I've got a *gris-gris* on me. You remember a Negro woman called Gros Mama Goula in New Iberia?'

'She ran a brothel?'

'That's the one. She'd like to shake up my cookie bag. She either sent some of her people over here to do this, or it was done by a guy named Jimmie Lee Boggs. But my guess is that the two of them are working together.'

'I just don't understand.'

'These are people who for one reason or another would like me to disappear. So they put on this *gris-gris* show. But whoever did this has probably spent some time in a southern prison. A frog with a nail through it means a guy had better jump or he's going to have a bad fate.'

I saw her face becoming more and more clouded.

'Bootsie, these guys are dimwits. They're always looking for something new or clever to dress up their act. When they do some bullshit like this, it's because they're running scared.'

'I've heard that name Boggs,' she said. 'I get the feeling he's taken very seriously.'

'All right, he's got the contract on Tony C. He's also the guy who shot me last summer. But I think Jimmie Lee's scared. It's turned around on him.'

'Dave, what in God's name are you doing? Why did you bring me here this morning?'

'I'm not sure, Boots.'

'God, you're incredible.'

'Maybe I don't think I'm doing right by you.'

This time her eyes saw meaning in my face.

'I hurt you real bad a long time ago. I don't want to do it again,' I said.

Her eyes kept looking up at me. I pulled up a chair and sat across from her.

'Maybe you have some regrets?' she said softly.

'I didn't say that.'

'You love the past, Dave. You love Louisiana the way it used to be. It's changed. Forever. We are, too. Maybe you're discovering that.' She smiled.

'I don't know. I don't learn anything very easily.'

Her eyes went down in her lap, and she brushed her fingers over the fine hair on the back of her wrist.

'Dave, did you do something that bothers you?' she said.

'No.'

'Are we talking about another woman?'

'I'm mixed up with a bunch of people I can't think straight about right now.'

She was quiet for a moment; then she said, 'Who is she?'

'I haven't been untrue to you.' The words sounded hollow, marital, the banal end of something.

'Is she one of Tony's crowd?'

'I'm in a situation where I'm going to have to hurt some people. I don't feel good about it. I got mixed up in it because I was shot by Jimmie Lee Boggs. Now I'm at a place where I don't understand my own feelings.'

'You're an undercover cop, aren't you?'

'I've gotten involved with people whom cops sometimes call lowlifes or geeks or greaseballs. Except I don't feel that way about all of them now, and I should. That's what it amounts to, Bootsie.'

'Do you want it over between us?'

'I don't think it can ever be over between us.'

'You shouldn't count on that,' she said, and I felt my heart drop.

'Can you tell me why you were over at Baylor?' I said.

'Not today. No more today.'

'You're going to close me out? You're not going to let me be your friend when you need one?'

'Do you love me or the past, Dave? Do you think I'm the past? Do I look like the past? Am I the summer of 'fifty-seven?'

Her eyes and her voice were kind, but I had no

answer for her or myself, and the room was so quiet that I could hear the rustle of banana leaves outside the window.

Three hours later I was sitting at a redwood table by the side of Tony's tennis court while he hit balls at Jess Ornella on the opposite side of the net. Jess wore a red sweatsuit and blue boat shoes and clubbed at the balls as though he were under attack. Three dozen balls must have littered the clay court, most of them on his side.

'I tell you what, why don't you get us some iced tea?' Tony said.

'I told you I ain't any good at games,' Jess said.

'You're doing good. Keep working at it. Your stroke's getting better all the time,' Tony said. He sat down at the table with me, patting his neck and face with a towel, and watched Jess walk toward the house. 'He looks like a hog on ice, but you ought to see him fly an airplane.'

'Jess?'

'His old man was a crop duster during the Depression. Jess can thread a needle with anything that has wings on it. One time he flew us upside down under a power line.'

Unconsciously I touched the stitches on my lip. They felt as tight and hard as wire.

'When are you getting them out?' he said.

'Tomorrow.'

'Something on your mind, Dave?'

'I guess I was still thinking about my apartment.'

'Don't go back there. Stay with me as long as you're in New Orleans. You don't need an apartment.'

'I'm still trying to figure out Boggs, too.'

'Why? You like trying to put yourself inside the head of a moron? Look, why do you think a guy like me is successful in this business? I'll tell you. A guy who can walk down the street and chew gum at the same time is king of the block. Take Jess there, and remember he's one of the few I trust, he thinks Peter Pan is the washbasin in a whorehouse.'

'Boggs is smarter than you think.'

'He's a psychopath. Look, the real badasses are in prison or the graveyard. If they're not there yet, they will be. About every two or three months I hear a rumor somebody's going to whack me out. And once in a while somebody tries. But I'm still hitting tennis balls. And a couple of other guys, guys who somebody wound up in Houston or Miami, Jess has driven down into Lafourche Parish and no telling what happened. So if you want into the life, Dave, you don't worry over it. Hey, come on, man, most people grow old and sit on the porch and listen to their livers rot.'

'I've got another problem, too, Tony. My people back in Lafayette want a chance to get their money back. A half million is a lot to lose.'

He picked up his racket cover and began pulling it over the head of his racket.

'They're not looking for a major buy,' I said. 'They just want to recover what they lost.'

He zipped up the leather cover and rested the racket across his thighs.

'Clete says there's a major score about to go down in the projects. I'd like to get in on it,' I said.

He nodded attentively, his eyes looking off into the trees.

'I hear you talking, Dave, but like I once said to

you, I don't do business at my house.' Then he glanced into my face.

'I respect that, Tony, but these guys back in Lafayette are turning some dials on me.'

'Fuck 'em.'

'I've got to live around there.'

'Hey, give me a break. Do I take care of you or not?' His small mouth made that strange butterfly shape.

'I'm just telling you about my situation.'

'All right, for God's sakes. We'll take a drive. You're worse than my wife.'

A few minutes later we were in the Lincoln, driving across the twenty-four-mile causeway that spans Lake Pontchartrain, with Jess and the other bodyguards behind us in the Cadillac. The sun was high in the hard, blue sky, and the waves were green and capping in the wind. Tony drove with his arm on the window, a Marine Corps utility cap pulled down snugly to the level of his sunglasses. His gray and black ringlets whipped on his neck. He looked out at a long barge whose deck was loaded with industrial metal drums of some kind.

'We used to fish and swim in the lake when I was a kid,' he said. 'Now the lake's so polluted it's against the law to get in the water.'

'New Orleans has changed a lot.'

'All for the bad, all for the bad,' he said.

'Can you tell me where we're going now?'

'A place I bet you've never seen. Maybe I'll show you my plane, too.'

'Can we talk now?'

'You can talk, I'll listen,' he said, and smiled at me from behind his glasses.

'These guys want to give me another fifty or sixty thou if I can buy into some quick action.'

'So?'

'Can I get in on the score?'

'Dave, the score you're talking about is all going right into the projects. It involves a lot of colored dealers and some guys out in Metairie I don't like to mess with too much.'

'You don't do business with the projects?'

'It's hot right now. Everybody's pissed because these kids are killing each other all over town and scaring off the tourists. Another thing, I never deliberately sold product to kids. I know they get hold of it, but I didn't sell it to them. Big fucking deal. But if you want me to connect you, I can do it.'

'I'd appreciate it, Tony. I figure this is my last score, though. I'm not cut out for it.'

'Like I am?' he said. His face was flat and expressionless when he looked at me.

'I didn't mean anything by that.'

'Yeah, nobody does. I tell you what, Dave, go into Copeland's up on St. Charles some Wednesday night. Wednesday is yuppie night in New Orleans. These are people who wouldn't spit on an Italian who grew up in a funeral home. But they got crystal bowls full of flake on their coffee tables. They carry it in their compacts, they chop up lines when they ball each other. In my opinion a lot of them are degenerates. But what the fuck do I know? These are people with law degrees and M.B.A.s. I went to a fucking juco in Miami. You know why? Because it had the best mortuary school in the United States. Except I studied English and

290

journalism. I was on the fucking college newspaper, man. Just before I joined the crotch.'

'I'm not judging you, Tony.'

'The fuck you're not,' he said.

I didn't try to answer him again. He drove for almost a mile without speaking, his tan face as flat as a shingle, the wind puffing his flannel shirt, the sunlight clicking on his dark glasses. Then I saw him take a breath through his nose.

'I'm sorry,' he said. 'When you try to get off crank, it puts boards in your head.'

'It's all right.'

'Let's stop up here and buy some crabs. If I don't feed those guys behind us, they'll eat the leather out of the seats. You're not pissed?'

'No, of course not.'

'You really want me to connect you?'

'It's what my people need.'

'Maybe you should let those white-collar cock-suckers make their own score.'

I had a feeling Clete would agree with him.

We ate outside Covington, then took a two-lane road toward Mississippi and the Pearl River country. Finally we turned on to a dirt road, crossed the river on a narrow bridge, and snaked along the river's edge through a thick woods. The water in the river was low, and the sides were steep and covered with brush and dried river trash.

'It's weird-looking country, isn't it?' Tony said. 'Have you ever been around here before?'

'No, not really. Just on the main highway,' I said. But I could never hear the name of the Pearl River without remembering the lynchings that took place in Mississippi in the 1950s and 1960s and the bodies that had been dredged out of the Pearl with steel grappling hooks. 'Why do you keep your plane over here?'

'A beaver's always got a back door,' he said. 'Besides, nobody over here pays any attention to me.'

We wound our way down toward the coast, splashing yellow water out of the puddles in the road. Then the pines thinned and I could see the river again. It was wider here, and the water was higher, and sunk at an angle on the near bank was an old seismographic drill barge. It was orange with rust, and its deck and rails and four hydraulic pilings were strung with gray webs of dried algae.

'What are you looking at?' Tony said.

'I used to work on a drill barge like that. Back in the fifties,' I said. 'They were called doodlebug rigs because they moved from drill hole to drill hole.'

'Huh,' he said, not really interested.

I turned and looked at the drill barge again. All the glass was broken out of the iron pilothouse, and leaves drifted from the tree branches through the windows.

'You want to stop and take a look?' Tony said.

'No.'

'We got plenty of time.'

'No, that's all right.'

'It makes you remember your youth or something?'

'Yeah, I guess,' I said.

But that wasn't it. The drill barge disturbed me, as though I were looking at something from my future rather than my past.

'You see that hangar and airstrip?' Tony said.

The woods ended, and up ahead was a cow pasture with a mowed area through the center of it, and a solitary tin hangar with closed doors and a wind sock on the roof.

'That's where you keep your plane?' I said.

'No, I keep my plane a mile down the road. Just remember this place.'

'What for?'

'Just remember it, that's all.'

'All right.'

We drove past the pasture and clumps of cows grazing among the egrets, then entered a pine and hackberry woods again. At the end of the shaded road I could see more sunny pastureland.

'I want to tell you something, something I haven't been honest about. Then I want to ask you a question,' Tony said.

'Go ahead.'

'I got a bad feeling, the kind you used to get sometimes in 'Nam. You know what I mean? Like maybe it was really going to happen this time, you were riding back on the dustoff in a body bag. I got that feeling now.'

'It's the withdrawal from the speed.'

'No, this is different. I feel like it's five minutes to twelve and my clock's ticking.'

'They didn't get you over there, did they? Blow it off. Guys like us have a long way to run.'

'Look, like I told you, the only guy working for me I can trust is Jess. But Jess couldn't think his way through wet Kleenex. So I'm going to ask you, if I get clipped, will you look after Paul, make sure that bitch takes care of him, keeps him in good schools, buys him everything he needs?'

'I appreciate the compliment, but—'

'Fuck the compliment. I want an answer.'

'Start thinking about a divorce, Tony, and get these other thoughts out of your head.'

'Yes or no?'

He looked at me, one hand tight on the steering wheel, and we bounced through a deep puddle that splashed water across the windshield.

'I'd do my best for him,' I said.

'I know you will. You're my main man. Right?' And he pointed one finger at me and coked his thumb, as though he were aiming a pistol, and popped his mouth with his tongue. Then he laughed loudly.

Late that afternoon I told Tony I was going to have the oil in my truck changed. I drove to a filling station by the shopping center and used the outside pay phone while the attendant put my truck on the rack. I caught Minos at his office and told him of the trip over to Mississippi.

'When do you think this shipment's coming in?' he said.

'Any day.'

'All right, we'll get the money in the bus locker for you. Now, let's talk about you getting wired.'

'Minos, I think there might be a problem here with entrapment. This isn't Tony's deal. I'm leading him into it.'

'Anywhere there's dope in Orleans or Jefferson Parish, he's getting a cut out of it.'

'I don't think that's true. He talked about some guys in Metairie running this deal.'

'I don't care what he says. Cardo's dirty when he gets up in the morning. Stop pretending otherwise.

Look, if somebody hollers later about entrapment, that's our problem, not yours.'

'I think we're shaving the dice.'

'It's not entrapment if this guy has fore-knowledge of a narcotics buy and he takes you into it.' He paused to let the exasperation go out of his voice. 'You've only got one thing to worry about, Dave – getting close to him with a wire. Now, we can do it two ways, with a microphone or a miniaturized tape recorder.'

'He's not going to do business in the house.'

'Which do you want to use?'

'How far can the microphone send?'

'Under the best conditions, without electric interference or buildings in the way, maybe up to a quarter of a mile.'

'I think I'll be better off with the recorder. That way we won't have to worry about reception prob-lems with the tail.'

'How do you want to pick it up?' he said.

'I have to go to the doctor's at ten tomorrow morning to get my stitches out. Have somebody at his office.' I gave him the address.

'Then that's about it for right now,' he said.

'Minos, there's one other thing that bothers me. Maybe I imagine it.'

'What?'

'Sometimes it's like he knows I'm still a cop. Like maybe he wants to take a fall.'

'Who knows? A guy who shoots speed up into his arm made a contract to destroy himself a long time ago. They all flame out one way or another. Who cares how they do it? Hang loose,' he said, and hung up.

That night I was watching television on the sun porch with Tony and Paul when the phone rang in the kitchen and the Negro houseman told me that I had a call. I picked the receiver up off the Formica counter, sat down on a stool, and put it to my ear. The counter gave on to the porch, and I could see Tony's and Paul's faces in the illumination of the television screen.

'Hello,' I said.

'Dave, it's Clete. Are you where you can talk?'

'We're watching television.'

'I dig you. Just listen, then. That redhead broad just called me at the club. From what I get, somebody beat the shit out of her. She wants to see you, but she doesn't want Cardo to know about it.'

'Uh-huh,' I said.

'She wouldn't tell me much. She sounds like one scared broad. She's staying at a friend's place out in Metairie. I've got the address.'

'I see.'

'Cardo's right there.'

'That's right.'

'Look, pick me up at the bar, and we'll drive out there tonight. Tell Tony you're lending me some money, I'm having trouble meeting the vig with one of his shylocks. He'll buy that. I owe those fuckers five large.'

'All right, Cletus. I'll see what I can do.'

I hung up the receiver and sat back down in front of the television set. I brushed at my pants leg distractedly.

'What's the trouble?' Tony said.

'Oh, nothing, really. Clete's having some money problems. He gets a little strung out sometimes. I

296

guess I'd better go see him. Would it bother you if I came in late?'

'No, here's the house key. Just tell the guys at the gate you'll be back late so they won't think it's somebody else, you know what I mean?'

'I'll be quiet coming in.'

'Sure, don't worry about it. Somebody's squeezing your friend?'

'A little problem with the vigorish.'

'Tell him to come see me about it. Maybe I can work it out.'

'That's good of you, Tony.'

It took me a half hour to drive to the bar on Decatur. Clete was waiting for me under the colonnade. It had started to mist, and he wore a brown raincoat over his sports jacket. I pulled to the curb, and he jumped in the truck. He read me the address in Metairie off a folded piece of paper, and I headed out of the Quarter toward Interstate 10.

'Who beat her up?' I said.

'She wouldn't say.'

'Why didn't she want Tony to know about it?'

'I didn't ask her. Dave, are you making it with her?'

'No.'

'Are you sure?'

'I told you no.'

'You didn't have just one flop in the hay with her?'

'You heard what I said, Clete.'

'Yeah, well, usually broads like that get remodeled after they let the wrong guy in the bread box. She called for you, not Cardo. What should I conclude on that, Streak? Or am I just full of shit?'

'I didn't talk to her. I don't know what happened. And you're pissing me off.'

We were silent in the cab of the truck. It started to rain harder, and I turned on the windshield wipers.

'I'm just trying to help, believe it or not,' he said.

'I know that, Clete.'

'I'm backing your play, and I don't care if I get paid for it or not.'

'What do you mean?' I looked over at him. Rainy patterns of light ran down his face.

'I didn't get any bucks from the DEA this week. I called Dautrieve, and he said I was terminated.'

'Are you kidding?'

'Wait a minute, don't get heated up. He said some other guys made the decision. He didn't have any control over it.'

'He should have told me.'

'Maybe he didn't have a chance to. Fuck it. Look, there's our exit up there. Welcome to Metairie, the only town in the United States to elect a Klu Klux Klansman and American Nazi as its state representative. What a depressing shithole. This place makes you think maybe the white race ought to be picking the cotton.'

'I've got to have a talk with Minos.'

'Talk all you want to. When you deal with the feds, you're dealing with people whose thought patterns are printed on computer chips. Besides, they all smell like mouthwash. Did you ever trust a guy who smells like mouthwash?'

She opened the apartment door on the night chain. She had on a short-sleeved terry cloth robe. Her right eye was a purple knot, and there was still a

298

crust of dried blood in one nostril. She slipped the chain loose and opened the door wide. Her arms were streaked with yellow and purple bruises, the kind that a man's clenched hand leaves. I could smell the Mentholatum that she had smeared on her skin. She closed the door and locked it again as soon as we were inside.

'I thought maybe you wouldn't come,' she said.

'Why?' I said.

'I don't know, it was just what I thought.' She talked carefully, as though the inside of her mouth were hurt. 'There's some beer and pop in the refrigerator if you want some.'

'Who did it, Kim?' I said.

'Jimmie Lee Boggs.'

'When?'

'This morning. Just after I got up. I opened the door to get the newspaper and he hit me in the face and knocked me back inside the room. I never had anybody hit me like that. I didn't believe anyone could hit that hard.'

I could hear the humiliation in her voice, see the shame in her face. I had seen the same look of debasement in victims of violence many times, and it was almost impossible to convince them that they were not deserving of their fate. I could feel Clete's awkwardness next to me.

'I think I'll take that beer,' he said, walking to the refrigerator. 'Then I'll just step out here on the balcony and have a cigarette.'

He slid open the glass doors that gave on to a small balcony with a barbecue grill on it, then closed them behind him and looked out over a lighted, weed-filled lake that was dented with rain.

She sat on the couch with her hands in her lap and her head bowed.

'Why didn't you think I'd come?' I asked again.

'Because you know I'm a snitch.'

'What else?'

Her eyes were averted. She looked small sitting on the couch. I sat down next to her. She turned her face up, then looked away again.

'What else, Kim?'

'Because you know I betrayed you. I told Lieutenant Baxter about the buy down at Cocodrie. That's why Jimmie Lee Boggs came after me. He said he figured it was either you or me who dropped the dime on him. He beat me all over the apartment. Then he twisted a towel in my mouth and filled the sink and held my head under the water until I almost passed out. He kept saying, "Gargle time, beautiful. Rinse out your mouth, now. Think about the canary I'm gonna stuff in it." He would have killed me if the landlady hadn't started banging on the door for the rent.'

She glanced sideways at my face.

'Why were you snitching for Nate Baxter?'

'My brother's a groom at the Fairgrounds. Lieutenant Baxter has him in jail for possession. He says he can upgrade the charge to conspiracy to distribute, and Albert – that's my brother – will get fifteen years in Angola.'

'Baxter put you inside Tony's crowd?'

'I already had the job at the club. All I had to do was become available.'

'Available?' I said.

'I said to Baxter, "What do you mean, exactly?" He says. "You've got a piece of equipment that'll

300

get you anything you want." He looks across his desk, then he goes, "That's big-picture clear, isn't it? Talk it over with your brother. Let me know what you decide. It doesn't matter to me, hon, one way or another."'

'You should have reported him, Kim.'

'Great. I work in a skin joint run by the Mafia, my brother's a druggie in custody, and I'm going to report a Vice lieutenant? Look, it doesn't matter what he said. I did what he wanted. I told him everything Tony was doing, I told him about you, I'm to blame for what happened down at Cocodrie.'

'You tried to warn me. Give yourself a little credit.'

'Are you going to tell Tony?'

'No. But as of tonight, you're out of the life, Kim. You don't go back to that job, or back to your apartment, or out to Tony's. I also advise you to stay away from Nate Baxter. He's a liar and a coward and a bully. Also, he doesn't have the power to upgrade your brother's charges. That comes out of the prosecutor's office. Believe me, your brother will be better off taking his own chances.'

She took a Kleenex out of her robe and touched one nostril with it. Her face had no makeup on it, and it looked shiny and white where it wasn't bruised.

'I don't know what to do,' she said. 'I only have a little money. I have to have a job.'

'Somebody's going to take care of you. I guarantee it.'

She put the Kleenex away and played with her fingernails.

'I have to ask you something,' she said.

'Yes?'

'It's not a very appropriate question, I guess, but there's no chance, is there? Not now.'

'Of what?' I said, although I already knew the answer.

'What I mean is, it's like when people do something to one another, or maybe to themselves, something shameful, it kills what might have been between them, doesn't it?'

'I don't know, Kim.'

'Yes, you do. It's why my brother Albert is the way he is. Years ago he had a wife and a little girl. Then one night he got drunk at a party and slept with another woman. So he had all this Catholic guilt about what he'd done, and rather than blow it off, he got his wife drunk and talked her into getting into the sack with another guy. All he got out of it was the knowledge that he couldn't love himself anymore, and so he doesn't think anybody else can, either.'

'I wouldn't try to figure it all out now, Kim.'

'Tony's right. We're the cluster fuck. The human race is.'

'Cynics and nihilists are two bits a bagful,' I said. 'Don't let them sell you that same old tired shuck. Listen, a man named Minos Dautrieve is going to contact you. He's an old friend with the DEA, so trust him. We're going to take care of you.'

'I was right, then. You're still a cop.'

'Who cares? The only thing that matters here is that you're out of the life. We're clear on that, aren't we?'

'Yes.'

I put my hand on her forearm.

'Kim, you stood up for your brother,' I said. 'Everything you did took courage. Most people aren't that brave. I think you're one special lady.'

She looked up at me. Her unswollen eye glimmered softly.

'Really?' she said.

'You bet. I've had some good people cover my back, like Cletus out there, but I'd put my money on you anytime.'

She smiled, and her free hand touched the backs of my fingers.

It was still raining when we left the apartment building and got back inside my truck.

'Your face looks like a thunderstorm,' Clete said.

'Nate Baxter,' I said.

'She was working for him?'

'Yep.'

'He's the guy mommies warned them about. I always had the feeling that if we ever had a Third Reich here, you might see Nate manning the ovens.'

'There's a bar up here on the corner. I want to stop and use the phone.'

'You're not going after Baxter?'

'Not now. But he's not going to get away with this.'

'Hmm,' Clete said, grinning in the dashboard light, his eyebrows flipping up and down like Groucho Marx's.

We went inside the corner bar, and Clete ordered a drink while I called Minos at his guesthouse from a phone booth next to a pinball machine. I told him about Kim, the beating she had taken from Jimmie Lee Boggs, the fact that she was an informant for Nate Baxter.

'Can you get her into a safe house?' I said.

'If she wants it.'

'Tomorrow morning.'

'No problem.'

'But I've got one. Why did you guys cut Cletus from the payroll?'

'I was going to tell you about it. It just happened today. I didn't have any say in it.'

'We had a deal.'

'I don't control everything here.'

'He saved my life out on the salt. I didn't see any DEA guys out there.'

'I'm sorry about it, Dave. I'm a federal employee. I'm one guy among several in this office. You need to understand that.'

'I think it's a rotten fucking way to treat somebody.'

'Maybe it is.'

'I think that's a facile answer, too.'

'I can't do anything about it.'

'Tell your office mates Clete has more integrity in the parings of his fingernails than a lot of federal agents have in their whole careers.'

'Drop by and tell them yourself. I'm not up to a harangue tonight. It's always easy to throw baboon shit through the fan when somebody else has to clean it up. We'll pick up the girl in the morning, and we'll get the tape recorder to you at your doctor's office. Good night, Dave.'

He hung up the receiver, and I could hear the pinball machine pinging through the plywood wall of the phone booth. Outside the window, the mist and blowing rain looked like cotton candy in the pink glow of the neon bar sign.

13

The next morning was bright and clear, and I went to the doctor's office off Jefferson Avenue and had the stitches snipped out of my head and mouth. When I touched the scar tissue above my right eyebrow, the skin around my eye twitched involuntarily. I opened my mouth and worked my jaw several times, touching the rubbery stiffness where the stitches had been removed.

'How does it feel?' the doctor asked. He was a thick-bodied, good-natured man who wore his sleeves rolled up on his big arms.

'Good.'

'You heal beautifully, Mr. Robicheaux. But it looks like you've acquired quite a bit of scar tissue over the years. Maybe you should consider giving it up for Lent.'

'That's a good idea, Doctor.'

'You were lucky on this one. I think if you'd spent another hour or so in the water, we wouldn't be having this conversation.'

'I think you're right. Well, thank you for your time.'

'You bet. Stay out of hospitals.'

I went outside into the sunlight and walked toward my truck, which was parked under an oak tree. A man in khaki clothes with a land surveyor's plumb bob on his belt was leaning against my fender, eating a sandwich out of a paper bag.

'How about a lift up to the park?' he asked.

'Who are you?'

'I have a little item here for you. Are you going to give me a ride?'

'Hop in,' I said, and we drove up a side street toward Audubon Park and stopped in front of an enormous Victorian house with a wraparound gallery. Out in the park, under the heavy drift of leaves from the oaks, college kids from Tulane and Loyola were playing touch football. The man reached down into the bottom of his lunch sack and removed a miniaturized tape recorder inside a sealed plastic bag. He was thin and wore rimless glasses and work boots, and he had a deep tan and liver spots on his hands.

'It's light and it's flat,' he said. He reached back in the sack and took out a roll of adhesive tape. 'You can carry it in a coat pocket, or you can tape it anywhere on your body where it feels comfortable. It's quiet and dependable, and it activates with this little button here. Actually, it's a very nice little piece of engineering. When you wear it, try to be natural, try to forget it's on your person. Trust it. It'll pick up whatever it needs to. Don't feel that you have to "point" it at somebody. That's when a guy invites problems.'

'Okay.'

'Each cassette has sixty minutes' recording time on it. If you run out of tape and your situation doesn't allow you to change cassettes, don't worry about it. Never overextend yourself, never feel that you have to record more than the situation will allow you. If they don't get dirty on the tape one time, it'll happen the next time. Don't think of yourself as a controller.'

'You seem pretty good at this.'

'It beats being a shoe salesman, I guess. You have any questions?'

'How many undercover people have been caught with one of these?'

'Believe it or not, it doesn't happen very often. We put taps on telephone lines, bugs in homes and offices, we wire up informants inside the mob, and they still hang themselves. They're not very smart people.'

'Tony C. is.'

'Yeah, but he's crazy, too.'

'That's where you're wrong, partner. The only reason guys like us think he's crazy is because he doesn't behave like the others. Mistake.'

'Maybe so. But you'd better talk to Minos. He got some stuff on Cardo from the V.A. this morning. Our man was locked up with the wet brains for a while.'

'He's a speed freak.'

'Yeah, maybe because of his last few months' service in Vietnam.'

'What about it?'

'Talk to Minos,' he said, got out of the truck, and looked back at me through the window. 'Good luck on this. Remember what I said. Get what you can and let the devil take the rest.'

Then he crossed the street and walked through

the park toward St. Charles, his attention already focused on the college kids playing football by the lake. The streetcar clattered loudly down the tracks in front of the Tulane campus across the avenue. I went to a small grocery store a few blocks down St. Charles, where the owner provided tables inside for working people to eat their lunch at, and called Minos at his office to see if he had relocated Kim in a safe house. I also wanted to know what he had learned about Tony's history in Vietnam, besides the fact that as an addict Tony had been locked up in a psychiatric unit rather than treated for addiction.

Minos wasn't in. But in a few hours I was to learn Tony's story on my own, almost as though he had saved a piece of forgotten memory out of my own experience and thrust it into my unwilling hands.

I took Bootsie to lunch at an expensive Mexican restaurant on Dauphine before I drove back out to Tony's. She looked wonderful in her white suit, black heels, and lavender blouse, and I think perhaps she had the best posture I had ever seen in a woman. She sat perfectly straight in her chair while she sipped from her wineglass or ate small bites of her seafood enchilada, her chin tilted slightly upward, her face composed and soft.

But it was too crowded for us to talk well, and I was beset with questions that I did not know how to frame or ask. I guess my biggest concern about Bootsie was a selfish one. I wanted her to be just as she had been in the summer of 1957. I didn't want to accept the fact that she had married into the Mafia, that she was business partners with the

Giacano family, that financial concern was of such great importance in her life that she would not extricate herself from the Giacanos.

For some reason it was as though she had betrayed me, or betrayed the youth and innocence I'd unfairly demanded she be the vessel of. What an irony, I thought: I'd killed off a large portion of my adult life with alcohol, driven away my first wife, delivered my second wife, Annie, into a nightmare world of drugs and psychotic killers, and had become a professional Judas who was no longer sure himself to whom he owed his loyalties. But I was still willing to tie Bootsie to the moralist's rack.

'What's bothering you?' she asked.

'What if we just give it all up? Your vending machine business, your connection with those clowns, my fooling around with the lowlifes and crazoids. We just eighty-six it all and go back to New Iberia.'

'It's a thought, isn't it?'

'I mean it, Boots. You only get one time on the planet. Why spend any more of it confirming yesterday's mistakes?'

'I have to tell you something.'

'What?'

'Not here. Can we be together later tonight?'

'Yeah, sure, but tell me what, Boots?'

'Later,' she said. 'Can you come for supper at the house?'

'I think I can.'

'You *think*.'

'I'm trying to tie some things up.'

'Would you rather another night?' She looked at a distant spot in the restaurant.

309

'No, I'll do everything I can to be there.'

'You'll do *everything*?'

'What time? I'll be there. I promise.'

'They're not easy people to deal with, are they? You don't always get to set your own schedule, do you? You don't have control over everything when you lock into Tony Cardo's world, do you?'

'All right, Bootsie, I was hard on you.'

'No, you were hard on both of us. When you love somebody, you give up making decisions just for yourself. I loved you so much that summer I thought we had one skin wrapped around us.'

I looked back at her helplessly.

'Six-thirty,' she said.

'All right,' I said. Then I said it again. 'And if anything goes wrong, I'll call. That's the best I can do. But I know I'll be there.'

And I was the one who'd just suggested we eighty-six it all and go back to Bayou Teche.

Her dark eyes were unreadable in the light of the candle burning inside the little red chimney on the table.

When I got back to Tony's house, I hid the tape recorder in my closet. The house was empty, so quiet that I could hear clocks ticking. I put on my gym shorts and running shoes, jogged for thirty minutes through the neighborhood and along Lakeshore Drive, then tried to do ten push-ups out on the lawn. But the network of muscles in my left shoulder was still weak from the gunshot wound, and after three push-ups I collapsed on my elbow.

I showered, put on a pair of jeans and a long-sleeved sports shirt, and walked out by the pool with a magazine just as Tony and Jess came through the front gate in the Lincoln, with the white limo behind them.

Tony slammed the car door and walked toward me, pulling off his coat and tie.

'Come inside with me. I got to get a drink,' he said. He kept pulling off his clothes as we went deeper into the house, kicking his shoes through a bedroom door, flinging his shirt and trousers into a bathroom, until he stood at the bar in his Jockey undershorts. His body was hard, knotted with muscle, and beaded with pinpoints of perspiration. He poured four inches of bourbon into a tumbler with ice and took a big swallow. Then he took another one, his eyes widening above the upended glass.

'I think I'm heading into the screaming meemies,' he said. 'I feel like somebody's puling my skin off with pliers.'

'What is it?'

'I'm a fucking junkie, that's what it is.' He poured from the decanter into his glass again.

'Better ease up on the fluids.'

'This stuff's like Kool-Aid compared to what my system's used to. What you're looking at, Dave, is a piece of cracked ceramic. Those guys are weirding me out, too. We're in my real estate office out by Chalmette, and I'm talking to my salespeople at a meet while the guys are milling around out there by the front desks. These salespeople are mostly middle-class broads who pretend they don't know what other kinds of businesses I'm in. So we end the meet and walk out to the front door and everybody is bouncy and laughing until they see the guys

311

comparing different kinds of rubbers they bought at some sex shop. It's like my life is part of a Marx Brothers comedy. Except it ain't funny.'

He put his head down on the bar. 'Oh man, I ain't fucking gonna make it.'

'Yeah, you will.'

'Have you ever seen a wet-brain ward at the V.A.? They wear Pampers, they drool on themselves, they eat mush with their hands. I've been there, man, and this is worse.'

'I've had dead people call me up long-distance. Do you think it gets any worse than that?' I said.

'You think that's a big deal? I'll tell you about a smell—' He stopped and drank out of his glass. The ice clinked against the sides. His eyes were dilated. 'Come outside, I want to show you something.'

He picked up the decanter and walked out the side door on to the lawn. Jess looked up from dipping leaves out of the pool.

'Hey, Tony, you forgot your pants,' he said, then he saw the expression on Tony's face and said, 'So it's a good day to get some sun.'

I followed Tony across the lawn, through the trees, and past the goldfish ponds and birdbaths and tennis court to the back wall of his property. A hooded air vent protruded from the ground close to the base of the wall.

'Find it,' he said.

'What?'

'The trapdoor.'

'I don't see one.'

He bent over and pulled an iron ring set next to a sprinkler head, and a door covered with grass sod raised up out of the lawn and exposed a short,

312

subterranean stairwell.

'It's an atom bomb shelter,' he said. 'But I heard the guy who built it used to pump the maid down here.'

We went down inside, and he clicked on a light and pulled the door shut with a hanging rope. The walls and floor were concrete, the roof steel plate. There were two bunk beds inside the room, a pile of moldy K rations in one corner, and a stack of paperback novels and a disassembled AR-15 rifle on top of a bridge table.

'I come down here when things are bugging me,' he said. 'Sometimes I make up a picnic basket and Paul and me spend the night down here, like we're camping. It's got a chemical toilet, I can hook up a portable TV, nobody knows where I am unless I want them to know.'

He sat down on the bunk bed and leaned back against the concrete wall. A dark line of hair grew up the center of his stomach from the elastic band of his underwear. He stirred the ice in his drink with his finger. Then he was quiet for what seemed a long time.

'After I got hit they didn't send me back to my old platoon,' he said. 'Instead I got reassigned to a bunch of losers. Or maybe they'd just been out too long. One guy had a scalp lock from a woman on his rifle, another guy gave a little boy a heat tab and told him it was candy. Anyway, I didn't like any of them. Which was all right, because they didn't like me, either, and they kept treating me like a newbie.

'So one night the lieutenant tells us to set up an ambush about four klicks up this trail, so we pass a real small ville by a stream after one klick and we go on another klick and finally everybody says, "Fuck it, we sandbag it, let the loot set his own ambush."

'But while we're sitting out there in the dark it's like everybody's got something else on his mind. It's hot and quiet, and water's dripping out of the trees and we're slapping mosquitoes and smelling ourselves and looking at our watches and thinking we got six more hours out here. Then the guy with the scalp lock on his rifle – his name was Elvis Doolittle, that's right, I'm not making it up – Elvis rubs his whiskers with his hand and keeps looking back down the trail and finally he puts a cigarette in his mouth. The doc says, "What the fuck you doing, Elvis?"

'He says, "I'm going back to the ville."

'Then nobody says anything. But everybody had seen these two teenage sisters with their mama-san in front of the hooch. And they know what Elvis is thinking. Then he says, "We'll leave Mouse and the new guy. Nobody'll know. That ville's got something coming anyway. That booby trap that got Brown. They set it."

'"You don't know that," Mouse says.

'"If they didn't set it, they know who did," Elvis says.

'Then they all talked it over and my heart started beating. Not because of what they were going to do, either, but because I was afraid to be left out on the trail with just one guy.

'Elvis turns to me and says, "You ever say anything about this, you ain't getting back home, man." Then they were gone. The trees were so thick all those guys just melted away into the blackness. You could hear monkeys clattering around in the canopy and night birds and sounds like sticks breaking out there in the jungle. Sweat was running out of my pot and my breath started catching in my throat. Then we hear something clank.

'Mouse whispers, "It's up the trail. It's up the fucking trail."

'I tell him to be quiet and listen, and he says, "It's NVA, man."

'I tell him to shut up again, but he says, "They dideed out on us, man. It ain't right. I ain't staying."

'His eyes look big as half-dollars under his pot, and I'm trying to act cool, like I got it under control, but the sweat keeps burning my eyes and my hands are shaking so bad it's like I got malaria. Then I hear something up the trail again.

'"That's it," Mouse says, "Let's get out of here."

'I put my hand on his arm. "All right, man, we go back to the ville," I say. "But what are you gonna do with what you see back there?"

'"I ain't gonna see nothing," he says. "It ain't my business. I got eighteen more days, then it's back to the world. I ain't gonna get pulled into no court-martial, either. You do what you want to, Cardo."

'He takes off, and a minute later I follow him, tagging along like a punk to something I don't even want to know about, all because I'm scared.

'When we get back to the ville, Elvis has put all the zips in their hooches and has sent the doc with a flashlight into the hooch that's got the two teenage sisters. The doc comes out and says, "They're clean," and then Elvis and this big black dude go in. About ten minutes later Elvis comes out fixing his fly and sees me and Mouse squatting by the trail.

315

'"You dumb shits," he says. "You get the fuck back up that trail."

'"I ain't gonna do it, Elvis," Mouse says.

'He grabs Mouse by the back of his shirt and pulls him up out of the dirt, just like you pick up a dirty clothes bag.

'"Fuck you, man. We're not going back up there by ourselves," I say. "We heard something clank up there. You dideed out on us. They get through, your ass is in a sling."

'He's frozen there, with Mouse hanging from his fist. He says, "What d'you mean, something clanked?"

'Before I can answer an old man runs across the clearing out of nowhere and tries to get in the hooch, where a couple of other guys are taking their turn inside. He's yelling in gook, and the big black dude his holding him by the wrists, and everybody's laughing. Then one of the sisters starts screaming inside, and more zips are coming out of their hooches, and it's all starting to deteriorate in a hurry. Elvis lets loose of Mouse and walks fast across the clearing just as the two guys come back out of the hooch.

'One of them is the guy who gave the kid a heat tab. He and Elvis look at each other, then the guy says, "The shit's already in the fire, man."

'The old man goes in the hooch, and there's more yelling inside, and Elvis says, "What'd you do to her?"

'The guy, the heat-tab guy, says, "Nothing you didn't."

'But the guy who was in there with him says, "He told her he'd kill her baby if she didn't blow him."

316

'By that time I just wanted to get out of there, so I don't know who threw the grenade. I was already headed down the trail when I heard it go off. But somebody threw it right in the door of the hooch, with the two sisters and the old man and maybe a baby inside. Then I started running. When I looked back I could see the sparks above the trees from the burning hooch. I don't know if they killed anybody else there or not. I never asked, and I never told anybody about it. The next day I volunteered to work in the mortuary at Chu Lai.'

'The mortuary?' I said.

'That's right, man. I peeled them out of the body bags, cleaned the jelly out of their mouths and ears, washed them down, embalmed them, and boxed them. Because I'd had it with the war. And I'd lost my guts, too. I just wasn't going out again. I didn't care if I was a public coward or not.'

He drank from the bourbon, then leaned forward on his thighs. He rubbed the sweat off the back of his neck and looked at his hand.

'Maybe it took courage to do that, Tony,' I said.

'No, I was afraid. There's no way around that fact.' His voice was tired.

'You could have gotten out of the bush in other ways. You could have given yourself a minor wound. A second Heart would have put you in a safe area. You think maybe it's possible you volunteered for the mortuary to punish yourself?'

He looked up at my face. The skin around his left eye was puckered with thought.

'You can beat up on yourself the rest of your life if you want to. But no matter how you cut it, you're no coward. I'll give you something else to think

317

about, too. On your worst day over there, you probably proved yourself in ways that an average person couldn't even imagine. It was *our* war, Tony. People who weren't there don't understand it. Most of them never wanted to understand it. But you ask yourself this question: would any grunt who was in the meat grinder judge you harshly? In fact, is there anyone at all who can say you didn't do your share?'

He widened his eyes and looked between his legs at the concrete floor. He pinched the bridge of his nose and made a snuffling sound. He started to speak, then cleared his throat and looked at the floor again.

'Better get some clothes on,' I said. 'You'll catch cold down here.'

'Yeah, I'll do that.'

'I guess I'll see you at the house,' I said.

'I lied about something. I don't use this place for Paul and me to camp. You see that AR-15? I used to come down here and sit in the dark with it and think about doing myself. When you turn off the light it's just like a black box, like the inside of a grave. I'd put the front sight under my teeth and let it touch the roof of my mouth and my mind would go completely empty. It felt good.'

I pushed on the trapdoor, which was made of steel and overlaid with concrete and swung up and down on thick black springs, and walked up the steps into the balmy November afternoon. The moss-hung oaks by the back wall were loud with blue jays and mockingbirds. I looked back down into the shelter and saw Tony still seated on the side of the bunk, his face pointed downward, the skin of his back as tight as a lampshade, bright with sweat.

I went up to the shopping center and called Minos at his office to find out about Kim, but he still hadn't returned. When I got back to Tony's house, the school bus had just dropped off Paul, and Jess was wheeling him inside.

'How you doing, Paul?' I said.

'Great. Special class got to go on the Amtrak train today.' He wore a striped trainman's hat, a checkered shirt, and blue jeans with a cowboy belt.

'I bet that was fun, wasn't it? Where's your old man?'

'Getting dressed.' He grinned broadly. 'Dad was exercising on the lawn in his underwear.'

'Why not? It's good weather for it,' I said, and winked at him.

'You got a phone message,' Jess said. 'From that friend of yours that runs the bar, what's his name?'

'Clete?'

'Yeah, he says to call him at the bar.'

'Thank you.'

'Dad said we all might go to a movie tonight,' Paul said.

'Well, I'm supposed to have dinner with a friend tonight.'

'Oh.'

'How about tomorrow night, maybe?' I said.

'Sure,' he said, but I could see the disappointment in his face.

Jess wheeled him up the ramp into the house, and I used the phone in the kitchen to call Clete.

'Where are you?' Clete said.

'At Tony's.'

'Can you talk, or do you want to call me back from somewhere else?'

'What is it?'

'Nate Baxter's in the bar.'

'I see.'

'He says he's here if you want to talk to him.'

'What's that supposed to mean?'

'You know Nate. Always looking inside his pants to make sure of his gender.'

'If it makes him happy, tell him I'll be looking him up one of these days.'

'He said one thing, though, that's a little bothersome. He said, "Tell Robicheaux I know he's got the broad stashed."'

The house was quiet except for the sound of shower water in the bathroom that adjoined Tony's bedroom.

'You there, Dave?' Clete said.

'Yes.'

'It sounds like our man knows a little more than he should.'

'What's he doing now?'

'Drinking at the bar.'

'I'll be there in a half hour.'

I told Tony that I had to run a couple of errands downtown, then I was going to Bootsie's for supper.

'Was that Bootsie on the phone?' he asked. He stood in his bedroom door, with a towel wrapped around his waist, raking the water out of his hair with a comb.

'No, it was Clete. He knows a guy who might give me a good deal on a boat.'

'I feel a lot better after a shower.' He stopped

320

combing his hair. 'Hey, tell me straight about something. Down there in the shelter, you weren't just playing with my head? I mean . . . we're not talking about a loss of respect here?'

'No.'

'Because I don't push myself on people.'

'You didn't push yourself on me.'

'You wanted to know what happened, I told you.'

I nodded without replying.

'But if a guy thinks less of me because of it, I don't hold it against him. We're clear on this?' he said.

'You're not the only guy who brought back a problem from there, Tony. I've got my own. Maybe they're worse than yours.'

'Yeah?'

'I got four of my men killed on a trail because I did something reckless and stupid. Everybody has his own basket of snakes to deal with.'

'Your vice has a little edge to it, Dave.'

'I think pride's a pile of shit.'

He laughed. 'You sure don't hide your thoughts, do you?' he said. 'How about bringing Bootsie out here for supper, then we'll all go to a movie.'

'It's kind of a private evening, Tony.'

'Paul was looking forward to it.'

'Then you should have told me earlier, podna.'

He nodded silently, then began dressing in front of a full-length mirror as though I were not there.

I didn't have time to worry any more about Tony's mood changes and his addict's propensity for trying

321

to control everyone and everything in his environment. In fact, maybe we were too much alike in that
regard, and for that reason I not only got along
better with him than I should have as a policeman,
I also saw my own menagerie of snapping dogs at
work inside him. When I got to Clete's Club, Nate
Baxter was by himself at the far end of the bar, one
shined brown loafer propped on the brass footrail.
He wore sharply creased tan slacks, an open-necked
yellow shirt, and a herringbone sports coat. His gold
watch and gold identification bracelet gleamed
softly in the light.

'You're looking sharp, Nate,' I said.

He tipped his cigarette ashes neatly into an
ashtray and took a sip from his highball glass, his
eyes looking at me in the bar mirror.

'You know a DEA agent by the name of Minos
Dautrieve?' he asked.

'He's out of Lafayette. Yeah, I know him.'

'He's in New Orleans now. He's running a sting.'

'Why tell the family secrets to me?'

'I underestimated you,' he said.

'I have to be somewhere in a few minutes. What
did you want to say to me, Nate?'

'She's my snitch. You shouldn't have messed
with her.'

'What are we talking about here?'

'You know what I'm talking about. You were in
her place out in Metairie. You got her stashed. But
it's not going to do you any good. She's our witness,
and she's going to testify for us. You can tell that to
Dautrieve for me if you want to.'

'You're going a little fast for me.'

'The girl she was staying with works in the same

322

club out on the Airline Highway. She told us you and Purcel were in her place. She said later some feds picked up the Dollinger broad. So I underestimated you. You've still got your badge, haven't you? But that doesn't mean you get to screw up our operation.'

'This is what you had to tell me?'

He tipped his cigarette ashes into the ashtray again. He still had not looked directly at me. He took a puff off his cigarette, then scratched his beard with one fingernail.

'You can tell Kim Dollinger she either comes in or we send her brother up the road,' he said. 'Don't let that broad jerk you around, Robicheaux. I could have charged her when we busted her brother. She was as dirty as he was.'

'Do you know that Jimmie Lee Boggs almost killed her?'

'You got a vested interest or something? We're talking about a snitch who was setting Tony C. up for a fall while she was banging him cross-eyed over in a beach house in Biloxi.'

'Listen—'

'No, you've got it wrong. You listen. We've worked on this case eight months. You guys come along and think you're going to wrap up Tony C. in a few weeks. In the meantime you don't inform us that you're working undercover, and then you've got the balls to grab my snitch.'

'You coerced her into prostituting herself.'

He turned his head and looked at me. The neon bar lights made the neatly trimmed edge of his beard glow with a reddish tinge.

'She was working at Tony C.'s club before she

323

ever came to our attention,' he said. 'He probably had to tie a board across his ass to keep from falling inside.'

I saw Clete walk out of his office in back and begin changing a light bulb over the bandstand. The back of the club was empty.

'You're a bad cop, Baxter. But worse, you don't have any feelings about people,' I said. 'There's a word for that – pathological.'

'Take somebody else's inventory, Robicheaux. I'm not interested. Here's what it comes down to. You fuck up this investigation, you keep getting in my face, causing me problems, I wouldn't count on the department protecting your cover. Anyway, I've had my say. Just stay away from me.'

He turned back to his drink and ran his tongue along his gums. I opened and closed my hands at my sides.

'You gonna have something, suh?' the black barman said.

'No, thank you,' I said.

I continued to stare at the side of Baxter's face, the grained skin on the back of his neck. I could hear my breath in my nostrils. Then I turned and walked toward the open front door. My body felt wooden, my arms and legs disjointed. The sun reflecting off a windshield outside was like a sliver of glass in the eye. I stopped, looked back, and saw Baxter go into the rest room by the bandstand.

When I pushed open the rest room door he was combing his hair in front of the mirror.

'If you do anything to hurt that girl again, or if you compromise my situation here in New Orleans, I'm going down to your office, in front of people,

324

and give you the worst day in your insignificant life,'
I said.

He turned from the mirror, slipped his leather
comb case out of his shirt pocket, blew in it before
he replaced the comb; his breath reflected into my
face. He used the back of his left hand to push me
aside.

I heard a sound like a Popsicle stick snapping
behind my eyes and saw a rush of color in my mind,
like amorphous red and black clouds turning in
dark water, and as though it had a life of its own my
right fist hooked into his face and caught him
squarely in the eye socket. His head snapped sideways, and I saw the white imprints of my knuckles
on his skin and the watery electric shock in his eye.

But I had stepped into it. His right hand came
out of his coat pocket with a leather-covered
blackjack, an old-fashioned one that was shaped
like a darning egg, with a spring built into the
braided grip. I tried to raise my forearm in front of
me, but the blackjack *whopped* across the top of my
left shoulder and I felt the blow sink deep into the
bone. The muscles in my chest and side quivered
and then seemed to collapse, as if someone had run
a heated metal rod through the trajectory of Jimmie
Lee Boggs's bullet.

I was bent forward, my palm pressed hard against
the throbbing pain below my collarbone, my eyes
watering uncontrollably, the lip of the washbasin a
wet presence across my buttocks. The expression in
Baxter's eyes was unmistakable.

'Just one more for the road,' he said softly.

But Clete pushed the door back on its springs
and stepped into the room like an elephant entering

325

a phone booth. His unblinking eyes went from me to the blackjack; then his huge fist crashed against the side of Baxter's head. Baxter's face went out of round, his automatic flew from his shoulder holster, and he tripped sideways over the toilet bowl and fell on top of the trash can in a litter of crumpled paper towels.

Clete grimaced and shook his hand in the air, then rubbed his knuckles.

'Are you all right?' he said.

'I don't know.'

'What happened?'

'He threatened to blow my cover.'

Clete looked down at Baxter in the corner. Baxter's eyes were half-closed, his mouth hung open, and one hand twitched on his stomach.

'You hit him first?' Clete said.

'Yep.'

Clete chewed his lip.

'He'll use it, then. That's not good, not good,' he said, and began making clicking sounds with his tongue. He reached down and patted Baxter on the cheek. 'Wake-up time, Nate.'

Baxter widened his eyes, then started to sit up among the wet towels and fell back down again. Clete lifted him by the back of his herringbone jacket and folded him over the rim of the toilet bowl.

'What are you doing?' I said.

'Freshen up, Nate. That's it, my man. Splash a little on your face and it's a brand-new day,' Clete said.

He flushed the toilet and pushed Baxter's head farther down into the bowl.

'That's enough, Clete,' I said.

Someone tried to open the door.

'This toilet is occupied right now,' Clete said. He lifted Baxter off the bowl and propped him against the wall, then squatted down and blotted his face with paper towels. 'Hey, you're looking all right, Nate. How many fingers am I holding up? Three. Look, three fingers. That's it, take a deep breath. You're going to be fine. Look, I'm putting your piece back in your holster. Here's your sap. Come on, look up at me, now.'

Clete patted Baxter's cheek again. The back of Clete's thick neck was red from the effort of squatting down. His stomach and love handles hung over his belt.

'Here's the way I see this deal,' he said. 'We write the whole thing off. It was just a bad day at Black Rock, not even worth talking about later. You had a beef, Dave had a beef, it's over now. Right?'

Baxter blinked his eyes and flexed his jaw as though he had a toothache. Water dripped out of his beard.

'Or you could go back to the First District and get into a lot of paperwork,' Clete said. 'Or you might want to cause Dave some grief with Tony C. But I don't think you're that kind of guy. Because if you were, it'd create some nasty problems for everybody. See, here's the serious part in all this. There's a hooker who comes into the bar. I usually don't let them in because they're bad for business. But I've known this broad since I was in Vice myself, and she's basically a nice girl and she respects my place and doesn't come on to the johns while she's in here. Anyway, she tells a funny story. She says you're getting freebies in the Quarter, and you made her ex-room-o cop your joint. I don't know, maybe she made it up. But you know how those broads are, they carry a grudge a long time. I don't think it'd take a lot to get one of them to drop the dime on you, Nate.'

Clete crimped his lips together and looked Baxter steadily in the eyes. Baxter's face looked as though he were experiencing the first stages of recognition after an earthquake. Clete closed the lid on the toilet and sat Baxter on top of it. His head hung forward. Clete touched him gently on the shoulder with two fingers.

'It ends here, Nate,' he said quietly. 'We're understood on that, aren't we?'

Baxter moved his lips but no sound came out.

'You don't have to say anything, as long as we have an understanding,' Clete said. 'Get yourself a couple of free doubles at the bar, if you want. I'm going to walk Dave outside now. It's a nice day. We're all going back outside into a nice day.'

Clete looked over the top of Baxter's head at me and made a motion toward the door with his thumb. I walked back out through the bar into the sidewalk under the colonnade. Clete followed me. The French Market and the tables in the Café du Monde were crowded with tourists now, and the street was heavy with afternoon traffic. Clete adjusted his tie, lit a cigarette with the lighter cupped in his big hands, and looked up the street as though he had nothing in his mind except a pleasant expectation of the next event in his life.

I rubbed my collarbone and the puckered scar of the .38 wound and straightened my back.

'How's it feel?'

'Like it's packed in dry ice.'

He felt along my shoulder with his thumb and forefinger. He saw me flinch.

'That's where he got you?'

'Yes.'

'There's no break. When your collarbone's broken there's a knot like a basketball.'

'Who's the hooker?'

'You got me. The ones I knew five years ago are probably hags now. Actually, they were hags then.'

'You're pretty slick, Clete.'

'What can I say?' He grinned at me. 'But one word of advice, noble mon. Think about going back to Bayou Teche and let New Orlenas go down the drain by itself. For some reason, Dave, having you in town makes me think of a man walking into a clock shop with a baseball bat.'

She had always loved roses and four-o'clocks. The flower beds in her lawn and the shaded areas around the coulee at her home on Spanish Lake had been bursting with them. Now she grew purple and gold four-o'clocks along the wall of her patio on Camp Street. They had already dropped their winter seeds like big black pepper grains on the worn bricks, but her yellow and hybrid blue roses still bloomed as big as fists. The western sky was streaked with magenta through the oak trees, and leaves floated across the tunnels of underwater light in the swimming pool. The air was heavy with the smoky taste of the meat fire in the hibachi, cool and bittersweet with the smell of fall, like the odor of burning sugarcane stubble, of pecans when they mold inside their husks under the tree.

She turned the steaks on the grill with a fork, her eyes watering in the smoke, and smiled at me. She wore leather sandals, faded designer jeans, and a black shirt with red flowers sewn into it. Her honey-colored hair was full of lights, and where it was trimmed on her neck it looked thick and stiff and soft and lovely to the touch, all at the same time.

She saw me press my hand to my shoulder again.

'Is there something wrong, Dave?' she said.

'No, I just have a little flare-up when the weather is about to change. I think it's going to rain. You know how it is this time of year. The leaves turn, then we have a real hard rain and we sort of click into winter.'

'It's too early for that,' she said. 'Besides, winter is never that bad here, anyway.'

'No, it's not. Boots, can I use your phone to call New Iberia? I need to check on Alafair.'

'Sure, hon.'

Alafair's voice made me want to leave New Orleans that night. Or maybe it made me want to escape even more the brooding premonition that seemed to hang between me and Bootsie like a secret both of us knew, but neither of us would broach.

She didn't have to tell me about the Baylor medical center in Houston: I had seen it in her eyes. It's a detached look, as if the person has stepped briefly around a corner and seen to the end of a long, gray street on which there are no other people. I'd flown in a dustoff loaded with wounded grunts, their foreheads painted with Mercurochrome *M*'s to indicate morphine injections, and the two who died before we reached battalion aid had had that look in their eyes, as though the hot wind through the doors, the steely *blat-blat* of the propeller blades, the racing green landscape below, were now all part of somebody else's filmstrip.

'It's bad, isn't it, Boots?' I said. I sat in the scrolled-iron patio chair by the pool and looked at the tops of my hands when I said it.

'Yes,' she said quietly.

'What's the name for it?'

'Lupus,' she said. Then she said, 'Systemic lupus. The full Latin name means "red wolf." Sometimes people get a butterfly mask on their face. I don't have that kind, though. It just lives inside me.'

I felt myself swallow, and I looked away from her eyes.

'You know what it is, then?' she said. She pushed the meat to the side of the grill and sat down across from me. Her hair was wreathed in smoke and the lighted turquoise shimmer off the pool.

'I've heard about it. I don't know a lot,' I said.

'It attacks the connective tissues. It starts in the hand sometimes and spreads through the joints. In the worst cases, when it's untreated, people look like they're wrapped in strips of plastic.'

I started to speak, but I couldn't.

'I didn't have medical insurance, no savings, nothing but the vending machine business,' she said. 'I couldn't just walk out on the business at twenty cents on the dollar.'

I saw a flicker of anger in her eyes, a spark, a recrimination that wanted to have its way. But it was only momentary.

Then she reached forward and touched me on the knee as though it were I who should be consoled.

331

'Dave, there're probably a hundred different degrees of lupus. Today it can be controlled. This new doctor I have in Houston has started me on a different kind of medication, with steroids and some other things. My problem is I ignored some warning sings, some swelling in my fingers in cold weather and stiffness in the joints, and I have some kidney damage. But I'm going to pull it off.'

'How long have you known?' I said. My voice sounded weak, as though I had borrowed it from someone else.

'For the last year.'

Her eyes moved over my face. She took my hand and held it on her knee.

'You shouldn't look like that,' she said.

'I've been getting on your case, Bootsie, criticizing you, telling you that you're mixed up with the greaseballs—'

'You didn't have any way of knowing, *cher*.'

'Boots—'

'Yes?'

'Bootsie, I don't know what to say to you.' I pressed my thumb and forefinger against my eyelids, but it didn't do any good. The wilted four-o'clocks, the black silhouettes of floating leaves, the flames in the grill, all became watery and bright like splinters of light shot through crystal. 'I majored in being a dumb shit. It's the one constant in my life.'

'I know you better than anybody else on earth, Dave. And no matter what you say, or what you believe, you never deliberately hurt anybody in your life.'

Then she stood up, her face smiling down at me, and sat in my lap. She held my head against her breast and kissed my hair and stroked her fingers along my cheek.

'You remember when we used to go to Deer's Drive-In and do this?' she said. 'I think yesterday is always only a minute away.'

I could feel the softness of her breast against my ear and hear the beating of her heart like a clock that told time for both of us.

14

In the hot darkness I smell the village before I see it – the wet reek of duck and hog shit, dead fish, moldy straw, boiled dog, stagnant pools of water coated with algae and mosquitoes. The air is breathless, so humid and still and devoid of movement that every line of sweat running down inside my fatigues is like the path of an insect across the skin. There is no light in the hooches, nor sound, and Marines sit listlessly on the ground, smoking, waiting for something, their weapons propped against their packs. They chew Red Man and unlit cigars, eat candy bars, and spit constantly between their legs.

Then for no reason that will ever make sense, somebody pulls the pin on a fragmentation grenade, releases the spoon, and rolls it inside a hooch. The explosion blows straw out of the bottom of the walls, lights the doorway in a rectangle of flame, sends a solitary kettle toppling end over end through the clearing. For a moment we can see the shapes of people inside, large ones and small ones, but they've given up, resigned themselves to this chance ending at the hands of an angry or fearful or bored boy from South Carolina or Texas, and their silhouettes settle on to the burning straw pallet like shadows flattening into the earth.

But the flames that crack through the sides of the hooch and lick up to the roof do not burn naturally. Instead, it is as though a high wind has struck the fire, fanned it into a vortex that burns with the clean, pure intensity of white gas. Then it becomes as bright and shattering to the eyes as a phosphorous shell exploding, and we wilt back from the heat into the wavering shadows at the edge of the clearing.

Behind me I hear thin-rimmed wire wheels rolling across the dirt, and I turn and watch Tony push Paul in his wheelchair toward the white brilliance of the fire. Tony's green utilities are sun-faded, caked with salt, streaked with sweat and mud and fecal matter from a rice paddy. He wheels Paul into the burning doorway, and I try to stop them but my feet feel as though they're wired together, and my hand looks like a meaningless, outstretched claw.

Tony's utilities steam in the heat; then he and Paul both burst into flame like huge candles. The fire has sound now, the road of wind in a tunnel, the whistle of superheated air cracking through wood, the resinous popping of everything that we are – skin and organ and bone.

But I am wrong about Tony and Paul. They have not found their denouement in a Vietnamese village. They emerge from the back of the fire and walk side by side into the jungle. Their bodies glow with a cool white brilliance, like a pistol's flare's, that is interrupted intermittently by the trunks of trees and tangles of vine as they go deeper into the jungle. The tripping of my heart is the only sound in the clearing.

Tony leaned forward in the chair next to my bed,

his head silhouetted against the early orange sun outside the window. He poked my shoulder with two stiff fingers.

'Hey, wake up,' he said.

'What?'

'You're having a real mean one.'

'What?' I was raised up on my elbows now.

'Do you always wake up with a chain saw in your head? Come on, get out of the rack. We got a lot to do today.'

I sat on the side of the bed in my underwear, my forearms propped on my thighs. I rubbed my face and looked again at Tony, trying to disconnect him from the dream.

'Did you get crocked last night or something?' he said.

'No.'

'All right, get dressed and let's eat breakfast.'

'What's going on, Tony?'

'You're going with me and Paul over to our fishing camp in Mississippi.'

'It's a school day, isn't it?'

'His school's closed for a couple of days. They've got to tear some asbestos out of the ceilings or something. You want to go or not?'

'I was going to do some things with Bootsie.'

'Today you put her on hold.'

'I don't think I want to do that.'

'Yeah?'

'I'm meeting her for lunch, Tony.'

'I owe you, I pay my debts. Are you interested or not?'

'What are you saying, partner?'

'Do you have fifty K in place?'

'Yes.'

'Where?'

'Don't worry, I can have it in an hour.

'So we eat breakfast, then you get it. At ten o'clock we're heading over for my camp. You're going to follow in your truck.'

'This is all a little vague.'

'You wanted the score. I'm giving you the score. It's a onetime offer. Are you in or out? Tell me now.'

'I'm in. When's it going down?'

'You don't need to know that.'

'Tony, I'm not sure I like being treated like a fish.'

'I don't know when it's going down. That's something I'll find out later. I told you I don't deal with these guys as a rule. But you want the action, so I'm making an exception.'

'Are you mad about something?'

'No, why?'

'You sound like you've got a beef.'

'I'd already promised Paul to take him to the camp today. Then last night I got a message at one of my clubs about your deal. So I'm kind of mixing business with a family trip. Which means I'm breaking one of my own rules, and I don't like that. But I don't go back on my word, either.'

'I'll get dressed and pick up my money.'

'Jess'll drive you.'

'You think I'm going to leave town?' I tried to smile.

'No offense, Dave, but anyone who does business with me does it in a controlled environment. *Anyone*.' He raised his eyebrows. They looked like grease-pencil lines drawn on his olive skin.

We ate cereal and toast and drank coffee in the glass-enclosed breakfast room while the Negro houseman helped Paul get dressed. The early sun had grown pale and wispy in the east, and clouds that were as black as oil smoke were forming in a bank over the Gulf.

'It might be a rough day for a fishing trip,' I said.

'It'll blow over,' he said.

He fiddled with his watchband, *tinked* his coffee spoon nervously against his saucer, looked out at the darkening line across the southern horizon. Then he said, 'You know where Kim might be?'

'No.'

'The manager at my club said she didn't come into work yesterday and she doesn't answer her phone. She didn't call you?'

'Why would she call me?'

'Because she digs you.'

He fluttered his fingers on the tablecloth. 'I'd better send a car out to her place,' he said. His eyes were narrowed, and they looked out through the glass and roved around the backyard. 'Maybe she split. Eventually most of them do. I thought she might be different.'

'Don't worry about her. She's probably all right,' I said.

One of Tony's bodyguards, a black-haired man of about twenty-five, came into the kitchen for coffee. He was barefoot and bare-chested, and his beltless brown slacks hung down low on his flat stomach. He looked at us without speaking, then filled his cup.

'Put a shirt on when you walk around the house,' Tony said.

The man walked back into the dining room without answering.

'It's a frigging zoo,' Tony said. 'I treat people with respect, I pay them decent wages, and they try to wipe their frigging feet on me. You know, I got a cousin runs a lot of action in Panama City. His wife tells him one day he's a drag, he's overweight, he's got bad breath, he's got a putz the size of a Vienna sausage, that the only thing he ever did for her was crush her two feet into the mattress every night. So she dumps him and starts making it with this county judge who's on the pad with the —— family in Tampa. Except she and the judge both get juiced out of their minds one night, and both of them get busted while she's blowing the judge in her Porsche behind this nightclub. She gets out of jail in the morning, hung over and trembling and her picture on the front page of the Panama City newspaper, and then she goes home and finds out my cousin had her Porsche towed back to her house, and she thinks maybe something's going right after all, my cousin's going to forgive her and square the sodomy charge with the city. Except she sees the Porsche is sitting flat on its springs because my cousin had a cement truck fill it up with concrete. I ought to take lessons from him.'

He looked again at the sky and at the trees blowing in the yard. He opened his mouth and scratched the tautness of his cheek with his fingernail.

'What's eating you, Tony?' I said.

'Nothing.'

'You haven't gotten back into pharmaceuticals, have you?' I smiled at him.

'I'm cool,' he said.

'You don't have to go into this deal. Let it slide if it doesn't feel right,' I said.

I watched his face. His eyes still roved the backyard. Back out, partner, I thought.

'I already committed you for fifty large,' he said. 'If you don't take it, I have to.'

'I have to call Bootsie.'

'I'll do it for you. While you go for your money with Jess. Nobody needs to know where we're going today, Dave.'

'All right,' I said. And there went my opportunity to tip Minos through the phone tap. Then I began to realize what was really on Tony's mind.

'I guess your little girl misses you,' he said.

'Yes.'

'After today it looks like you'll have everything you need to make your investors happy.'

'I guess I will.'

'To tell you the truth, Dave, I don't think I want to get into distribution over in Southwest Louisiana. There're too many potential problems there, conflicts with the Houston crowd. I don't need it.'

'Suit yourself.'

He didn't answer.

'I'll brush my teeth, then I'll be ready to go with Jess,' I said.

He nodded and made lines on the tablecloth with his cereal spoon. Through the glass the southern sky was as dark as gunmetal, and white veins of lightning pulsated and trembled in the clouds.

I brushed my teeth, rinsed my mouth, and spit into the lavatory. Too bad, Tony, I thought. I didn't know you were a closet Rotarian.

I had seen his kind before. They come into AA and unload some terrible moral guilt, or perhaps the whole travesty of their lives: then they begin to feel better. The ego begins to reassert itself, the tongue licks across the lips for maybe another try at the dirty boogie, and they decide to deep-six the people who've witnessed their moment of weakness and need.

So I had become Tony's disposable confessor. Wrong way to think, Tony, I thought. You commit the crime, you do the time. One way or another, you do the time.

Jess drove me to the bus depot, where I picked up the fifty thousand dollars the DEA had put in a locker for me. For a moment I thought I was going to lose Jess so I could phone Minos.

'I've had a knot in my bowels for two days,' he said, gripping his belt buckle with his fist and frowning with his whole face.

'Go use the men's room and I'll get a cup of coffee. We've got time.'

He thought about it and bent his knees slightly as though he were breaking wind.

'No, there's piss all over the toilet seats. I'll wait,' he said. 'Besides, Tony's acting weird again. When Tony gets weird, he needs somebody around him.'

'Weird about what?'

'Late last night he says to me, "It's all ending, it's all ending." I say, "What the fuck does that mean, Tony?"' Two Catholic nuns in black habits walked past us. 'He wouldn't answer me. He just walks off and stands in the middle of the dark tennis court like a statue. He stood out there half an hour.'

Back at the house Jess and one of the gatemen began loading fishing rods, food, and camping gear into the Lincoln and the Cadillac. A soft rain clicked on the trees in the yard. I told Tony I was going into my bedroom to pack an overnight bag; then I locked my bathroom door, took down my khakis, and taped the miniaturized recorder inside my thigh. I could activate it by simply dropping my hand and appearing to scratch my leg.

What an absurdity, I thought: I had invested all this energy and effort in nailing a man who had nothing to do with my life, who had never harmed me, who lived on the raw edges of narcotic madness. The story about Tony that Jess had told me in the bus depot was no mystery. Psychologists sometimes called it a world destruction fantasy. The recovering addict and drunk are suddenly cut off from their source: they have no fire escape, and the building is burning down. They wake in the middle of the night with a nameless terror and drag it with them like a gargoyle on a chain into their waking hours. Sometimes they can't breathe; their hearts race, blood veins dilate in the brain, a pressure band forms on one side of the head as though someone were tightening a machinist's vise into the bone. The only image that will adequately describe the fear is right out of the Revelation of Saint John the Divine: The beast is climbing up out of the sea, and the edges of the sky are blackening like an enormous sheet of dry paper held against a flame.

Psychologists will say that this is a reenactment of the birth experience. But the words bring no solace, no more than they can to the infant who, just delivered from the womb, waits for the slap of life.

In the meantime, while I was planning to weld the cell door shut on a driven creature like Tony Cardo, I had done little to keep my promise to Tante Lemon and Dorothea to prevent Tee Beau Latiolais from eventually being electrocuted at Angola. And while Tee Beau was twisting in the wind, trying to hide behind a pair of dark glasses in a pizza joint on the corner of St. Charles and Canal, the center of downtown New Orleans, a psychopath like Jimmie Lee Boggs was able to run around painting brain matter on walls in three states.

I tucked in my flannel shirt, buttoned my khakis, buckled my belt, and looked into the mirror. One way or another, it's show time, I thought, and carried my overnight bag and the briefcase with the fifty thousand out to the driveway just as Tony was latching the safety belt across Paul in the front seat of the Lincoln. Paul grinned happily at me from under a blue fishing cap with a white anchor stitched on it.

'Dad's going to take us out in the boat after it stops raining,' he said.

'Yeah, they school up in this weather. They'll be in close to shore, too,' Tony said. 'Dave, keep between us and the Caddy.'

'I won't get lost.'

'You might. We're going to take Interstate Ten

343

instead of the back road. Stay in my rearview mirror, okay?'

'You got it,' I said.

So I lost all hope of contacting Minos, and I was on my own. We bounced out the front gate in a caravan. The rain was moving across Lake Pontchartrain in a gray sheet, and the yellowed palm fronds on the esplanade clattered and stiffened in the wind.

The fishing camp was on the lower portion of the Pearl River basin, not far from the Gulf. It was built of unpainted cypress, with a rusty tin roof, and was set back on a sandy bluff above the river, so that the screened-in gallery had to be supported by stilts. The camp was surrounded by live oaks, and the tops of the willows on the bank grew to eye level on the gallery. It was still raining, and the wind off the Gulf blew a fine mist out of the trees into the screens.

But it was snug and warm inside the cabin, paneled with knotty pine, the floors covered with bright yellow linoleum, the kitchen outfitted with a butane stove, a microwave, and a double-door refrigerator. On the back porch, which gave on to the access road, was a freezer filled with frozen ducks, rib-eye steaks, and gallons of ice cream.

Tony and Paul sat at the kitchen table, tying leaders and huge lead weights and balsa wood bobbers to the saltwater rods and reels. In the front room, Jess and the four bodyguards who had followed in the Cadillac played *bourré* and drank canned beer at a plank table. They were a strange lot to watch, a juxtaposed contrast of the generational changes that had taken place inside the mob.

Jess Ornella was what mob people used to call a soldier. He was built like a hod carrier and looked dumb as dirt and probably was. Tony said that Jess had been in trouble all his life – with the nuns and brothers, truant officers, cops, social workers, probation officers, landlords, jailers, the draft board, bill collectors, wives, and prison psychiatrists (one had recommended that he be lobotomized). He had done time in the Orleans Parish jail for writing bad checks, committing bigamy, and setting fire to a restaurant for refusing him service. In Angola he had been a 'big stripe', a name given to those who were considered dangerous or incorrigible, and who usually stayed in lockdown in the Block. He always gave me the feeling that he could destroy a house simply by running back and forth through its walls.

But the others came from a different mold: young and lithe, tanned year-round, they wore gold chains and religious medallions and thick identification bracelets, and had a hungry look in their eyes. You knew they wanted something, but you weren't sure what it was, in the same way that you stare into a zoo animal's eyes and see an atavistic instinct there that makes you step back involuntarily. They constantly touched the flatness of their stomach, the boxed hairline on their neck, the gold watchband on their wrist; they made cigarette smoking a stylized art form. They seldom smiled, except with women who were new to them, and they talked incessantly about money, either about the amount they had made, or were about to make, or that someone else had made. Like women, they dressed for their own sex, but usually their loyalties went no further than a sentimental attitude towards their parents, whom in reality they seldom saw.

Jess accepted me because Tony had moved me into his house, perhaps just as he would not question Tony's choice of lawn furniture. But the others did not speak to me, other than to reply to a direct question. Jess saw me watching the game with a cup of coffee in my hand.

'You want to play?' he said, and started to move his chair aside.

But the men sitting on each side of him remained stationary. One of them had the deck of cards in his upturned palm and a matchstick in his mouth.

'Cecil just *bourréd* the pot. Wait till we play it out,' he said. His eyes never left the game.

'That's all right. I lose too much at the track, anyway,' I said.

No one looked up or acknowledged my statement, and I went back into the kitchen and began making a sandwich on the sideboard. Rain dripped out of the oak trees in back, and the dirt yard was flooded with a wet green light.

'Dad says we're going out on the salt even if it doesn't stop raining,' Paul said. 'We can put the rods in the sockets and stay in the cabin.'

'Sure, this is good tarpon weather,' I said. 'On a day like this you bounce the bait through the wake and the tarps will hit it so hard the rod will end all the way to the gunwale.'

'Are you glade you came, even though it's raining?' Paul said.

'Sure.'

'Dad says you're probably going to move back home with your little girl.'

I looked at Tony. He had one eye closed and was threading a nylon leader through the eye of a hook.

'Yes, I guess that's true, Paul,' I said.

'Can we come see you? And ride your horse?'

'Anytime you want to.'

Tony tied a blood knot with the leader and snipped off the loose end close to the hook's eye with a pair of fingernail clippers. He held the hook by the shank and pulled on the leader to test the strength of the knot. 'There,' he said to Paul. 'They won't bust that one.'

He wore bell-bottomed denims, a long-sleeved candy-striped shirt, and his Marine Corps utility cap with the brim propped up. His eyes avoided mine, and like his hired help who rode in the Cadillac he did not speak to me unless to answer a question, or to indicate to me that I could entertain myself with whatever was available in the camp.

I walked out under the dripping trees, then down under the screened gallery supported on stilts. The riverbanks were thick with wet brush and wild morning glory vines, and because the river emptied into the Gulf and its level was affected by the tides, trotlines were strung at crazy angles between tree trunks and logs and stakes driven into the mud. The tide was out now, and the highest water level of the river was marked by a gray line of dead hyacinths along the banks. Thunder boomed and rolled out over the Gulf, and the air was charged with the electric smell of ozone. The tree trunks glistened blackly, the canopy overhead and the scrub brush and canebrakes and layers of rotting leaves literally

347

creaked with moisture. I though of Alafair and Bootsie and realized that I had never felt more alone in my life.

Later, inside, the phone on the kitchen wall rang. Tony answered it, and after he said hello, he listened without speaking, and looked at me over the top of Paul's head. Then he hung up the receiver and said, 'Let's take a ride, Dave. Paul, I have to take care of a little business with Dave. You stay here with Jess, and I'll be back in an hour.'

'What about Dave?' Paul asked.

'He's got to do some stuff. We'll see him later.'

'Aren't you going fishing, Dave?' Paul said.

'We'll see how it works out. I might have to take off for a while,' I said.

'I thought you were going with us.' He was turned sideways in his wheelchair to talk to me. His blue jeans looked brand-new and stiff and too big for him.

'I might have to go back home,' I said. 'I've been gone a long time.'

'Your little girl wants you to come home?'

'Yes, she does.'

He nodded, picked up a piece of leader, and began poking it in a crack on the table.

'Are you coming back to visit at all?' he said.

'I'd like to take you fishing to some places I know around New Iberia. The bass are so big there we have to knock them back into the water with tennis rackets.'

His whole face lighted with his smile.

Tony and I rode in my pickup truck, and the

white Cadillac full of his hoods followed us up the dirt road that bordered the river. The chuckholes were deep and full of rainwater, and we bounced so hard on the springs that Tony had to prop one hand against the dashboard. I rubbed my thigh with my palm and used my thumb to hit the small button on the side of the tape recorder. Before we had left the camp, Tony had put on a raincoat and dropped his chrome-plated .45 automatic in the pocket. I banged through another chuckhole, and the .45 clanked against the door handle. Tony pulled his raincoat straight and kept the weight of the gun on his thigh.

'You think you might need that?' I asked.

'I carry it so I *won't* need it.'

'Did you ever have trouble with these guys?'

'These are guys who operate on the bottom of the food chain. They're not a bold bunch.'

'You don't think highly of them.'

'I don't think about them at all.'

'I appreciate what you're doing for me.'

'You've already told me that, so forget it. Look, my son likes you. You know why? It's because children recognize integrity in adults. I've got some advice for you, Dave. After this score, get out of the business. It's not worth it. There's not a morning I don't get up thinking about the IRS, the DEA, city dicks like Nate Baxter, cowboys who'll clip you just to get invited over to a certain guy's table at the Jockey Club in Miami. It's like they say about marriage: You do it for money and you'll earn every nickel of it.'

'I guess a guy makes his choices, Tony,' I said, and looked at the side of his face.

He turned his head slowly and looked back at me.

'That's right,' he said, 'and I'm making one now. When I got put in with the wet brains at the V.A., there was a lot of talk in the therapy sessions about character defects. I've got lots of those, but lying's not one of them. I choose to honor my word, and I don't like righteousness in people, particularly when they're talking about my life.'

He rubbed the moisture off the front glass with his sleeve. Beyond the tunnel of trees we could see pasture and sky up ahead.

'There's my airstrip. We only have another mile to go,' he said. 'Dave, after you get your goods, I think we say good-bye.'

'All right, Tony.'

'You think I'm a hypocrite, don't you?'

'I've got too many problems of my own to be taking other people's inventory.'

'Before you write me off, I want you to understand something. You helped me a lot, man. But right now I've got some heavy shit to work through – with my habit, my douche-bag wife, these fuckheads in Houston and Miami – and I've got to simplify my life and concentrate on Paul and nobody else. That's the way it is.'

He waited for me to reply.

'You're not going to say anything?' he asked.

'It all works out one way or another.'

'Yeah, that's the way I figure it. *Semper fi*, Mac, and fuck it.' He rolled down the window, let the mist blow inside, and took a deep breath. A bolt of lightning splintered into the tree line at the south end of the pasture where Tony kept his plane. The air smelled as metallic and cold as brass.

A mile farther on we drove out of the hackberry and pine trees into the pasture with the mowed airstrip and tin hangar that Tony had told me to remember on our first trip to the Pearl River country. Two cars and a van were parked in front of the hangar, and the hangar's main door was slid open about three feet. The surrounding fields were pale green and sopping wet, and from horizon to horizon steel-gray clouds roiled across the sky.

'The plane's not in yet, or these guys wouldn't still be hanging around,' Tony said. 'I'll stay with you through the buy, then I'll ride back in the Caddy and you're on your own.'

'All right, Tony.'

'Make sure you're satisfied with the quality of everything before you leave. Don't think you can go back to these guys with a complaint. They're basically punks, and they won't make it right. In fact, they usually try to cannibalize each other whenever they have a chance.'

'Where's the plane coming in from?'

'They make out like it's a direct connection from Colombia. But I think it's coming out of Florida. There're a lot of abandoned housing developments in the Everglades. So they use these paved roads out in the saw grass for airstrips. What the Miami crowd doesn't need or doesn't want, because maybe the prices are going down too fast, they lay it off on these guys.'

I drove along a two-cart dirt road through the pasture to the front of the hangar. Through the

351

opening door I could see the canary-yellow wings of a crop-duster biplane and rows of industrial metal drums and bright silver liquid propane tanks. I cut the ignition. In the rearview mirror I saw the white limo stop behind me. No one got out.

'What is this place?' I said.

'The guy who owns it is a local peckerwood who runs a farm-supply business or something. Look, Dave, when we go in there, I talk and you just hand them the money.'

'What about them back there?' I nodded toward the limo.

'They're paid to watch my back, not my business dealings. Come on, let's go.'

We walked through the wet grass and drizzling rain and stepped inside the dryness of the hangar. It was immaculately clean; there was another biplane, a red one, at the far end, and a small green John Deere tractor next to it, but there was not a spot of oil or a tread mark from a tire on the concrete floor slab. By a windowed side office were a picnic table and benches that had probably been moved in from outside, because there were pieces of grass on the bottoms of the legs. A fat man in rumpled brown slacks and a T-shirt was turning and flattening hamburger patties on a hibachi with a spatula. The smoke drifted off in the draft created by an opening in the far door that gave on to the mowed landing strip. Three men sat at the table. Two of them had their backs to us, and the third man was telling them a story, gesturing with his hands, and he did not look at us. On one end of the table was a washtub filled with crushed ice and green bottles of Heineken.

We walked a few feet forward and then stopped. To my right, stacked in a row along the front sliding door, were more metal drums, each of them containing dry chemical fertilizers, and at the end of the drums was a fingernail-polish-red Coca-Cola machine, the old kind with a big, thick lead-colored handle. Tony's eyes were rivited on the picnic table.

I looked at him.

'It's the wrong guys,' he whispered.

'What?'

'The black guys aren't there. The black guys are always in on the score.'

Then I heard the Cadillac's transmission in reverse, backing across the wet ground.

'It's a hit. It's a fucking hit. Get out of here,' Tony said, and he shoved me with one arm toward the opening in the door just as Jimmie Lee Boggs stepped out from behind the Coca-Cola machine and threw a pump ventilated-rib shotgun to his shoulder and let off the round in the chamber.

It was a deer slug, a solid, round piece of lead as thick as the ball of your thumb, and it whanged off a metal barrel just in front of us and ricocheted into the tin wall of the hangar. Tony and I both dove between the barrels at the same time. I heard Boggs eject the spent shell on to the cement and ratchet another into the chamber. Tony was squatted down, breathing hard, his chrome-plated .45 held at an upward angle. I was standing, pressed back against the wall, and I got my .45 out of my fatigue jacket pocket, slid back the receiver, and eased a hollow-point round into the chamber. The men who had been drinking beer and cooking hamburgers at the picnic table had fallen to the floor or piled inside the office below the level of the windows.

Tony tried to look around the side of the barrel, and Boggs fired again, this time a round that was loaded with buckshot. It scoured off the side of the barrel behind us and ripped a pattern of five holes that I could cover with my fingers in the tin wall. Then somebody inside the office started firing with a pistol, probably a revolver, for he let off five rounds that danced all over the concrete; then he stopped to reload. When he did I aimed by .45 with both hands over Tony's head and fired at the office until my palms were numb from the recoil. My ears roared with a sound like the sea, and the breech locked open on the empty clip. The hollow-points blew holes as big as baseballs out of the toppled picnic table and sent triangular panes of glass crashing into the office's interior, but the lower half of the office wall was built of cinderblock, and the hollow-points splintered apart inside the concrete and did no harm to the men on the floor.

My hands were shaking as I pulled out the empty clip and shoved a full one into the .45's magazine. Tony raked his springlike curls back with his fingers.

'We're seriously fucked,' he whispered.

'We wait them out,' I said.

'Are you kidding? If Jimmie Lee or one of those other guys gets outside, he can come around behind us and put it to us through the wall. It's a matter of time. I only got this clip. What have you got?'

'You're looking at it.'

The skin of his face was dry and tight, his eyes as darkly bright as when he'd been loaded on black

354

speed. He began breathing deeply in his chest, as though he were trying to oxygenate his blood. He looked at the big, round silver tanks of liquid propane that were lined against the adjacent wall.

'No,' I said.

'You heard stories about it. But I lived through it, man. The captain called it right in on top of us.'

'Don't do it, Tony.'

'Bullshit. You got to go out there on the screaming edge. That's the only place you win. You don't know that, you don't know anything.'

I wanted to put out my hand, push his gun down toward the floor, somehow in that last terrible moment exorcise the insanity that lived in his soul. Instead, I stared down at him numbly while he pivoted on one knee, aimed at a propane tank, and fired. The automatic leapt upward in his hand, and the round clanged off the top of the tank and hit an iron spar in the wall. He rested one buttock on his heel, propped his wrist across his knee, lowered his sights, and pulled the trigger again.

This time the round hit the tank dead center and cored a hole in it as cleanly as a machinist's punch. The propane gushed out on the cement, its bright, instant reek like a slap across the face.

His .45 lay on the floor now, and his hands were trembling as he tore a match from a matchbook and folded the cover back from the striker. I could hear the men inside the office moving around on top of the broken glass.

'Tony—,' I said. I was pressed back against the wall, between the barrels. The air was thick and wet with the smell of the propane.

'What?' he said.

355

'Tony—'

'It's the only way, man. You know it.'

I touched my religious medal and closed my eyes and opened them again. My heart was thundering against my rib cage.

'Do it,' I said.

'Listen, you get out of this and I don't, you keep your fucking promise. You look after my son.'

'All right, Tony.'

Boggs stepped out wide from behind the Coca-Cola machine and fired a pattern of buckshot that *thropped* past my ear and blew the top off a metal barrel. It rolled in a circle on the cement. Tony struck the loose match in his hand, touched the other matches with the flame, and flipped the burning folder out into the pool of propane.

The pool burst into white and blue flames; then the fire crawled up the silvery jet of propane squirting from the tank. I heard a window crash on the far side of the Coca-Cola machine, and I heard the men inside the office fighting with one another to get out the office door; but now Tony and I were out from behind the barrels, unprotected, and running for the opening in the hangar door.

The ignition of the propane tanks, the fertilizers, the air itself, was like a bolt of lightning striking inside the building. Through the hangar door I saw the rain falling outside, the sodden fields, the wind ruffling the tree line, then Tony hit me hard on the back and knocked me through the door just as the whole building exploded.

His body was framed against the flash, like a tin effigy silhouetted against a forge. He tumbled across the ground, his clothes smoking, his hair singed and stinking like a burnt cat's. The heat was so intense I couldn't feel the rain on my skin. We stumbled forward, past my pickup, into the field, as Jimmie Lee Boggs floored his van down the two-track road. Behind us, for only a moment, I heard screams inside the fire.

But Tony was not finished yet. He sat down in a puddle of water, his knees pulled up before him, aimed the .45 with both hands, and let off two quick rounds. One tore through the van's back panel, but the second spiderwebbed the window in the driver's door and blew out the front windshield. It hung down like a crumpled glass apron, and the van careered off the road, whipping the grass under its bumper, spinning divots of mud from under the tires.

'Suck on that one, Jimmie Lee,' Tony said.

The van seemed to slow as it made a wide arc through the field; then it lurched on its back springs as the driver shifted down, righted the wheel, and hit the gas again. The tin sides of the buildings were white with heat, as though phosphorous were burning inside; then they folded softly in upon themselves, like cellophane being consumed, and the roof crashed on to the cement slab. Boggs's van hit the main dirt road and disappeared into the corridor of trees.

Tony tried to get to his feet, but gave it up and sat back down in the water. His face was drawn and empty and dotted with mud.

'I'm going to leave you and come back for you, Tony. I'm borrowing your piece, too.' I took the .45 gingerly from his hand and eased the hammer back down.

He wiped his eyes clear with the back of his wrist and looked up and down my trouser legs. Then his hand felt inside my thigh, almost as though he were molesting me. His mouth shaped itself into a small butterfly, and his eyes roved casually over my face.

'Where's your backup people?' he said.

'I don't know. My guess is, though, they've got the road sealed on each end.'

'Yeah, that'd make sense.'

'Will you wait for me here?'

'I'm going to start walking back.'

'I don't think it'd be good for you to meet the guys in the limo.'

'My limo's in the bottom of a pond by now, and those guys are halfway across Lake Pontchartrain.' Then he said, 'Was Kim in on it?'

'No. I never saw her before I got involved with your people.'

'That's good. She's a good kid. Do me a favor, will you?'

'What?'

'Get the fuck away from me.'

I didn't answer him. I got in my pickup and followed Jimmie Lee Boggs's sharply etched tire tracks down the dirt road bordered on each side by pine and hackberry trees, and cows that poked through the underbush and lowed fearfully each time lightning snapped across the sky.

I didn't have to go far. His van was in a ditch opposite the old seismograph drill barge that was sunk at an angle on the other side of the river. I stopped my truck, stuck Tony's .45 inside my belt, and walked up on the driver's side of the van. The light was gray through the trees, and the air had the cold smell of a refrigerator that has been closed up too long with produce inside. The driver's door was partly open, and the dashboard and steering column were littered with chips of broken glass, and painted with blood.

I pulled the door wide open and pointed the .45 inside, but the van was empty. Twelve-gauge shotgun shells, their yellow casings red with bloody finger smears, were scattered on the passenger's seat and on the floor. A paintless, narrow, wooden footbridge, with a broken handrail and boards hanging out the bottom, spanned the river just downstream from the drill barge. Deep foot tracks led from the opposite side of the bridge along the mudbank through the morning glory vines and cypress roots to the starboard side of the barge, which rested at an upward angle against the incline.

The slats on the bridge were soft with rot, and three of them burst under my weight as loud as rifle shots. The river's surface was dented with water dripping from the trees, and the incoming tide on the coast had raised the river's level, so that the line of dried flotsam along the bank waved on the edge of the current like gray cobweb.

I walked along the bank through the underbrush to the bow of the barge, where the drill tower sat. The hull was rusted out at the waterline, and there were tears in the cast-iron plates like broken teeth. I grabbed hold of the forward handrail and stepped over it on to the deck. The deck was slippery with moldy leaves and pine needles, and somebody's boots had bruised a gray path from the gunwale to the door of the pilothouse.

I put my .45 in my left hand, slipped Tony's out of my belt with my right hand, and pulled the hammer back on full cock with my thumb. The inside of the pilothouse was strewn with leaves and empty wood crates that once held canned dynamite, primers, and spools of cap wire. In one corner were the shriveled remains of a used condom, and somebody had spray-painted on the bulkhead the initials KKK and the words JOE BOB AND CLAUDINE inside a big heart. At the rear of the pilothouse were the door and the steel steps that led down into the engine room.

I put my back against the bulkhead and looked around the corner and down the steps into the half-flooded room below. The water was black and stagnant and streaked with oil, and somebody had tried to retrieve the huge engine on a hoist, then abandoned his task and left it suspended on chains and pulleys inches above the water.

Then I heard something move in the water, something scrape against the hull.

'You're under arrest, Boggs,' I said. 'Throw your shotgun out where I can see it, then come up the steps with your hands on your head.'

It was silent down below now.

'If you're hurt and can't move, tell me so,' I said. 'We'll have you in a hospital in Slidell in a half hour. But first you've got to throw out the shotgun.'

The only sounds were the rain dripping in the water and the tree limbs creaking overhead. Sweat ran out of my hair, and the wind blowing through the windows was cold on my face.

'Look, Boggs, you're in an iron box. It all ends right here. If I open up on you, there's no place you can hide. Use your head. You don't have to die here.'

Then I heard him moving fast through the water, from out of a corner that was tilted at an upward angle against the bank, into full view at the bottom of the steps, his neck and shoulder scarlet with blood, his face and threadlike hair and drenched T-shirt strung with algae and spiderwebs. But he was hurt badly, and the tip of the shotgun barrel caught on the handrail of the steps just as I began firing down into the hold with both pistols.

The bullets ricocheted off the steps and the hull, sparking and whanging from one surface to the next. He dropped the shotgun into the water and tried to cover his face with his arms. But he lost his balance on the sloping floor and toppled forward into the machinist's hoist and suspended engine block. The chains roared loose from the pulleys, and Jimmie Lee Boggs crashed against the flooded bottom of the hull with the engine block and the tangle of chains squarely on top of his loins and lower chest. The blood drained from his face, and he reared back his head and opened his mouth in an enormous O like a man who couldn't find words for his pain.

I set both pistols on the floor of the pilothouse and walked down the steps into the water. The water was cold inside my socks and against my shins, and from the corner I smelled the sweet, fetid odor of a dead nutria whose webbed feet bobbed against the hull. The waterline was up to Boggs's neck, his grease-streaked hands rested on top of the block like claws, and he breathed as though his lungs were filled with some terrible obstruction.

I reached down under the water and caught the end of the crankshaft with both hands and tried to lift it. I strained until my shirt split along my back, and I slipped on the layer of moss and algae that covered the floor and stumbled sideways against the hull. My knee hit the side of his head.

'I'm sorry,' I said.

He cleared his throat and rubbed one eye hard with his palm, but he did not speak.

'Can you move at all?'

He shook his head.

'I've got a jack in the truck,' I said. 'I'll go get it and come back. But you're going to have to do something for me, Jimmie Lee.'

His elongated spearmint-green eyes looked up into mine. The pupils were like tiny burnt cinders.

'Can you talk to me?' I said.

'Yeah, I can talk.' His voice was thick with phlegm.

'When I come back I want you to tell me what happened to Hipolyte Broussard. I want you to tell me who stuffed that oil rag down his mouth. Are we agreed on that?'

'Why do you give a fuck?'

'Because Tee Beau Latiolais is a friend of mine. Because I'm a police officer.'

His eyes looked away at the rust-eaten line of holes in the hull. Where there had been light from the outside, the river current was now eddying inside the barge. His face was bright with sweat.

'Get me out of here, man. The tide's coming in,' he said.

I climbed hurriedly up the steps, got the jack and a three-battery flashlight out of the equipment box in the bed of my truck, made my way across the footbridge, and climbed back down into the engine room. I clicked on the flashlight and balanced it on a step so that the beam struck the hull above where Boggs was pinned. His skin looked bone-white against the blackness of the water.

I wedged the base of the jack between the tilted floor and the side of the hull and fitted the handle into the ratchet socket. I snugged the top of the jack against the engine block and started pumping the handle.

'Come on, Boggs, talk to me. It's not a time to hold back,' I said.

He strained his chin upward to keep it out of the water.

'The colored kid didn't kill the redbone. Fuck, man, get the sonofabitch off me,' he said.

'Who did?'

'The woman did.'

'Which woman?'

'Mama Goula. Who do you think, man?'

'How do you know this, Jimmie Lee?'

'I was out there. The redbone was under the bus, banging on the brake drums, yelling at the kid. The bus fell on him and the kid took off running. Come on, man, I'm busted up inside.'

'Keep talking to me, Jimmie Lee.'

'Mama Goula had brought some chippies out to the camp. She found the redbone and poked the rag down his throat with her thumb.'

I felt the engine block move slightly; then the jack handle slipped out of the socket and my knuckles raked against the hull. Boggs pushed with both hands against the block, his neck cording with the strain.

'Hang on,' I said, and reset the jack flush against the hull with the other end inserted against the engine's crankshaft. I jacked the handle slowly with both hands, a notch at a time, to try to move the engine's weight on Boggs's legs so he could sit up higher out of the water.

'Why did she want to kill Hipolyte?' I asked.

'She didn't want to split the action. It was a perfect chance to clip the redbone. She knew everybody would blame the kid. Fuck, hurry up, man.'

'Why would they blame Tee Beau?'

'The redbone was queer for him. He wanted to make the kid his punk.'

I eased the jack up another notch, saw it shift the block perhaps a half inch, and then I clicked it up another notch. It popped loose from the crankshaft with such force that it broke through the water's surface like a spring. Boggs's mouth opened breathlessly.

'You sonofabitch, you're gonna tear my insides out,' he said.

'Listen, I've got to find a piece of hose or some pipe.'

'What?' His eyes were filled with fright.

'I've got to get you something to breathe through.'

'No! You get that jack under the block.'

I held it up in my hand.

'It's stripped, Boggs,' I said.

'Oh man, don't tell me that.'

'Come on, we're not finished yet. I'll be right back.'

I hunted through the pilothouse and fore and aft on the deck, but anything of value that could be

364

removed from the barge had long ago been taken by scavengers. Then I recrossed the bridge and tore the radiator hose out of my truck. When I climbed back down into the engine room, Boggs's head was tilted all the way back, so that his ears were underwater and only his face was clear of the surface.

I knelt by him and put my hand under the back of his head.

'Take a breath and lift up your head so you can hear me,' I said.

Then I said it again and nudged the back of his head. He straightened his neck and looked at me wide-eyed, his mouth crimped tight, his nostrils shuddering at the waterline.

'We're going to hold this hose as tight as we can around your mouth,' I said. 'Ill stay with you until the tide goes out. Then I'll get help and we'll pull this block off you. You've got my word, Jimmie Lee. I'm not going anywhere. But we've got to keep the hose sealed against your mouth. Do you understand that?'

He blinked his eyes, then laid his head back in the water again, and I pressed the hard rubber edges of the radiator hose around his mouth.

We held it there together for fifteen minutes while the water climbed higher and covered his face entirely. His hair floated in a dirty aura about his head, and his eyes stared at me like watery green marbles. Then I felt the rubber slip against his skin, heard him choke down inside the hose, and saw a fine bead of air bubbles rise from the side of his mouth.

I tried to screw the hose tighter into his mouth, but he had swallowed water and was fighting now.

At first his hands locked on my wrists, as though I were the source of his suffering; then his fists burst through the surface and flailed in the air, and finally caught my shirt and tore it down the front of my chest. I pushed the hose down at him again, but there was no way now he could blow the water out of it and regain his breath.

Then one hand came up from the shirt, and felt my face like a blind man reaching out to discover some fragile and tender human mystery, and a last solitary air bubble floated from his throat to the surface and popped in the dead air.

15

Tony had walked almost all the way back to his fishing camp when I slowed the truck abreast of him under a row of moss-hung oaks. It had stopped raining now, and out in the pasture the cows had broken out of their clumps and were grazing in the grass. The hair on the back of Tony's head was singed the color of burnt copper. He glanced sideways at me, indifferently, and kept walking.

'Get in,' I said.

He jumped over a puddle in front of him and brushed a wet branch out of his face. I let the truck idle slowly forward in first gear.

'Come on, Tony. Get in,' I said.

'Is this a bust? If it is, do it by the numbers. I've got lawyers that'll eat your lunch.'

I braked the truck at an angle in front of him and popped open the passenger door.

'Don't act like a sprout, Tony,' I said. 'I want to tell you something.'

He paused, looked over the fields, pinched his nose, then got in the truck and closed the door. His clothes smelled like smoke and ashes. A volunteer fire truck passed us and splashed a curtain of yellow water across my windshield. Tony watched the fire truck disappear down the road through the back window. Finally, he said, 'Jimmie Lee got away from you?'

'No.'

'You popped him?'

'He drowned.'

'Drowned?'

I told him what happened down in the engine room of the drill barge.

'Then I guess it's a red-letter day for you, Dave. You got to watch Jimmie Lee shuffle off with the hallelujah chorus, and you get to be the narc who made the case on Tony C.'

'Is that the way you read it?'

'I told you once, everybody cuts a piece out of your ass one way or another. Except don't bank your promotion or your pay raise yet, Dave. What you've got here is entrapment. Also, I don't think you've got enough on that tape to get them real excited at the U.S. Attorney's office. You're the DEA, right?'

'Indirectly.'

'I'll put in a word for you. I'll tell them you really did your job well.'

The road bent close to the river again, and up ahead I could see Tony's fish camp and the Lincoln convertible parked in the back under the trees. Smoke rose from the chimney and flattened in the salt breeze off the Gulf. I pulled the truck on to the shoulder of the road and cut the engine.

I took Tony's .45 from the pocket of my fatigue jacket and handed it to him. He looked back at me strangely.

'Here's the lay of the land, Tony,' I said. 'I think you've got a big Purple Heart nailed up in the middle of your forehead. Everybody is supposed to feel you're the only guy who did bad time in Vietnam. You also give me the impression that somebody else is responsible for your addiction and getting you out of it. But the bottom line is you sell dope to people and they fuck up their lives with it.'

'I think maybe it's you who's got the problem with conscience, Dave.'

'You're wrong. As of now you're on your own. As far as I know, you died in that fire back there. I don't think a county medical examiner, particularly in a place like this, will ever sort out the bones and teeth in that hangar. If you disappear into Mexico with Paul and stay out of the business, I think the DEA will write you off. I doubt if your wife will be a problem, either, since she'll acquire almost everything you own.'

He chewed on his lip and looked up the incline at the camp.

'You've got your plane, you've got Jess to fly it, you've got that fine little boy to take with you,' I said. 'I think if you make the right choice, Tony, you might be home free.'

'They won't believe you.'

'Maybe you inflate your importance. Twenty-four hours after you're off the board, somebody else will take your place. In a year nobody will be able to find your file.'

He made pockets of air in his cheeks and switched them back and forth as though he were swishing water around in his mouth.

'It's a possibility, isn't it?' he said. He bit a

hangnail off his thumb and removed it from his tongue. 'Just pop through a hole in the dimension and leave a big question mark behind. That's not bad.'

'Like you said to me the other day, it's always about money. Stay away from the money, and the Houston and Miami crowd will probably stay away from you.'

'Maybe.'

'But any way you cut it, it's *adiós*, Tony.'

'My ranch is outside a little village called Zapopan. Maybe you'll get a postcard from there.'

'No, I think your story ends here.'

He pulled the clip from the handle of his .45, slid back the receiver, removed the round from the chamber, and inserted it in the top of the clip. He tapped the clip idly against the chrome-plated finish of the pistol, then put his hand on the door handle.

'I don't guess you're big on shaking hands,' he said.

I rested my palm on the bottom of the steering wheel and looked straight ahead at the yellow road winding through the trees.

'Say good-bye to Paul for me,' I said.

I heard him get out of the truck and close the door.

'Tony?' I said.

He looked back through the window.

'If I ever hear your dealing dope again, we'll pick it up where we left off.'

'No, I don't think so, Dave. I have a feeling your cop days are about over.'

'Oh?'

He leaned down on the window jamb.

'Your heart gets in the way of your head,' he said. 'If you don't know that, the pencil pushers you work for will. They'll get rid of you, too. Maybe you won't accept any thanks from me, and maybe I won't even offer you any, but my little boy up there says thank you. You can wear that in your hat or stick it in your ear. So long, Dave.'

He walked up the pine-needle-covered slope toward the back of the camp. He took his Marine Corps utility cap from his back pocket, slapped the soot off it against his trousers, and fitted it at an angle on his head. I drove slowly down the road past the camp, the truck lurching in the flooded potholes, and saw him open the screen door and smile at someone inside.

I came out of the trees and drove through a winter-green field that was filled with snowy egrets and blue herons feeding by a grassy pond. Ahead I could see the coast, the palm fronds whipping in the wind, and the waves cresting and blowing out on Lake Borgne and the Gulf. The air was cool and flecked with sunlight and smelled like salt and distant rain. And I realized that in the west the sun had broken through the gray seal of clouds, and left a rip in the sky like a yellow and purple rose.

Epilogue

Tony was right. Minos didn't believe me, particularly after I gave him a tape recording that contained a long blank space between the fire in the airplane hangar and Jimmie Lee Boggs's watery statement about Tee Beau's innocence in the murder of Hipolyte Broussard. But I didn't care. I had grown weary of federal agents and wiseguys, narcs and stings and brain-fried lowlifes, and all the seriousness and pretense we invest in the province of moral invalids. I had decided it was time to let someone else wander about in that neon-lit moonscape, where we constantly try to define the source of our national discontent, until our unstated addictions target an antithetically mixed, quixotic figure like Tony Cardo, and lead us away from ourselves.

I don't know what happened to him. The DEA found his Lincoln, his only means of transportation, at the camp, but they matched the tire treads to fresh tire tracks at the hangar where he kept his plane. Perhaps he paid somebody to drive the Lincoln back to the camp; however, the DEA also found his plane still in the hangar. One of Minos's fellow workers, one who was enraged at the fact that the additional fifty thousand dollars given me in the sting had been burned up in the hangar fire, theorized that Tony had had someone else fly a plane into the airstrip and pick him up, Paul, and Jess Ornella. But federal agents in Guadalajara who visited Tony's ranch outside Zapopan reported that Tony had not been seen in the area for almost a year. The next time I saw Minos in Lafayette, to plan a fishing trip, I mentioned Tony's name. He yawned, picked up a file folder off his desk, and showed me a photo of a man whose facial features looked back at me with the dirty luminescence and dark clarity characteristic of booking-room photography.

'You know this guy?' he said.

'No.'

'He lives in Metairie. He's a new boy on the block. We'd like very much to get him into our gray-bar hotel chain. He—'

But now it was I whose eyes began to glaze, and who tried not to yawn at the sound of the rain on the oak trees outside the window.

Two months later I received a creased and dog-eared envelope postmarked in Lake Charles. Inside it was a color photograph of Paul smiling in a fighting chair on the stern of a sport fishing boat. Squatted down next to the chair, with a four-foot tarpon held in both arms, the enormous hook still protruding from its dead mouth, was Jess Ornella, his jailhouse tattoos as blue against his tan as the sea behind him. With his back turned to the camera was a shirtless man in a huge Mexican sombrero who was baiting a mullet on a feathered spoon. His curly hair was cut short and glistened with sweat above his tiny ears. In the background was a biscuit-colored beach with a few hot-looking, wilted palm trees on it and a desiccated wooden dock, strung with drying butterfly nets, that extended out into the surf.

Someone had written in ballpoint on the back of the photograph:

You said around New Iberia you have to knock the bass back into the water with a tennis racket. That's pretty good. But you ought to try this place. The reefs are so crowded with kingfish there's not room for them all. Just yesterday I saw a couple of them walking down the highway carrying their own canteens. We're living on warm breezes and bananas fried in coconut oil. I'm clean and free, Dave. The tiger went away. Maybe you ought to get yourself a Roman collar, or at least by now I hope you've lost the badge and your dipshit colleagues. Face it, you dug being in the life. Even Jess thought you were one of us. That'd worry me.

Stay solid,
Pancho Gonzales

Tee Beau Latiolais was given a new trial, but before trial date Gros Mama Goula cut a subpoena server's face with a razor and fled New Iberia and the zydeco bar and hot-pillow joint she had operated for thirty years, and the prosecutor's office dropped the murder charge against Tee Beau. But some black people out in the parish said Gros Mama had the powers of a *loup-garou*, and had changed herself into ball lightning. They said when

374

the fog was white among the cypress trunks, people would see a tangle of pink light roll across the lily pads and dead water and explode against the levee. The grass on the bank would be scorched black, and snakes would writhe on the baked dirt.

But Tee Beau was not one to stay locked in a bunch of mojo fear, or even worry any longer about the months of sexual humiliation and shame that Hipolyte Broussard had inflicted on him. He and Dorothea were married, and today she works as a waitress in a seafood restaurant out on the St. Martinville road. Tee Beau owns his own taxicab. On Sundays he drives Tante Lemon and Dorothea to church in it, and for some reason they look like triplets inside, all three of their heads barely above the bottom level of the windows. Sometimes they make a special trip past my house and leave me a fat jar of cracklins, what we call *graton*, made with ground-up Tabasco peppers, and the first bite is such a shock to my mouth that sweat runs out of my hair. But every time Tante Lemon gives me another quart, she pats my hand confidently and says, 'You eat that, you, and I gonna give you mo'. Just like your daddy give me fish when I didn't have no food, me, I be comin' out and give you mo'.'

Saint Augustine once said we should never use the truth to injure. So the edge of my coulee is lined with spaded-in holes that contain dozens of mason jars which one day an archaeologist will probably dig up and identify as artifacts used by an ancient cult in a corn-god burial.

This started out as a story about my own fear, or rather about a time in my life when, because of an injury, I was not sure who I was, when I had to wait

375

each night for a protean figure of my own creation to define me as something weak and loathsome and undeserving of breath. Instead, it became a story of others, people I discovered to be far more brave in their way than I am. And I suppose that what I have learned is a lesson that the years, or self-concern, had begun to hide from me, namely, that the bravest and most loyal and loving people in the world seldom have heroic physical characteristics or the auras of saints. In fact, their faces are like those of people whom you might randomly pull out of a supermarket line, their physical makeup so nondescript and unremarkable that it's hard to remember what they looked like ten minutes after they walk out of a room.

Kim Dollinger is the manager of Clete's Club on Decatur now, and Clete has a private investigator's license and an office two blocks from the First District headquarters. He's made enough money running down bail jumpers to pay off all his debts to Tony's old shylocks. He still tries to fight his weight problem by clanking iron up and down in the back of his office and jogging through Louis Armstrong Park in his Budweiser shorts and LSU football jersey, which the black kids from the Iberville welfare project treat like the appearance of a dancing hippo in the middle of their day. People in the Quarter say he and Kim have become an item, but probably not as Clete had expected. When we go out for dinner together she mashes out his cigarettes in the ashtray, cancels his drink order from the bar, and orders low-cholesterol food from the menu for him. But he doesn't complain, and his eyes are gentle when he looks at her.

Bootsie cut her losses and sold out her vending machine business to one of her former in-laws, and that December she and I were married in St. Peter's Church in New Iberia. We took Alafair with us to Key West, where the water is warm year-round, and the late-afternoon sun boils into the Gulf like a molten red planet. At night light-fish swim among the coral like electrified wisps of green smoke. In screened-in restaurants by the water's edge we ate big dinners of oysters on the half shell, fried shrimp, and conch fritters, and we trolled for bonefish in the flats and dove Seven-Mile Reef south of the island. At fifty feet the water was as clear and green as Jell-O, shimmering with sunlight, the sand as white as ground diamond, and I watched Bootsie swim deep into the canyons of fire coral, indifferent to the spiked nests of sea urchins and the dark, triangular shapes of stingrays. Her tanned body would be beset with bluefish; then she would kick her flippers, clouding the water below her with sand, and dispel them like a sudden shuddering of thin metal blades.

Minos persuaded the DEA to replace the boat I lost south of Cocodrie, and he said that actually the DEA was happy with the work that I had done for them, because Tony was gone and the man who had moved in on his action, one of the Houston crowd, had evidently been having an affair with Tony's wife. They spent a lot of their time quarreling, even throwing drinks at one another on one occasion, in public places.

But my financial debts are paid off, and I've given up law enforcement, at least for the time being. Bootsie and I run our boat-rental and bait business on the bayou. We barbecue chickens and links of sausage for midday fishermen, and we seine for shrimp out on the long green roll of the Gulf. It's still winter, but we treat winter in South Louisiana as a transitory accident. Even when the skies are black with ducks, the oak and cypress limbs along the bayou teeming with robins, the eye focuses on the tightly wrapped pink buds inside the dark green leaves of the camellia bush, the azaleas and the flaming hibiscus that have bloomed right through the season. South Louisiana is a party, and I've grown old enough to put away vain and foolish concerns about mortality, and to stop imposing the false features of calendars and clocks upon my life, or, for that matter, upon eternity.

Sometimes in the evening, when I'm closing up the bait shop and my shoulder twinges from picking up crates of Jax and Pearl beer, when the wind lifts the moss on the dead cypress in the marsh and blows red embers from a burnt cane field into the darkening sky, I think of juju magic and *gris-gris* charms, I think of Tony and Paul, Kim and Clete, Dorothea, Tee Beau, and Tante Lemon, even ole Jess Ornella, and I have to pause, almost fearfully, at the beating of my heart. Then I see Bootsie and Alafair walk down from the lighted gallery to get me for supper, hand in hand through the pecan trees, and I turn keys in locks and Bootsie and I go back up the path, with Alafair swinging from our arms, our mismatched shadows fused into a single playful shape under the rising moon.